"If we hurry, we can re̶ ̶ ̶ ̶ ̶ ̶ ̶ ̶ ̶ ̶ arise," said the Mardukaɳ

Roger's software translated. "He says we'd better get moving or something nasty is going to happen."

"Did he indicate what?" Pahner asked.

"He called it the *yaden*. No context." He turned to the Mardukan and tried his toot's voice control function. "What are the *yaden*?"

Roger discovered that the software was giving him images in response to some form of subcommunication involving his background, the gestures of the Mardukan, and known words. In this case, it obviously had no clear translation, but the general outline, although startling, was clear. He almost laughed.

"He says the *yaden* are vampires."

"Oh," Pahner said blandly. "So we should move out?"

"Yes," Roger said. "He has a problem with something that apparently comes out only at night. He wants to hurry to make it to his village before whatever it is comes out."

"That's going to be tough," Pahner said consideringly. "We've got a pass to cross, then quite a bit of jungle."

"Then I suggest that we'd better get moving," Roger said.

As the sun set behind the mountains, the Mardukan became more and more voluble in his worries, and translations became clearer. "Prince Roger, we must hurry. The *yaden* will suck us dry."

"How large and fierce are these *Yaden*?" Roger asked.

"They are neither large nor fierce," said Cord. "They are stealthy. They will slip into a camp and select one or two. Then they overcome them and suck them dry. This valley is thick with them."

"Oh, great," Roger groaned. "We're in the Valley of the Vampires."

MARCH
UPCOUNTRY

DAVID WEBER
JOHN RINGO

MARCH UPCOUNTRY

This is a work of fiction. All the characters and events portrayed in this book are fictional, and any resemblance to real people or incidents is purely coincidental.

A Baen Books Original

Baen Publishing Enterprises
P.O. Box 1403
Riverdale, NY 10471
www.baen.com

ISBN: 0-7434-3538-9

Cover art by Patrick Turner

First paperback printing, May 2002
Second paperback printing, July 2002

Library of Congress Cataloging-in-Publication Number 00-051940

Distributed by Simon & Schuster
1230 Avenue of the Americas
New York, NY 10020

Production by Windhaven Press, Auburn, NH
Printed in the United States of America

This book is dedicated to our mothers.

To Alice Louise Godard Weber,
who put up with me, taught me,
edited me, believed in me,
and encouraged me to believe I could
be a writer...
despite all evidence to the contrary.
I love you. There. I said it.

To Jane M. Ringo,
for dragging me to places I didn't want to go
and trying to make me eat stuff that would
turn a monkey's stomach.
Thanks Mom.
You were right.

CHAPTER ONE

"His Royal Highness, Prince Roger Ramius Sergei Alexander Chiang MacClintock!"

Prince Roger maintained his habitual, slightly bored smile as he padded through the door, then stopped and glanced around the room as he shot the cuffs of his shirt and adjusted his cravat. Both were made from Diablo spider-silk, the softest and sleekest material in the galaxy. Since it was protected by giant, acid-spitting spiders, it was also the most expensive.

For his part, Amos Stephens paid as little attention as possible to the young fop he had so grandly announced. The child was a disgrace to the honorable name of his mother's family. The cravat was bad enough, and the brightly patterned brocade jacket, more appropriate for a bordello than a meeting with the Empress of Man, was worse. But the hair! Stephens had served twenty years in Her Majesty's Navy before entering the Palace Service Corps. The only difference between his years in the Navy and his years in the Palace was the way his close-cropped curls had shifted from midnight black to silver. The mere sight of the butt-length golden hair of the farcical dandy Empress Alexandra's younger son had become always drove the old butler absolutely mad.

The Empress' office was remarkably small and spare, with a broad desk no larger than that of a middle-level manager in any of the star-spanning corporations of Earth. The appointments were simple but elegant; the chairs sensible, but elaborately hand-crafted and covered in exquisite hand-stitching. Most of the pictures were old master originals. The one exception was the most famous. "The Empress in Waiting" was a painting from life of Miranda MacClintock during the "Dagger Years," and the artist, Trachsler, had captured his subject perfectly. Her eyes were open and smiling, showing the world the image of an ingenuous Terran subject. A loyal upholder of the Dagger Lords. In other words, a filthy collaborator. But if you stared at the painting long enough, a chill crept over your skin and the eyes slowly changed. To the eyes of a predator.

Roger spared the painting one bare glance, then looked away. All of the MacClintocks lived under the shadow of the old biddy, long dead though she was. As the merest—and least satisfactory—slip of that lineage, he had all the shadows he could stand.

Alexandra VII, Empress of Man, regarded her youngest child through half-slitted eyes. The carefully metered bite of Stephens' ironic announcement had apparently gone over the prince's head completely. Roger certainly didn't seem affected by the old spacer's disdain in the slightest.

Unlike her flamboyant son, Empress Alexandra wore a blue suit of such understated elegance that it must have cost as much as a small starship. Now she leaned back in her float chair and propped her cheek on her hand, wondering for the hundredth time if this was the right decision. But there were a thousand other decisions awaiting her, all of them vital, and she'd spent all the time she intended to on this one.

"Mother," Roger said insouciantly, with a micrometric bow, and glanced at his brother in the flanking chair. "To what do I owe the honor of being summoned into two such august presences?" he continued with a slight, knowing smirk.

John MacClintock gave his younger brother a thin smile and a nod. The galaxy-renowned diplomat was dressed in a conservative suit of blue worsted, with a practical damask handkerchief poking out of one sleeve. For all that he looked like a doltish banker, his poker face and sleepy eyes hid a mind as insightful as any in the known worlds. And despite the developing paunch of middle-age, he could have become a professional golfer . . . if the job of Heir Apparent had allowed the time for it.

The Empress leaned forward abruptly and fixed her youngest with a laser stare. "Roger, We are sending you off-planet on a 'show the flag' mission."

Roger blinked several times, and smoothed his hair. "Yes?" he replied carefully.

"The planet Leviathan is celebrating Net-Hauling in two months—"

"Oh, my God, Mother!" Roger's exclamation cut the Empress of Man off in mid-sentence. "You must be joking!"

"We are not joking, Roger," Alexandra said severely. "Leviathan's primary export may be grumbly oil, but that doesn't change the fact that it's a focal planet in the Sagittarius sector. And there hasn't been a family representative for Net-Hauling in two decades." *Since I repudiated your father*, she didn't bother to add.

"But, Mother! The smell!" the prince protested, shaking his head to toss an errant strand of hair out of his eyes. He knew he was whining and hated it, but the alternative was smelling grumbly oil for at least several weeks on the planet. And even after he escaped Leviathan, it would take several more weeks for Kostas to get the smell out of his clothes. The oil made a remarkable musk base; in fact, it was in the cologne he was wearing at the moment. But in its raw form, it was the most noxious stuff in the galaxy.

"We don't care about the smell, Roger," snapped the Empress, "and neither should you! You will show the flag for the dynasty, and you will show Our subjects that We care enough about their reaffirmation of alliance to the Empire to send one of Our children. Is that understood?"

The young prince drew himself up to his full hundred ninety-five centimeters and gathered the shreds of his dignity.

"Very well, Your Imperial Majesty. I will, of course, do my duty as you see fit. It is my duty, after all, is it not, Your Imperial Majesty? *Noblesse oblige* and all that?" His aristocratic nostrils flared in suppressed anger. "Now I suppose I have some packing to oversee. By your leave?"

Alexandra's steely gaze held him for a few moments more, and then she waggled her fingers in the direction of the door.

"Go. Go. And do a good job." The "for a change" was unstated.

Prince Roger gave another micrometric bow, turned his back quite deliberately, and stalked out of the room.

"You could have handled that better, Mother," John said quietly, after the door had closed on the angry young man.

"Yes, I could have." She sighed, steepling her fingers under her chin. "And I should have, damn it. But he looks too much like his father!"

"But he *isn't* his father, Mother," John said quietly.

"Unless you create his father in him. Or drive him into New Madrid's camp."

"Try to teach me to suck eggs, why don't you?" she snapped, then inhaled deeply and shook her head. "I'm sorry, John. You're right. You're always right." She smiled ruefully at her older son. "I'm just not good at personal, am I?"

"You were fine with Alex and me," John replied. "But Roger's carrying a lot of loads. It might be time to cut him some slack."

"There isn't any slack to cut! Not now!"

"There's some. More than he's gotten in the last several years, anyway. Alex and I always knew you loved us," he pointed out quietly. "Roger's never been absolutely sure."

Alexandra shook her head.

"Not now," she repeated more calmly. "When he gets back, if this crisis blows over, I'll try to . . ."

"Undo some of the damage?" John's voice was level, his mild eyes unchallenging, open and calm. But then, he looked that way in the face of war.

"Explain," she said sharply. "Tell him the whole story. From the horse's mouth. Maybe if I explain it to him it will make more sense." She paused, and her face hardened. "And if he still is in New Madrid's camp, well, we'll just have to deal with that as it comes."

"But until then?" John met her half-angry, half-saddened gaze levelly.

"Until then we stay the course. And get him as far out of the line of fire as possible."

And as far from power as possible, as well, she thought.

CHAPTER TWO

Well, at least he's an athlete. Watching the prince drift out of the free-fall and flip to a lithe touchdown on the padded landing area, Company Sergeant Major Eva Kosutic had to admit that she'd seen experienced spacers handle the maneuver worse. *Now if he'd only grow a spine.*

First Platoon of Bravo Company, Bronze Battalion, The Empress' Own Regiment, was drawn up at attention in serried ranks on the forward side of the shuttle boat bay. The platoon's turnout was better than the Fleet's, which was only to be expected. The Bronze Battalion might be the "lowest" in the hierarchy of The Empress' Own, but they were still among the most elite bodyguards in the known universe. And that meant both the deadliest *and* the best looking.

It was Eva Kosutic's job to make sure of that. The thirty-minute Guard Mount had been, as always, precise and painstaking. Every centimeter of the uniform, equipment, and toilette of the individual Marines had been minutely inspected. In the five months she'd been

Sergeant Major of Bravo Company, Captain Pahner had never found a single fault after she'd checked over the troops. And he never would, if Eva Kosutic had anything to say about it.

Admittedly, there were very few "gigs" for her to find. Before winning assignment to "The Regiment" all candidates went through an exhausting washout course. The five-week Regimental In-Processing, or RIP, was designed to remove the wannabes and combined all the worst aspects of commando training with intense inspections of uniform and equipment. Any Marine found wanting— and most were—was sent back to his unit with no hard feelings. It was understood that "The Regiment" accepted only the best of the best of the best.

Once a recruit survived RIP, of course, he found another hierarchy to deal with. Almost all of the recent "Rippers" were assigned to Bronze Battalion, where they had the inexpressible joy of guarding an overbred pansy who'd rather spit on them than give them the time of day. Most of them suspected that it was just another test. If they stayed hardcore and professional for eighteen months, they could either take a promotion to stay in Bronze or else vie for a position in Steel Battalion and protect Princess Alexandra.

Personally, Eva Kosutic was counting down. One hundred and fifty-three days and a wake-up, she thought, as the prince stepped off the landing mat.

The last notes of the Imperial Anthem died, and the ship's captain stepped forward and saluted.

"Your Royal Highness, Captain Vil Krasnitsky, at your service! Might I say what an honor it is to have you with us on the *Charles DeGlopper*!"

The prince gave the ship's captain a languid one-handed wave, and turned to look around the boat bay. The petite brunette who'd trailed him out of the tube stepped forward and around him with an almost unnoticeable flare of her nostrils and took the captain's hand.

"Eleanora O'Casey, Captain. It's a pleasure to be aboard your fine vessel." Roger's former tutor and current chief of staff gave the captain a firm handshake and looked him directly in the eye, trying to project some semblance of leadership since Roger was in one of his sulks. "We've been told there's not a crew in this class that can touch yours."

The captain glanced sideways at the distant nobleman for only a moment, and then turned back to the chief of staff.

"Thank you, Ma'am. It's good to be appreciated."

"You've won the Tarawa Competition two years in a row. That's proof enough for this poor civilian." She gave the captain a blinding smile and nudged Roger lightly with her elbow.

The prince turned to the captain and gave him a thin, remote, and fairly meaningless smile. The captain, blinded by the sight of royalty, gave a sigh of relief. Presumably, the prince was pleased and his career would avoid the shoals of royal disfavor.

"May I introduce my officers?" Krasnitsky asked, turning to the line of waiting personnel. "And if His Highness wishes, the ship's company is prepared for inspection!"

"Perhaps at a later time," Eleanora suggested hastily. "I believe His Highness would prefer to be shown to his cabin."

She smiled at the captain once more, already rehearsing her future explanation that the prince had suffered a slight case of motion sickness in the free-fall tube and that was why he was distracted. The excuse was weak, but having "spacephobia" would go over better with the ship's crew than explaining that Roger was being a pain in the ass on purpose.

"I understand completely," the captain said sympathetically. "Changing environments can be stressful. If I might lead the way?"

"Lead on, Captain. Lead on," Eleanora said with yet another blinding smile. And another elbow jab to Roger.

Just let us make it to Leviathan without Roger embarrassing me too hideously, she thought earnestly. *Surely that isn't asking too much!*

"Oh, Christ on a Crutch. It's Mouse."

Kostas Matsugae looked up from the day-jackets he was unpacking from their traveling containers. The equipment bay was rapidly filling with Bronze Barbarians . . . and from the way they were putting their own equipment into lockers, it looked to be a permanent arrangement.

"What is the meaning of this?" the diminutive valet asked, in a precise, spare voice.

"Oh, don't get your titties in a wad, Mouse," the first speaker, one of the longer service privates, said. "There's only so much space on one of these assault transports. I guess you're gonna have to shoehorn into the space heavy-weapons would take up. Hey, all," the private went on, raising his voice slightly to be heard over the conversations and clatter of equipment. "Mousey's in the compartment. So nobody start doin' the nasty on the benches."

One of the female corporals sashayed past the middle-aged valet, stripping out of her dress uniform as she went.

"Mousies, how I love them. Mousies is what I love to eat."

"Nibble on their toesies, nibble on their tiny feet!" the rest of the platoon chorused.

Matsugae sniffed and went back to unloading the prince's accoutrements. His Highness would want to look his best for dinner.

❖   ❖   ❖

"I'm not going to take dinner in the damned mess," Roger said petulantly, pulling at a strand of hair. He knew he was being a spoiled brat, and, as always, it drove him crazy. Of course, the whole situation seemed expressly designed to drive him mad, he reflected bitterly, and gripped his hands together until the knuckles went white and his forearms quivered.

"I'm not going," he repeated adamantly.

Eleanora knew from long experience that arguing with him was probably a lost cause, but sometimes, if you ground away at one of Roger's sulks, he came out of it. Sometimes. Rarely.

"Roger," she started calmly, "if you don't take dinner the first night, it will be a slap in the face to Captain Krasnitsky and his officers. . . ."

"I'm *not* going!" he shouted, and then, almost visibly, gathered control of his anger. His whole body was shivering now, and the tiny cabin seemed too small to contain his rage and frustration. It was the captain's cabin, the best one on the ship, but compared to the Palace, or even the regal ships of the Empress' Fleet that Roger had traveled on previously, it was the size of a closet.

He took a deep, cleansing breath, and shrugged.

"Okay, I'm being an ass. But I'm still not going to dinner. Make an excuse," he said with a sudden boyish grin. "You're good at that."

Eleanora shook her head in exasperation, but had to smile back. Sometimes Roger could also be disarmingly charming.

"Very well, Your Highness. I'll see you tomorrow morning."

She took the single step backward to open the hatch and stepped out of the cabin. And almost ran over Kostas Matsugae.

"Good evening, Ma'am," the valet said, skipping aside

despite an armful of clothing and accoutrements. He had to dodge again to avoid running into the Marine standing guard outside the door, but the Marine remained utterly expressionless and motionless. Any humor she might have felt at the frantic hopping about of the valet was quashed by iron discipline. The members of The Empress' Own were renowned for their ability to remain stone-faced and still through virtually anything. They occasionally had contests to determine who had the most endurance and stoicism. The former sergeant major of Gold Battalion held the record for endurance: ninety-three hours at attention without eating, drinking, sleeping, or going to the bathroom. It was the last, he'd admitted, which had been the hardest. He'd finally passed out from a combination of dehydration and toxin buildup.

"Good evening, Matsugae," Eleanora replied, and fought her own urge to smile. It was hard, for the fussy little valet was so bedecked with outfits that it was almost impossible to find him under the pile. "I'm sorry to say that our Prince won't be taking dinner in the mess, so I doubt he really needs those," she continued, gesturing with her chin at the mass of clothes.

"What? Why?" Matsugae squeaked from somewhere under the pile. "Oh, never mind. I have the casuals for after dinner, so I suppose that will do." He gave his neck a little twist, and his balding head and round face rose like a toadstool from the pile of clothing. "It's a terrible shame, though. I'd picked out a lovely sienna suit."

"Maybe you can calm him down with some clothes." O'Casey's smile took on a tinge of resignation. "I seem to have set him off, instead."

"Well, I can understand his being upset," the valet said with another sharp squeak. "Being sent off to the back of beyond on a pointless mission is bad enough, but to send a prince of the Blood Royal on a barge is simply the worst insult I can imagine!"

Eleanora pursed her lips and frowned at the valet.

"Don't go making it any worse than it already is, Matsugae. Sooner or later, Roger has to begin taking up his responsibilities as a member of the Royal Family. And sometimes that means sacrifices." *Like maybe the sacrifice of enough time to get a staff to go with the "Chief,"* she added silently. "He doesn't need his sulks encouraged."

"You care for him in your way, Ms. O'Casey, and I will care for him in mine," the valet snapped. "Push a child around, despise him, revile him and cast out his father, and what do you expect to get?"

"Roger is no longer a child," she retorted angrily. "We can't coddle, bathe, and dress him like he is one."

"No," the valet replied. "But we can give him enough space to breathe! We can make an image for him and hope he grows into it."

"What, an image of a clotheshorse?" the chief of staff shot back. It was an old and worn argument that the valet seemed to be winning. "He's grown into *that* one beautifully!"

The valet stared back at her like a fearless mouse confronting a cat.

"Unlike some people," he sniffed with a glance at her painfully plain suit, "His Highness has an appreciation for the finer things in life. But there's more to His Highness than a 'clotheshorse.' Until some of you begin to acknowledge that fact, however, you'll get exactly what you expect."

He glowered at her for an instant longer, then gave yet another sniff, hit the latch for the hatch with an elbow, and stepped into the cabin.

Roger leaned back on the bed in the tiny cabin, eyes shut and tried his best to radiate a dangerous calm. *I'm twenty-two years old*, he thought. *I'm a Prince of the*

Empire. I will not cry just because Mommy is making me angry.

He heard the blast-door of the cabin open and shut, and knew immediately who it was; the cologne that Matsugae wore was almost overpowering in the small compartment.

"Good evening, Kostas," he said calmly. Just having the valet present was soothing. Whatever anyone else thought, Kostas always took him at his face value. When that value was below par, Kostas would tell him, but when it had merit on its own level, Kostas would acknowledge it where no one else would.

"Good evening, Your Highness," Kostas said, already laying out one of the light *gi*-like chambray outfits the prince preferred to lounge in. "Will you want your hair washed this evening?"

"No, thank you," the prince responded with unconscious politeness. "I suppose you heard I'm not taking dinner in the mess?"

"Of course, Your Highness," the valet responded as the prince rolled upright on the bed and looked sourly around the cabin. "Pity, really. I had a beautiful suit picked out: that light sienna one that complements your hair so well."

The prince smiled thinly. "Nice try, Kosie, but no. I'm just too frazzled to be polite at dinner." He slapped the sides of his head with both hands in frustration. "Leviathan I could take. Net-Hauling I could take, grumbly oil and all. But why, oh *why*, did Mother Her Regalness choose to send me on this goddamned tramp freighter?"

"It isn't a tramp freighter, Your Highness, and you know it. We needed room for the bodyguards, and the alternative would have been to detach a Fleet carrier. Which would have been a bit much, don't you think? I will admit, though, that it's a bit . . . shabby."

"Shabby!" The prince gave a bitter laugh. "It's so worn I'm surprised it can hold atmosphere! It's so old I bet the hull is welded! I'm surprised it's not driven by internal combustion engines or steam power! John would've gotten a carrier. *Alexandra* would've gotten a carrier! But not Roger! Oh, no, not 'Baby Roj!' "

The valet finished laying out the various outfits to be chosen from in the limited space of the cabin and stood back with a resigned expression.

"Will I be drawing a bath for Your Highness?" he asked pointedly, and Roger gritted his teeth at the tone.

"So I should stop whining and get a grip?"

The valet only smiled very slightly in return, and Roger shook his head.

"I'm too worked up, Kosie." He looked around the three-meter-square space and shook his head again. "I wish there was someplace I could work out in peace on this tub."

"There's an exercise area adjacent to the Assault Complement Quarters, Your Highness," the valet pointed out.

"I said in peace," Roger commented dryly. He generally preferred to avoid the troops that filled the compartment. He'd never actually worked out around the Battalion, despite being its nominal commanding officer, because he'd had his fill of weird looks and sniggers behind his back in four years at the Academy. Getting the same treatment from his own bodyguards would be hard to take.

"The majority of the ship's company is eating at the moment, Your Highness," Matsugae pointed out. "You would probably have the gym to yourself."

The thought of a good workout was awfully attractive. Finally Roger nodded his head.

"Okay, Matsugae. Make it so."

As the dessert was cleared, Captain Krasnitsky looked significantly at Ensign Guha. The mahogany-skinned young woman blushed a darker hue, and stood up, wine glass in hand.

"Ladies and gentlemen," she said carefully, "Her Majesty the Empress. Long may she rule!"

After the chorused "The Empress," the captain cleared his throat.

"I'm sorry His Highness is unwell, Captain." He smiled at Captain Pahner. "Is there anything we can do? The gravity, temperature, and air pressure in his cabin are as close to Earth normal as my chief engineer can make them."

Captain Pahner set down his almost untouched wine glass and nodded to the captain. "I'm sure His Highness will be fine." Various other phrases crossed his mind, but he carefully suppressed them.

After the completion of this voyage, Pahner would move on to a command slot on a very similar ship. But larger. As with all COs in The Empress' Own, he was already on the promotion lists for the next grade, and at the completion of his rotation, he would take over as the commander of the 2nd Battalion, 502nd Heavy Strike Regiment. Since the 502nd was the primary ground combat unit of Seventh Fleet—the Fleet usually found in any face-off with the Saints—he could expect to see regular action, and that was good. He had no love of war, but the heat of battle was the only possible place to truly test whether a person was a Marine or not, and it would be good to be back in harness.

With over fifty years in the service, enlisted and officer, the two commands—Empress' Own and Heavy Strike—would be as good as it got. From there on out, it would all be downhill. Either retirement, or else colonel and then brigadier. Which was as good as saying a desk job: the Empire hadn't fielded a regiment in a couple of centuries. It was a somber thought that he could see a light at the end of the tunnel and it was a grav-train.

Captain Krasnitsky waited for further elaboration, but decided after a moment that that was all he was getting from the taciturn Marine. With another frozen smile he turned to Eleanora.

"Has the rest of the staff gone ahead to Leviathan to prepare for the Prince's arrival, Ms. O'Casey?"

Eleanora took a slightly deeper gulp of wine than was strictly polite, and looked over at Captain Pahner.

"I *am* the rest of the staff," she said coldly. Which meant that there had *not* been anyone to send ahead as an advance party. Which meant that once they got there, she would be running her ass off trying to set up all the minor details the staff should be handling. The staff that she was apparently chief of. That mysterious, magically invisible staff.

The captain was now well aware that he was wandering through a field of landmines. He smiled again, took a sip of wine, and turned to the engineering officer at his left to engage in casual chitchat that wasn't going to tick off a member of the Imperial Household.

Pahner moistened his lips with his wine again and looked over at Sergeant Major Kosutic. She was chatting quietly with the ship's bosun, and caught the look and simply raised her eyebrows as if to say, "Well, what you want me to do about it?" Pahner shrugged millimetrically in reply, and turned to the ensign at his left. What could any of them do about it?

CHAPTER THREE

Pahner tossed the electronic memo pad onto the desk in the tiny office of the Assault Complement Commander.

"I think that's about all the planning we can do without actually seeing the dirtside conditions," he told Kosutic, and the sergeant major shrugged philosophically.

"Well, frontier planets full of rugged individualists rarely spawn assassins, anyway, Boss."

"True enough," Pahner admitted. "But it's close enough to both Raiden-Winterhowe and the Saints to have me twitchy."

Kosutic nodded, but she knew better than to ask most of the questions that came to mind. Instead, she fingered her earlobe, where the sun-painted skull and crossbones glittered faintly, and then glanced at the antiquated watch on her wrist.

"I'm going to take a turn around the ship. Find out how many of the posts are asleep," she announced.

Pahner smiled. In two tours with the Regiment, he'd never found a post other than fully alert. You just didn't make it this far if you were the type to even *slouch* on guard duty. But it never hurt to check.

"Have fun," he said.

Ensign Guha finished sealing her ship boots and looked around the cabin. Everything was shipshape, so she picked up the black bag at her feet and touched the stud to open her cabin hatch. Somewhere in the depths of her mind a little voice was screaming. But it was a quiet voice.

She stepped out of the cabin, turned to the right, and shouldered the ditty bag. The bag was unusually heavy. The materials within would have been detected in the security sweep of the ship which was standard operating procedure before a member of the Imperial Family took transit . . . and they had been. And then accepted. The assault ship was designed to take a full Marine complement, after all, which included all of their explosive "loadout." The six ultradense bricks, formed out of the most powerful chemical explosive known, should do the job perfectly. The thought was a pleasing one, and, of course, her own position as logistics officer gave her full access to the material. Even more pleasing. Taken all in all, she practically scintillated with pleasure.

Her cabin was on the outer rim of the ship, along with most of the personal quarters, and she had a long trip to Engineering. But it would be a happy trip . . . despite the quiet little screams within.

She strode down the passage, smiling pleasantly at the few souls about in the depths of ship-night. They were few and far between, but no one questioned the logistics officer. She'd been taking deep-night strolls for her whole tour, and it was put down to simple insomnia. And that was fair enough, for she did suffer from insomnia, however far from "simple" it might be on this particular night.

She traveled the curved passages of the giant sphere, taking elevators to lower levels on a circuitous route that brought her closer and closer to Engineering. The route was designed to avoid the Marine guards scattered at strategic locations around the ship. Although their detectors wouldn't spot the demolitions unless she got very close, they would easily detect the fully charged power cell of the bead pistol in the same bag.

The horizon of the gray painted passages shrank as she neared the center of the vast ball. Finally, she exited one last elevator.

The passage beyond was straight for a change, the far end sealed by a blast-door. To one side of the blast-door, covering the controls, was a single Marine in the silver-and-black dress uniform of the House of MacClintock.

Private Hegazi came to attention, one hand sliding automatically towards his sidearm as the elevator opened, but he relaxed again almost immediately when he recognized the officer. He'd seen her any number of times on her perambulations of the ship, but never by Engineering.

Guess she got bored, he thought. *Or maybe I'm about to get lucky?* Nonetheless, his duty was clear.

"Ma'am," he said, remaining at attention as she neared. "This is a secure space. Please exit this secure area."

Ensign Guha smiled faintly as an aiming grid dropped across her vision. Her right hand, hidden inside the bag, flipped the bead gun off of safe, and triggered a five-round burst.

The five-millimeter steel-coated, glass-cored beads were accelerated to phenomenal speeds by the electro-magnets lining the barrel. The weapon's recoil was tremendous, but all five of the beads had cleared the barrel before recoil began to take effect. Ensign Guha's hand was thrown violently out of the now smoking bag, but the beads continued their flight towards the Marine guard.

Hegazi was fast. You had to be in the Regiment. But he also had less than an eighth of a second between the instant his instincts shrilled a warning and the impact of the first bead on his upper chest.

The outer layer of his heavy uniform was a synthetic that simulated buff wool but was fire resistant. It wasn't ballistic resistant. The next layer, however, was kinetic reactive. As the beads struck, the polymers of the uniform reacted instantaneously, their chemical bonds shifting under the imparted energy to change the textile from soft and flexible to solid as steel. The armor had weaknesses and was vulnerable to cuts, but it was light, and well-nigh impregnable to small-arms fire.

Yet any material has a breaking point. In the case of the Marines' uniform armor, that point was high but not infinite. The first bead shattered on the surface, the metal and glass bits flicking out in a fan to pepper the underside of the Marine's chin even as his hand reached once more for his own sidearm. The weight was coming off his feet as he started to drop to a kneeling position when the second bead hit a few centimeters above the first. This bead also shattered, but the extra energy began to splinter the molecular bonds of the resistant material.

The third bead did the trick. Coming in on the heels of the second and slightly lower, it shattered the kinetic armor like glass, finally throwing some of its mass into the now unprotected Marine's sternum.

Ensign Guha wiped the blood off of the keypad and attached a device to the surface temperature scanner.

She shouldn't have had the codes to enter Engineering, or the facial features, for that matter. But any system is subject to compromise, and this one was no exception. The security systems saw the IR features of the *DeGlopper*'s chief engineer and received the correct codes timed in just the way the chief would have tapped them. She stepped through the open blast-doors and looked around, pleased but not surprised that there was no one in sight.

The engineering spaces of the ship were huge, taking up well over one-third of the interior volume. The tunnel drive coils and the capacitors to feed them took up the majority of the space, and their keening song filled the vast compartment as they sucked in energy voraciously and distorted any concept of Einsteinian reality. The light-speed limit could be violated, but it required immense power, and the tunnel drive gobbled up internal volume almost as greedily as it did energy.

But the field of the tunnel drive system was more or less fixed and independent of mass. Like the phase drive, there was a specific limit to the maximum volume of the field which could be generated, but the mass within that field was unimportant. Thus the huge ship carriers of the various Imperial and republican navies that battled among the stars. And thus the vast size of the interstellar fleet transports.

But all of it depended on power. Enormous, barely controlled power.

Ensign Guha turned to the left and followed the curving passage as the tunnel drive thumped out its keening star song.

Kosutic nodded at the guard on the magazine deck as she stepped back out the hatch. The guard, a newbie from First Platoon, had stopped her at the hatch and insisted that she pass the facial temperature scan and

key in her code. Which was exactly what she was supposed to do, which was the reason for the sergeant
major's nod of approval. However, Kosutic also made a
mental note to talk to Margaretta Lai, the trooper's
platoon sergeant. The trooper had clearly loosened up
when she recognized the sergeant major, and she needed
to learn to doubt everything and everyone. Eternal
paranoia was the entire purpose of the Regiment. There
was no other way to guard effectively in this day and
age.

Despite early gains in processing, it had taken
humanity nearly a millennium after the invention of
the first crude computers to develop a system of
implanted processors that interfaced completely with
human neural systems without adverse side effects. The
"toots" were still cutting edge and being constantly
refined . . . and they were a security planner's nightmare, because they could be programmed to take over
a person's body. When that happened, the unfortunate
victim had no control over his own actions. The
Marines called people like that "toombies."

Some societies used specially modified toots to control the actions of convicted criminals, but in most
societies, including the Empire of Man, such a use of
the hardware was illegal for all but military purposes.
The Marines themselves used the system to the full-
est as a combat aid and multiplier, but even they were
wary of it.

The big problem was hacking. A person whose toot
had been "hacked" could be forced to do literally anything. Just two years ago, someone had mounted an
assassination attempt on the prime minister of the
Alphane Empire by using a human official with a
hacked toot. The hacker had never been found, but
once the security protocols were solved, it had been
a ludicrously simple thing to do. The toots were

designed for radio-packet external data input, and a small device disguised as an antique pocket watch had been found in the official's possession. It was speculated that it had been given to him as a gift, but wherever it had come from, it had taken his toot over. It was as if the official had been possessed by a demon hidden in the ancient Pandora's box.

Since then, all members of the Regiment and all close servitors of the Imperial Family had been required to go through random scans, and the security protocols of their toots had been updated yet again. Kosutic knew that, but she also knew there was no such thing as a perfect defense.

She made a note to hunt down Gunny Lai on her toot and smiled at the ambiguity of her own actions. She'd started off in the Marines before the day of the devices; but she'd become as dependent on them as everyone else. It was a humorous irony, in a bitter sort of way, that she now saw them as the single biggest threat to her charges.

She stepped onto the elevator and checked the duty roster again. Hegazi was on Engineering. Good troop, but new. Too new. Hell, they were all too new; eighteen months was just enough time to get very good at their jobs, then most went on to Steel. The few who stayed were rarely the best. She thought of Julian and laughed. Of course, there was best and best. But she intended to remind Hegazi, who was a good troop overall, that he needed to be totally one hundred percent paranoid at all times.

She stood in the pool of the Marine's blood. She hadn't bothered to check his pulse; nobody who'd lost that much blood was alive, and she was too busy considering what to do to waste time on pointless gestures. She didn't consider for long—the Marines didn't exactly

pick ditherers as the senior noncoms of The Empress'
Own—but there was always enough time to screw up,
so there had to be enough to make the right move, as
well.

She tapped her communicator.

"Sergeant of the Guard. Full load out to Engineering. We have a breach. Do not sound General Quarters."

She cut the communication. The guards would contact Pahner, and the assassin wouldn't be alerted, for
the Marine communicators were encrypted. Of course,
the saboteur—and sabotage had to be what the killer
contemplated—could have left any of half a dozen telltales along his backtrail to warn him that he'd been
discovered.

Kosutic plucked the sensor wand off the dead guard's
belt and swept the hatch. No obvious traces there. She
keyed in the entry code and went through the hatch fast
and low as it opened. The blood was already coagulat-
ing, and the body was cooling, so the assassin probably
wasn't on the far side of the hatch. But Eva Kosutic
hadn't survived to be a sergeant major by depending on
"probably."

"Engineering, this is Sergeant Major Kosutic," she said
into her communicator. "Do not, I say again, do *not*
sound an alert. We have a probable saboteur in Engineering; your guard is dead." She swept the sensor wand
around. There were heat traces everywhere, but most
went straight ahead. All except one. A single trace split
off from the pack, heading to the sergeant major's left,
and it looked fresher.

"What?" the communicator demanded incredulously.
"Where?"

"It looks like somewhere in quadrant four," she
snapped. "Get on your scanners and vids. Find them."

There was a moment of silence from whoever was
on the other end of the line. Then—

"Roger," the communicator responded.

She hoped like hell it wasn't the saboteur.

Ensign Guha paused and looked left and right. She brought up a measuring grid and used it to locate the precise point she needed on the right-hand bulkhead, then reached into her satchel and extracted a one-kilo shaped charge. She stripped the covering plastic off the bottom, affixed it to the bulkhead with the provided adhesive, and examined her handiwork for a moment, to ensure it wasn't going anywhere. Then she pulled a pin and depressed a thumbswitch. A small red light blinked on, then went out; the bomb was armed.

She turned to her left once more and continued her circuit. Only three more to go.

Captain Pahner closed the front of his chameleon suit and configured his helmet to seal the whole system as the elevator descended. Gunnery Sergeant Jin, already suited, stood beside him with Kosutic's helmet slung at his side and her chameleon suit over his shoulder. The standard issue Marine suits offered better ballistic protection than dress uniforms, faded the wearer into the background, and were designed for vacuum work. They weren't as good as combat armor, but there wasn't time for full armor. He had one platoon warming theirs up anyway, of course, but if this didn't go down in the next few minutes his name wasn't Armand Pahner.

"Eva," he snapped into the helmet mike. "Talk to me."

"Three so far. One-kilo shaped charges right over plasma conduits. They've got anti-tamper devices in them. I can smell it."

"Captain Krasnitsky, this is Captain Pahner," Pahner said sharply. *Surprise is a mental condition, not reality,* he reminded himself. "We have to shut down those conduits."

"We can't," Krasnitsky answered. "You can't just shut off a tunnel drive. If you tried it, you'd come out at a random point somewhere in a nine-light-year radius sphere. And the plasma has to be slowed down, anyway. If you just try to shut off it . . . backfires. We could lose everything."

"If we were about to be hit in Engineering by enemy fire," Pahner asked, "what would you do then?"

"We'd be under *phase* drive!" Krasnitsky snapped back. "You can't *be* hit in tunnel space. There's no procedure for this!"

"Shit," Pahner said quietly. It was the first time anyone had ever heard him swear. "Sergeant Major, get the hell out of there."

"I don't see any timers."

"They're there."

"Probably. But if I can get the shooter . . ."

"They could be on a dead-man's switch," Pahner said, gritting his teeth as he stepped off the elevator. "This is an order, Sergeant Major Kosutic. Get out of there. Now."

"I'm closer to getting out going through the shooter than going back," Kosutic said mildly.

Pahner looked at the first bomb. As Kosutic had said, there were no telltales but it smelled like it had anti-tamper devices. He turned to the sergeant of the guard, Sergeant Bilali from First Platoon, who looked as cool as a cucumber for someone standing within a few feet of a bomb that could go off at any moment. The private next to him wasn't quite as cool; she was watching the sergeant's back and breathing deeply and regularly. It was a common method of dealing with combat stress, which she obviously was. Pahner arched an eyebrow at Bilali.

"Demo?"

"On the way, Sir," the sergeant replied crisply.

"Okay," Pahner said with a nod and a glance around. If the bomber gave them time, they could try blowing the bombs in place. The explosion of a charge placed next to one of them would tend to break up the plasma jet from a shaped charge, and the bulkheads were armored to protect the plasma conduits. Without a shaped-charge jet, there was no way the explosions would penetrate. Of course, that assumed that they didn't go off before the demolition teams could get to them.

"'If you can keep your head when all about you . . .'" Pahner whispered, thinking furiously.

"Excuse me, Sir?"

"Is there someone following up the Sergeant Major?"

"Yes, Sir," Bilali said. "There are teams coming from either end, and we have one cutting across the middle of Engineering, as well."

"Okay, we all know we're brave, but there's a fine line between hardcore and stupid. Let's get the heck out of here and seal this passage in case these things go off."

"Roger that, Sir." The expression on Bilali's midnight-black face didn't even flicker as he touched his communicator. "Guard. Everyone but the point teams, out of the passage. Seal it at both ends." The passage made a circuit of the ship. Although there were side connections, those stayed sealed as a matter of course. It was only the central passageway hatches that remained open. And the intervening blast-doors. If worse came to worst . . .

"Captain Krasnitsky," Pahner said, "what happens if we shut all the doors and the bombs detonate anyway?"

"Bad things," a female voice snapped. "This is Lieutenant Commander Furtwangler, Chief Engineer. First of all, the blast-doors aren't designed for multiple plasma failures. They might not stop it from flooding Engineering. And even if they do keep the plasma from killing

us all, we still drop out of TD. We probably don't
get the drive back with that much damage, and even
if we do, we lose most of our range. Satan only knows
what secondary damage would occur. Bad things," she
repeated.

Pahner nodded as the blast-doors shut on his Marines.
Bad things seemed to be happening all over.

Kosutic had noted the pattern of placement, and as
the sixth blast-door came up, she leapt forward, skid-
ding on her stomach into view of where the next bomb
would be.

Ensign Guha triggered a burst of beads that shrieked
through where the sergeant major would have been had
she come around the corner running upright. The kick
from the powerful pistol threw it up over the ensign's
head despite her two-handed grip, and she never had
time to get back on target.

Eva Kosutic was a veteran of a hundred firefights and
fired thousands of bead rounds every week just to keep
in practice. No hacked assassination program, however
well-designed, could beat that experience. Her own bead
pistol tracked onto the young ensign's throat, and she
triggered a single round.

The five-millimeter bead was accelerated to four
kilometers per second in its twenty-centimeter flight up
the barrel. When it struck the ensign's neck, one centimeter to the left of her trachea, it shattered, converting
all of its kinetic energy to explosive hydrostatic shock
in a fraction of a second.

The ensign's head exploded off her body and was
thrown backwards as the severed carotids jetted blood
all over the unarmed bomb at her feet.

Before the decapitated body had hit the floor, Kosutic
was up and running. The armed bombs were probably
remotely triggered, but they would also have a backup.

Any plan this meticulous was bound to have a backup. The simplest would be a timer, but a good addition would be a dead-man's switch controlled by the assassin's toot. When the ensign died, which she more or less had just done, the toot would send out a signal—probably when all brain activity ceased—to detonate the bombs. But although the ensign-zombie was for all practical purposes dead, brain activity in a case of severance continued for a few seconds. Which was why the sergeant major had shot her in the throat, not the head.

All of the bombs were behind Eva Kosutic, and she intended to ensure that they stayed as far away as possible. She keyed her communicator. *"Fire in the hole! Shut all blast-doors!"* she shouted as she leapt over the sprayed blood and past the ensign's head, still accelerating.

Captain Pahner had just opened his mouth to repeat the sergeant major's order when there were a whole series of thumps, and the world went sideways.

CHAPTER FOUR

Roger was never sure afterwards if it was the General Quarters alarm or the rough hands of the Marines that startled him awake.

The Marines' faces were unfamiliar to his mostly sleeping brain in the dim red emergency lights, under the banshee howl of the alarm, and he reacted violently as he was slammed roughly into a bulkhead. As a member of the Imperial Family, his toot was equipped with several bits of software not available to the general public, including a complete "hardwired" hand-to-hand combat package and an "assassin" program which did several interesting things. Moreover, the prince had always been athletic. He held black belts in three separate "hard" martial arts, and his *sensei* (not surprisingly) was one of the best in the entire Empire of Man.

With all of that going for him, he was *not* a safe person to jump upon, without warning, in the dark, whatever Bravo Company might have thought of him. Even taken by surprise in a sound sleep, he managed to kick backward, trying for a knee strike as one arm was wrenched to the left and inserted in a sleeve. Considering his surprised, sleep-groggy state, it was a remarkably well-executed attempt . . . and accomplished absolutely nothing.

If the members of The Empress' Own were surprised by his response, they had a surprise or two for him, as well. Like the fact that *their* toots offered hardwired booster packages of their own . . . and that all of them had spent even longer training in the martial arts than he had. He was spun around and struck in the solar plexus for his troubles.

The two Bravo Company privates seemed unconcerned by his chokes and gasps as they expertly stuffed him into an emergency vac suit, and once they had him in the suit, with his helmet on, they sat on him. Literally. He was pushed roughly to the deck, where the two bodyguards pinned him down and sat on him, weapons trained outward.

Due to the oversized cretin sitting on his chest, he couldn't reach his suit controls, and since the com was in its default "off" mode, he couldn't even call Captain Pahner and order him to get these slope-browed bruisers to let him up. Although he was technically their commander, the privates paid no attention to his first few queries, shouted through the plastron of the helmet. As soon as he realized his efforts were ineffective, he gave up. The hell if he was going to be ignored by these goons.

After what seemed an eternity, but couldn't have been more than ten or fifteen minutes, the compartment hatch opened to reveal two Marines in battle armor. The guards sitting on him stood up, one of them giving him a hand to help him to his feet, and left the compartment. The two new guards, faceless nonentities behind the flickering visors of their powered armor, sat him on the bed and sandwiched him between them, weapons trained outward once again. But in this case, the weapons were a quad-barreled heavy bead gun and a plasma cannon trained, respectively, toward the door and toward the next compartment. If boarders came slicing through the wall, they were in for an uncomfortable surprise.

He now had time to examine the vac suit and found that—surprise, surprise—the com was limited to the emergency "Guard" frequency only. It was an unforgivable sin, roughly comparable to eating one's own young, to use that frequency in anything but a true emergency. That was a lesson (one of the few) he'd learned quite painfully during his mandatory ordeal at the Academy, and since the troopers didn't seem to be hostile—just very, very determined to keep him safe—this probably didn't count as a "true" emergency. So no communicator.

Which left him to ponder what was going on with virtually no data. There was air, but the emergency lights were on. He reached for the latches on his suit to take the helmet off, but one of the armored Marines tapped his hand away from them. The tap was obviously intended to be polite but firm, but the pseudo-muscles of the armor turned it into a stinging slap.

Rubbing his knuckles, Roger leaned over until his helmet was in contact with the Marine's.

"Would you mind telling me what the hell is going on?"

"Captain Pahner said to wait until he got here, Your Highness," a female soprano, badly distorted by the helmets, responded.

Roger nodded and leaned back against the bulkhead, flipping his head inside the helmet to try to make his ponytail lie flat and smooth. So, either there'd been a coup, and Pahner was in on it, or there'd been some sort of emergency, and Pahner wanted to be able to give him a complete report rather than a garbled version second- or third-hand.

If the second scenario were correct, well and good. He would just cool his heels here for a while, then find out what the problem was. If it was a case of the first scenario . . . He looked at the armored Marine with the bead cannon pointed at the door. There was probably a snowball's chance in hell that he could actually wrest it away from the Marine and kill Pahner with it, but if this was a coup, his life was worth less than spit anyway. Might as well go out like a MacClintock.

He walked mentally back over every step of the event, and noticed that the floor had stopped vibrating. The background hum of the various life-support and drive systems had become so familiar that it was unnoticed, but now, with it gone, its absence was obvious. If those systems were off-line, they were in deep trouble indeed . . . which at least militated against the coup theory.

Then he thought about the two troopers who'd dragged him out of bed. They'd suited him up and literally sat on him for a good ten minutes before anyone showed up to relieve them. And they hadn't had suits. If the cabin had lost pressure, they would have died rapid and unpleasant deaths. So the privates, at least, thought he was worth keeping alive. Which also argued against the coup theory.

They'd also risked their lives to protect him, and while that willingness to risk or lose their lives to keep their charges alive was assumed on the part of the Imperial Family, Roger had never been in an emergency. There'd never been a situation in which his bodyguard's life was threatened. Well, there'd been that one disastrous encounter on a vacation, but the bodyguard was never actually in danger, whatever the young lady had threatened. . . .

But in this case, two people whose names he didn't even know had risked an awful death to protect his life.

It was a confusing thought.

❖   ❖   ❖

Nearly two hours passed before "Captain" Pahner appeared, accompanied by Captain Krasnitsky. Pahner was in a chameleon suit, while the ship's captain was in a Fleet skin suit, with his helmet flopped back out of the way.

Pahner nodded to the two guards, who left the cabin, closing the hatch behind them. Roger took a good look at Krasnitsky, and promptly waved him into the station chair at the small desk. While the Fleet captain collapsed into the seat, Pahner touched the stud to lock the hatch, then turned and faced the prince.

"We have a problem, Your Highness."

"Oh, really, Captain? I hadn't noticed." The prince's voice was muffled through the plastron of the helmet. After a moment's fumbling, he released the standard catches and dumped the helmet on his bunk. "By the way," he continued sourly, "there wouldn't happen to be a skin-suit in *my* size on board, would there?"

"No, Your Highness, there wouldn't," Pahner answered stoically. "I've already checked. That detail was overlooked. As were others, apparently." He turned to the miserable-looking captain. "If you'd care to continue, Captain Krasnitsky?"

The captain rubbed his face and sighed.

"We were sabotaged, Your Highness. Badly."

"Sabotaged?" the prince repeated incredulously. "By whom?"

"Now *that* is the million-credit question, Your Highness," Pahner admitted. "We know the who as in 'who actually did the sabotage.' That was Ensign Amanda Guha, the ship's logistics officer."

"What?" Roger blinked in confusion. "Why would she do that?"

Captain Krasnitsky opened his mouth to answer, then looked at Pahner, and the Marine shrugged his shoulders and continued. "We're not positive, of course, but I believe she was a toombie."

"A toot zombie?" Roger's eyes widened. "Here? Are there any more?" Then he shook his head at the stupidity of his own question. "We wouldn't know, would we?"

"No, Your Highness, we wouldn't," Pahner replied with considerable restraint. "However, there are some indications that she was the sole toombie. It's vanishingly unlikely that anyone else in the Company is at risk. Everyone who is expected to have contact with you is regularly swept and has up-to-date security protocols. And everyone in the ship's company was swept before the voyage. Including Ensign Guha. But we found a device in her cabin. . . ."

"Oh, shit," Roger said.

"I can think of at least twenty ways the device could have made it on board," Pahner continued. "However, that's not the most pressing issue at the moment."

"Your Highness," Captain Krasnitsky said finally, with a nodded thanks at Pahner, "Captain Pahner is correct. How they got to Guha is less important than what she did to us, I'm afraid. She managed to attach explosive devices to several of the tunnel drive plasma conduits. When they went off, we nearly lost Engineering entirely from an unvented plasma core leak. When the plasma breach was detected, the automated systems were *supposed* to shut off deuterium flow, but the next bead in the magazine was a worm program that she apparently dumped into the control systems. It cut out the safety interlocks, so the plasma kept venting. . . ."

The captain stopped and wiped his face, trying to find the right words to report the disaster, but Pahner did it for him.

"We've lost all but one fusion plant, Your Highness," the stone-faced Marine said. "Tunnel drive is off-line. Phase drive is off-line. The chief engineer got the flow shut down manually, but a plasma blast took her out right after she did it. And she was our only fully qualified engineering repair officer."

"A physical and cyber attack." The prince sounded stunned. "Against a member of the Imperial Family?"

"Yes, Your Highness," Pahner said with the bleak smile of the truly pissed professional. "Lovely, don't you think? And it wasn't as if they were going to stop there. We've got worm programs and viruses in every major subsystem: Navigation, Fire Control—"

"And Environmental," Krasnitsky interrupted with a shake of his head. "Well, had. I'm pretty sure we got them all wiped out, but we've taken some heavy casualties in Engineering, and—"

"I was 'pretty sure' there wasn't anything like them on board to begin with!" Pahner snapped angrily. "We need to be more than 'pretty sure,' Captain."

"Agreed, Captain," the captain said shortly. He stood and straightened his back. "Your Highness, with your permission, I need to get back to my ship. I have high hopes that we can make sufficient repairs to get us to a habitable planet. Although," he turned and looked at the granite-faced Pahner again, "the system we have to make for . . ."

He let his voice trail off and shrugged, and Roger nodded, with a dazed expression.

"Of course, Captain. You need to get back to work. Good luck. Call me if you need anything."

He realized how fatuous the last sentence sounded even as it dropped from his lips. What the heck could he do that trained and experienced crew members couldn't? Cook? But the already exhausted captain paid no attention to the silliness of the remark. He simply bowed, and stepped past Pahner and out of the cabin.

The hatch closed behind him, and Pahner gave the prince another bleak smile.

"What the Captain didn't mention, Your Highness, is where we're headed."

"Which is where?" the prince asked warily.

"Marduk, Your Highness."

The prince searched his memory, but found nothing. A quick check of his implanted database found the planet, but it was simply listed as a Class Three imperial planet. A toot had a fairly large memory, but much of it was taken up by the interaction protocols. The remainder was filled with data which, in Roger's case, anyway, was selected at the user's discretion. Now the entry flashed across the surface of his consciousness as figures and pictures scrolled across his vision. Most of the data was textual and symbolic, the better to crowd into the memory allocation, and he frowned thoughtfully as he scanned it. The world maintained an imperial post with what sounded like very limited landing facilities, but it wasn't even an associate member—just a place where the Empire had planted its flag.

"It's one of ours," he stated carefully.

"Nominally, Your Highness. Nominally," Pahner snorted. "There's a port, but no repair facilities— certainly none capable of repairing one of these assault ships. There's an automated refueling post over one of the gas giants which is owned by TexAmP, but the port is locally managed. Out on the back of beyond like it is, who knows what's actually going on?"

Pahner consulted his own toot and frowned much more unhappily than Roger had.

"The only intel note I have on the region is that the Saints might be active out here. On the other hand, Your Highness, out here on the frontier about half the time you turn around there's a Saint SpecOps team nosing under the tent." He smiled faintly. "Of course, they probably feel the same way about us."

Pahner consulted his notepad, with its much greater memory, and frowned again.

"The locals are hostile and primitive, the fauna is vicious, the mean temperature is thirty-three degrees centigrade, and it rains five times a day. The region is notorious for Dream Spice smuggling, and piracy is rampant. Of course." He shook his head. "Frankly, Your Highness, I feel like I'm taking you down Fourteenth Street at oh-three hundred on a Saturday night in August dressed in thousand-credit chips."

Fourteenth Street had been in existence since the days when Imperial City had been the District of Columbia, the capital of the former United States, and it had never been a good place to wander. But that was the last thing on Roger's mind at this particular moment, and he rubbed his face and sighed.

"Is there any good news?" The question had a note of a whine in it, and he kicked himself for being such a shit. Everyone else was busting their butts to save his sorry ass. The least he could do was not whine about the situation!

Pahner's face tightened.

"Well, you're still breathing, Your Highness. So I haven't failed my charge yet. And I think the Captain can get the ship *to* Marduk, which is a blessing. At least in a military ship they can reroute the fixed control runs, although that's going to take a week or more, with most of the Company pitching in alongside the crew to do, pardon the pun, grunt work.

"It's good news that the senior engineer was in the compartment in the middle of the night and reacted fast enough to shut down an out of control reaction. It's good news that we're on a military ship. It's good news that we only got knocked six or seven light-years off course, and not clear into Saint territory. It's good news that we're still breathing. But other than that, no. I can't think of any."

Roger nodded. "You have an interesting definition of good news, Captain. But I see your point. What can I do to help?" he asked, carefully controlling his voice.

"To tell you the truth, Your Highness, the best thing you can do is to stay in your cabin and out of the way. All your presence would do would be to distract the crew and make my guys have to run around using up extra oxygen. So, if you'd stay put, I'd appreciate it. I'll have your meals delivered."

"What about the gym?" Roger asked, his eyes flicking around the tiny cabin.

"Until Environmental comes back online, none of us are going to be doing much working out, Your Highness. Now, if you'll excuse me, I have to get back to work."

Without waiting for permission, Pahner hit the hatch key and let himself out. The hatch cycled shut behind him, leaving Roger to stare at the walls that seemed smaller than ever.

And to listen for the returning circulation of air.

CHAPTER FIVE

Prince Roger's patience had worn thin.

The better part of a day had passed since the crudely repaired, shuddering tunnel drive had kicked off and the in-system phase drive had cut in, and he was tired of being good. He'd been stuck in his cabin, half the time in this ill-fitting vac suit, for three weeks while the repairs proceeded and the ship limped through tunnel space toward Marduk, and the noise and vibration of the patched-up drive systems hadn't been designed to make him any happier about it.

The TD normally emitted a smooth, almost lulling background hum, but the jury-rigged repairs had produced something that whined, shuddered, and sometimes seemed to threaten to tear the ship apart. Pahner and Captain Krasnitsky had been careful to underplay the problems on their infrequent visits to update him, but the repairs weren't much more than "5k cord and bubble gum," according to Matsugae, who'd become friendly with some of the guards. They'd held together, though, and the awful journey was almost over. All they had to do was land on Marduk and commandeer the first imperial ship back to Earth. He might even end up being able to avoid Leviathan completely. Problem solved, crisis resolved, danger past. So Roger, Prince of the House MacClintock, was not by God going to stay cooped up, incommunicado, in his stinking cabin.

He smoothed down his hair, patted a few stray strands into place, touched the hatch control, and stepped out into the passage. The stink in the dim corridor was even worse than in the cabin, and for a moment he considered donning his helmet. But he was obviously clumsy putting it on and taking it off, and damned if he was going to give these Myrmidons a reason to laugh at his expense. He turned to one of the armored guards.

"Take me to the bridge," he ordered in his most imperious tone. He wanted to be absolutely clear that he was done cowering in his cabin.

Sergeant Nimashet Despreaux cocked her head inside her helmet and regarded the prince from behind the shield of her flickering visor. The helmet system was intended to cause the eye to shift away, enhancing the effect of the chameleon camouflage they all wore. But it also made it impossible for anyone on the outside to see a Marine's expression, and, after a brief pause, she stuck her tongue out at him and turned toward the bridge. She also sent a biofeedback command to the radio control and opened a channel to Captain Pahner.

"Captain Pahner, this is Sergeant Despreaux. His Highness is headed for the bridge," she reported flatly.

"Roger," was the terse reply.

It was going to be interesting to be a fly on the wall for this one.

They finally cycled through the double airlock system to the bridge, and Roger looked around. He'd familiarized with the *Puller*-class at the Academy, but he'd never actually been on the bridge of one before. The company-sized assault transports were the backbone of the Corps support groups, which meant they were under-emphasized by the Academy. An Academy graduate wanted to be posted to Line or Screen forces, where the promotions and the action were, not to an assault barge. Might as well captain a garbage scow.

But this garbage scow had survived the crisis, and that said a lot for the captain and crew, Academy graduates or not.

There was evidence of the damage even on the bridge. Scorch marks on the communications board indicated an overload in the maser com, and most of the front panels were missing from the control stations. Control runs were normally formed directly into the hull structure when a ship was grown, but since military ships had to assume that they would suffer combat damage, there were provisions for bypassing them with temporary systems. In this case, hastily installed relays, some of them even made out of *wire*, for God's sake, snaked across the floor, and the compartment was filled with the faint pulse of optic transmissions leaking from the joints.

Roger stepped over the cables littering the deck and joined the captain where he and Pahner were examining the tactical readout. The hologram of the system buckled and rippled as the crippled tactical computers struggled to keep it updated.

"How are we doing?" he asked.

"Well," Captain Krasnitsky answered with a grim, utterly humorless smile, "we *were* doing fine, Your Highness."

As he finished speaking, the General Quarters alarm sounded. Again.

"What's happening?" Roger asked over the wail, and Captain Pahner frowned and shook his head.

"Unidentified warship in the system, Your Highness. They're over a day away from intercept, but we don't know what else might be lying doggo nearby."

"What?" Roger yipped, his voice cracking in surprise. "How? But—" He stopped and tried to put on a better face. "Are they part of the sabotage? Could they be waiting for us? And who are they? Not imperial?"

"Captain?" Pahner turned to the ship's commander.

"Currently, who they are is unknown, Sir. Your Highness, I mean." For once, the captain wasn't flustered by the presence of royalty. The overriding necessity to fight his ship was all he had mind for, and the last three weeks of hell had burned out most of his other worries. "Our sensors are damaged, along with everything else, but it's definitely a warship from the phase drive signature. The filament structure is too deep for it to be anything else." He frowned again and thought about the rest of the questions.

"I doubt that they're part of some deeply laid plan, Your Highness. When the tunnel drive was damaged, it threw us badly off our planned flight path. I doubt that the conspirators, whoever they were, could believe we're still alive, and if they'd made preparations to 'make sure of the job,' they would have done so in systems closer to our base course. Marduk is off our baseline by almost a full tunnel jump, almost seventeen light-years. I don't see how anyone could have anticipated our ending up here.

"So, no, I don't think they're 'waiting for us,' but that doesn't necessarily make their presence good news. The drive and emissions signatures look kind of like a Saint parasite cruiser, but if that's so, that means the Saints have had a Line carrier in-system."

"And that means the Saints have probably taken the system," Pahner snarled.

The ship captain smiled thinly and sniffed, tapping the edge of the crippled tactical display. "Yes, it does."

"So the planet is under hostile control?" Roger asked.

"Possibly, Sir. Your Highness," Krasnitsky agreed. "Okay, probably. The orbitals, at least. They haven't necessarily taken over the port."

"Almost certainly," Pahner concluded. "Captain, I think we need a council. Myself and my officers, His Highness, your officers who are available. We have time?"

"Oh, yes. Whoever this is, he waited to bring up his phase drive until we were deep enough inside the tunnel wall to be sure no merchant could make it back out without being overhauled. Which probably means our signature is changed enough from our damage that he thinks we're a merchie instead of an assault ship. But even with our accel towards the planet and his accel towards us, we have several hours to decide what we're going to do"

"What are our choices?" Roger asked. The blinking red icon of the possible hostile cruiser held his eyes like a lodestone, and Krasnitsky smiled faintly.

"Well, there isn't much choice, is there, Your Highness? We can't space out . . ."

" . . . so, we'll have to fight," Captain Krasnitsky said.

The wardroom was crowded. Besides Krasnitsky, there were his executive officer, the acting engineer, and the acting tactical officer. On Bravo Company's side of the table there was Prince Roger, who was flanked by Eleanora O'Casey and Captain Pahner. In addition, Pahner had brought two of his three lieutenants. According to the ideal universe of The Book, there were supposed to be seven lieutenants a line company, but that happy state of affairs was rarely found in dreary reality. It was especially hard to find in The Empress' Own, which had even higher standards for its officers than its enlisted men.

In general, the need for an executive officer and "chief of staff" for a company commander was seen as overriding the need for a platoon leader, so Third Platoon was officerless. Its platoon sergeant, who normally would have been in the meeting, was busy getting it prepared for whatever the CO decided to do, and the navigator was on the bridge, bluffing the oncoming cruiser which was looking more and more like a Saint parasite.

"I don't want anyone to have any doubts," Krasnitsky went on. "We might win, and we might not. Usually, I'd say we could take a single cruiser—we've got more missiles, and heavier, and we've got him licked on beam armament." He paused and stared at the deckhead for a moment. "We've got all the normal advantages of a tunnel drive ship. We aren't mass-limited; the drive only cares about our volume, so we can afford to mount ChromSten armor, which he can't. That right there is a major factor, since it will shrug off some of the missiles that get through, whereas ours will all hammer him. And we've got more internal volume, so we can absorb more of the damage that does get through.

"The downside is, we're in sad shape. We can hardly accelerate at all, and our sensors and targeting systems are screwed. We're a damned big target, too, so it's not like they're going to miss. All the normal disadvantages of a TD ship, with a few extra thrown in. So we'll take damage, no question. Even if we win, we'll be in worse shape than we are now."

He paused again and looked around the compartment. The Marines, combat veterans all, looked grim but determined. His own people, none of whom had actually been through a ship-to-ship action, looked a bit white, but focused. The prince's chief of staff was trying very hard to look as if she had any idea at all of what was going on. The prince, though . . . The prince was a sight. It was obvious that, whatever else he'd taken at the Academy, no-win simulations hadn't been on the program. As the briefing had gone on, his eyes had just gotten rounder and rounder. . . .

"What about punching the assault shuttles?" Pahner asked, leaning a chin on one fist and looking so calm he appeared almost disinterested. Krasnitsky had dealt with some cool Marines in the course of his career, but the commander of the prince's bodyguard was obviously one of those rare people who simply got calmer when disaster loomed. The Fleet officer was willing to bet that the Marine's blood pressure and heartbeat were so low they were dropping off the scale.

"I'd suggest loading them," Lieutenant Commander Talcott, *DeGlopper*'s XO said, "but don't punch them. Putting their additional armor between the Prince and incoming fire would be good, but you'd have a helluva time making the planet without us from here."

"Have we received any transmission from the other ship?" Eleanora asked.

"Not yet," Krasnitsky said. "Lag. The soonest we can expect to receive a com is sometime in the next half hour, and they'll be receiving our own message about the same time. And before you ask: we're the Nebula Lines freighter *Beowulf's Gift*, out of Olmstead. We've had a tunnel drive failure, and we're looking for a port to await a repair ship."

"Whether they believe it or not," snorted Lieutenant Gulyas, the Second Platoon leader. Since Marine companies were designed to operate independently, which meant their COs needed their own *de facto* staffs, he also wore the "hat" of intel officer.

"Indeed," Lieutenant Commander Talcott said. "Just as much as we believe them."

"There's no reason for them to suspect us," Captain Krasnitsky pointed out. "With our phase drive damage, we can't make any sort of acceleration, and the damage also masks our tendril signature. Frankly, we do look like a damaged freighter. They'll practically have to do a hull map to tell the difference."

"By which time," Sublieutenant Segedin declared, "we'll have them locked up and ready to blast." The acting tactical officer seemed to be looking forward to the action. Nervous but ready, like a racehorse at the starting gate. "The good news is how long they waited to fire up. They have to be assuming we're a merchie, so they'll come calling for us to heave to or follow them to the planet. We'll play along, but not decel. The closer we get to the planet, the better."

"We're down one missile tube," Talcott commented. "The local server was flattened by the power surges, and we're out of spares, but that leaves us seven. And all the laser mounts are online. Fire control is . . . spotty. But it should hold for a short engagement."

"So the ship blasts the cruiser," Prince Roger said, twining a golden strand of hair around one finger. "Then what? How do we get back to Earth?"

"Then the port submits, or we drop kinetic weapons on it, Your Highness," Pahner said flatly. "And after that, we wait for a ride home."

"And if the carrier comes back?" Roger was surprised at how calm he sounded. He looked at the piece of hair in his hand as if in surprise, and then patted it back into place. "I mean, the cruiser had to be dropped off by a carrier, right? And a carrier has collapsed armor and even more missiles than we do. Right?"

Pahner and Krasnitsky shared a look, and Pahner answered.

"Well, Your Highness, I think we'll have to cross that bridge when we come to it. It could just be lying low somewhere. But," he glanced at Segedin, "what about other ships in the system? Other cruisers or destroyers?"

"Right now, we don't detect any," the acting TACO replied. "But if the cruiser hadn't lit off its drive, we never would have detected him, either. There could be a carrier or another cruiser—or a hundred little fighter bastards—out there, and we'd have no idea."

"Okay," Pahner said, "we'll cross that bridge when we come to it, too." He turned to the Marine lieutenants who were making notes on their pads. The electronic devices would convert the entire meeting to text for reading, but the notes brought out the highlights. "Get the assault boats prepped. Full loadout. When we hit orbit, we should be prepared for a hot drop on the port."

"Are we talking an extended fight here, Sir?" Lieutenant Sawato asked. The First Platoon leader was the senior lieutenant and *de facto* operations officer for the company. If there was going to be an extended fight, it would be her job to ensure that the plans were in place to support it.

"No." Pahner shook his head. "We'll call on them to surrender. If they do, we'll drop on them like a ton of lead. If they don't, we'll hit them with kinetic strikes, *then* drop on them like a ton of lead. We'll work up a full mission order around that in the next few hours. Take this as a warning order. "

"Will that be strictly necessary, Major?" Eleanora asked. "I mean, you're the Bronze Battalion, not an enforcement company. It's your job to protect Prince Roger, not to retake planets from people like the Saints. If we hold the orbitals, can't we just wait for reinforcements to arrive and handle the situation on the ground?"

Pahner looked at her woodenly for a moment.

"Yes, Ma'am. I suppose we could," he said finally. "But, frankly, I think it's important that whoever has taken over the system understand that when you dick around with an imperial base, all it gets you is bloody and bruised. More to the immediate point, we might end up hiding on the ground. I'd prefer that base be neutralized if we do."

"You mean if the cruiser's support ship comes back?" Roger asked.

"Yes, Your Highness. Or if it's still around somewhere," Pahner replied shortly.

"Will His Highness be on the assault?" Krasnitsky asked in a diffident tone.

"Yes!" Roger said quickly, his face lighting at the thought of getting off the ship.

"No!" Pahner and O'Casey spoke simultaneously, and it was difficult to say which sounded more emphatic. They looked at each other, then at the prince. The two of them flanked him like lions at the gate, and O'Casey leaned out over the table to fix his eye, since he was steadfastly looking across the table at Captain Krasnitsky.

"*No*," she said even more firmly.

"Why not?" Roger asked, wincing inwardly as he heard his own whining tone. "I can carry my own weight!"

"It's too dangerous," O'Casey snapped. "The very idea is ludicrous!"

"If we're performing an assault, Your Highness, I can't have my troops guarding you at the same time," Pahner pointed out in her support.

"*My* troops," Roger said petulantly. He hated the tone, but he didn't know how else to say it. "*Mine*, Captain. I'm the battalion commander; you work for me." He smoothed his hair and pulled a couple of imaginary wayward strands into place, and Pahner's face turned to clenched-jawed iron.

"Yes, Your Highness, you are." He leaned back,

crossed his arms, and gazed impassively up at the deckhead. "What are your orders, Sir?"

Roger had already opened his mouth to protest the next infringement on his prerogatives, and the sudden lack of resistance left him with his mouth hanging wide. He had absolutely no idea what orders he should give, nor did he want to give any. He just wished that people would start treating him like an adult and the commander of the battalion instead of an appendage only important as something to guard. But suddenly the image of a Marine, out of his chameleon suit, exposed to vacuum, sitting on his own vac suited chest, waiting to see if the ship was going to depressurize, flashed across his vision, and he knew he had to find a way out of the corner he'd painted himself into. He thought about the conversation which had been going on around him, to the point of doing a quick check of his toot. The device had been set to a one-minute memory storage, a technique that had stood him in good stead in school and on numerous social occasions, and he felt a surge of relief as he spotted an out.

"Well, Captain, I think we should get started on drafting an operations order while the platoons prep the shuttles. We'll settle who's going to be included on the mission in the operations order." He glanced sideways at Eleanora, but she refused to meet his eye, as did the embarrassed-looking officers across the table. "Do you have anything further, Captain Krasnitsky?"

"No, Your Highness," Krasnitsky said. "I think that's it."

"Very well," the prince said. "Let's get to it!"

Krasnitsky looked at Pahner, who nodded, and with that, the meeting adjourned.

CHAPTER SIX

"Prince Roger to the bridge, please. Prince Roger to the bridge."

The intercom announcement, backed by a ping on his implant, caught Roger at an inopportune time. He was finally being fitted for a suit of armor, and the process was not going well.

The decision had been made, not without some heated discussion, that although Roger would not be permitted to join any assault on the port facilities, he would go down with the second wave of technical support from the ship. It was only half a victory, from his perspective, but at least Pahner had admitted that since there might still be some hostile fire, breaking out a suit of armor and fitting it to the prince was probably a good idea.

Roger suspected that the captain's rationale was intended as much to get the Marines' charge out of his hair as anything, but it only made sense to put as much security around the Imperial Person as possible. Unfortunately, the fitting was going to be interrupted, and he felt some trepidation as he looked over at the armorer who was glaring at the intercom with his lips drawn back in a snarl.

Since good armorers were much harder to find than good guards, and since their function was an "out of sight, out of mind" one, armorers assigned to The Empress' Own went through a far less stringent winnowing process than the guards and faced only one true criterion: extreme competence. And when there weren't enough volunteers, extremely competent armorers were sometimes "volunteered." This occasionally led to the assignment of persons who, while more or less suitable to take out in public, were not the sort with whom Roger normally dealt.

"So what do we do now?" the prince asked, staring at a hand frozen in an alloy gauntlet. The gauntlet's interface was proving cranky, and the armorer had been deeply engrossed in the debugging process when the announcement came in.

"Will, Yer Highness," said the slight Marine, whose name tag read *Poertena*, "I guess we git a pocking can opener and cot you out."

It took Roger a moment to translate the sergeant's thick Pinopan accent. Pinopa was a world of widespread archipelagoes and tropical seas which had been settled in the first wave of slow-boat colonization by refugees from the Dragon Wars in Southeast Asia, and although the planet's official language was Standard English, the Pinopan had obviously grown up in a non-English household. Despite the accent, Roger was pretty sure he had "pocking" translated correctly. He hoped, however, that the corporal was exaggerating the rest.

"Should I call them and tell them I'm busy?" Roger asked, unsure how they were going to get him out of the ill-fitted armor in any short period of time. Normally, it was a matter of hitting controls which opened the armor along numerous seams, but given the problems this particular suit had been evincing, the experienced armorer had locked down and tagged out most of the controls. The alternative, in which he wasn't particularly interested, was the possibility of intercepting several hundred amps of current or getting cold-cocked by a flailing fist. Now it would be necessary to reconnect all the contacts before the prince could be extracted.

"New, Yer Highness. I'll have you out in a pocking minute. Tell them yer gonna be ten mikes, and that'll cover it. Besides, I got all this udder pocking suits they need pix." His arms swept around the Armory, where half a dozen suits were up on racks awaiting repair. "Pocking gun-bunnies alles breaking t'eir suits. Pocking passers."

The armorer crossed the room to a disused tool chest and extracted a one-meter wrench. He dragged the mass of metal back over to the prince, who was immobilized by the armor, and looked the noble right in the eye.

"Now, Yer Highness," the slight, dark Marine said, grinning nervously, "t'is ain't gonna hurt a bit."

He swung the giant wrench back like a batter, and, with a grunt of effort, slammed its head into the left upper biceps of the suit with all his might.

Roger grimaced when he realized what was about to happen, but other than an unpleasant vibration, the only effect on the suit was that the connection from the arm piece to the shoulder popped free. The collapsed molecules of the ChromSten armor barely noticed the impact, but Poertena dropped the ersatz hammer and shook his hands.

"Pocking vibration."

He looked at the disconnected arm in satisfaction, then picked the wrench up and maneuvered to the other side.

"I used to use a hammer fer t'is." The right biceps

was disconnected with another grunt of effort and another noisy clang. "But my cousin-in-law, he said, 'Ramon. Gets you a wrench, pudder-mocker.' So I gets a wrench. An' tee pudder-mocker was right." He dropped the wrench and reached up into the gap created by the detached arm piece. "Wonce you get tee arms detached, it all over but tee counting." He slid his small hand and forearm up along the prince's back. Roger could feel him fumbling for something, then there was a release of tension as the seam along the rear of the suit's carapace opened. Unfortunately, the suit bent at the shoulders, and that trapped the armorer's forearm in the gap. "Pock," was his only comment. Then—

"Prince, can you sock it op an' push you shoulders pack?"

With a few more contortions, the prince found himself standing in the middle of scattered bits of powered armor. He looked down at his singlet, and chuckled. "So much for modesty."

The armory hatch whooshed opened and a female sergeant in chameleon dress stepped in. She had a cool face with high Slavic cheekbones, and her long brown hair was done up in a bun at the back of her head. The rippling distortion of the chameleon fabric denied any impression of shape, but her quick tread and lithe movements indicated a high level of athleticism. She didn't bat an eye at the half-naked prince or the scattered armor.

"Your Highness, Captain Pahner requests your presence on the bridge."

"Com the Captain and tell him that it took a bit to get out of the armor," Roger said testily. "I'll be there in a minute."

"Yes, Your Highness," the sergeant said blandly and tapped the transmitter button on her side as Roger began getting dressed in the clothes he'd chosen for these few, tense hours. He'd considered combat dress, but decided that it was just too uncomfortable and finally chosen a safari outfit made of a brushed cottonlike material. It wouldn't be appropriate for combat, but it gave a fine aura of adventure and was much more pleasant than the chameleon cloth everyone else had changed into.

Roger watched the sergeant surreptitiously as he dressed. At first, he thought that she was wiggling her jaw to work a bit of food out of her teeth, but he eventually realized that she was having a long subvocal discussion or argument with someone. The throat microphone was almost invisible against her long, tanned neck, and the receiver, of course, was embedded in her mastoid bone.

Finally he was dressed, and he gave the multipocketed shirt a tug and flipped off a bit of lint.

"Ready."

The sergeant touched the hatch control, but stayed behind as the prince left, escorted by the two guards in the passage outside. As the hatch closed, she turned to the armorer who was reassembling the suit on a mannequin rack.

"Poertena," she said in severe tones, "did you do the hammer thing to the Prince?"

"Of course I didn' do tee hammer ting," the armorer said nervously. "I don' do tee hammer ting no more."

"Then what the hell is that wrench doing on the floor?"

"Oh, t'at. I don' do tee hammer ting, I do tee wrench ting."

"Poertena, you start fucking around with the Prince, and Pahner will have your ass for breakfast."

"Pock Pahner," the armorer snapped, gesturing around the compartment. "You see t'at? I got six pocking sets of pocking armor to get ready. You see Pahner help-ing? You see you helping? I gonna go get reamed by Pahner, or I gonna pix suits?"

"If you need help, ask!" The sergeant's blue eyes flashed, and she crossed her arms and glared at the half-pint armorer. "We're finished loading the boats. I've got two squads sitting around with their thumbs up their butts. They can be down here in a second."

"I don' need a buncha ham-fist clowns pocking up my suits," the armorer said petulantly. "Every time I gets help, they pock up my suits."

"Okay," the sergeant said with a nasty smile. "Tell you what. I'll get Sergeant Julian to help you."

"Oh, nooo," Poertena said as he realized that he'd put himself in a trap with his bitching. "Not Julian!"

"Hey, Troop!" Julian entered the weapons bay, walked up to the nearest trooper, who was a recent join from Sixth Fleet, put a hand on her shoulder, and grasped her hand for a firm handshake. "Glad you could make it." He gestured with his chin at the plasma rifle the trooper was preparing to disassemble. "You need some help with that there plasma thingamajig?"

The plasma rifle was the IMC's version of a squad automatic weapon. It weighed six kilos, and was sup-plied by external powerpacks which weighed two kilos each and were good for three to twelve shots, depend-ing on the weapon's discharge settings. The "basic load" for a plasma gunner was twelve packs, the gunners normally carried up to thirty packs in their rucksacks, and their squad mates usually distributed another thirty among them. If there was one thing in the universe a Marine squad hated, it was running out of plasma ammo.

This particular squad from First Platoon had gath-ered in the bay for one last cleaning of weapons, and since the plasma rifle had a mass of subcomponents, it was natural that the gregarious Julian, from Third Platoon, would offer to help. The new private had just started to smile when her fire team leader spoke up.

"Don't do it, gal," Corporal Andras said.

"What?" Julian affected a hurt expression. "You don't think I can help this rookie trooper?"

The trooper, Nassina Bosum, had just spent six months in the Husan Action before reporting as a Bronze Barbarian. She opened her mouth to retort angrily that she was anything but a rookie, but was cut off by her team leader.

"Oh, you'll help all right. . . ." Andras muttered.

"Seven seconds," Julian said with a smile, and the corporal eyed him beadily.

"No way." There were over forty subcomponents in the M-96 plasma rifle. There was no way to disassemble it completely in seven seconds. Not even for the legendary Julian.

Julian reached into a breast pocket and extracted a chip. "Ten creds says I can do it in seven seconds."

"Impossible!" Bosum snapped, forgetting the implied insult. The standard was over a minute; nobody could disassemble a plasma rifle that fast.

"Put your money where your mouth is," Julian said with a smile, and tossed the chip onto the table.

"I'll take some of that," a grenadier said from down the table, and the squad leader, Sergeant Koberda, pushed forward to manage the piles. Finally there were two chips on Julian's side, and a pile of five- and ten-credit chips opposite.

"Who bet on Julian?"

"I did," Andras said sourly. "He's taken my money every other time."

"We ready?" Julian asked, his hands hovering over the plasma rifle.

"Uh, hang on," said one of the bead riflemen, pulling a helmet out from under his station chair and putting it on his head. "Okay," he said, tapping a control so that the ballistic-protection visor extruded. "Fine by me."

Sergeant Koberda touched the plasma gunner on the shoulder.

"You might wanna step back," he said with a little warning wrinkle of the nose. He suited action to words himself, then put his arms over his head, and the gunner saw others do the same.

"Wha . . . ?" Bosum began, but the squad leader had already activated the timer in his toot and said: *"Go!"*

Removing the compression pin to begin the disassembly process took the longest, just over a third of a second. The new troop watched in awe until the first magneto ring bounced off her skull. Then she realized that pieces of the weapon were flying all over the compartment and started to yell for the sergeant to stop . . . just as the last bit of component flew across the open space and bounced off a bulkhead.

"Done!" Julian yelled, raising his hands.

"Six point four-three-eight seconds," Koberda announced morosely, consulting his toot as he kicked aside a capacitor.

"Thank you, thank you, ladies and gentlemen," Julian said, bowing and splitting the heap of chips into two equal piles. He slid one across to Andras, picked up his own, extracted a bundle of other chips large enough to choke a unicorn, and added the squad's offerings to the bundle. "Always a pleasure," he added, and headed for the next compartment.

Corporal Bosum looked around the compartment, trying to figure out where all the pieces of her weapon had gotten to.

"Does he do this often?" she asked sourly.

"Every chance we give him," Andras said. He picked

up a capacitor ring and tossed it to her. "But sooner or later, he's gotta lose."

"Sergeant Julian to the Armor Bay," chimed the intercom. "Sergeant Julian to the Armor Bay."

"Oh, man," Koberda said. "That was Despreaux. Despreaux, Poertena, and Julian all in the same compartment! I'd rather be on the bridge!"

Roger tugged down the skirts of his safari jacket and flipped off an imaginary bit of fluff before nodding at the guard to trigger the hatch command. The guard waited patiently, then tapped the green square and stepped through the hatch to do an automatic sweep for hostiles. What the sweep turned up was a massive amount of tension.

Roger stepped over the now tape- and padding-covered control runs and crossed to the tac center. He took a stance with his feet shoulder-width apart and his hands behind his back, nodded coolly at Krasnitsky and Pahner, and then glanced at the rippling tactical display. His cool demeanor vanished abruptly, and his hand flew forward to point at the red icon in the hologram.

"Look! There's a—"

"We know, Your Highness," Pahner said stonily. "Another cruiser."

"It hasn't moved out yet," Krasnitsky said with a sigh. "It's probably warming up its pulse nodes because we haven't slowed down." He rubbed his stubbly jaw and sighed again. "The XO has been hailing the first one. It wants us to begin decelerating to prepare for boarding. It's claiming to be an imperial cruiser, HMS *Freedom*, but it's not. For one thing, the *Freedom* is a cruiser carrier, not a cruiser. For another, its captain has a Caravazan accent."

"Saints." Roger's mouth felt dry.

"Yes, Your Highness," Pahner said. He didn't comment on the obviousness of the conclusion. "Probably," he corrected. "Whoever they are, the worst-case scenario is Saints. So we assume it's them."

"But, Captain," the prince said, looking at Krasnitsky, "can your ship win against *another* cruiser?"

Krasnitsky looked around the bridge. Not a hair had twitched, but he knew better than to have *that* discussion in public.

"Perhaps we should step into the briefing room," he suggested.

Once the hatch had closed, he turned to the prince. "No, Your Highness. There is zero chance that we can survive taking on two cruisers. We're not a full-scale Line ship, just a heavily armed and armored transport. Were we at full strength, without damage, maybe. As it is, there's no chance."

"So what do we do?" Roger looked from Pahner to Krasnitsky. "We have to surrender, right?"

It was Pahner's turn to sigh. "That's . . . not really an option, Your Highness."

"Why ever not?" Roger asked. "I mean," he turned to the grim-looking Fleet officer, "you're going to *die* if you don't!"

Pahner bit his tongue on a sharp rejoinder, but Krasnitsky simply nodded. "Yes, Your Highness, we will."

"But why?" Roger asked, his eyes wide in amazement. "I mean, I know it isn't the proper thing to surrender, but you can't run, and you can't win. So why not?"

"He can't risk their getting their hands on you, Your Highness," Pahner snapped finally.

"But . . ." Roger began, then stopped to think about it. He pulled his ponytail in frustration. "Why not? I mean, what could they do with . . . with *me*, for God's sake? I mean, I could understand if it was Mother, or John, or even Alexandra. But who the heck cares about

Roger?" he ended a trifle bitterly. "I don't know any secrets, and I'm not in immediate line for the throne. Why *not* turn me over to them?"

The prince's face hardened with resolution.

"Captain, I insist that you surrender. As a matter of fact, I order you to. Honor is all well and good, but there is a line between honor and stupidity." He lifted his chin and sniffed. "I will surrender to them myself, with honor. I'll show them who's a MacClintock." The stance would have been improved if there hadn't been a slight quiver in the pronouncement.

"Fortunately, Your Highness, you're not in my chain of command," Krasnitsky said with a wry smile for the bravado. "Major Pahner, I'm going to go get ready for the change in plans. Do you want to try to explain it to him?" With that, he nodded at the prince and left the compartment.

"What?" the prince gasped as the hatch closed behind him. "Hey! I gave you an order!"

"As he said, Your Highness, you're not in his chain of command," Pahner said with a shake of his head. "But you might at least thank him for committing suicide, not berate him."

"There's no reason for them not to surrender," Roger said stubbornly. "This is just stupid!"

Pahner cocked his head and looked at the prince darkly.

"What happens if the Saints get their hands on you, Your Highness?"

"Well," Roger said, thinking about it. "If they tell the Empire, it's war, or they hand me back over. I suppose they could force a few concessions, but they don't want a war."

"And what if they don't tell the Empire right away, Your Highness?"

"Uhmmmm . . ."

"They can't tamper with your toot, Your Highness; not with *its* security protocols. But what about psychotropic drugs?" Pahner tilted his head to the other side and raised an eyebrow. "What then?"

"So I make funny noises and bark like a dog," Roger scoffed. Until they were finally fully banned, psychotropic drugs had been common at comedy clubs for the terminally humorless.

"No, Your Highness. My guess—and I'm not privy to these sorts of scenarios—but my guess is that they would have you babble all the state secrets that you know to their 'free and independent' news services."

"But that's the point, Captain Pahner," Roger said with another laugh. "I don't *know* any state secrets."

"Sure you do, Your Highness. You know all about the Empire's plans to invade Raiden-Winterhowe."

"Captain," the prince said warily, "what are you talking about? Not only are we at peace with Raiden-Winterhowe, but taking them on would be stupid. They've got nearly as good a navy as we do."

"In that case, Your Highness," Pahner said with another smile, "what about the Empire's conspiracy to enslave all the alien species we can find and to terraform planets that have been reserved because of their unique flora and fauna?"

"Captain Pahner, what are you *talking* about?" the prince demanded. "I've never heard of any of this! And that sounds like Saint rhetoric. . . ." He stopped. "Oh."

"Or about how your imperial mother eats fetuses for breakfast, or about—"

"I get the point!" the prince snapped. "You're saying that if they get their hands on me I'll be their mouthpiece for all that bullshit they're always spouting."

"Whether you want to or not, Your Highness." Pahner nodded. "And I don't even want to *think* about what they'll do with your big game hunting record. For that matter, it would make the lives of the rest of the Family worth less than a plugged millicred. If they could kill the rest of the Family, that would make you heir."

"Parliament would impeach me," Roger said with a bitter laugh. "Hell, Parliament would probably impeach me even if the Saints *weren't* putting words into my mouth. Who the hell is going to trust *Roger* at the controls?"

"It takes two-thirds to impeach, Your Highness," the captain said darkly.

"Are you suggesting that the Saints could influence a third of Parliament?" Roger was beginning to think he'd stepped through a looking glass and into some sort of weird fantasy universe. There'd always been bodyguards around him, certainly, but no one had ever seriously suggested that he might be a target of another empire's designs. He'd always assumed that the guards were there mainly for show or to keep off the occasional overly smitten female fan. Now he suddenly realized that what they were there for was . . . sitting on his chest, waiting for the air to evacuate.

"Why?" he asked, quietly, wondering what would make people serve and protect someone that even he didn't like looking back at him in the mirror.

"Well," Pahner replied, not understanding the true question, "the Saints want to ensure that humanity doesn't expand further into uncontaminated worlds. It's a religion to them." He paused, unsure how to go on. "I'd assumed that you'd been briefed, Your Highness."

Actually, it was common knowledge. The Church of Ryback had a few outlets in the capital, all heavily financed by the Saints, and they ran regular commercials. For that matter, it was a common subject for discussion in civics and history classes, which made Pahner wonder about the prince's education. Asking what the Saints wanted made no sense at all, given that

O'Casey had been Roger's tutor for years and she had a quadruple doctorate in, among other things, history.

"No. No, that's not what I meant. I meant . . ."

Roger looked into the bleak face of the Marine and realized that this was not a good time to get the question off his chest. And even if he asked it, Pahner—as most people seemed to do when Roger asked questions— would probably just provide some opaque answer that ensured deeper confusion.

"I meant, 'What.' What do we do now?"

"We're going to go for the longshot, Your Highness," Pahner said, nodding now that the question made sense again. He suspected that something else had gone on in that airhead, but what it had been he neither knew nor particularly cared. There was a mission to perform, and it looked to be a long one.

"We're going to reload the boats. With the cruiser topside, taking the port by assault is out. So we're going to have to land on the planet and make our way to the port on foot. We can't let anyone know we're there, or they'll slaughter us, so we're going to have to come in on a ballistic approach and land quite a way around the planet from the port. Marduk was an afterthought to the Empire, so it's never been fully surveyed, and there's no satellite net, so the port won't be able to detect us as long as we stay out of line of sight. Once we reach the port, we capture a ship and head for home."

It sounded easy put like that. Right.

"So we're going to land on the backside then take the shuttles across . . . um, I can't remember the term. Low to the ground so they don't get spotted?"

"Nape of the Earth," Pahner answered somberly. "No, Your Highness. Unfortunately, we're going to have to launch nearly five light-minutes out. We're going to put three platoons and a few support personnel from the ship in four assault shuttles: enough room for a reinforced company. The rest of the load is going to be fuel for deceleration. When we're down, if we have enough fuel to do a couple of klicks we'll be lucky."

"So how are we going to get to the port?" Roger asked, dreading the answer.

"We're going to walk, Your Highness," the captain said with a grim smile.

CHAPTER SEVEN

"It says here, 'Marduk has a mean gravity of slightly greater than Earth normal, and is a planet of little weather change,'" Sergeant Julian said, reading off his pad. He'd managed, along with Poertena, to get two more suits up and running before the call came to drop everything and change the loadout on the shuttles. Currently, they were unloading.

He was perched on one silver wing of an assault shuttle as his squad moved out nonessential materials. The space-to-ground assault craft's variable geometry wings could sustain in-air flight at speeds as low as a hundred KPH or as high as Mach three, but it also had hydrogen thrusters for space maneuvering. Similar to a ground support pinnace, it had lighter weapons and a single top-mounted quad-barreled bead cannon, and thus correspondingly more room for personnel and equipment.

"'. . . with a median temperature of thirty-three degrees and a median humidity of ninety-seven percent,'" he continued. There'd been nothing in the

Marine databases on the planet, but it turned out that one of the corporals in Second Platoon had a *Fodor's Guide to the Baldur Sector*. Unfortunately, it offered only a limited amount of data on the planet . . . and what data there was only made a gloomy situation worse. "Jesus Christ, that's hot!"

"Oh, just fucking great," Lance Corporal Moseyev said as he trotted out of the shuttle with a case of penetrator ammunition in his hands. "I only had three weeks and I was transferring to Steel!"

"'The native culture is at a stagnant level of low-grade firearms technology. Politically, the Mardukans—' Hey, there's a picture!"

The Mardukan native, a four-armed biped from a hexapedal evolutionary line, was pictured next to a human wiredrawing for size. From the scale, the Mardukan was the height of a grizzly bear, with broad, long feet on the ends of long, backcurved legs. The hands of the upper and lower arms were about the same size, with the upper shoulders wider than the lower, which were in turn wider than the hips. The upper arms ended in long, fine, three-fingered hands with one fully opposable thumb each. The hands of the shorter, lower arms were heavier and less refined, with a broad opposable pad and two dissimilar fingers. The face was wider and flatter than a human's, with a broad nose and small deep-set eyes. Two large horns curled up and back over the head. They were obviously functional weapons; the inner curve looked razor-sharp. The rubbery-looking skin was a mottled green and had an odd sheen to it.

"What's that?" Moseyev asked, pointing to the sheen.

"Dunno." Julian tweaked the cursor over the skin and rolled up the magnification. "'The skin of the Mardukan is covered in a polycy . . . polyss . . . in a something something coating that protects the species from casual cuts and the various harsh funguses of its native jungle home," he read, then thought about it for a second. "Ewww."

"It's covered in *slime*," Moseyev laughed. "Yick! Slimies!"

"Scummies!" Sergeant Major Kosutic snapped from the hatchway, and strode into the launching day. "I thought you were told to get the extraneous equipment out of the shuttle, Julian?"

"We were getting updated on the mission, Sergeant Major!" Julian was suddenly at attention, the pad held alongside his trousers. "I was briefing my squad on the enemy and conditions!"

"The enemy are the fucking Saints or pirates or whatever-they-are that hold the port." Kosutic stalked up to stand so close to the braced sergeant that he could smell her breath mint. "The scummies are what we're going to have to cut our way through to get there. Your mission, right now, is to get the shuttle unloaded—not to sit around on your ass cracking wise. Clear?"

"Clear, Sergeant Major!"

"Now get your asses to work. We're on a tight time schedule."

"Moseyev!" Julian said, turning hastily back to his squad. "Get your team unloading that ammo. We don't have all day-cycle! Gjalski, your team on the powerpacks. . . ."

"Not the powerpacks," Kosutic said. "Leave all of them. We're going to add extra, as a matter-of-fact. Thank Vlad we don't have a heavy weapons platoon with us."

"Sergeant Major," Julian asked as the squad began to scurry around, "you called the Mardukans 'scummies.' Where'd you hear that?"

"Knew somebody that went through here once." The sergeant major pulled at an earlobe. "Didn't sound like much fun."

"Are we really gonna have to walk all the way across the damn world?" Julian asked, aghast.

"There ain't many choices, Sergeant," the sergeant major snarled. "You just stick with the mission."

"Roger, Sergeant Major." The sergeant glanced at the "scummy" on the pad. It looked big and nasty . . . but, then, that also described the IMC. "Will comply."

There weren't a lot of options.

"Okay, I want options, people," Pahner said, and looked around the briefing room. "First of all, let's be clear about something: what's the mission?"

The group was limited to the prince's party: himself, Pahner, O'Casey, and the three lieutenants. O'Casey was panning through the limited data on Marduk on a pad. The old-fashioned academic always seemed to prefer holding data in her hand. Roger, for his part, had looked at it nine ways from Sunday already on his toot, and there wasn't much good in it.

"Take the port while avoiding detection," Lieutenant Sawato answered. The slight officer gestured at the limited-scale map depicted in the hologram over the table. It had been extracted from the *Fodor's*, and, with the exception of the area around the port, offered virtually no detail. "Land on the northeast coast of this large continent, cross a relatively small ocean, and move inland to take the port."

"Sounds easy," Lieutenant Gulyas snorted. He was about to go on, but Pahner raised a hand.

"You forgot one thing, Lieutenant," Pahner told Sawato mildly. "While insuring the security of His Highness Prince Roger."

Roger opened his mouth to protest, but was elbowed by O'Casey. He knew those elbows of old, and knew better than to try to go on.

"Yes, Sir," Sawato said to Pahner, but with a nod to Roger. "That was, of course, assumed."

"You know what they say about assumptions," Pahner said. "Let's not assume Prince Roger's safety, okay? The Navy has a plan for getting us onto the planet, and there's not a thing we can do to affect that. But we need to do everything we can to ensure that item above all else. His Highness' security is job one."

He looked around to make sure the other officers understood that and then nodded.

"In that case, I think we need to look at the conditions and threats next." He turned to Lieutenant Gulyas. "Conall, normally that would be your brief. However, I've been talking to Doctor O'Casey, and she has some insights." He turned to the civilian. "Doctor?"

"Thank you, Captain," she replied formally, and tapped the display to bring up a picture of Marduk. "You are all, by now, familiar with the limited data we have on Marduk and its inhabitants.

"Marduk is classified as a Type Three world," she continued, and tapped another control. This time the picture was a large beast of some sort, with six stumpy legs, an armored forehead, and a triangular, fang-filled maw. The human scale model next to it indicated that the creature was a bit larger than a rhinoceros.

"That, by the way, is probably the same classification Earth would have had at the same technological and development level. Marduk, however, has not only an unfriendly climate—it's extremely hot and steamy, which will have a negative effect on electronics—but also unfriendly inhabitants and wildlife. This particular specimen, called a damnbeast, is a good example. The first survey crew ended up shooting several specimens. The planet is warm enough that the dominant species are all cold-blooded, which makes a higher ratio of predators to prey possible. Whereas a mammal this size would require half a million hectares to support, one of these has a territory of less than forty thousand hectares." She smiled faintly. "And this is the only recorded carnivore species listed in our onboard data bases. Further inquiries referenced the official Survey Service report."

She smiled again at the general groan.

"The resident autochthons, the Mardukans, are at a pre-steam level of technology. Obviously, their tech level varies from area to area of the planet, but some of their most advanced cultures have discovered gunpowder, although that's scarcely uniform and even the ones which have it don't have anything resembling mass production or cartridge weapons."

She tapped another control, bringing up a view of some odd weapons.

"These are the primary projectile weapons of the Mardukan societies which have mastered gunpowder: the matchlock arquebus and the hooped bombard. These weapons were used on Earth in the distant past, primarily in Europe, although the arquebus was rapidly superseded by flintlock muskets, and then rifles. The hooped bombard is a distant cousin of one of your Marine howitzers."

She brought up another screen, this time a map of the Mediterranean.

"The Mardukan sociological climate has few direct counterparts in human history, but there are similarities to the Earth during the early Roman Republic. The Mardukans are broken up into city-states and small empires that are distributed along fertile river valleys, so these areas between the rivers are primarily barbaric. Although the barbarians do have a few gunpowder weapons, they rely primarily upon spear-hurlers and lances. The precise nature of the barbarian tribal structure is unknown."

"Why is it unknown?" Lieutenant Gulyas asked, wondering where she'd gotten all this information.

"Well, probably because they ate the researchers," O'Casey said deadpan, then grinned. "Or because it's never been researched. From what I've been able to find, anything more than a thousand klicks or so from the spaceport is very much terra incognita. Either way, the data in my database stopped there."

"Where did you have that?" Gulyas asked curiously.

"I always travel with my history and sociology databases," O'Casey said with another smile. "I need them to work on papers." She turned back to her pad.

"To continue, not only are the barbarians at war with each other—when they're not raiding the borders of the city-states—but the city-states are continually at war with each other, as well. Any state of peace can be assumed to be a temporary truce, awaiting the slightest spark to ignite a war." The smile she gave the officers of this time was grim. "I think that we can assume a Marine company is going to constitute a spark."

She paused for a moment, then shrugged.

"That pretty much exhausts the primary data. I'll make the full outtake available to you right after the meeting."

"Thank you, Doctor," Pahner said somberly. "That was a nice overview. I'm sure you also noticed that we can eat the food. The biochemistry's a long way from Earth standard, but our nanites ought to be able to break down anything we can't digest naturally, and they should keep anything in the local biosystem from actively poisoning us. On the other hand, not even the nanites can put in what isn't there, so we'll require supplements, especially of vitamins C and E and several amino acids. Which means we'll be humping those." He looked up when there were no groans from the lieutenants. "No complaints? My, we must be feeling sobered."

"We've been discussing it, Sir," Lieutenant Sawato admitted. The XO shook her head. "I listed out all the parameters, but, as Lieutenant Gulyas indicated, there are tremendous problems."

"True." Pahner leaned back and rested his chin on his hand. "Tell me what they are."

"First of all, Sir, there's the matter of time. How long will it take us to cross a world?"

"A long time," Pahner replied calmly. "Months."

The entire compartment seemed to draw a deep breath as someone finally said the words. They were no longer talking about a short drop on the planet, but about an extended stay. They had all realized it, but no one had wanted to say it.

"Yes, Sir," Lieutenant Jasco said into the silence after a moment. The tall, broad CO of First Platoon was in charge of logistics, and he shook his leonine head. "I don't see it, Sir. We don't have the food or the power. We carry combat rations for two weeks, and power for one week's use of the armor, but we're looking at three to six months to cross the planet. We may be able to forage, and our nanites will help with digestion problems, but if we're going to be dealing with hostiles, foraging will be limited. And given the intensity of the threat, we need the powered armor to survive, but it won't begin to last that long. With all due respect, and not wanting to be a quitter, I don't see a way to do this mission, Sir."

"All right." Pahner nodded. "That's your input. Does anyone see a way to accomplish the mission?"

"Well, we can strip the ship of spare power systems," Lieutenant Gulyas suggested. "There are powerpacks all over the place."

"How do we get them where we're going?" Jasco shook his head. "It's a situation of diminishing returns when you overload suits carrying stuff—"

"We can preposition caches!" Gulyas gestured enthusiastically with his hands. "We send out a team that puts down a cache. Some of the team stays behind to guard it, while the rest come back to get supplies. They take them to the cache and use some of the cache to take them a little further. They leave a team with that cache and go back for supplies. . . ."

"We'd be defeated in detail if we strung ourselves out that way," Sawato said severely.

"And that would take *six times* as many supplies!" Jasco snapped.

"We could carry the armor," Roger suggested diffidently, and looked around at the lieutenants. Jasco rolled his eyes and leaned back and crossed his arms, while Gulyas and Sawato simply refused to meet his gaze. "It would save power . . ."

"Ahem," Jasco said. "Your Royal Highness, with all due respect . . ."

"I think," Roger said, "that it would be better in these sorts of meetings to use my proper military rank."

Jasco cast a quick glance at Pahner, but the captain returned it blandly, and the lieutenant was suddenly reminded of one of those Academy tests where there was no right answer.

"Yes, um, Colonel. As I was saying, the suits weigh nearly four hundred kilos apiece," he continued with a not particularly friendly chuckle.

"Oh," Roger said with a chagrined expression. "I . . . oh."

"Actually," Pahner said quietly, "that was exactly what I had in mind." He looked around at the stunned lieutenants and smiled kindly. "Ladies and gentlemen, you are a credit to your training. 'Hit 'em hard and hit 'em low, grab their balls and don't let go,' right?"

The lieutenants smiled at the Academy drinking song. Even though most officers in the IMC, like

Pahner himself (although usually with less . . . spectacular career summaries) were former enlisted, it was well known in the officers corps.

"Well, we will indeed hit these 'scummies' hard and low when we have to. But we don't have the power to smash our way across the planet, so we're going to have to make treaties when possible, trade when necessary, and only kick ass as a last resort. When we kick ass, we'd better kick ass with a vengeance, but we parley first.

"One platoon each day, on a rotating basis," he continued, "will be detailed as bearers. We will carry one squad's armor. We'll take Second Squad of Third Platoon's; they have the most veterans and the highest combat scores, currently." He looked at Roger, obviously weighing pros and cons, then nodded. "And we'll take the Prince's. He doesn't have much background in it, but it goes along with ensuring his survival.

"But we have to remember that crossing the planet only gets us halfway to our objective. The real mission is to take the port and get our hands on a ship home, and we'll need the armor to take the port even more than we should need it on the way there. Initially, until we get the lay of the land, we'll keep one team in armor at all times. Once we become comfortable with our ability to survive, we'll make our way in normal uniforms to conserve power until we reach the port.

"Initially, we'll maintain our security with bead rifles and plasma weapons. But we can assume that they, too, will become exhausted. So from our first encounter with the Mardukans, we will ensure that all Mardukan weaponry is gathered, and we'll begin training with it."

He looked at the lieutenants again. Jasco, at least, appeared to think he'd lost his mind. The other two were trying, unsuccessfully, to keep their thoughts off their faces, but the prince, to give him credit, just seemed confused. It amused Pahner to turn the lieutenants' worldview on its ear; making them think was good for them, whatever the junior officers might believe. In the case of the prince ... Pahner found himself moving from annoyed towards amused, which was another surprise.

Pahner had always considered the prince his charge, but never one of "his" officers. Or, for that matter, whatever the Table of Organization might say, his superior. But now the captain realized that what he actually had on his hands was a terribly confused, brand-new lieutenant. And since "Captain" Pahner had spent a good part of his life as "Gunny" Pahner, teaching confused lieutenants the rules of the game, the prince suddenly switched from a hindrance to a challenge. A tough challenge—Pahner had never seen a lieutenant with a lower likelihood of making a decent officer—but an approachable one, nonetheless. And the only kind of challenge worth facing was a tough one. With that realization, the mission, in Pahner's mind, suddenly went from impossible to simply very difficult.

"Train with scummy weapons, Sir?" Lieutenant Jasco asked, looking at the other officers. "What are we going to do with them? Sir?"

"We'll use them to hold off attacking Mardukans or hostile fauna until heavier weapons come online. And when we get to the point that our power supplies are at the minimum necessary, in my opinion, to take the port, we'll use them exclusively."

"Sir?" Lieutenant Sawato said diffidently. "Are you sure about this? Those—" She gestured at where the hologram had been. "Those ... weapons aren't very good."

"No, Lieutenant, they aren't. But we'll just have to learn to get by. Our chameleon suits have limited ballistic protection, so we'll be highly resistant to fire from their arquebuses. As for lower-velocity weapons like spears and lances and swords and everything else . . . we'll deal with that as it comes.

"Now," the captain continued. "What, other than charges for the weapons and armor support, are our largest issues?"

"Communication," Lieutenant Gulyas said. "If we're going to trade and negotiate, we have to be able to communicate. We have a 'kernel' of the Mardukan language, but that's for one dialect on the subcontinent surrounding the base. We don't have any kernels for other areas. Without kernels, our toots can't translate for us."

"I can work on that," O'Casey said. "I've got a good heuristic language program I use for anthropological digging. I may have some trouble communicating with the first few groups we run across, but once I pick up a regional language base, even vast dialect changes won't affect things. And I can create kernels for other toots."

"Well, that's that one solved," Pahner said with a smile. "But you'll need to get that program to other toots. We can't have you as a point failure source."

"That might be a problem," she admitted. "It's big. It will take a very capable toot to handle it. I've got one custom designed for me, but without a huge amount of processor capability and storage, this program runs like a slug."

"I'll load it," Roger said quietly. "Mine's . . . pretty good." There was a slight, general chuckle at the understatement, for the Imperial Family's implants' abilities were almost legendary. "We might have some trouble loading it, but I'll guarantee I can run it."

"Okay," Pahner said. "What's next?"

"Food," Lieutenant Jasco said. "We don't have the rations for the trip, and we can't forage and carry the

armor and keep the Prince safe all at once." His tone
was respectfully challenging.

"Correct," Pahner acknowledged calmly. "And what
is the answer to *this* dilemma?"

"Trade," O'Casey said definitively. "We trade high-
tech items for whatever the Mardukans use for portable
wealth. That might not be metals, by the way. The
ancient North Africans traded salt. But whatever they
use here, we trade the largest mass of advanced technology at the first city-state for our basic needs and a
'nest egg,' and then portion the rest out slowly as we
go."

"Exactly." Pahner's nod was firm. "So, what do we
have that would make good trade goods?"

"Firestarters," Jasco said promptly. "I saw a case of
them in the supply room last week." He consulted his
pad. "I've got an inventory here—let me cross load."

He set his pad down on the table to transmit the
inventory data, and the other lieutenants and O'Casey
captured the data and began perusing it while Roger was
still pulling out his own pad. By the time he had it
opened and configured to receive, Jasco had cut the
transmission and was back to looking at the data.

"Lieutenant," the prince said in a lofty tone, "if you
don't mind?"

Jasco looked up from the lists in surprise. "Oh, sorry,
Your Highness," he said, and set the list to transmit
again.

Roger nodded as his pad picked up the data.

"Thank you, Lieutenant. And, again, it's 'Colonel'
under these circumstances."

"Yes, of course . . . Colonel," Jasco said, going back to
his data.

"What do we see?" Pahner asked, apparently ignoring the byplay. He didn't have a pad out, nor had he
received a download.

Roger transferred the data to his toot and put his own pad away. He would've taken the data straight into the toot from Jasco's pad, but the implant had so many security protocols that filtering through the pad had been easier and faster. As Roger was going through these circumlocutions, the officers and O'Casey were studying the inventory.

"Virtually anything in here would be tradable," and O'Casey said, her eyes bugging out at the thought. "Space blankets, chameleon liners, water carriers . . . not boots. . . ."

"We'll be space- and mass-limited," Pahner noted. "The ship's going to have to drop us fairly far out, and we'll have to come down in a long, slow spiral to avoid detection. That means internal add-on tanks of hydrogen, and those will take up volume and mass. So the higher the potential profit, the better."

"Well," O'Casey continued, "not uniforms. Rucksacks. There are five spares; that might be good. Spare issue intel-pads? No. What are 'multitools'?"

"They're memory plastic tools," Lieutenant Sawato said with a nod. "They come with four 'standard' configurations: shovel, ax, pick-mattock, and boma-knife. And you can add two configurations."

"We've got fifteen spares," Jasco said, flipping through the data. "And each Marine in the Company has one."

"Of course," Gulyas observed with a chuckle, "some of those have some . . . odd secondary settings."

"What?" Sawato smiled. "Like Sergeant Julian's 'out of tune lute' setting?"

"I was actually thinking of Poertena's 'pig pocking pag' setting," Gulyas snorted.

"I beg your pardon?" O'Casey blinked, and looked back and forth between the two lieutenants.

"The armorer controls the machine that resets the adjustable configurations," Pahner told her in a resigned tone. "Julian used to be Bravo's armorer before Poertena. Both of them are jokers."

"Oh." The prince's ex-tutor considered for several seconds, then snorted as she finally completed the translation of "pig pocking pag" in her head. "Well, in this case the setting makes sense. We're going to need lots of . . . large bags to carry equipment."

CHAPTER EIGHT

"Hey, Julian, old puddy!" Poertena yelled across the shuttle bay. "Gimme a hand what t'is pag!"

"Jesus Christ, Poertena!" Julian hefted the carry handles on the outside of the quivering memory plastic sack. "What the pock . . . I mean, what the heck do you have in here?"

"Every pocking ting I could pocking pack," the armorer answered. "Tee pocking suits don' run on t'eir pocking own. You know t'at!"

"What the hell is in here?" Julian asked, reaching for the mouth of the sack. It was heavy as hell.

"Get chore pocking hands out o' my pocking pag!" Poertena snarled, slapping at the offending member.

"Look, if I'm gonna help you hump it, I'm gonna know what the hell I'm carrying." Julian popped the sack opened and looked in. "Jesus Christ, Poertena!" he repeated. "The fucking *wrench*?"

"Hey!" the little Pinopan shouted, practically hopping up and down in fury. "You got your pocking way of doin' it, an' I got *my* pocking way! You never can get people out, they power goes off? Huh? Have to blow tee pocking seals! Only ting holding t'em seals is tee pocking secondary latches! You get tee secondary latches loose, you got tee armor open, and tee seals not damaged! Bot *no*! Big time billy badass soldier always gotta blow tee pocking bolts!"

"That's what it says to do in the manual," Julian said, throwing his hands up in the air. "Not *bang* on 'em until they come apart!"

"*Hey!*" Sergeant Major Kosutic shouted from the entrance to the bay as she strode across to break up the incipient fight. "Am I gonna have to jack both of you up?" she asked, glaring up at Julian.

"No, Sergeant Major," he said. "Everything's under control." He should have known she'd show up. She popped up like a damned Djinn every time anything got out of whack.

"Well, keep it strack! We've got a hard, cold mission to perform, and we don't need any sand in the gears. Do you understand that?"

"Yes, Sergeant Major!"

"And, Poertena," the sergeant major said, rounding on the braced Pinopan. "One, you'd better learn not to tell any more sergeants 'pock you' in public, or I will have your ass. Do you understand me?"

"Yes, Sergeant Major," Poertena said, looking for a convenient rock to melt away under.

"Two, you'd better learn a new word to replace 'pock,' because if you say it *one* more time in my hearing, I will *personally* tear off your stripes and feed them to you—raw. You are in The Empress' Own now, not whatever rag-bag line outfit you came from. We do not say 'pock' or 'rap' or any of those other words. We *especially* do not say them while rigging the pocking *Prince*. Do I make myself pocking clear?" she finished, pounding a rock-hard index finger into the lance corporal's chest.

Poertena's eyes flickered for a moment in panic. "Clear, Sergeant Major," he answered, finally, obviously unsure if he could get along without his verbal comma.

"Now what's in the Santa bag?" she snarled.

"My pock . . . my tools, Sergeant Major," Poertena answered. "I gotta have my po . . . my tools, Sergeant Major. Tee armor don' run by itself!"

"Sergeant Julian?" the sergeant major said, turning to the sergeant who'd started to drop out of his braced position as Poertena seemed to be getting the worst of the chewing out.

"Yes, Sergeant Major?" Julian snapped back to attention.

"What was your objection? You seemed to have one."

"We have mass limitations, Sergeant Major!" the NCO barked. "I objected to certain of Lance Corporal Poertena's tools that I didn't believe were strictly necessary, Sergeant Major!"

"Poertena?"

"He doesn't like my po . . . my wrench, Sergeant Major," the lance corporal answered somewhat sullenly. He was fairly sure he was going to lose the tool.

The SMaj nodded and opened the bulging sack. She glanced at the packrat's nest inside, and nodded again. Then she turned to the armorer and fixed him with a glare.

"Poertena."

"Yes, Sergeant Major?"

"You know we're humping across tee whole . . . this whole planet, right?" the top sergeant asked mildly.

"Yes, Sergeant Major." Poertena didn't brighten up; he'd been on the receiving end of mild and bitter before.

The NCO nodded again, and pulled on her earlobe. "Because of your unique position, you will probably be exempt from helping to hump the ammo, power, and armor."

Kosutic looked around the bay, then back into the sack.

"But I'm not going to have any of these people carrying unnecessary stuff," she growled.

"But, Sergeant Major—"

"Did I ask you to speak?" the NCO snapped.

"No, Sergeant Major!"

"As I say, I'm not going to have anyone carrying unnecessary stuff," she continued, fixing the Pinopan with a frigid eye. "However, I'm not going to tell you, the armorer, what you really need to do your job, either. I'm going to leave that entirely up to you. But I *will* tell you that nobody else in the Company is going to hump one item *for* you. Is that perfectly clear?" she ended, with another rock-hard index finger, and the armorer gulped and nodded his head.

"Yes, Sergeant Major." He winced internally at what that meant.

"You are being given slack on what you've got to carry," Kosutic said, "*because* you have your own stuff to hump. Not, by Satan, so that other people can hump it for you. Clear?"

Index finger.

"Clear, Sergeant Major."

"So, if you want your hammer, or wrench, or whatever, fine. But *you*—" index finger "—are gonna hump it. Clear?"

"Clear, Sergeant Major." Poertena's voice sounded more strangled than ever, not least because Julian stood grinning at him behind Kosutic's back. The sergeant major gave the armorer one last glare . . . then turned to the squad leader with cobralike speed.

"Sergeant Julian," she said mildly, "I'd like a moment of your time out in the passage."

Julian's smile froze, and he cast a burning glare at the Pinopan before he followed the top sergeant out of the shuttle bay. Poertena, for his part, could have cared less about the glare. He was trying to figure out how to fit two hundred liters of tools into a ten-liter space.

"We can't fit that in," Lieutenant Jasco said, slowly and carefully so that Lieutenant Gulyas could understand. He pointed to his pad, where the loading program was already in the yellow. "We're . . . gonna . . . be . . . overloaded," he continued in the simplest possible terms, and Gulyas gave him a friendly smile that stopped at the eyes. Then he reached up to clap the much larger platoon leader on the shoulder.

"You know, Aziz, you're an okay guy, most of the time. But from time to time, you're a real prick." He went on as the other lieutenant's face colored up. "We need trade goods. We need ammo. We need power. But if we don't have enough supplements to last the whole trip, we're all gonna die anyway!"

"You've stripped the ship of every last vitamin and herbal remedy!" Jasco snapped, slapping the hand off his shoulder. "We don't need three hundred kilos of supplements!"

"No," Gulyas agreed. "By exact calculation, we need two hundred and thirty precisely balanced kilos for six months with no casualties. If we take no casualties. And if we stay six months. Neither of those is likely, so we probably need less. But what about waste? And we don't *have* the *precise* supplements we need. And what about a trooper's opening up his kit and finding that mold has eaten his stash overnight? If we don't have enough supplements, we're all *dead*. So we've gotta have all the supplements we can hump; it's that simple."

"We're overloaded!" Jasco snapped, waving the pad. "It's *that* simple!"

"Can I be of assistance, gentlemen?" Sergeant Major Kosutic appeared as if by magic between the two lieutenants. "I only ask because some of the troops seemed to be interested in this discussion, as well."

Gulyas looked around the shuttle bay and noticed that work had almost stopped as the troopers slowed down to watch the two lieutenants argue. He turned back to the sergeant major.

"No, I think we have it under control." He looked at Jasco. "Don't we, Aziz?"

"No, we don't," the junior lieutenant said stubbornly. "We're running out of room for the loading. We can't afford three hundred kilos of supplements."

"Is that all we're taking?" Kosutic sounded surprised. "That doesn't sound like enough. Hang on." She keyed her throat mike, and used her toot to bring the two lieutenants into the circuit. "Captain Pahner?"

"Yes?" came the growled response.

"Priority. Supplements, or trade goods?" she asked.

"Supplements," Pahner said instantly. "We can raid instead of trade if we have to, but all the trade goods in the ship won't keep us alive without supplements. The order of priority is fuel, supplements, food, the suits for Third Platoon, power, ammo, trade goods. Each person may bring ten kilos of personal gear. How many kilos of supplements do we have?"

"Only three hundred," Kosutic answered.

"Damn. I'd hoped for more. We'll have to eke it out with rations. We go on short rations from the moment we board the shuttles. And confiscate all the pogie bait. Most of it won't have much in the way of nutritional value, but it's something. No more than one ration per day, and we hope we have one a day all the way through."

"Understood," Kosutic said. "Out here." She raised her eyebrows at the lieutenants. "Does that clear the air, Sirs?"

"Yes, Sergeant Major, it does," Jasco said. "I still don't think we're going to run out, though."

"Sir, may I make an observation?" the sergeant major asked, and Lieutenant Jasco nodded.

"Of course, Sergeant Major." He was an Academy graduate, with a previous stint as a platoon leader and four years in the IMC under his belt, but the sergeant major had been beating around the Fleet long before he was born. He might be stubborn, but he wasn't stupid.

"In a situation this screwed up, Sir, planning for the worst is just good sense. For example, I would strongly suggest that you not put all the supplements on one bird. Or any other point failure source, such as spare ammo or power. Spread it across the shuttles. When the shit hits the fan, there's no such thing as being overparanoid."

She nodded and stepped lightly out of the shuttle bay, and Jasco stood shaking his head as he looked at the pad in his hand.

"Do you think she was looking at the load plan?" he asked Gulyas.

"I dunno. Why?"

"Because I had *all* the spare food, ammo, and power on Shuttle Four!" the logistics lieutenant said angrily, and shut the pad with a snap. "It would have carried the heavy weapons platoon in a standard drop, and since it was empty . . . What a cherry mistake! Damn, damn, damn it to hell! Time to start cross-loading."

"And that, Your Highness," Pahner said, gesturing towards the memo pad, "is why I don't consider it advisable for you to bring the three cartons of personal gear."

The wardroom was empty, except for the two of them, although Doctor O'Casey was expected soon.

"But what am I going to wear?" the aghast prince

asked. He pulled at the chameleon fabric of the uniform he'd changed into. "You can't expect me to go through each day every day in *this*? . . . Can you?"

"Your Highness," Pahner said calmly, "each of the military personnel will be carrying on his own back six spare pairs of socks, a spare uniform, personal hygiene equipment, five kilos of proteins and vitamin supplements, rations, additional ammunition and power packs for their weapons, additional ammunition for squad and company level weaponry, a bivy tent, his multitool, a rucksack fluid pouch with six kilos of water, and up to ten kilos of personal gear. The load will total out at between fifty and sixty kilos. In addition, the entire Company will be switching off carrying powered armor and additional trade goods, ammunition, and powerpacks."

He cocked his head and regarded his nominal commander steadily.

"If you order the Company, in addition to all these necessities, to carry your spare pajamas, morning clothes, evening clothes, and a dress uniform in case there's a parade, they will." The company commander smiled thinly. "But I find the idea extremely . . . ill advised."

The prince looked at the officer in shock and shook his head.

"But who's going to be carrying all that stuff for *me*?"

Pahner's face became closed and set as he leaned back in the station chair.

"Your Highness, I've already made arrangements for the support material for Doctor O'Casey to be distributed and field gear to be issued for Doctor O'Casey and Valet Matsugae." The captain regarded the prince steadily. "Am I to assume from that question that I should make the same arrangements for *your* personal gear?"

Before Roger could even think of a proper reply, he found his mouth, as usual, running away with itself.

"Of course you should!" he half-snapped, then nearly quailed as Pahner's face darkened. But he'd already climbed out on the limb; might as well saw with abandon. "I'm a *prince*, Captain. Surely you don't expect me to carry my own bags?"

Pahner stood and placed his hands flat on the tabletop. Then he drew a deep, calming breath, and let it out.

"Very well, Your Highness. I need to go make those arrangements. By your leave?"

For just a moment, the prince appeared to be about to say something, but finally he made a small moue of distaste and waved a hand in dismissal. Pahner gazed at him silently, then gave a jerky nod and strode around the table and out the hatch, leaving the prince to contemplate his "victory."

CHAPTER NINE

Captain Krasnitsky leaned back in his command chair and rotated his shoulders in his skin suit.

"All right. Let's bring the ship back to General Quarters, if you please, Commander Talcott."

The captain hadn't slept in thirty-six hours. He'd had a sonic shower before climbing back into the stinking skin suit, but the only thing keeping him going at this point was Narcon and stimulants. The Narcon was to keep him from going to sleep. The stimulants were to keep him thinking straight, since the *only* thing the Narcon did was prevent sleep.

Even with the combination, his brain felt wrapped in steel wool.

"Wait until they open fire, Commander," he repeated, for what seemed the thousandth time. "I want to get as close as possible."

"Aye, Sir," Talcott said, with rather less exasperation than Krasnitsky thought he would probably have shown in the commander's position.

The captain's mouth tried to quirk a smile, but his amusement was fleeting, and his mind flickered back over his options with a sort of feverish monotony.

DeGlopper was an assault ship, not a true warship, but she was a starship, out-massing the in-system cruiser by nearly a hundred to one, and had enormously heavy ChromSten armor. The combination of mass and armor meant she could take damage that would shatter her opponent. But she was also slower, and not only were her sensors damaged, but her entire tactical net had taken a hit from the sabotage. So like any blind, drunk bruiser faced with a clear-eyed and nimble, but much smaller, foe, she wanted to grapple. She only had a good right remaining, but one uppercut was all it would take.

The plan called for her to maintain the appearance of a damaged freighter, desperate to make landfall, for as long as possible. She was finally starting to decelerate, and the cruiser was piling on all the gravities of deceleration it could stand, as well, but the transport would still flash by the smaller ship at nearly three percent of light-speed. At those velocities, there would be a very, very limited envelope of engagement.

Which meant every shot had better hit.

"We're coming into radar and lidar detection range, Captain," Commander Talcott said a few minutes later. "Should we paint their hull?"

"No. I know we'd get better lockup, but let's play unarmed merchie as long as we can. Be ready to paint them the minute they do it to us, though. And we're going to be close enough that our antiradiation HARMs should be in range. When they paint us, launch a flight."

"Aye, Sir," Talcott said, and moved over beside the ship's defensive systems officer.

Now if the shuttles only came through it alive.

❖   ❖   ❖

Prince Roger hunched closer to the tiny display, trying to discern anything from it, but the same flickering and distortion that had been evident on the bridge's tactical plot was even more pronounced on the smaller flat screen of the shuttle.

"Give it up, Your Highness," Pahner suggested, and there was actually an edge of humor in his voice. "I've tried to follow ship-to-ship battles on these things when the systems were all *working*. All you're going to do is strain your eyes."

Roger rotated in the station chair to face him, careful where he put his feet, arms, and hands. Nearly his first action on boarding the shuttle had been to smash a readout as the unfamiliar powered armor lived up to its reputation for strength. And for clumsiness in the hands of the untrained.

The station chairs were designed for use by armored or unarmored Marines, so they were hardened. The same could not be said for all the items surrounding them, and there wasn't much space in which to move. The simple fact was that a shuttle loaded with troops and supplies was always overcrowded.

The troops in the cargo bay sat packed like sardines in four rows, two back-to-back down the center of the bay, and one down either side, facing inward. The rows were composed of memory plastic cocoons, but the cocoons were thin walled to either side, so that their occupants were practically shoulder to shoulder, and each row faced another, so close that the Marines' knees intertwined. Their individual weapons and rucksacks were on their knees, piled on top of each other, and each cocoon top sprouted a combat helmet, currently configured to do service as a vac helmet for the chameleon suit of the trooper inside it.

Between a near-total inability to move their legs, the fact that the slightest movement resulted in punching a neighbor, and the fact that getting up or out required going through four layers of gear, it was no place for a claustrophobe. But at least troops in chameleon suits didn't have to worry about how to go to the bathroom. Since the suits were designed for space combat, they had all the comforts of home.

There were armored suits scattered through the cocoons as well, and halfway down the compartment the rows of troops were abruptly broken by a mass of hydrogen cylinders. The red painted battle steel ovals, each the size of an old-fashioned natural gas tank, were piled halfway to the shuttle roof and strapped down nine ways from Sunday. The shuttle might crash, a nuclear-tipped missile might detonate at point-blank range, but nothing was going to move those cylinders. Which was the point. If they kicked loose during the maneuvers of the shuttles or their mothership, the passengers might as well give up and open their suits to vacuum, because without the hydrogen in those tanks, the shuttles would never be able to make reentry.

Beyond the cylinders, which were placed just forward of the shuttle's center of gravity, was the rest of the armored squad and general cargo. In the case of this shuttle, putting the armored squad behind the cylinders, along with the cargo, which had a higher density than the troopers forward of the cylinders, balanced out the load. Since the ships were going to have to make a nearly "dead stick" atmospheric reentry, balance of the cargo was critical. But the whole setup made for terrific crowding.

At least Roger didn't have to put up with the conditions in the cargo bay, but the small compartment he shared with Pahner wasn't all that much better. It offered just enough room to swing a cat . . . assuming it was a very small cat. It contained two tactical stations, wedged into the starboard side of the shuttle, forward of the cargo compartment that separated it from the cockpit. It was the most hardened part of the ship, which was one of the reasons Roger was there, and it also had umbilicals, like those in the cargo bay, to provide local power and recycling support to armor or vac suits. But the low overhead (the position was wedged in above the starboard forward thruster plenum) and the limited space to move around meant that it, also, was no place for a claustrophobe. And just to make the crowding complete, Pahner and Roger's rucksacks hung from the cramped compartment's forward bulkhead.

Roger managed to get his knees out from under the tac station without breaking anything else and looked at the back of Pahner's helmet.

"So," he said testily, "what do we do now?"

"We wait, Your Highness," the company commander replied calmly. He seemed to have gotten over his anger at the prince's refusal to carry his own gear. "The waiting is supposed to be the hardest part."

"Is it?" Roger asked. He found himself out of his depth. This was something he'd never planned for—not that he'd been given many options in planning his life— and it was something he wasn't prepared for. He was accustomed to the challenge of sports, but one reason he had embraced that sort of challenge was because no one had ever taken him seriously enough to make any others applicable to him. Now he was face to face with the greatest challenge of his life . . . and making a mistake on this ballfield would mean death.

"It is for some," Pahner replied. "For others, the worst part is the aftermath. Counting the cost."

He turned his own chair to face the prince, trying to decipher what was going on behind the flickering ball of the boy's faceplate.

"There's going to be a pretty high cost to this operation," he continued, carefully not allowing his tone to change. "But that happens sometimes. There are two sides to any wargame, Your Highness, and the other side is trying to win, too."

"I try very hard not to lose," Roger said quietly. "I discovered early on that I didn't care for it a bit." The external speaker was the highest quality, but the sound still echoed oddly in the little compartment.

"Neither do I, Your Highness," Pahner agreed, turning back to his command station. "Neither do I. There aren't any losers in The Empress' Own. And damned few in the Fleet."

"We just got painted, Sir." Commander Talcott's quiet tone was totally focused. "Sensors confirm that it's a Saint lidar. A Mark 46." He looked up from the tactical system. "That's standard for a *Muir*-class cruiser."

"Roger," Krasnitsky said. "They'll realize their mistake in a moment. Go active and open fire as soon as you have a good lock."

Sublieutenant Segedin had been poised for the order like a runner in the blocks, and his hand stabbed the active emissions button just as the launch alarm sounded.

The Saint parasite cruiser was underarmed for the engagement. Although she was large for an in-system ship, she and her sisters were nothing compared to a starship.

Since the tunnel drive was dependent on volume, not mass, starships could be made extremely large and incredibly massive. Max-hull warships were over twelve hundred meters in diameter, and all interstellar warships were plated with ChromSten collapsed matter armor. That armor normally represented a third of the total mass of a ship, but since their systems were volume dependent, it hardly mattered. They also had immense room for missiles, and the capacitors that drove their tunnel drives gave them enormous storage for their energy batteries.

But once they were inside the TD limit, they found themselves limping along on phase drive, and phase drive *was* mass dependent. Which meant that starships were relatively slow and awkward to maneuver.

That was where the parasites came in.

Parasite cruisers and fighters could be packed into max-hull warships in terrific numbers. Once the starships entered a system, they could send out their cruisers and fighters to engage the enemy, but the cruisers were designed to be fast and nimble, rather than heavily armored, and lacked the ChromSten of starships. But *this* cruiser had come well within *DeGlopper's* engagement range and was at the mercy of the heavier ship.

The CO of the Saint parasite quickly realized that he'd screwed up by the numbers. His initial launch started with a single missile, which had clearly been intended as a "shot across the bows," but the rest of his broadside followed swiftly. Within moments, a half-dozen missiles came scorching towards the assault ship, and the next broadside followed seconds later.

"He's firing at his launchers' maximum cycle rate, Sir!" Segedin announced, and Krasnitsky nodded. The Saint captain was firing as rapidly as he could, using a "shoot-shoot-look" tracking system. It would take nearly four and a half minutes for the missiles to cross the distance between the two ships, which meant that at his current rate of fire, he would have shot his magazines dry before the first salvo impacted. It was exactly what Krasnitsky would have done in his place, because given the difference in the sizes and power of the two opponents, the cruiser's only chance at this point was to overwhelm and destroy the heavier ship before they closed to energy range.

But that wasn't going to happen.

"All right, let's delta vee," he told Segedin. "I want a max delta towards this Saint P-O-S. Take him, Tactical!"

"Aye, Sir!"

Radar and lidar had an iron lock on the cruiser, and despite the crippling effects of Ensign Guha's sabotage, the tactical computers quickly finalized firing solutions.

DeGlopper was a four-hundred-meter-radius sphere. She was an assault ship, which meant she had to build in room for six shuttles, but that left more than enough room for missile tubes and ample magazines, and the missiles in those magazines were larger and heavier than any parasite cruiser could carry. Now all eight of her launchers began hammering fire at the Saint, and mixed in with her more dangerous missiles were jammers and antiradiation seekers.

It looked like a totally unfair fight, but *DeGlopper's* tactical net was far below par. Most of her missiles were under autonomous control, which meant the transport's computer AI couldn't adjust their flight profiles to maximum effect. And it also meant her point defense was far less effective than normal.

"Vampires! I have multiple vampires inbound!" There was a series of thuds as the ship's automated defenses reacted to the inbound missiles. "We have auto-flares and chaff. Some of the vampires are following the decoys!"

"And some of them aren't!" Krasnitsky snapped, watching his own plot. "Sound the collision alarm!"

Some of the Saint missiles were picked off by countermissiles and laser clusters. Others were sucked off course by active and passive decoys, and the entire first salvo was destroyed or spoofed. But one missile from the second salvo, and three missiles from the third, got through, and alarms screamed as pencils of X-ray radiation smashed into the ChromSten hull.

"Direct hit on Missile Five," Commander Talcott

reported harshly. "We've lost Number Two Graser, two countermissile launchers, and twelve laser clusters." He looked up from his displays and met Krasnitsky's eyes across the bridge. "None of the damage hit any of the shuttles or came near the magazines, Sir!"

"Thank God," the captain whispered. "But still not good. Navigation, how long to beam range?"

"Two minutes," the Navigator reported, and smiled evilly. She'd successfully fooled the Saint captain for hours, playing the role of a panicked merchant skipper while he reviled her parentage, knowledge, and training. Now let him suck laser!

"Hit!" Segedin called. "At least one direct missile hit, Sir! She's streaming air!"

"Understood," Krasnitsky replied. "How are we doing on the computers?"

"Rotten, Sir!" Segedin snapped, euphoria vanished. "I had to shift resources to the defensive systems. Most of the birds are flying on their own at this point."

"Well, this will be over soon," the captain said, just as another salvo of Saint missiles came streaking in. "One way or another."

CHAPTER TEN

Roger grabbed the arms of the command chair as another concussion rocked the shuttle like a high wind.

"This," he remarked quietly, "is not fun."

"Hmmm," Pahner said noncommittally. "Check your monitors in the troop bay, Sir."

The prince found the appropriate control and tapped it, turning on the closed-circuit monitors in the troop bay. What they revealed surprised him: most of the troops were asleep, and the few who were awake were performing some sort of leisure activity.

Two had electronic game pads out and appeared to be competing in something with one another. Others were playing cards with hard decks or, apparently, reading. One even had a hard copy book out, an old and much thumbed one from the look. Roger panned around, looking for anyone he recognized, and realized that he only knew three or four names in the entire company.

Poertena was asleep, with his head thrown back and his mouth wide open. Gunnery Sergeant Jin, the dark,

broad Korean platoon sergeant of Third Platoon, had a
pad out and was paging slowly through something on
it. Roger scrolled up the magnification on the monitors,
and was surprised to see that the NCO was reading a
novel. He'd somehow expected it to be a military
manual, and he spun the magnification still higher,
curiously, so that he could read over the sergeant's
shoulder. What he got was a bit more than he'd bar-
gained for; the sergeant was reading a fairly graphic
homosexual love story. The prince snorted, then spun
the monitor away and dialed back on the magnification.
The sergeant's taste was the sergeant's business.

The monitor stopped as if by its own volition on the
face of the female sergeant who'd summoned him from
the armor fitting. It was a face of angles, all high cheekbones and sharp chin with the exception of the lips,
which were remarkably voluptuous. Not a pretty face,
but arguably a beautiful one. She was looking through
a pad as well, and for a reason he wasn't sure he would
have cared to explain, he hunted until he found a
monitor that would permit him to look over her shoulder.
He panned the camera down, and felt a sudden rush
of relief—although exactly why he was glad that what
she was reading was the briefing on Marduk was something he didn't care to consider too deeply.

Flipping back over to the original monitor, he zoomed
in on the sergeant's chameleon suit. There it was. On
the right . . . breast. *Despreaux.* Nice name.

"Sergeant Despreaux," Pahner said dryly, and the
prince hit the trackball and panned the monitor off the
name.

"Yes, I recognized her from when she crashed my fitting," he said hurriedly. "I was just realizing how few
of these guards I know by name." He cleared his throat
uncomfortably, happy, for some reason, that the captain
couldn't see his face.

"Nothing wrong with getting to know their names," Pahner said calmly. "But what you might want to catch is their attitudes," he continued, as another salvo slammed into the ship.

"We just lost Graser Four and Nine, and Missile Three. We're down twenty-five percent on our counter-missile launchers. More on the laser clusters," Commander Talcott said. He didn't bother to add that *DeGlopper* had also suffered severe hull breaching, since everyone on the bridge could feel the draw of the vacuum around them. The executive officer had just turned toward the captain, when there was a crow of delight from Tactical.

"There she blows!" the sublieutenant shouted. The Saint cruiser had come apart under the hammer of the missiles, without even having come to grips at energy weapon range.

"Put us back on course for the planet—and shift to Evasion Able Three!" Krasnitsky snapped to the helmsman. "We're not out of the woods yet. There are still incoming missiles."

"Yes, Sir," Segedin agreed with a triumphant grin. "But we still got her!"

"Yes, we did," Talcott whispered so quietly that only Krasnitsky could hear. "But what about her mate?"

The tac officer shut down the guidance channels to the remainder of the offensive missiles and shunted all the processor power they'd been using to the defenses. Then he picked up half the defensive net and waded in. Between the added processor power, the loss of the cruiser's support, and the addition of Segedin's experience, the remainder of the missiles were quickly shredded. All that was left, for the time being, was to pick up the pieces.

❖   ❖   ❖

"So that's it, Your Highness," Captain Krasnitsky finished, looking up from the pad in his hand. His skin suit was sealed, and the orange vacuum warning light behind him was clearly visible. "We used less than half our missiles in this engagement, but the other cruiser has already broken orbit and is accelerating towards us. We'll drop your shuttles in two hours, and it will take us longer than that to get patched up and restore pressure again. So I would suggest that you stay where you are, Your Highness."

"Very well, Captain," the prince said. He was aware that all the captain was seeing was the distorted ball of his powered armor's helmet-visor, and he was just as glad. He was beginning to understand why *DeGlopper* had to, effectively, commit suicide, but he was still uncomfortable with it.

Pahner's company, at least, were official bodyguards for the Imperial Family, with the tradition of taking rifle beads to protect their charges; "catching the ball" as it was called. But the company's personnel had to survive—some of them, at least—if they were to accomplish their mission of keeping him alive; *DeGlopper*'s entire crew had to *die* to do that. Spoiled he might be, but not even Roger MacClintock was immune to the sense of guilt that produced. Yet nothing in Krasnitsky's tone or attitude suggested that he had ever even considered any other course of action. In the captain's place, Roger suspected that he might be thinking about how . . . convenient it would be if something happened to remove the prince from the equation. After all, if Roger were dead, there would be no reason for Krasnitsky's remaining crew to die to save him, now would there? Somehow, the fact that Krasnitsky and all of his people seemed totally oblivious to that glaringly logical point only made him feel guiltier.

"I suppose we'll talk again before separation," he said after a moment, awkwardly. "Until then, good luck."

"Thank you, Your Highness," the captain said with a tiny nod. "And good luck to you and the Company, as well. We'll try to do the *DeGlopper* name proud."

The communications screen blinked out, and Roger leaned back and turned to Captain Pahner. The Marine had doffed his helmet and was scratching his head vigorously.

"Who was DeGlopper, anyway?" the prince asked, fumbling with the controls and latches of his own helmet.

"He was a soldier in the American States, a long time ago, Your Highness," Pahner said, cocking his head at the angle Roger had begun to recognize as a subtle sign that he'd stuck his foot in it. "There was a plaque right outside the cabin you were in, listing his medal and the citation for it. He won their equivalent of the Imperial Star. When we get back to Earth you can look up the citation."

"Oh." Roger pulled the pin and let his hair down so that it cascaded across the back of the armor, then scratched his scalp with both hands at least as vigorously as Pahner. "We weren't in these things all that long. What makes your head itch so badly?"

"A lot of it's psychosomatic, Your Highness," Pahner said with a snort. "Like that itch between your shoulder blades."

"Agggh!" Roger rolled his shoulders as well as he could in the constricting armor and squirmed, trying to rub his back against the internal padding. "You would have to mention that!"

Pahner just smiled. Then he frowned ever so slightly. "Can I make a suggestion, Your Highness?"

"Yesss?" Roger replied doubtfully.

"We're not going anywhere for two hours. I'm going

to go roust out the troops and tell them they can undog their helmets and do a little stretching. Give them about a half-hour, and then come down and talk to a few of them."

"I'll think about it," Roger said dubiously.

He did, and his thoughts didn't make him all that happy.

CHAPTER ELEVEN

Chaplain Pannella placed his hands behind his back and sniffed.

"Lord Arturo isn't going to be happy," he observed.

Captain Imai Delaney, skipper of the Caravazan Empire parasite cruiser *Greenbelt*, refrained from snarling at the ship's chaplain. It wasn't the easiest restraint he'd ever exercised, and it got even harder as he looked around and recognized his bridge officers' stunned disbelief. He drew a deep breath and wiped his face. They'd obviously gotten sloppy, and "not happy" was a very pale description of what Lord Arturo would be when he heard about this one.

At the same time, he understood exactly how it had happened. There had been no problems at all since the two parasites had been put on station, and they were mainly there to make sure that no one noticed the Saint presence in the system. They'd let a few transports—the ones with registered schedules—through and taken a few of the tramps as prizes. But their primary job wasn't commerce raiding; it was supporting the tactical operations that were being staged through the system, and it had become routine. Too routine.

"It's a *Puller*-class transport," the tactical officer reported as he studied his readouts. "There was one flash of nearly full power. They're masking their drive, somehow, but that flash was clear."

"Why would the Earthies send in a single armed transport?" the chaplain demanded. "And why is its acceleration so low?"

The captain decided that screaming would probably be unwise, however tempting. The answer to both questions was obvious, but if he simply stated them bluntly he might be accused of "insufficient consideration" for the chaplain's feelings and opinions. As if a chaplain should have a voice in military matters!

He looked around the bridge. His officers' uniforms were the somber and slightly off-color tones that bespoke preparation in low-acid processes. The textiles were all natural, too . . . which meant that unlike in most navies, if there was a sudden shipboard fire the crew was subject to immolation.

Captain Delaney had been aboard an Empie parasite cruiser once. The bridge had been all cool tones and smoothly rounded edges; on his own ship, the edges were jagged and unfinished. Finishing and "trim" were considered unnecessary frills. Unnecessary frills used excess energy. Excess energy, eventually, was bad for planetary environments. So, no trimming for *Greenbelt's* bridge.

The same philosophy extended throughout the ship. Everything looked rough hewn and badly fitted. Oh, it worked. But it wasn't as smooth as it would have been aboard a damned Empie warship. Nothing was . . . not even the command relationships. On an Empie ship, the captain was king. He might be under the command of an admiral, but on his own ship he was lord and master.

On the Saints' ships, though, the chaplain always had to be considered. Adherence to the tenets of the Church of Ryback was as important, to the higher-ups, as capability. So besides fighting the damned aristos for command slots, Captain Delaney had been fighting the Church for his entire career.

Not that there was going to be any difference of opinion about what to do in this instance.

"I believe she might be damaged," he said, allowing no trace of his thoughts to color his tone. "That one burst of power is probably all their phase drive could stand."

"Well . . . I suppose that makes some sense," the chaplain said doubtfully. "What are we going to do about it?"

We *are going to kill it*, Delaney thought. *Which would be easier to do if you would just get your eco-freak butt back to the chapel and off my bridge!*

"The data from *Green Goddess* indicates that the enemy's tactical net is probably damaged," he said aloud. He scratched his beard and thought about it. "We'll stay at the edge of the powered missile envelope and pound her to scrap. She can't maneuver, and we should have the better tac net." He nodded his head in self-agreement. "Yes. That should work."

"How much damage will we take?" the chaplain asked nervously. "Damage repair will do great harm to the environment. We must limit our use of resources in every way we can. And it will surely damage the *ki* of the crew."

"Do you want the ravening imperialists to fully colonize this world?" Delaney asked rhetorically. "That ship is filled with Marines, carrying their humanocentric infestation with them to new worlds. What would you have me do? Let them go?"

"No," the chaplain snapped, shaking his head. "They

must be destroyed. The infestation must be ripped out root and branch. This fine world shall not be polluted by man!"

Fine world, indeed, the captain thought behind a smile of agreement. *It's a green hell. Killing these Marines is probably doing them a favor.*

Sergeant Major Kosutic reached across the narrow compartment and tapped the prince's chief of staff on the shoulder.

"You can undog your helmet now," she said, suiting action to words and removing her own.

O'Casey undid the latches clumsily, and looked around the cramped compartment.

"Now what?" she asked.

"Now we wait a couple of hours, and hope His Evilness Who Resides in the Fire decides we get to live," Kosutic answered, scratching the back of her neck. She set down the helmet and reached under the command station. "Aha!" she said, and pulled out a long plastic tube with a faint ripping sound.

"What is that?" O'Casey asked, looking up as she opened her pad to begin an entry.

"It's a wiring harness cover." Kosutic leaned forward and inserted the flexible tube into the neck of her suit. "Most of these shuttles have had them stripped out already." She began rubbing the corrugated tube up and down her back. "Ahhh," she gasped. "I forgot mine, by Satan."

"Oh," Eleanora said, suddenly noticing the itchiness of her own back. "Can I, um, borrow it?"

"Check by your left knee. I don't mind your borrowing it, but you might as well find your own. Best back scratcher ever created."

Eleanora found the wiring harness where the sergeant major had indicated and pulled its cover out.

"Ooooh," she sighed after a brief try. "Boy, this is good!"

"And for telling you that deep, dark secret, known only to Old Marines," Kosutic said, "you have to tell me something."

"Like what?"

"Like what's eating the Prince," Kosutic replied, propping her heels on the command station in front of her.

"Hmmm," Eleanora said thoughtfully. "That's a long story, and I'm not sure how much of it you're cleared for. What you know about his father?"

"Just that he's the Earl of New Madrid; that he's on the watchlist, which means he doesn't get within a planet of the Empress; and that he's quite a bit older than the Empress."

"Well, I'm not going to get into why he was banished from Court, but Roger not only looks like his father, he acts very much like him. New Madrid is a gorgeous man, who's a terrible dandy. And he's also very much involved in The Great Game."

"Ah." Kosutic nodded. The intrigues of the Empire had gotten deeper and deeper during the reign of Emperor Andrew, Alexandra's father. While things had never, quite, come to the point of outright civil war, they seemed to be edging closer to it. "So is the Prince involving himself in the Game?" she asked carefully, and Eleanora sighed.

"I'm . . . not sure. He's been in contact with some of the known conduits in his sports clubs. I mean, one of the other fellows on his polo team is a known member of New Madrid's clique. So, maybe. But Roger hates politics with a purple passion. So . . . I'm not sure."

"You should know."

"Yes, I should," the chief of staff admitted. "But it's not the sort of thing he would confide in me. I'm an appointment of his mother's."

"Is he . . . conspiring against the *Empress*?" Kosutic asked even more carefully.

"I doubt that very much," Eleanora said. "He seems to truly love his mother, but he might be being used as a dupe. The way he acts, the . . . frivolity. It just doesn't make any sense. With his background, with what his father did, Roger has to realize that presenting such a front lays him open to charges of following in New Madrid's footsteps. So half the time I'm certain he's doing it on purpose, and the other half . . . I just don't know."

"Maybe it's a double-blind," Kosutic suggested. "He might be putting on these airs as a cover for being really, really capable?"

She was aware that she was engaging in wishful thinking, but there had to be at least a shred of light in the darkness. Otherwise, the Marines had stuck their heads into a guillotine for an enemy of all they held dear.

"I doubt it," Eleanora said with a grim chuckle. "Roger's just not that subtle." She gazed down at her pad for several moments, then sighed. "And, frankly, however subtle he is or isn't, he's always been the odd one out in the Imperial Family."

She tapped at the pad's controls for several seconds, then closed it and turned her chair to face the sergeant major.

"At the expense of possible *lese majeste*," she said, "Roger can act like a real pain in the ass sometimes. No, let's be honest—he can *be* a real pain in the ass. But I think it's fair to point out that it's not entirely his fault."

"Ah?" Kosutic kept her face carefully expressionless, but mental ears pricked at the chief of staff's tone. Despite the fact that Bronze Battalion was specifically charged with the task of guarding the Heir Tertiary, and despite the amount of time the Bronze Barbarians had

spent in their charge's presence (not with any particular sense of pleasure for either party), no one in the
company really *knew* Roger at all. O'Casey obviously did,
and if she was prepared to give Kosutic any insight at
all into the prince, the sergeant major was more than
ready to listen.

"No, it's not," O'Casey told her, and shook her own
head with a crooked smile. "He's a MacClintock, and
everyone knows that all MacClintocks are brave, trust-
worthy, fearless and brilliant. They're not, of course, but
everyone *knows* they are, anyway, and the fact that
Crown Prince John and Princess Alexandra actually live
up to the stereotype—like their mother—only makes it
even harder on Roger. The Crown Prince has a record
as a diplomat anyone could envy, and even without her
family connections, Princess Alexandra would be
respected as one of the finest admirals in the Fleet.
And then there's Roger. Decades younger than the
others, always on the outside, somehow . . . the classic
'bad boy' of the Imperial Family. The never-do-well,
spoiled, pampered aristocrat." She paused and cocked
her head at the sergeant major.

"Sound familiar?" she asked with a quirky half-grin.

"Well, yes, actually," Kosutic admitted. It wasn't
something any Marine, and especially any member of
Bronze Battalion, had any business admitting to anyone, anytime, anywhere, but she admitted it anyway,
and O'Casey chuckled without humor.

"I thought it might. But when you consider the cloud
his father is under, the fact that no one really knows
where Roger himself stands, and the fact that the
Empress' own attitude towards him often seems . . .
ambiguous," she chose the word with obvious care, "it's
probably inevitable that he should turn out at least a
bit that way." She snorted sadly. "Kostas Matsugae and
I have argued about it often enough, but I've never

disagreed with Kostas' insistence that Roger wasn't exactly dealt the fairest possible hand. But where Kostas and I differ is on where we go from where we are *now*. I wasn't Roger's first tutor, you know. In fact, I've only been with him for a little over six years, so I wasn't there when he was a hurt little boy dealing with the unfairness of life. I can feel for that little boy's pain, I suppose, but I have to be more concerned with getting Roger the theoretical adult to face up to the fact that life isn't fair and learning to deal with it as a MacClintock and as a prince of the Empire. And," she admitted heavily, "I don't seem to be doing a very good job of it."

"Well," Kosutic told her, picking her words with equal care, "I can't say I envy you. I've done my share of kicking wet-behind-the-ears lieutenants into Marine officers, but the Corps gives me a lot better support structure for that kind of thing than you seem to have."

"It *would* be nice if I could use the sort of judo I've seen you using on Captain Pahner's officers," O'Casey agreed wistfully. "But I can't. And, frankly, Roger has a positive genius for digging in his heels. He may not be the overachiever his brother and sister are, but he's certainly got every bit of the MacClintock stubbornness!"

She paused with a sudden laugh, and Kosutic raised an eyebrow at her.

"What's funny?" the sergeant major asked.

"I was just thinking about Roger and stubbornness," O'Casey replied. "Well, that and God's peculiar sense of humor."

"I beg your pardon?"

"Have you ever been to the Imperial War Museum?" the academic asked, and the Marine nodded.

"Sure. A couple of times. Why?"

"I take it you've seen the Roger III Collection, then?" Kosutic nodded again, though she wasn't at all sure where O'Casey was headed with this. Roger III had been one of the many unreasonably capable emperors the MacClintock Dynasty had produced, and, as seemed to be the norm among his relatives, he had been a man of passionate (and, some would say, peculiar) interests. One of them had been military history and, particularly, that of Old Earth between the twelfth and sixteenth centuries, CE, and he had assembled what was probably the finest collection of arms and armor from the period in the entire history of the human race. When he died, he had bequeathed the entire collection to the Imperial War Museum, where it had become and remained one of its star attractions.

"Ever since Roger III's time," O'Casey went on a bit obliquely, "the continuance of his hobby interest in ancient weaponry has been something of a tradition in the Imperial Family. Oh, there's an edge of affectation to it, of course—something that makes good PR as a 'family tradition' that imperial subjects can ooh and ah over—but there's also more than a little truth to it. The Empress and the Crown Prince, for example, can spend hours explaining more than you ever wanted to know about things like Gothic armor and Swiss pikemen." She grimaced with so much feeling that Kosutic chuckled.

"But not Roger," the academic continued. "I said he can be stubborn? Well, he dug his heels in and flatly refused to have anything to do with the 'tradition.' I suppose it was a fairly harmless way to express his rebellion, but he was certainly . . . firm about it. Maybe it's partly because it was all started by another Roger who also happens to have been another of those MacClintock figures everyone *respects*—unlike our Roger—but despite his family's very best efforts, he never showed the least interest in the entire subject, which is a pity really. Especially now."

"Now?" Kosutic gazed at her for a moment, then

barked a laugh as understanding struck. "You're right," she said, "it *would* be handy if he knew anything about it, given the local tech level on Marduk."

"Absolutely," O'Casey agreed with another sigh, "but that's our Roger all over. If there's a way to do it wrong, he'll find it every time."

Roger watched Pahner make his way down the center transom of the shuttle bay and shook his head. With the troops squashed into the shuttle like old-fashioned sardines in a can, the only way to move up and down the troop bay was by walking on the transom on which the center seats were mounted. That meant, of course, that he was walking at head level to the seated Marines.

The problem was that while Pahner was in a relatively light and fairly nimble skin suit, which he'd donned in preference to armor for just this reason, Roger was wrapped in ChromSten. He could no more make his way down that narrow strip in armor than he could walk a tightrope, and he rather doubted that any of his bodyguards would feel happy about being stepped upon, however daintily, by armor that weighed as much as a tyranothere.

"Well, Your Highness?" Pahner asked as he reached the end and swung easily to the floor.

"I'm going to have a hard time making my way down the bay in this," Roger said, gesturing at his armor. Pahner glanced at the gray battle steel and nodded.

"Take it off. We're going to be rattling around for a couple of hours."

"Take it off where? There's not enough room in the compartment."

"Right here," Pahner said, gesturing at the small open area. The patch of deck was the only open area in the bay, a tiny sliver of room for the shuttle crew to move around in. A ladder led up from it to a small landing with two hatches, one to the command compartment, and the other to the bridge. There was another hatch on the troop level portside. It was a pressure door leading to the exterior.

"Right here?" Roger juggled the helmet under his arm to give himself a moment to think while he looked around. Most of the guards were still doing their own things. A few had gotten up to move around, but most of those had headed to the rear of the bay where the palletized cargo afforded room to stretch out. It seemed awfully . . . public, though.

"I could get your valet," Pahner said with a faint smile. "He's back there," he continued, gesturing towards the rear of the troop bay.

"Matsugae?" Roger's face brightened. "That would be grea— I mean, yes, of course, Captain. Do you think you could fetch my valet?" he ended in a refined drawl.

"Well," Pahner said, his face closing down again, "I don't know about 'fetch.'" He banged the nearest sleeping guard on the shoulder. "Pass the word for Matsugae."

The Marine yawned, shoved the next Marine in line, passed on the word, and promptly went back to sleep. A few moments later, Roger saw the small form of the valet emerge from under a pile of rucksacks. He bent down and spoke to someone, then climbed onto the transom and made his way toward the prince.

Vertical pillars ran up from the transom to the roof every two meters, and if Matsugae was far less nimble on the uncertain footing than Captain Pahner had been, he had the overall idea down. He would hold onto a vertical, then move forward of it, using it to balance as he shuffled out on the transom as far as he could before making a hopping lunge for the next. Using this technique, he slowly made his way forward to the prince's position.

"Good—" the valet paused, obviously checking the

clock in his toot "—evening, Your Highness." He smiled. "You're looking well."

"Thank you, Valet Matsugae," Roger said, much more careful to maintain his formality in front of so many listening ears. "How are you?"

"Very well, Your Highness. Thank you." Matsugae gestured to the rear of the compartment. "Sergeant Despreaux has been a mine of helpful information."

"Despreaux?" Roger lifted an eyebrow and leaned sideways to look down the line of troops, and caught the brief flash of a refined profile.

"She's a squad leader in Third Platoon, Your Highness. A very nice young lady."

"Given their resumes," Roger said with a smile, "I doubt that you could categorize any of the young ladies in The Empress' Own as 'nice.'"

"As you say, Your Highness," Matsugae said with an answering smile. "How can I be of service?"

"I have to get out of this armor and into something decent."

Matsugae's face crumpled.

"I'm sorry, Your Highness. I should've known. Let me go get my pack." He started to scramble up onto the transom again, preparing to retrace his route.

"Wait!" Roger said. "I have a uniform packed up in the command compartment. I just need help getting out of the armor."

"Oh, well then," Matsugae said, climbing back down. "If Captain Pahner could give me a hand? I don't actually know all that much about armor, but I'm willing to learn."

As they disconnected the armor's various latches and controls, Roger became curious.

"Matsugae? Am I to understand that you have spare uniforms for me in your pack?"

"Well, Your Highness," the valet said almost shyly,

"Sergeant Despreaux told me that you weren't able to bring all your clothes. And why. I didn't feel it appropriate that you have only one suit of armor and a single uniform, so I packed a few extra outfits along. Just in case."

"Can you carry it?" Captain Pahner sounded skeptical. "Of course, if that's *all* that you're carrying . . ."

"I will admit, Captain," the small valet said in a pert voice, "that I'm not carrying the weight of ammunition most of your Marines are. However, I *am* carrying my full equipment load and a share of the squad load for the headquarters group. His Highness' gear is, so to speak, my ammunition allotment."

"But can you carry it?" Pahner repeated darkly. "Day after day."

"We shall simply have to see, Captain," Matsugae replied calmly. "I think so. But we shall have to see."

He returned to his task of peeling the prince, and Roger soon found himself once again standing in the midst of scattered pieces of armor.

"I'm forever putting this stuff on and taking it off." He brushed an imaginary fleck of dust from the singlet he'd worn under the armor as Matsugae scrambled up the steps to the command compartment.

"Not for much longer, Your Highness," Pahner pointed out. "Once we land on the planet, it will hardly ever be used. But if we need it, we're *really* going to need it."

CHAPTER TWELVE

"What else do we need?" O'Casey asked, thumbing through the list of supplies the Marines had loaded.

"Whatever it is, it better not weigh much," Kosutic replied. The sergeant major was doing a recalculation of fuel use, and she looked up with a grimace. "I don't think we have much margin."

"I thought you could glide one of these things in," Eleanora said uncomfortably. It was hardly her area of expertise, but she knew that the shuttles' swing-wing configuration gave them a tremendous glide ratio.

"We can." Kosutic's tone was mild. "If we have a runway, that is." She gestured at one of the monitors, where the small map from the *Fodor's* was displayed. "Do you see many airports? In glide mode, one of these things needs a nice, old-fashioned runway. You try to land without one, and you might as well give your soul to His Wickedness."

"So what happens if it were running out of fuel, then?"

"Well, if we were headed in for a standard atmosphere

118

insertion, we could correct at the last minute and do some atmospheric skipping to slow down. The problem is, if we do an orbit, we'll be detected. Then the whole plan goes out the airlock, and we have a cruiser and the garrison hunting us dirtside.

"If, on the other hand, we do a steep reentry—which, by the way, is what we're planning—and run out of fuel, we'll just pancake."

"Oh."

"Make a hell of a hole," Kosutic snorted.

"I can imagine," O'Casey said faintly.

"I imagine that this is about where we should be detecting the Saint, Sir," Sublieutenant Segedin said.

"Understood." Captain Krasnitsky looked at the helmsman. "Prepare for course change. Quartermaster, pass the word to the Marines to prepare for separation."

"They should have detected us by now," Captain Delaney said. "Why are they still decelerating for the planet?"

"Could they still intend to land their Marines?" the chaplain asked, leaning over the tactical display beside him.

Delaney's nose wrinkled at the sour smell of the chaplain's unwashed cassock. Washing among the faithful was an occasional thing, since it used unnecessary resources. And such harmful chemicals as deodorants were, of course, right out.

"They must," Delaney mused. "But they're still too far out." He smiled as the display changed. "Ah! Now we have a feel for their sensor damage. There's the course change."

"Prepare for separation. Five minutes," the ennunciator boomed.

Roger looked up in surprise from his conversation with Sergeant Jin. The Korean was surprisingly well versed on current men's fashions, and after Roger had circulated briefly around the compartment (doing his best imitation of Mother at a garden party), he'd settled down for a long talk with the sergeant. Better that than a long talk with the fascinating Sergeant Despreaux. Something told him that getting "interested" in one of his bodyguards in a situation like this one probably was a bad idea. Not that it would have been a *good* idea under any circumstances, he reflected with a familiar moodiness.

"You'd better get your armor back on, Sir," Jin said, glancing at the chameleon suit Roger had changed into. "It'll take you at least that long."

"Right. Talk to you later, Sergeant." Roger had become accustomed to walking the transom, and now he sprang lightly onto it and skipped forward, swinging gracefully from pillar to pillar.

"Show off," Julian muttered as he shifted the rucksack across his knees. It wasn't particularly uncomfortable, since it was supported by his armor, but the confinement got to him after a while.

He'd been awakened by the prince's circuit, and hadn't yet gotten back to sleep. He realized that his responses to the fop's rote questions had been a bit surly, but the prince hadn't seemed to notice.

"I don't think he was showing off," Despreaux said tartly. "I think he was hurrying up front."

Julian raised an eyebrow. Since Despreaux was seated across from him, it gave him the perfect opportunity to needle her, and it would have violated his most deeply held principles to pass it up.

"Ah, you're just jealous because he has better hair than you do."

She glanced sideways to get a glimpse of the rapidly undressing prince.

"It is nice," she murmured, and Julian's mouth dropped open as the realization dawned on him.

"You *like* him, don't you? You've got the hots for the *Prince*!"

Her head snapped back around, and she glared at the other squad leader.

"That is the stupidest thing— Of course I don't!"

Julian started to tease her further, but then the full implications hit him. There was no way the Regiment would allow one of the guards to carry on with a member of the Imperial Family. He looked around, but all the other troopers seemed to be asleep or had earbuds in. Fortunately, no one had caught his earlier outburst, and he leaned forward as far as the packed equipment permitted.

"Nimashet, are you nuts?" he hissed softly. "They'll have your ass for this!"

"There's nothing going on," she replied just as quietly, fingering the gray chameleon cover of the rucksack on her knees. "Nothing."

"There'd better be nothing!" he whispered fiercely. "But I don't believe it."

"I can handle it," the sergeant said, leaning back. "Don't worry about me. I'm a big girl."

"Sure you are. Sure." He shook his head and leaned back as well. *What a cock-up*, he thought.

On the opposite side of the transom, Poertena managed to turn a laugh into a cough. He rolled his head around as if half-asleep, and coughed again. *Despreaux and the Prince*, he thought. *Oh, t'at's pocking funny!*

"What's so funny, Sir?" Commander Talcott asked. The XO had just returned from a survey of the ship, and the news wasn't good. Four of *DeGlopper's* eight missile launchers had taken enough damage to put them out of play for the next bout, and the dead cruiser's fire had gouged deep wounds into the ChromSten-armored hull. Some of them threatened loaded magazines, and although the laser-pumped fusion warheads wouldn't detonate from impact, the power systems of the missile drives would ... and take the entire ship with them.

But at least the phase drive had suffered no further damage. In fact, it was actually in better shape than for the last encounter, so they'd have a few more gravities to play with and more time on the power. And while they'd lost launchers, they'd also used less than half the total missile inventory against their first opponent, so the next fight would be nearly even.

Except for the cruiser's ability to dance rings around them.

"Oh, I was just thinking about our ship's namesake," Krasnitsky answered the question with a grim smile. "I wonder if *he* ever thought 'What the heck am I doing this for?'"

Roger watched the external monitors as the giant docking hatches opened. The perfect blackness of space beckoned as the tractor moorings cut loose, and the shuttles drifted forward. As they cleared the ship's field, *DeGlopper's* artificial gravity fell away, and they were in freefall.

"I forgot to ask, Your Highness," Pahner said tactfully. "How are you in microgravity?" He carefully avoided any mention of the excuses O'Casey had made to explain the prince's "indisposition" the first evening aboard.

"I play null-gee handball quite a bit," the prince said in an offhand manner as he swiveled the monitor around to watch the ship disappearing in the distance behind

them. "I don't have any problems with freefall at all."
He smiled evilly for just a moment. "Eleanora, on the
other hand . . ."

"I'm gonna *diiie*," the chief of staff moaned, clutch-
ing the motion sickness bag to her mouth as another
wave of wracking nausea washed over her.

"I've got a Mo-Fix injector around here somewhere,"
Kosutic said with the half-malicious chuckle of one who
possessed a cast-iron stomach. Even the smell of the
ejecta was survivable; it wasn't like she hadn't smelled
it before.

"I'm allergic." Eleanora's voice was muffled by the
plastic bag. Then she leaned back and zipped the bag
shut. "Oh, Goddd. . . ."

"Oh," Kosutic said in more sympathetic tones. She
shook her head. "We're going to be out here for a couple
of days, you realize?"

"Yes," Eleanora said miserably. "I do realize that. But
I'd forgotten these shuttles don't have artificial gravity."

"I don't think we can rotate, either," the sergeant
major told her. "We're going to do a long, slow burn.
I don't think we can do that and rotate at the same
time."

"I'll live . . . I think." The chief of staff suddenly ripped
the bag open and buried her face in the contents.
"*Arrggg.*"

Kosutic leaned back and shook her head.

"I can see this is gonna be a great trip," she said.

CHAPTER THIRTEEN

"On a scale from one to ten," Captain Krasnitsky muttered, "I give this trip a negative four hundred."

He coughed and shook his head to clear the mist of blood the cough brought up. The instructions on the box were fairly clear. Now if he could just hold together long enough to enter the codes.

Finding the keys for this particular device had been tough. Talcott, who'd had one, had been cut in half on his way back from Engineering. And, of course, the third had been in the suit of the acting engineer. He'd felt awful about having to cut it off of her to get to the device, but he'd had no choice. Tactical had had the fourth, and Navigation the fifth; those two had been easy to snag after the hit on the bridge.

Somewhat to his surprise, the ship had held together. And now, the Saints, after receiving the surrender transmission and the recording of the prince ordering Krasnitsky to surrender, were practically salivating. Capturing the prince would set every member of the ship's crew up for life, even in the austere Saint theocracy.

There was no plot here in the armory, but he didn't need one to know what was happening. He could hear the parasite cruiser docking onto the larger ship, and the concussion as the Saint Marines forced the airlocks for boarding.

Lessee. If I have all five keys, but only one activator, I have to set a delay. Okay. Makes sense.

"Captain Delaney, this is Lieutenant Scalucci." The Caravazan Marine paused and looked around the bridge. "We've taken the bridge but no prisoners. We are encountering resistance from the crew. So far, no prisoners. They're fighting hard—some of them in powered armor—and not surrendering as I would've expected. We have yet to encounter the Prince's body-guards." He paused and looked around again. "There's something about this I don't like."

"Tell him to keep his opinions to himself!" Chaplain Panella snapped. "And find the Prince!"

Captain Delaney glanced at the chaplain, then keyed his throat mike.

"Continue the mission, Lieutenant," he said. "Be careful of ambushes. They apparently haven't surrendered after all, whatever their captain said."

"It doesn't appear that way, Sir. Scalucci, out."

The captain turned to face the chaplain squarely.

"We'll find the Prince, Chaplain. But losing people doing it is stupid. I wish we'd had a pinnace to send the Marines over." An unlucky hit to the boat bay, unfortunately, had settled that. "If the Prince weren't on board, I'd put this down as a trap!"

"But he is," the chaplain hissed, "and there's no way they'd risk *his* life playing some sort of ambush game!" He grinned like a rabid ferret. "Although, if they had any sense, they'd cut his throat themselves to keep him out of our hands. Imagine what we can do with a member of the Imperial Family of that damned 'Empire of Man'!"

"Captain!" It was Lieutenant Scalucci. "The shuttle bays are empty! The shuttles must have already punched!"

The Saint captain's eyes flew wide.

"Oh, pollution!" he swore.

"The Saint is matching the last known accel of the *DeGlopper*," Pahner said.

"How can you tell?" Roger asked, eyes aching from the strain of staring at the tiny screen. "I can't tell a thing from this."

"Bring up the data records, instead," Pahner advised. "I've always said there's no reason we couldn't have larger screens in these things. But the command station was an afterthought in the design, and nobody's ever changed it."

"Well, we will!" the prince smiled as he banged the side of the recalcitrant instrument. "Oops."

He'd forgotten the power of the armor, and he withdrew his hand carefully from the fist-sized hole driven into the side of the workstation.

Pahner spun his own chair around and typed commands on the secondary keyboard at the prince's station. The now flickering monitor switched from a wider view of power sources in near space to a list of data.

"There's the last known velocity and position of the *DeGlopper*," the captain said. "And there's her current probable position and velocity." He sent a command through his toot, and a different screen came up. "And this is the Saint data."

"So they're alongside?" Roger asked, noting the obvious similarities in the data.

"Yep. They've matched course and speed with the

DeGlopper. Which means they fell for Krasnitsky's little deception hook, line, and sinker."

Roger nodded and tried to reflect some of the Marine's satisfaction, but it was hard. It was odd, he thought. Pahner was military, like Krasnitsky, and he knew as well as Roger that the Fleet captain and his entire crew were committing suicide to cover their escape. Somehow, the prince would have expected that to produce more emotion in the Marine. He'd always suspected that people who chose military careers had to be a little less . . . sensitive than others, but Pahner had been quick to let *him* know, however respectfully, whenever he stepped on one or another of the Marines' precious traditions or attitudes. So why was Pahner so detached and clinical over what was about to happen when he himself felt a hollow void of guilt sucking at his stomach?

This wasn't the way things were supposed to happen. People weren't supposed to throw away their lives to protect *him*—not when even his own family had never seemed quite certain he was worth keeping. And when gallant bodyguards and military personnel offered to lay down their lives for their duty, weren't they supposed to get something out of it besides simply *dying*?

The questions made him acutely uncomfortable, and so he decided not to think about them just at the moment and reached for some other topic.

"I didn't sound all that good on the recording," Roger said sourly.

"I think you sounded perfect, Your Highness," Pahner said with a grin. "It certainly suckered the Saints."

"Uh-huh," Roger acknowledged even more sourly. Until he'd heard the edited playback of him ordering the officers to surrender which Krasnitsky had sent to the Saint cruiser, he hadn't realized how truly childish he'd sounded. "Surrender with honor." What poppycock.

"It worked, Your Highness," Pahner's voice was much colder, "and that's all that matters. Captain Krasnitsky has them right where he wants them."

"If there's anyone left to detonate the charge."

"There is," Pahner said firmly.

"How do you know? Everybody could be dead. And unless there's at least one officer left who knows the codes . . ."

"I know, Your Highness." There was no doubt at all in Pahner's reply. "How? Well, the Saint cruiser is still alongside. If it had captured one of the crew and made him talk, it would be accelerating away at top speed. It isn't; so the plan has to be working."

And God bless, Captain, the Marine thought quietly, allowing no trace of his inner anguish to show as he watched the data codes and thought of the men and women about to die. *You've done your part; now we'll do ours to make it worth something. He's a pain in the ass, but we'll keep him alive somehow.*

"It's not working," O'Casey said to herself.

The sergeant major had drifted into the troop bay to buck up the troops, leaving the civilian to fend for herself. Which was ironic, because Eleanora was feeling seriously in need of bucking up herself. Of course, even the sergeant major might have gotten tired of the smell, which could help explain whose morale she'd decided to improve.

To take her mind off the situation, O'Casey had started reviewing the plan—if it was really fair to call it that. From the moment the second cruiser had been spotted, there'd been no time for anything as deliberate and orderly as formulating anything Eleanora O'Casey would have called "a plan." Everything had been one frantic leap of improvisation after another, and she'd been sure something vital had to have been overlooked. For that matter, she still was, but she'd never had time to stop and reflect, and now she was feeling so out of sorts and woozy that her brain was scarcely in shape for critical analysis.

Unfortunately, it was the only brain she had, and despite its grumpy complaints, she insisted that it apply itself to the problem.

They'd loaded the trade goods. She'd suggested adding refined metals, as well, but Pahner had rejected the suggestion. The captain hadn't felt that the weight-to-cost ratio would make metals worth carrying, and besides, most of the material available consisted of advanced composites, impossible for local smiths to work at the Mardukans' technology level. And, as Pahner had pointed out, material that couldn't be adapted to the locals' needs would be effectively useless to them.

There'd been no great stock of "precious" metals or gems on the ship, either. A smidgen of gold was still used in some electronics contacts, but there'd been no way to get it out. Captain Pahner had ruthlessly appropriated the small store of personal jewelry, but there hadn't been a great deal of that, either. At least what there was ought to be very attractive to a barbarian culture, even though it was little more than costume jewelry by the standards of the Empire of Man. She doubted that anyone on Marduk had ever heard of a synthetic gem!

But even if one assumed that Mardukans valued such items as highly as human cultures of comparable tech levels had valued them, there simply weren't enough of them to even begin to meet their needs. The trade goods would be worth far more in the long run, yet Eleanora still felt she was missing something. Something important. It bothered her that she had all this incredible store of knowledge about ancient cultures and—

Knowledge.

❖   ❖   ❖

Chief Warrant Officer Tom Bann ran the calculations for the fifteenth time. It was going to be close, closer than he liked. If everything went perfectly, they were going to have less than a thousand kilos of hydrogen when they landed. To a groundhog, that might have sounded like a lot; a pilot, on the other hand, knew that it was nothing over the distance they were traveling. The margin of error was more than that.

He glanced at the monitor and shook his head. He was a "Regiment" pilot, not one of the shuttle pilots assigned to *DeGlopper*, but it still hurt to watch a sacrifice like that. They were all Fleet, whether they were Marines or Navy, and Krasnitsky had sure taken the highroad. He shook his head again and looked at the number. It would really suck if it all turned out to be for nothing.

"Hello? Pilot?" He didn't recognize the voice in his earbud at first, but then he realized it was the prince's chief of staff.

"Yes, Ma'am? This is Warrant Bann." He wondered what the airhead wanted at a time like this. It had better be important to interfere in a deathwatch.

"Can we still get a connection to the ship's computers?"

Bann thought about all the things wrong with the request and wondered where to start.

"Ma'am, I don't think—"

"This is important, Warrant Officer," the voice in his earbud said firmly. "Vital, even."

"What do you need?" he asked warily.

"There's a copy of the *Encyclopedia Galactica* in my personal database. Why we didn't bring it with us, I don't know."

"But . . ." Bann said, thinking about the problems of connecting to the ship. Even if there were surviving antennae, he'd have to use a whisker laser, and with the Saints attached to the hull, there was a good chance that they would detect it, which would give away the shuttle's location.

"I know there's hardly anything on Marduk in it," O'Casey said quickly, anticipating part of his objection, "but there *is* data on early cultures and technologies. How to make flintlocks, how to make better iron and steel. . . ."

"Oh." The warrant officer nodded in his helmet. "Good point. But if I try to connect with the ship, we might be detected. And then what?"

"Oh." It was O'Casey's turn to pause in thought. "We'll have to take the chance," she said after a moment, her voice firm. "This data could make or break the expedition."

Bann thought about it as he warmed up the laser system. He saw her argument—it could be vital data—and there certainly wasn't much time to kick the idea around. If he tried to find Captain Pahner's blacked-out shuttle first to ask for permission, *DeGlopper* would almost certainly be gone before they could get anything. Which meant that *he* had to decide if it was worth endangering the entire mission to get some possibly useless data.

On the whole, he decided, it was.

"Whisker laser!" The lieutenant at Ship Defense Control turned towards her superior. "It appears to be sending a data request to the Empie assault ship. From . . . two-two-three by zero-zero-nine!"

"The shuttles," Delaney said. "It's the shuttles, trying to sneak away to the planet."

"We're too far out," the chaplain objected. "You said so yourself. They can't brake and make a reentry. And even if they could, we'd still be here to control the planet."

"True." Delany nodded. "But they *could* hide on the surface for a time."

"Only until the carrier detected them," Panella said dismissively. "They'd be mad to try to sneak down to the surface. Besides, we can still run them down, and we would've detected them soon after they started their deceleration."

"Maybe," the captain said dubiously. "But those shuttles use a hydrogen reaction jet that's fairly hard to detect much beyond a light-minute." He scratched his beard in thought about it for a moment. "Still, you're right. They must have expected to be detected."

He thought for a moment more, and in his eyes flew open wide.

"Unless they know we won't be here *to* detect them!" He wheeled to his bridge crew.

"Detach the ship! *Detach now!*"

"What to download?" O'Casey asked the empty compartment. "What? What, what? Come on, load!" she snapped.

Warrant Officer Bann had experienced great difficulty finding a connection, but Eleanora was in now, and waited as the final connects were made. When the screen finally came up, she sent the command through her toot.

"Search 'survival,' " she whispered, watching the results of the query come up. "Scroll down, scroll down, 'hostile flora and fauna' download, 'medicine' download. Search 'fuels, shuttle.' Scroll down. 'Expedient' download. Search, 'military, primitive.' Refine, 'arquebus.' Scroll down, scroll." She kept one eye on the loading diagram. The whisker laser was a relatively small bandwidth system, and the first download on hostile flora and fauna survival wasn't complete yet. She hissed, and then shook her head as a default message came up. "Four

thousand three hundred eighty-three articles. *Damn*."
She didn't have time for this.

"Refine . . . 'generals.' Refine, 'greatest.' " She viewed
the results. There was only one name she recognized
offhand, despite her doctorate in history. She'd been
more interested in societal developments than in military destructiveness, and arquebuses were as distant as
ancient Rome and its fabled legions. But one name stood
out in both the military and societal continuum.

"Download, 'Adolphus, Gustavus.' "

"Damn," Pahner snarled.

Roger nodded, more comfortable with the information now. "Disconnection."

"Yes," the captain replied in a quiet voice, watching
the simple text "TOS" which had replaced the data feed
from DeGlopper. *Termination of Signal.* Such a . . .
sanitary acronym. The letters held his eye, and then the
sensor readouts on the Saint cruiser disappeared, as well.

"Ah," he said sadly, and Roger nodded again.

"Well," the prince said after a moment, trying to
lighten the atmosphere, "at least they got them."

Without even turning around, he felt the temperature in the compartment drop, and swore at himself for
putting his foot into his mouth yet again. He'd been
wrong about the Marine's lack of feeling, he realized.

"Yes, I suppose they did. Your Highness," Pahner said
flatly.

"Damn!" Eleanora shouted, slamming her hand down
on the panel. The transmission had shut off in mid-line,
and she'd only gotten part of the way through the entry
on Gustavus Adolphus, King of Sweden.

She'd hunted for other data after entering that article,
and as she had, she'd realized the incredible reach of the
information available. The Marines could use data on

improved metallurgy, agriculture, irrigation, and engineering. On chemistry, biology, and physics. It had all been sitting there the whole time, available for translation to pads or even toots. They could've loaded the whole thing into individual toots and had a walking encyclopedia!

But only if she'd thought of it in time.

"What's wrong?" Sergeant Major Kosutic asked, coming back into the compartment. She glanced at the monitors and nodded. "Oh. The *DeGlopper*'s gone. But they got the Saint."

"No, no, no. That's not it!" O'Casey snapped, banging the workstation again. "I realized after you'd gone that I had the whole universe in my hand. I had a copy of the *Encyclopedia Galactica* in my personal system on the ship. I hardly used it, because it was only outline information. But there were all *sorts* of things that we could've downloaded if we'd only thought of it in time. I started grabbing articles, but the signal terminated on me."

"Oh? Did you get anything?"

"Yeah," O'Casey replied as she brought up the data. "I think I got the most critical stuff. Survival and hostile environments, survival first-aid, something on expedient shuttle fuels and the beginning of a download on a general from Earth when they used arquebuses." She frowned and looked at the files. "The one on shuttle fuels looks a little slender."

Kosutic's mouth worked as she tried not to smile while the academic brought up the data on shuttle fuels.

"Oh. According to this, the field expedient shuttle fuel can be made by using electricity to break down water and—"

"And there's a system on the shuttle that can do it," Kosutic interrupted. "They get the power from solar cells . . . and it takes about four years to fill a shuttle's tanks."

"Right." O'Casey turned from the monitor. "You already knew that?"

"Yep," Kosutic admitted, still fighting back a grim chuckle. "And before anyone joins the Regiment, she goes through a Satan-Be-Damned course that includes combat survival skills. In fact, Captain Pahner is a survival instructor."

"Oh," O'Casey said. "Damn."

"Don't worry about it," Kosutic advised her, and this time the sergeant major allowed her chuckle to escape. "The Empire's worlds have an enormous variety of tech levels, and the Marines recruit from almost all of them. You'd be amazed by the stuff some of the troops know. When we need something done, most of the time there'll be a troop who has the skill. You just watch."

"I hope you're right."

"Trust me. I've been riding herd on Marines for almost forty standard years now, and they *still* surprise me sometimes."

"In that case, I guess we just sit here and wait for the landing," O'Casey said sourly.

"Pretty much," Kosutic agreed. "You play pinochle?"

CHAPTER FOURTEEN

"Oh, joy."

Pahner tapped the monitor control, but the picture didn't get any better. Not that there was anything wrong with the sensors or their readouts.

For the last three days the shuttles had been on a pursuit arc headed to overtake the planet from behind. The port was on a small continent or a large island, depending on how one chose to look at it, and their flight plan had been carefully calculated to bring them down just on the far side of the local ocean. That would have put them within a thousand klicks of their objective, and the Mardukans were supposed to have seafaring capability, so most of the trip could be accomplished on shipboard. All they'd have to do would be to hire a ship or ships to carry them across.

It had been, Pahner admitted modestly, a neat and tidy plan. The only real drawback had been that it pushed the parameters of the shuttles' range envelope. The deep-space burns required to put them on the proper intercept course for the planet had consumed so much of their total fuel that they had just enough left to complete their approach and land.

Unfortunately, there was a ship in orbit above the port.

She was powered down, or *DeGlopper* would have detected her, but she was probably the carrier for the parasite cruisers. And whoever she was, parked in that position, she would be able to detect and track the shuttles' reentry unless they landed, literally, on the far side of the planet.

The good news was that the second Saint cruiser obviously hadn't realized the shuttles had escaped—or, at least, hadn't realized in time to alert her carrier. If she had, the carrier would have moved to watch the side of the planet which the port's sensors couldn't cover in order to prevent the shuttles from sneaking in. The *bad* news was that the carrier's mere presence, and the diversion that would force upon them, would add some ten thousand kilometers to their dirtside journey.

And, of course, that they wouldn't have enough fuel for the landing, anyway.

"Oh, this is bad," Roger said, looking over the captain's shoulder. "Very, very bad."

"Yes, Your Highness," Pahner said with immense restraint. "It is."

He and the prince had been at close quarters for three days, and neither was in the best mood.

"What are we going to do?" Roger asked, and that faint edge of whine was back in his voice.

Pahner was spared the necessity of an immediate response by the attention chime of the communicator. He managed not to let his relief at the interruption show as he hit the button that acknowledged the com request. Rather than answer immediately, however, he switched the system to holo-mode and waited patiently. It wasn't a long wait, and he smiled thinly at the series of holograms which soon hovered in the compartment.

"I take it that you've all noticed our friend," he said dryly once his audience—all three lieutenants, all four pilots, Sergeant Major Kosutic, and Eleanora O'Casey—was complete.

"Oh, yeah," Warrant Bann said. "The planned IP is out, and so are aborts one and two."

"We should have had a plan in place for this!" Chief Warrant Officer Dobrescu snapped. The pilot of Shuttle Four looked at Pahner as if this were all his fault. Which, in a way, it was.

"That's true enough," Bann said, "but the fact is that we never did have the fuel for a conventional powered landing, no matter where we set down. We needed that atmospheric braking even to hit the prime site."

"Which site is completely out of the question with that damned carrier sitting there," Pahner pointed out. It was, he decided, almost certainly the most unnecessary observation he'd ever made, but he made himself continue with the thoroughly unpalatable corollary. "We'll have to land in the backlands, instead."

"We can't," Dobrescu said. "You can't land one of these things in a jungle unpowered!"

"What about these white patches?" Roger asked, and Pahner and all of the holograms turned to look at him as he tapped the limited chart he'd been feverishly reviewing. The map on the handheld pad had been prepared from a cursory spatial survey and had virtually no detail, but certain features stood out, and he tapped the image again.

"I don't know what they are," Pahner said. He took the pad and gazed thoughtfully at the irregularly shaped patches in a mountainous region on the far side of the planet from the port. "Whatever they are, they aren't created structures; they're too big for that."

He started to say that they wouldn't help, then stopped. They weren't jungle or water or mountain, and that was about all the planet had to offer. So what were they?

By now others were studying their pads.

"I think . . ." Lieutenant Gulyas began, then stopped.

"You think what?" Warrant Bann asked. He too was drawn to the white patches.

"They're one of two things," Gulyas said. "I can't tell if they're above or below sea level, but if they're low enough, I *think* they might be dry lakebeds."

"Dry lakebeds on a jungle world," Dobrescu snorted. "That's rich. And very convenient if they are. But if we aim for them and they're not, we're dead."

"Well," Bann replied, "a planet is a damned big place, Chief. There almost have to be dry lakebeds on it *somewhere*, and we're dead anyway if the carrier sees us or we auger into a mountainside. Might as well try the possible lakebeds and hope."

"I agree with Lieutenant Gulyas," Roger said. "That's why I pointed them out. This looks like the sort of folded mountain formation where you'd get them. If the mountains folded around them and cut off their water sources, that would leave dry lakebeds." He scanned across the rest of the map. "And there are others, closer to the port. See? It's not just here."

"But the rest of the world is swamps, Your Highness," Dobrescu pointed out. "You need desert terrain for dry lakes, and why would there be desert only there?"

"I'd say that whole mountain range is probably arid," Pahner said. "The surface color is brown, not green. And there are other arid regions—they're just few and far between. So there's a good chance these really are dry lakes."

He gazed at the pad a moment longer, then set it aside and looked back at the pilots.

"Whether we're in agreement or not, the possibility that they're lakebeds is our only way out. So begin recalculating for an extended burn to slow us and a sharp descent behind the planet for a dead stick landing."

Dobrescu opened his mouth to protest, but Pahner held up his hand.

"Unless there's an alternative plan, that's what we're going to do. *Do* you have an alternative?"

"No, Sir," Dobrescu replied after a long moment. "But, with all due respect, I don't like the idea of risking His Highness' safety on a guess."

"Neither do I. But that's exactly what we're going to do. And the good news is, that we're going to be risking the rest of our lives right along with his. So if it doesn't work, none of us will have to explain it to Her Majesty."

After they'd hit zero G and the likelihood of being shot out of space by the cruiser had passed, the troops had floated around the troop bay, lacing into their low-grav hammocks and chilling out. Three days on the shuttle without a damned thing they had to do but sleep were on the order of heaven to most of the experienced Marines. But as they neared the planet and landing, the hammocks and loose gear were secured, and the troops buckled down and put on their mission faces. It had been a nice little interlude, and everyone felt fairly refreshed.

Of course, there were still a few small problems to deal with.

"Hold on a second," Julian said as the shuttle began to skip through the outermost reaches of atmosphere. "Are you trying to tell me that they *think* there's a landing zone?"

"More or less." Despreaux smiled. "It looks like there is, but, you know, we don't exactly have the best maps in the galaxy."

"Oh, this is *truly* good," Julian said, slamming his

helmet into place while the assault shuttle began to shake and shudder. "Wrrflmgdf," he continued, as the helmet muffled his voice.

"What was that?" Despreaux held a hand up to her ear as she reached for her own headcover. "I think I missed it."

"What I *said* was," Julian cut in his suit speaker to tell her, "this is truly fucking good!"

"What's the problem?" Despreaux settled her helmet and brought her own speakers online. "Just another day in the Marines."

"This is the sort of shit I wrangled my way into the Regiment to avoid," Julian snarled, wiggling deeper into the enveloping memory plastic of his cocoon as the shuttle hit another bump. "If I wanted to make lousy drops on hostile planets under insane commanders I could've stayed with Sixth Fleet."

Despreaux laughed.

"Oh, Zeus, that's rich! You were in the Sixth?"

"Yep, under Admiral Helmut, Dark Lord of the Sixth." He shook his head in memory. "Now there was a character. Kill you as soon as look at you."

Despreaux smiled, and her eyes crinkled as the shuttle gave another lurch. "You know you love it."

"Like hell!" Julian shouted as the roar of reentry filled the compartment and began to grow. He worked his tongue at a bit of ration caught between his teeth for a moment, and looked around quizzically.

"Is it just me, or do we seem to be coming in a little faster than usual?"

"We're too steep!" Bann shouted, and his hand cocked, ready to override the automated reentry system if the computer got confused.

"Stay on profile," Dobrescu said calmly. "We're in the pipe. It's just a shaky pipe, is all."

"We're exceeding parameters!" Bann snapped. Shuttle Four felt as if it were shuddering apart, and there was zero maneuver fuel left. All the pilot could do was hang on and hope she stayed together. "I've got overheating on all surfaces, and stress warnings on the wings!"

"We are exceeding the manual numbers," Dobrescu admitted as his toot flashed a series of numbers across his vision. Every system was in the yellow, but he'd performed over two thousand drops in training and combat, and had a far better feel for the real, as opposed to the specified, capabilities of the rugged drop shuttles than whatever dweeb had written the manual. "The computer doesn't like that, but the numbers are conservative. We'll be fine."

"This is insane!"

"Hey, you're the one who said 'go for the lakebeds'!" Dobrescu chuckled nastily. Then shrugged. "Would you rather be target practice for that carrier?" he asked in a milder tone. There was no answer. "Then shut up and hang on."

The shuttles flashed across the eastern ocean at five times the speed of sound, and the thunder of their crossing hammered the uncaring waves. Their speed dropped steadily, and the outer barrier range of mountains—the upthrust giants that turned the region beyond into a desiccated wasteland—reared before them. They swung out their wings, clawing now for enough speed and lift to make the tiny dots of their possible landing areas, and the faces of their pilots were grim and taut.

The craft were heavily laden, and even with their wings swept forward for maximum lift, their greatest danger now was that they would simply fall out of the sky. They had to retain altitude to cross the soaring ranges, yet maintain a tightly calculated flight path to their hoped-for landing areas, and the final descent would be steep and tricky.

Shuttle Four cleared the final ridge by barely nine meters, and Warrant Officer Bann let out a whoop.

"*Yeeha!* That's a dry lake if I've ever seen one!"

The glittering white salt bed reflected the intense G-9 sun like a mirror. The pilots' helmet visors darkened automatically, and their eyes swept back and forth over the glowing instrument readouts projected onto their visor heads-up displays.

The dangers of landing on salt lakes were as old as flight. The flat, white expanses made perfect airports but for one thing: perspective. With nothing to give a feeling of depth, a pilot trying to land visually was unable to determine whether he was going to land or just dig a big, nasty hole. The answer, of course, was technology, and the shuttle pilots pulled in their heads like turtles and shut out everything but their instruments. Radar and lidar range finders measured airspeed, velocity over ground, flight-angle, and all the other myriad variables that made the difference between a landing and a fireball and pronounced them correct. Nonetheless, each pilot continued to monitor his systems, hoping that no further demons would rear their ugly heads at the last moment and snatch defeat from victory.

Chief Warrant Dobrescu checked his instruments, studied the computer-calculated glide path on his HUD, and shook his head. They were actually doing it. He'd given up on performing any sort of decent landing when they picked up the Saint carrier; now it seemed that the entire company might actually make it to the ground intact.

Then the hard part would start.

CHAPTER FIFTEEN

Julian popped the seals on his helmet, took a sniff of the air, and grimaced as the temperature overcame the residual cool from his suit chiller.

"Christ, it's hot!"

The sweat that instantly popped out on his skin disappeared just as quickly. The blinding light from the salt flats was mixed with a light, parching wind, and the temperature was at least forty-nine degrees Standard—over a hundred and twenty degrees in the antiquated Fahrenheit scale still used on a few backward planets.

"Whew, this is gonna be funnn."

He gave a brief, unamused chuckle, and beside him Lance Corporal Russell juggled her grenade launcher into the crook of her arm and popped her own helmet.

"*Yah!* It's like being in a furnace!"

There was nothing to be seen but the four shuttles, scattered over a kilometer or so of blazing, empty salt, and the distant mountains. Julian's squad, as the only one with armor, had been unloaded first. The ten troopers had spread out with scanners on maximum, but they were barely detecting microorganisms. The salt was as dead as the surface of an airless moon—deader than some, for that matter.

Julian sent a command to his toot and switched to the company command frequency.

"Captain Pahner, my squad doesn't detect any sign of hostile zoologicals, botanicals, or sentients. The area appears clear."

"I see." The captain's tone was as a dry as the wind in Julian's face. "And I suppose that's why you took off your helmet?"

The sergeant rolled his tongue in his cheek and thought for a moment.

"Just trying to use all possible sensory systems, Sir. Sometimes smell works where others don't."

"True," the captain said mildly. "Now put it back on and set up a perimeter. I'll have the rest of Third move out to support. When they're in place come into the center as a reserve."

"Roger, Sir."

"Pahner, out."

"Modder pocker."

Poertena dropped the case of grenades onto the stack, wiped sweat off his face, and looked around. He'd spoken quietly, but Despreaux heard him, and she snorted as she ticked the item off her list. Despite the intense heat, she looked as cool as if she were standing in snow.

"Don't worry," she said. "We're nearly finished unloading. Then the fun begins."

Poertena took on the cross-eyed, inward look characteristic of someone communicating with his toot.

"Modder . . . we've been at t'is for hours!" He looked toward the horizon, where the sun was still well up. "When do tee sun go down?"

"Long day, Poertena," Despreaux said with another

cool smile. "Thirty-six hours. We've got nearly six more until dusk."

"Pock," Poertena whispered. "T'is suck."

"And you know what's really gonna suck?" Lance Corporal Lipinski demanded of the universe in general as he affixed a large square of solar film to the top of his rucksack. All members of the company had been issued squares. The combined area was designed to partially recharge the powerful superconductor capacitors that drove the human technology. While the power gathered would never support the company's bead guns, plasma rifles, and powered armor, it would serve to maintain a charge in their communicators and sensors.

"What?" Corporal Eijken asked.

The Bravo Team grenadier jerked at the belt feed over her shoulder. If the feed wasn't aligned perfectly, the grenades had a tendency to jam, and that was something she really didn't want to happen. They were going to be walking a long way through really bad stuff. That much had already become evident.

The company had unloaded and prepared through the remainder of the day and into the night. As the sun went down, the temperature went with it, and by local midnight it was well below freezing. Even with their chameleon blankets, it had been a long, miserable night, and many of the troopers remembered why they'd signed up for the Regiment in the first place. Pride of position was certainly one reason, but another was so that they wouldn't have to do stuff like huddle under a thin covering in below-freezing temperatures on a surface hard enough for an interplanetary transport landing apron.

They'd been up and at it again before dawn, loading rucksacks and overbags, piling the spare gear on stretchers, and generally preparing to move out. As the

sun came up, the cold came off, but now it was building into another scorcher. Which made for a certain
amount of bitching, no matter how good the troops.

"What's really gonna suck," Lipinski replied, "is humping all of *his* gear."

He gestured cautiously with his chin in the direction
of the prince, and Eijken shrugged.

"It's not that much spread across the Company. Hell,
I've been in companies where the CO makes his clerk
carry his gear."

"Yeah," Lipinski agreed quietly, "but they're not good
companies, are they?"

Eijken opened her mouth to respond, but stopped as
Despreaux left a gaggle of NCOs and headed their way.

"Company," the grenadier said instead, and she and
Lipinski trotted towards the sergeant as she made an
"assemble here" gesture at her scattered squad. Despreaux waited until everyone had gathered around, then
pulled out her water nipple.

"Okay, drink."

The water bladders were integral to the combat harness of the chameleon suit: a flexible plastic bladder that
molded into a trooper's back under his rucksack. The
bladder held six liters of water, and had a small, efficient chiller driven by a mechanical feedback system. As
long as the trooper was moving, the chiller was running.
It didn't make icewater, but what it produced was
generally at least a few degrees below ambient temperature, and that could be awfully refreshing.

"Uh, I gotta get mine," Lipinski said.

Sergeant Despreaux waited as the lance corporal and
a private from Bravo Team retrieved their combat har-
nesses and the others took swigs from their bladders.
Once everyone had gathered again, she glanced around
mildly.

"The next time I see anyone without her harness,"

she noted, and then glanced pointedly at one of the plasma gunner's flat bladders, "or with an empty water bladder, I'm putting her on report. Your nanites may help you keep going even when you dehydrate, but only to a point."

She glanced around the team again, and then shrugged one shoulder. It was the one her rifle was slung over.

"And I'm also gonna put you on report if I see anyone without a weapon again. We don't know a thing about this planet, and until we do, we will consider it hostile at all times. Understood?"

She listened to the chorus of agreement, then nodded.

"The Captain is going to give a little talk before we get started. Get your teams together and get loaded up. We've got fifteen minutes before move-out. I want you to mostly finish your bladders, then refill from the tanks on the shuttles. I want you sloshing when we start out." She glanced around one more time. "Let's go over this again. Drink?"

"Water," the squad responded, more or less in unison and with a few smiles.

"When?"

"Always."

"How much?"

"Lots."

"And carry . . . ?"

"Your weapon."

"When?"

"At all times."

"Very good," she said with a blinding smile. "You're a credit to your squad leader." She gave them a wink and headed back over to where Sergeant Major Kosutic was standing.

❖   ❖   ❖

Kosutic waited until the company's NCOs had gathered around, then raised an eyebrow.

"Well?"

"Just like you said," Julian said, taking a sip of water from the bladder in his armor. "Nobody had finished his water. Only a couple had refilled."

"Same here," Koberda said. "You'd think they'd learn. We're all vets, and we all went through RIP. Hell, most of us have spent time in Raider units! This is just same shit, different day."

"Uh-huh." Kosutic nodded in agreement. "How's your water level, George?"

"What?" Koberda's hand tapped the bladder on his back. "Oh." The bladder was mostly full, and Kosutic chuckled as he popped the drinking tube into his mouth.

"This is gonna be a long mission, By His Wickedness," she said, scratching her ear. "And we need to get the right habits right at the beginning. Most of your troops think they're tough. Hell, they *are* tough. But there's tough and there's tough, and, frankly, they're the wrong kind of bad news for this. Give me a bunch of fringe world mercenaries for an op like this one. We're used to having everything on a silver platter, and all we gotta do is drop, kick ass, and go home. This is about staying in the fight for months. That's not something we train for or plan on.

"The troops are gonna get worn out. They're not gonna want to eat. They're not gonna want to drink. They're not gonna want to keep alert. They are not, By His Evilness, going to care.

"So you've gotta be their momma and their poppa. You've gotta make them eat. You've gotta make them drink. You've gotta make sure they keep up their hygiene. You've gotta make sure they keep up their heads.

"Let the troops keep on the lookout for the bad guys. You squad leaders and platoon sergeants have to keep an eye on the troops.

"And I'll keep an eye on *you*," she finished with a laugh. "Now, drink!"

"Have you had anything to drink this morning, Your Highness?" Captain Pahner asked as he watched the prince unpack his weapon.

The rifle would have been a point of contention if Armand Pahner had had an ounce of strength left for silly arguments. He had nothing against the weapon as a hunting rifle: the Parkins and Spencer eleven-millimeter magnum was a gem among heavy caliber rifles. True, it was a "smoke-pole" rather than a bead gun, but the selectable action weapon (it could be fired in either bolt-action or semi-automatic mode) was the end product of over a millennia of development. The big, chemical-propelled round had excellent penetration and muzzle energy, and in the hands of an expert, it was deadly out to nearly two kilometers with the Intervalle 50x variable hologram scope mounted on it.

Yet whatever its virtues, it was also incredibly heavy, nearly fifteen kilos, and used nonstandard brass-cartridge rounds, which meant the prince would be unable to trade ammunition with the other weapons. Eventually, the prince's own ammo would run out, and he would be left with an extremely expensive, very heavy stick.

But Armand Pahner was done arguing with the arrogant young prick. About most stuff.

"Not recently," Roger replied with a headshake as he snapped the receiver into the walnut stock.

"Then might I suggest that His Highness drink water?" Pahner said through gritted teeth. He knew that the prince had all the military's nanite and toot enhancements, and a few that even his bodyguards didn't have. But he still had to have some water in his veins for the nanites to swim in.

"You can suggest it," Roger said with a slight smile.

"And I even will, in a minute. But I'm going to get my rifle assembled first."

"Very well, Your Highness," Pahner said after a calming breath. It was hot as the hinges of hell already, and he didn't need this. "We're going to be moving out in a few minutes." The captain smiled faintly. "O'er Marduk's sunny plain."

"I'll be there," Roger said with a glance at the captain. The Marine's last phrase had not made sense to the prince, but he had other things to worry about, and he started loading ammunition into his combat vest. The handspan-long cartridges would eventually cover the chameleon cloth harness, actually providing an ersatz armor. He had a pack at his feet which was intended to accept additional rounds, and there were loops sewn into the legs of his combat suit. He would eventually be covered in bullets.

God help us if he gets hit by a stray bead, Armand Pahner thought.

Pahner glanced at Poertena. The armorer was racked out in the shade under one net-draped wing of the shuttle. The captain knew most of the troops had bitched about hauling the camo nets into place and staking them down, but he'd been adamant. The shuttles' hulls and wings were essentially one huge crystal display; as long as their internal power held out, their programmable skins could produce better reactive camouflage than a chameleon suit or even powered armor. But even though the power requirement wasn't huge, it was more than enough to eventually drain the shuttle capacitors, at which point the craft would stand out like elephants on a golf course if anyone happened to overfly them and look down. Even if that hadn't been the case, the best reactive skins in the universe couldn't do much about the shadows they cast, so he'd ordered the nets out. Not only would they take over when the power did run out, but they broke up the artificial angularity of the shuttle hulls and wings, which also broke up the artificiality of the shadows they cast.

Roger, predictably, had considered it a waste of time, although at least he'd managed to restrict *his* bitching about it to Pahner himself instead of whining in front of the troops. The captain had wanted—badly—to ask why he'd been so upset when no one was asking *him* to do the grunt work, but he'd decided against it after only a brief struggle. They'd already gone around and around about his decision to maintain a round-the-clock listening watch on all frequencies. It would only require a single trooper to monitor them through the sophisticated com equipment engineered into his helmet, which would hardly pose a crippling drain on their manpower. Despite that, the prince had done a deplorably poor job of concealing his opinion that worrying about possible communications traffic when the entire mass of the planet lay between them and the only high-tech enclave on it made no sense at all, and Pahner had no doubt that Roger had written him off as a terminally paranoid security dweeb.

Fortunately, the captain had discovered that he was remarkably immune to worries about the prince's good opinion of him, and Roger's arguments hadn't changed his mind about the listening watch *or* the camo nets. No doubt the prince was right when he pointed out that the chance of anyone coming in low enough to see the shuttles, assuming there was any reason to be looking in the first place, on the completely opposite side of the globe from the only spaceport or landing facility on the entire planet was virtually nonexistent. Armand Pahner, however, was not in the habit of exposing his people or his mission to avoidable risk, however remote, even if the "extra work" did piss them off.

And it was remarkable how the troops' attitude had shifted when the sun came back up and they realized what nice shade the nets provided for anyone who could come up with an excuse to get under them. Like Poertena, who looked indecently comfortable as he snored with his head propped on a gigantic rucksack. The captain wondered, briefly, what was in it, then walked over and kicked the Pinopan on the sole of his boot. The armorer's eyes popped open, and he scrambled to his feet.

"Yes, Sir, Cap'n?"

"Circulate around. Leader's conference. Here. Now."

"Yes, Sir, Cap'n," Poertena acknowledged, and trotted off towards the knot around Kosutic, bead rifle at high port.

Pahner turned and looked towards the distant mountains. Trees were faintly visible on the lower slopes.

CHAPTER SIXTEEN

The trees were spindly and very tall. There were branch scars on their lower surfaces, but the first actual limbs were nearly twenty meters up the trunk. From there, the trunk continued upwards another ten or twenty meters in a spreading crown. They looked misshapen, like some sort of odd, oversized toadstools. The bark was generally gray and smooth, but some of the trees showed gouges that reached nearly to the spreading crowns.

Roger glanced up at the trees through the extruded plastron of his helmet and shook his head.

"Bad sign. Strop marks," he commented. There'd been chatter about the gouges on the tactical net, but he was still having a hard time making out what everyone was talking about. Now, looking up the trees, some of the comments made more sense.

"Pardon me, Your Highness?" Eleanora said, pausing to take a couple of deep breaths. The pace Captain Pahner had set wasn't fast—he knew better than to rush forward in terrain about which he had no knowledge—

but combined with the heat, it was terribly debilitating to a woman who'd practically never set foot outside a city. She'd kept up with the Marine company so far, but only by dint of iron determination, and it was obvious that she was exhausted.

The company had been walking for nearly six hours, marching for fifty minutes and then taking a ten-minute water break as per doctrine for the environmental conditions. It had taken them that long to get off the salt flats, and now they were entering an alluvial outflow from the mountains. The outflow, unlike the salt flats, had some vegetation. But not much, and the trees that made up the majority of it were widely spaced. And scarred.

"Strop marks," Roger repeated, absently offering the academic the left arm of his armor to support some of her weight. The prince was sweating profusely, but didn't look particularly worn. That might have something to do with carrying less gear than the rest of the company or being in powered armor, but mostly it had to do with the fact that he preferred being on safari to anything else.

He'd traveled, hunted, and studied in more unpleasant, out-of-the-way places than almost any of the Marines realized. And he rarely hunted game that didn't hunt back.

"Marks on a tree like that come from two things," he explained. "Animals eating the bark, and territory marking. And if it were bark-eaters, *all* the trees would be marked."

"So," O'Casey asked with another gasp, "what does that mean?" She knew it should be obvious, but she was wilting in the heat. She checked her toot and suppressed a whimper. Twenty minutes until the next rest.

"It means that there's a something around here that's territorial," Roger said with a glance at the marks high overhead. "Something really, *really* big."

❖   ❖   ❖

Sergeant Major Kosutic watched the point guard, PFC Berent, from Julian's squad. The company was moving with two platoons forward of the headquarters unit, and one behind, and they'd started with Third Platoon forward, since Third had the only squad with armor. The private on point not only had her suit sensors on maximum, she had a hand-held scanner in her left hand. The hand-helds were more sensitive than the suits' systems, and this one was dialed to maximum. So far, though, there'd been no signs of the predators the brief entry on the partial planetary survey report had alluded to. Kosutic had just opened her mouth to make a comment on that to Gunny Jin when the point held up a closed fist. Almost as one man, the company jerked to a stop.

"Well, if we run into whatever it is," Eleanora said, taking a deep gulp of water, "just let it kill me, okay?" She suddenly realized that she was talking to herself and that the whole company had stopped. "Roger?" she said, and turned to look back.

Pahner had a repeater of the scout's data on one-quarter of his visor, and general data on the company and its formation on two other quarters. The fourth was left for figuring out where to put his feet. Currently, the only one he was paying attention to was the repeater from the scout.

The beast that had come into sight around a pile of boulders was dark brown and nearly as high in the shoulder as an elephant, but longer and wider. The head was armed with two long, slightly curved horns that looked useful for fighting or digging, and the neck was protected by a ruff of armor. Massive shoulders were covered in armored scales that faded back to pebbly hide, and it had six squat, forward-thrust limbs and a fleshy tail that flailed back and forth as it pounded from left to right across the company's path. As it ran, it bugled in rage at whatever it was chasing.

The captain examined it for just a moment. The beast was fearsome looking, but a closer examination confirmed his initial judgment. There was no sign of canines or any analog; only grinder teeth were revealed when it opened its maw to scream. Nor did the beast have the sort of long, lean look one found in virtually all predators. It was undoubtedly something to keep an eye on and could be a problem, but it wasn't a carnivore, and was therefore unlikely to attack the company.

"All units," he said, knowing that the tac-comp in his communicator would set the radio to all-frequency broadcast. "Don't fire. It's an herbivore. I say again, do not fire."

There was chatter on the net, and although Roger's inexperience with the com link kept him from following it at all clearly, he could certainly understand its excited overtones. He looked at the creature and its paws. They were odd for a desert creature, webbed and clawed like those of a carnivorous toad. And it was just about the right length and design to be able to rear up on those trees. It was obviously an herbivore, but it was just as obviously a part of whatever herd had marked these trees as its territory. That put it in the "dangerous" slot, and Roger wasn't about to let it circle around and hit the company from behind like a Cape buffalo, or a Shastan rock toad. Or go and get the rest of the herd to squash them all to paste.

He put the rifle to the shoulder and drew a breath. *Lead it, easy squeeze.*

❖   ❖   ❖

Pahner's jaw dropped as the giant beast snapped at its side. It turned on its tail once, then slammed over sideways in a self-made hurricane of dust and gravel. The ground shuddered underfoot with the impact, and it lashed and snapped at the air for several seconds until it was still. He watched it for one sulphurous moment more, and took a deep breath.

"*Okay! Who the hell fired?!*" There was complete silence on all the nets. "I *said*, 'who fired?'!"

"That would be His Highness," Julian said ironically.

Pahner cut out the snickering on the squad leaders' net and turned to where Roger stood with a smoking rifle propped on his thigh. The prince had the Parkins and Spencer set for bolt action, and Pahner watched as he jacked the spent round out of the chamber and caught it in midair. He pulled a fresh round out of his vest, chambered it, and put the empty case where the new one had been. Each of the movements was precise, but jerky and over-muscled. Then he reached up and cleared the chameleon field from his helmet so that he could meet Pahner's eye.

Pahner stepped over to where the prince stood and switched to the command frequency they alone shared.

"Your Highness, could we talk for a moment?"

"Certainly, Captain Pahner," the prince said sardonically.

Pahner looked around, but there was nowhere to have a private conversation. So he touched the control that opaqued the prince's visor again.

"Your Highness," he began, then drew a deep, calming breath. "Your Highness, can I ask you a question?"

"Captain Pahner, I assure you—"

"Your Highness, if you please," Pahner interrupted in a strangled tone. "May. I. Ask. You. A. Question?"

Roger decided at that moment that discretion was better than valor.

"Yes."

"Do you want to live to get back to Earth?" Pahner asked, and Roger paused before responding carefully.

"Is that a *threat*, Captain?"

"No, Your Highness, it's a *question*."

"Then, yes, of course I do," the prince said shortly.

"Then you'd better get through your overbred, airheaded brain that the only way we are going to survive is if you don't *fuck me over every time we turn around*!"

"Captain, I assure you—" the prince started to respond hotly.

"*Shut up!* Just shut up, *shut up*! You can have me relieved once we get back to Earth! And I am *not* going to wrap you up in ropes and carry you the whole way, although right now that sounds like a good idea! But if you don't get a grip and start figuring out that we are *not* on some backwoods adventure where you can go and blast anything in sight and walk away without consequences, we are all going to get *killed*. And that would *really piss me off*, because it would mean that I *failed* to get you back to Earth so that I can *give you back to your mother in one goddamned piece*. That is *all* I care about, and if you don't get with the program, I will *sedate* you and *carry* you to the spaceport *unconscious on a stretcher*! Am I making myself absolutely, positively, crystalline clear?"

"Clear," Roger said quietly. He realized there was no way he could possibly explain the situation as he saw it to the enraged captain. He also realized that with the helmets opaqued and on a restricted frequency, no one else had heard the dressing down.

Pahner paused for a moment longer, looking around the desolate wasteland. It might look flat, but he knew

it hid dozens of little dips where enemies and predators could be hiding. The whole march, for months on
end, was going to be like that. And all the Marines, as
opposed to the civilians they were guarding, knew that.
He shook his head and switched to the all-hands
frequency.

"Okay, show's over. Let's move out."

Great. Just great. Just what a unit in a situation like
this needed: an obvious argument in the chain of command right at the start.

"Woo, hoo, hoo," Julian whispered on his suit mike.
"I think the Prince just caught himself a nuke."

"I bet Pahner didn't even ask why he took the shot,"
Despreaux said.

"He *knows* why Princy took the shot," Julian shot
back. "Big, bad big-game hunter saw the biggest game
in town. Time to try out the rifle."

"Maybe," Despreaux admitted. "But he *is* a big-game
hunter. He's dealt with big nasty animals a lot. Heck,
he does it as a hobby. Maybe he knew something Pahner
didn't."

"The day you find out something the Old Man
doesn't know," Julian commented, "you come look me
up. But bring some CarStim; I'll need it for the heart
attack."

"I t'ink he just like to kill stuff," Poertena said
soberly. They'd reached the carcass of the giant herbivore, and he examined more closely. It would have
made a fair trophy for any hunter.

Despreaux glanced over at the armorer. Despite the
huge rucksack that made him look like an ant under a
rock, he'd come up behind them so quietly she hadn't
noticed his presence.

"You really think so?"

"Sure. I hear about his trophy room," Poertena said,

sipping water out of his tube. "There are all sorts of t'ings in there. He likes to kill stuff," he repeated.

"Maybe," Despreaux repeated, then sighed. "If so, I hope he can learn some control."

"Well, I guess we'll see the next time we have a contact," Julian said.

"*Contact!*" the point guard called.

CHAPTER SEVENTEEN

Kosutic tapped a bead rifle outward.

"There are three people covering one scummy," she commented to the trooper as she stepped past him. "Watch your own Satan-Be-Damned sector."

" . . . just appeared out of nowhere," the point guard was saying as the sergeant major walked up. The PFC waved the sensor wand at the scummy. "Look, there's hardly any readout!"

"That's what your eyes are for!" Gunnery Sergeant Jin snapped. He looked at the scummy standing quietly just outside the perimeter, and shuddered. He hadn't seen the being until the point yelled, either.

The Mardukan stood two and a half meters tall. He—it was clearly and almost embarrassingly a "he"—carried a figure-eight shield nearly as tall as he was. A lance that was even taller was cast over one shoulder, and he had a large, leather covering thrown over his head. It was obviously an attempt at a parasol, and his need for something like it was clear. Given the fact that Mardukans were covered in a water-based mucus, the fact that he could have survived all the way to the edge of the salt flats was amazing. He should have been dead of dehydration long before he got this far.

Kosutic tossed her bead rifle over one shoulder in a manner similar to the way the Mardukan carried his spear, stepped past the three troopers covering the stranger, and held out one hand, palm forward. It wasn't a universal sign of peace, but humans had found it to be close.

The Mardukan gabbled at her, and she nodded. The gesture meant no more to him than his handwaving at the horned beast did to her. He could be angry that they'd killed his pet, or happy that they'd saved his life. Her toot took a stab at the language, but returned a null code. The local dialect had very little similarity to the five-hundred-word "kernel" they'd loaded into the toots.

"I need O'Casey up here quick," she subvocalized into her throat mike.

"We're on our way," Pahner responded. "With His Highness."

Kosutic held up one hand again, and turned to look over her shoulder. As she did, she noticed the two bead rifles and the plasma gun still leveled at the apparently benign visitor.

"Go ahead and lower them, Marines. But keep them to hand."

She half-turned at the crunch of gravel, and smiled at the group approaching from the center of the company's perimeter. The diminutive chief of staff was virtually invisible behind the bulk of Pahner and Roger's armor. And surrounding Roger was a squad from Second Platoon that looked ready to level the world. All in all, it looked like a good time to fade, and she bowed to the visitor and drifted backwards, wondering how it would go.

❖   ❖   ❖

Eleanora O'Casey wasn't a professional linguist. Such people not only had specially designed implants, they usually also had a flair for language that interacted with their toots so that the final translation was synergistically enhanced. She, on the other hand, was dependent on an off-the-shelf software package and a general knowledge of sentient species to carry her through. There were quite a few "ifs" in that equation.

The regions around the spaceport used a four-armed bow as a sign of parley. Unfortunately, there were a variety of nuances to it—none of which had been very clear in the explanation—and she had only two arms.

Here went nothing.

D'Nal Cord examined the small being before him. All of the beings in this tribe—they looked like *basik*, with their two arms and waggling way of walking—were small and apparently weak. However, most of them blended into the background as if they were part of it. It was probably an effect of their strange coverings, but it was also disconcerting. And some weapon or magic among them had killed the *flar* beast. Both features bespoke great power. And since the *flar* beast had nearly had him, it also spoke of an *asi* debt. At his age.

The being bowed in a nearly proper fashion and gabbled at him in a strange guttural tongue. It was different from the words which had been spoken between the beings.

"I seek the one who killed the *flar* beast," he answered, gesturing at the aggressive herbivore. The beasts burrowed during the day in the dry hills, and he'd been blinded by the light of Artac shining off the sands, beaten down by the heat and dryness and, truth to tell, feeling his age. He hadn't noticed the depression around the snorkel at the surface, and he'd survived only because it had been a rogue bull with no herd mates to help it kill him. And because of the altruistic act of a stranger.

Damn him.

The slight one at the fore spoke again.

" . . . kill . . . flor . . ."

Cord spoke very slowly this time.

"I . . . seek . . . the . . . one . . . who . . . killed . . . the . . . *flar* . . . beast. That rogue bull over there, you ignorant little *basik*."

"I need the second person, damn it," Eleanora gritted through her teeth. She touched her chest. "I . . . Eleanora." She pointed at the Mardukan, hoping it would understand.

The scummy gobbled and clacked at her again. It seemed to be becoming agitated. As well it should, for it was terribly hot and dry out here for it. Which brought up an idea.

"Captain Pahner," she turned to the CO. "This is going to take a while. Could we set up some sort of shelter from the sun?"

Pahner looked up at the height of the sun and consulted his toot.

"We've got three more hours of daylight. We shouldn't stop for the night."

Eleanora started to protest, but Roger held up a hand at her, and turned to Pahner.

"We need to communicate with these people," he said, gesturing at the scummy with his chin. "We can't do that if this guy dies of heatstroke."

Pahner took a breath and looked around as he suddenly realized that the comment was coming in on the command frequency. Apparently the prince had listened to the previous lecture about debating in front of the troops. But he was still wrong.

"If we take too long, we'll run out of water. We only

have so much supply. We need to get into the lowlands where there's resupply."

"We need to communicate," Roger said definitely. "We take as much time for that as Eleanora needs."

"Is that an order, Your Highness?" Pahner asked.

"No, it's a strong suggestion."

"Excuse me." Eleanora couldn't hear them, but she could tell that they were debating and thought she ought to make a point. "I'm not talking about all night. If I can get this guy into some shade and get him a little water and humidity, this will probably go fairly fast."

Roger and Pahner turned to glance at her, then turned featureless faceshield to featureless faceshield and debated some more. Finally, Pahner turned back to her.

"Okay."

A couple of privates, impossible to tell apart in identical uniforms and camouflage helmets, came forward and rapidly erected a large tent. The temperature inside wasn't going to be all that wonderful, but they sprayed a few milliliters of water around on the inside of the walls, and the evaporation both cooled it a bit and raised the humidity. The relief would be brief, but it would help the Mardukan.

Cord stepped inside the structure and sighed. It was not only cooler, it was not so dry. His *dinshon* exercises had prevented complete desiccation, but the experience had been anything but pleasant. This was still far too arid for permanent survival, but it was a welcome respite. He nodded to the small interpreter (such as he was) and the two slightly larger beings in their strange hard coats like stang beetles.

"My thanks. This is much better."

He also noted the two additional beings in the background. Their strange weapons weren't pointed at him, but he'd seen bodyguards enough among the city magnates to recognize them for what they were. He wondered which of them was the leader.

"I'm Eleanora," O'Casey said, gesturing at herself. Then she pointed, carefully, at the Mardukan. Pointing in some cultures was an insult.

"D'Nal Cord . . ." The rest was a senseless gabble.

"*Flar* beast?" she asked, hoping to get more context.

"I . . . knowledge . . . *flar* beast . . . kill."

"You want to know how the beast was killed?" she said in the best approximation of the local dialect her toot could create. The known words were increasing, and she felt that the toot would soon have a full kernel. But understanding was still elusive.

"No," the Mardukan said. " . . . killed the *flar* beast? You?"

"Oh," Eleanora said. "No," she answered, gesturing at Roger. "It was Roger." She stopped as she realized that she'd just pointed out the prince for retribution if the act was considered hostile.

Roger tapped a control and cleared his visor of its concealing distortion.

"It was I," he said. His toot had been loaded with the same program, and he'd been following Eleanora's progress. For that matter, his toot had considerably more processor capability than hers, and he suspected that his own program might have made more progress than hers. He was pretty sure, for example, that he was further along on the Mardukan's body language. The individual seemed at least partially unhappy, but not really angry. More like resigned.

The Mardukan, Cord, stepped toward Roger, but paused as the two Marines in the background hefted their weapons. He reached out, carefully, and placed his hand on Roger's shoulder. There was a gabble of syllables.

" . . . brother . . . life . . . owe . . . debt . . ."

"Oh, shit," Eleanora said.

"What?" Roger asked.

"I think," she said with a snort, "that he just said the something like you saved his life and that makes you his blood-brother."

"Oh, hell," Pahner said.

"What?" Roger repeated. "What's wrong with that?"

"Maybe nothing, Your Highness," Pahner said sourly. "But in most cultures like this, those things are taken seriously. And sometimes it means the brother has to join the tribe. On pain of pain."

"Well, we're probably heading in the direction of his tribe," Roger pointed out. "I'll drink the deer's blood, or whatever, and then we'll pass on through. Nice story to tell at the club, and all that."

Eleanora shook her head.

"And what happens if you have to stay with the tribe or it's going to be a big problem?"

"Oh," Roger said. Then, "Oh."

"This is why you don't shoot until you have to," Pahner told him on the side circuit.

"Let me see if I can talk our way out of this," O'Casey said.

"Fat chance," Pahner muttered.

" . . . Chief Roger . . . regrets . . . honor. Travel . . . way . . . pass . . ."

Cord laughed.

"Well, I'm not all that happy about it, either. I was on a very important spirit quest when he had the temerity to save my life. Don't you people have any couth? Never mind. That doesn't matter a *rid* fly's fart. I still have to follow him around like a demon-spawned *nex* for the rest of my life. Oh well. Maybe it will be short."

He watched the little spokesman working through the translation, and finally gestured impatiently.

"This tent is nice, but if we hurry we can reach my village before the *yaden* arise. Unless you have skin like a *flar* beast, we'd best be under cover. I suppose you can cut up the *flar* and use it for cover, but it would take time. Time we might not have."

"I think he said—"

"Tough noogies," Roger finished with a laugh. "He said we're just going to have to live with it. And something about hurrying."

"I didn't get that full a translation," Eleanora said with a shake of her head. "And there was more than the basic cultural background. There's something definitely sticky about this translation. I got a real gender malfunction, at first. It's settled down to male though."

She glanced at the naked Mardukan and then away.

"Of course, I don't see how it could possibly mistake the gender," she added with a smile.

"I got most of it," Roger said. "I think I'm more attuned with him or something. He also says we'd better get moving or something nasty is going to happen."

"Did he indicate what?" Pahner asked.

"He called it the *yaden*. No context. I think it's related to night." He turned to the Mardukan and tried the toot's voice control function. "What are the *yaden*?"

Roger discovered that the software was giving him images in response to some form of subcommunication involving his background, the gestures of the Mardukan, and known words. In cases where it had clear translations, it shut down the direct auditory feed and substituted the "translated" words. But in this case, it obviously had no clear translation, so it was giving ephemeral images of possible translations, and the general outline, although startling, was clear. He almost laughed.

"He says the *yaden* are vampires."

"Oh," Pahner said blandly.

"He's very emphatic about it, though," Elenora said, nodding in agreement. "Yes, I get that, too, now. Vampires. You're good with this, Roger."

Roger smiled in pleasure at the rare compliment.

"You know I like languages."

"So the scummy thinks we should move out?" Pahner asked, just to keep things straight.

"Yes," Roger said, somewhat coldly. He was beginning to develop a distaste for the epithet. "He has a problem with something that apparently comes out only at night. He wants to hurry to make it to his village before whatever it is comes out."

"That's going to be tough," Pahner said consideringly. "We've got a pass to cross, then quite a bit of jungle. We'll barely make it up to the top of the ridge before dark."

"He seems to think we ought to be able to make it before dark without *too* much trouble," Eleanora put in.

"He may be right," Pahner responded. "But if he is, then his village has to be a lot closer than I think he's suggesting."

"Then *I* suggest that we'd better get moving," Roger said.

"No question there," Pahner agreed. "First we've got to get this tent taken down, though."

"Hang on." Roger pulled his drinking tube down. "Here," he said, gesturing with it to the Mardukan. "Water."

They didn't have that word yet, so he used Standard. To demonstrate, he took a drink out of it and dribbled a few drops onto his hand to show the Mardukan what it was. Cord leaned forward and took a swig off of the tube. He nodded at Roger in thanks, then gestured to leave the tent.

"Yeah," Roger said with a laugh. "I guess we're all on the same sheet of music."

But playing in different keys.

It quickly became apparent to Roger where the disconnect between Cord's and Pahner's estimated travel times lay. Cord's giant legs drove him forward at a far quicker pace than humans were able to maintain. The Marines, had they been less heavily encumbered, could have jogged and kept up with the Mardukan, but Matsugae, O'Casey, and the Navy pilots were unable to make anything like the same rate of movement. As the sun set behind the mountains and the alluvial outflow narrowed into a mountain gorge, the Mardukan became more and more voluble in his worries, and translations became clearer and clearer.

"Prince Roger," Cord said, "we must hurry. The *yaden* will suck us dry if they find us. I'm the only one with a cover cloth." He gestured to his leather cape. "Unless you have those 'tents' for everyone?"

"No," Roger said. He grasped a boulder and pulled himself up onto it. The vantage point gave him a clear view of the company scattered up and down the narrow defile. The tail of the unit was just starting up the narrow, steep canyon while the head was nearing the top. As mountain canyons went, it wasn't much, but it was slowing them as the heavily laden troopers struggled up the ravine, pulling themselves from boulder to boulder. They blended into the background well, but for the flash of solar panels on the rucksacks and the occasional reflection off a weapon's barrel. The parties with the stretchers were in particularly bad straits, wrestling their heavy and cumbersome loads over rocks and around corners. All in all, the company was moving very slowly.

"No, we don't have enough large tents for everyone.

But we have other covers, and everyone has a personal bivy tent. How large and fierce are these *yaden*?"

Cord mulled over a few of the words that obviously weren't quite right.

"They are neither large nor fierce. They are stealthy. They will slip into a camp full of warriors and select one or two. Then they overcome them and suck them dry."

Roger shuddered slightly. He supposed that it could be superstition, but the description was too precise.

"In that case, we're just going to have to post a good guard."

"This valley is thick with them," Cord said, gesturing around. "It is a well-known fact," he finished simply.

"Oh, great." Roger jumped nimbly down off the boulder. "We're in the Valley of the Vampires."

CHAPTER EIGHTEEN

The wind was constant and enervating. It blew through the pass incessantly, funneling from the high-pressure upland desert to the lower pressure jungles. It dried the surroundings here at the head of the pass, creating one last patch of arid ground before the all-enveloping triple-canopy rain forest barely a hundred meters below.

Captain Pahner looked down at that canopy and, for the sixth time, reconsidered his decision to stop in the pass itself. Cord hadn't cared one way or the other; he insisted that anything short of returning to his village was a veritable death sentence, and now he sat by a fire as the cold settled in. Pahner didn't blame him a bit; the cold-blooded scummy would be virtually somnolent once the full cold hit.

The Marine scratched his chin for a moment, pondering what they'd so far learned from the native. He was forced to admit, albeit grudgingly, that Roger had had a point about the need to acquire the ability to communicate with the locals as quickly as they could. And the delay for the initial conversation probably hadn't mattered all that much in the end. Not that Pahner intended to say anything of the sort to Roger . . . or even to O'Casey. There could be only one commander, especially in a situation as extreme as this, and whatever the official table of organization might have said, "Colonel" His Royal Highness Prince Roger wasn't fit to be trusted with the organization of a bottle party in a brewery.

Now that the moment of pure, incandescent rage which had possessed him when the young jackass went right ahead and killed the *flar* beast had passed, the captain rather regretted his language. Not because he hadn't meant it, and not because it hadn't needed saying—not even, or perhaps especially, because of the potential impact their little *tête-à-tête* might have upon the future career of one Captain Armand Pahner (assuming the captain in question survived to worry about career moves). No, he regretted it because it had been unprofessional.

On the other hand, it seemed to have finally started making an impression on the sheer arrogance and carelessness which seemed to be two of the prince's more pronounced characteristics. Which was the reason Pahner had no intention of admitting that *this* time the kid might have had a point. The last thing they needed was for the prince to feel justified in continuing to butt heads with the professional who was his only chance of getting home alive.

Setting that consideration aside, however, it was beginning to look as if Cord might prove very valuable indeed, at least in the short run, and the debt he felt he owed to Roger might actually work out in the company's favor. It appeared that the Mardukan was a chief or shaman of the tribe whose territory they were about to enter, and that suggested that Roger might just have secured the best introduction and intermediary they could hope for.

Exactly why he'd been headed towards the lakebed remained less clear. He insisted that he'd been on some sort of vision quest, and it seemed evident that whatever problem he'd been seeking answers to must be pressing to drive him into such a hostile environment, but just what that problem was remained elusive despite his efforts to explain it. On the other hand, his conversations with Roger and Eleanora during the hike to this first camp had nearly completed the task of gathering a workable kernel for the language program. By tomorrow, translations should be as clear as the software could make them.

Pahner allowed himself a few more seconds to hope that would be the case—it would be really nice to have *something* break their way—and then put that particular problem away in favor of more immediate concerns. He turned and walked back through the camp perimeter, running one last personal visual check. Everything was in place: directional mines set, laser detectors on sweep, thermal detectors up and watching. If anything tried to get through those defenses, it had better be invisible or smaller than a goat. He completed his check and crossed to where Sergeant Major Kosutic waited with the portable master panel slung over her shoulder.

"Turn it on," he said, and she nodded and hit the trip switch. Icons flashed on the panel as the sensors came online and the weapons went live, and he watched her eyes move as she ran the visual checklist. Then she looked up at him and nodded again.

"Okay, everybody," Pahner announced, using both his external suit speakers and the all-hands frequency. "We're live. If you have to take a dump or a piss, do it in the latrine."

The latrines, like everything else about the camp, met the guidelines for a temporary camp in hostile territory. The latrines had been set up on the jungle side of the camp, and were dug to regulation depth and width. Inside the sensor parameter, each two-man team had dug in its own foxhole, and most of the party would sleep in them. The two-meter trenches were uncomfortable, but they were also safe. Those who weren't assigned to a fire team, like the Navy personnel (or Roger), had erected temporary shelters with their one-man "bivy" tents within the perimeter enclosed by the foxholes, and the company would maintain fifty percent watch all night long, with one trooper covering the other as he or she slept. It was a technique which had kept armies relatively safe on multiple worlds and through thousands of wars.

Relatively safe.

"How are the troops, Sergeant Major?" he asked quietly. He didn't like having to ask, but the constant wrestling with Roger was dragging him away from the troop time he preferred.

"Worried," Kosutic admitted. "The marrieds, especially. Their spouses and kids will have gotten the word by now that they're dead. Even if they make it back after all, it's going to be hard. Who's going to provide for their families in the meantime? A death bonus isn't much to live on."

Pahner had considered that.

"Point out to them that they're going to be up for plenty of back pay when they get home. Speaking of which, we're going to have to get some sort of a pay cycle in place when we get to whatever passes for civilization on this ball."

"Long way off to think about," Kosutic pointed out. "Let's make it through this night, and I'll be happy. I don't like this *yaden* thing. That big scummy bastard doesn't look like the type to scare easy."

Pahner nodded but didn't comment. He had to admit that the Mardukan shaman had him spooked, too.

❖   ❖   ❖

"Wake up, Wilbur." Lance Corporal D'Estrees nudged the grenadier's boot with her plasma rifle. "Come on, you stupid slug. Time to take over."

It was just past local midnight, and she was more than ready to rack out for a couple of hours. They'd been trading off, turn and turn about, since sunset, while it got colder and colder. There'd been a few little things moving in the jungle below, and the sort of strange, unfamiliar noises any new world offered. But nothing dangerous, nothing to write home about. Even with both of the planet's double moons below the horizon, there was enough light for their helmets to enhance it to a barely dusky twilight, and there'd been nothing doing. Just hours to wait and watch and think about the straits the company was in. Now it was Wilbur's turn and the bivy tent was calling to her. If she could just get the stupid bastard to wake up, that was.

The grenadier was sleeping in his bivy, a combination of one-man tube-tent and sleeping bag less than a meter behind the foxhole. If it dropped in the pot he could be in the hole in a second; *would* be in the fox-hole before he was fully awake. It also kept him in reach to be awakened for guard duty, but it had been a long day and it looked like he was sleeping pretty hard.

Finally, she got annoyed and flipped on her red-lens flashlight. It had the option of infrared, but prying open an eyelid and shining infrared in was an exercise in frustration.

She pulled back the head of the tent to flash the light in the sleeping grenadier's eyes.

Roger rolled to his feet at the first yell, but he could have spared himself some bruises if he'd just stayed put. The instant he came upright, two Marines tackled him and slammed him straight back down on the ground.

Before he could sort out what was happening, there were three more troopers on his chest, and more around him with weapons trained outward.

"Get off me, goddamn it!" he yelled, but to no avail. The limits of his command authority were clear; the Marines would let him make minor choices, like whether they lived or died, but not large ones, like whether *he* lived or died. They ignored his furious demands so completely that in the end he had no choice but to settle for chuckling in bemusement.

Several minutes passed, and then the pile began to erupt as arms and legs disentangled. There were a few good-natured wisecracks that he pointedly did not hear, and then a hand pulled him to his feet. He noticed in passing that it was as dark as the inside of a mine, and he was wondering what had changed their minds and convinced them to let him up when his helmet was placed on his head and the light amplifiers on the visor engaged. Pahner was standing in the doorway of the tent.

"Well," the captain said wearily, "we've had a visit from your friend's vampires."

The grenadier was twenty-two, stood a shade over a hundred seventy centimeters, and, according to his file, weighed ninety kilos. He'd been born on New Orkney, and he had light reddish hair that ran thick on the backs of his freckled hands.

He no longer weighed ninety kilos, and the freckled hands were skeletal and yellow in the beam from the flashlight.

"Whatever it was," Kosutic said, "it sucked out just about every drop of blood in his body." She pulled up the chameleon cloth and pointed to the marks on his stomach. "These are at all the arteries," she said, turning the head to show the marks at the neck. "Two punctures, side-by-side, just about the width of human canines. Maybe a little closer."

Pahner turned to the lance corporal who'd been the grenadier's buddy. The Marine was stonefaced in the light from the lamp as she faced the company and platoon leadership with a dead buddy at her feet.

"Tell me again," Pahner said with iron patience.

"I didn't hear a thing, Sir. I didn't see a thing. I was not asleep. Private Wilbur did not make a sound, nor were there any significant sounds from the direction of his hooch."

She hesitated.

"I . . . I might have heard *something*, but it was so faint I didn't pay it any attention. It was like one of those sounds in a hearing test, where you can't really tell if it was a sound or not."

"What was it?" Kosutic asked, checking the inside of the bivy tent for any indication of what had slipped in and out of the camp with such deadly silence. The small, one-man tents were shaped like oversized sleeping bags with just enough room inside for a person and his gear. Whatever had killed the private had entered and left the tent without any apparent trace.

"It . . . sounded like . . . a bat," the plasma gunner admitted unhappily, fully aware of how it was going to sound. "I didn't think anything of it at the time."

"A bat," Pahner repeated carefully.

"Yes, Sir," the Marine said. "I heard a real quiet flapping sound once. I looked around, but nothing was moving." She paused and looked at the semicircle of her superiors. "I know how it sounds, Sir. . . ."

Pahner nodded and looked around.

"Fine. It was a bat." He drew a deep breath and looked back down at the body. "To tell you the truth, Corporal, it sounds like just another creature on another world we don't know much about.

"Bag him now," he told Kosutic. "We'll have a short service and burn him in the morning."

The Marine body bags could be set to incinerate their contents, which allowed bodies to be recovered rather than left behind. After the cremation, the bag was rolled up like a sleeping bag around the ashes and became just another package which could be carried with a minimum of weight and space.

"A bat," he muttered, shaking his head again as he walked back into the darkness.

"Don't worry about it, Troop," Gulyas told D'Estrees definitively with a tap on the arm. "We're on a new planet. It might have real vampire bats, and those are sneaky suckers, let me tell you." The lieutenant had grown up in the mountains of Colombia, where vampire bats were an old and known enemy. But *Terran* vampire bats didn't suck a corpse dry.

"It might have been real vampires," the corporal said dubiously.

The morning dawned with a sleepy, nervous company of Marines praying the fierce G-9 star back into the sky. After recovering the mines and sensors and conducting a brief service for Wilbur, they moved out down the valley on the jungle side of the mountains with a much more cautious attitude toward their new home.

Roger continued to walk with Cord as they moved down the gentler valley on the western side of the range. The pass was high and dry, which gave it some of the temperature characteristics of the desert beyond, and the morning was very cool when they first broke camp. The low temperature caused the Mardukan to move slowly, almost feebly; the isothermic species was obviously not designed for cold weather. But as the day progressed and the sun cleared the peaks at their backs, the oppressive heat of the planet came on full force and the shaman awoke fully, shook himself all over, and gave the grunt Roger had come to recognize as Mardukan laughter.

"Woe for my quest, but I will be happy to leave these awful mountains!"

Roger had been looking around at the banded formations in the walls of the valley and thinking the exact opposite. They were beginning to reach the low hanging clouds, the second cloud layer that obscured the lowland jungles, and the humidity was already increasing. Along with the gathering heat it made for conditions well suited to a steam bath, and he wasn't particularly elated by the thought of wading deeper into them.

But for now, the steep valley had temporarily plateaued, and Roger stepped aside from his slot in the column again as he paused to examine the small cirque. The valley was obviously a product of both runoff and glaciation, so temperatures must have been much lower at some point in the planet's geologic history. The remnants of that geologic event had produced a valley of surpassing beauty to a human's eyes.

The kidney-shaped valley was centered by a modest lake, about a half-hectare in area, fed from small streams that plumed down the rocky walls, and a primary stream that was apparently intermittent stretched up into the heights. The company had already refilled its bladders from the pool, and the water had been proclaimed not only gin-clear but fairly cool.

The upper and lower ends of the valley were marked by moraines, small mounds of stones, which had been dropped by the glacier in its retreat. The upper moraine would have been a perfect spot for a house with a breathtaking view of the lake and the jungles laid out below it. By the same token, the lower moraine could have provided a prime source of building materials.

The striated walls of the valley were clearly a product of the uplift that had formed the entire chain, but their strata indicated that at one point, long, long, long ago, they'd been part of a plain or shallow seabed. Roger noted evidence in different places of both coal and iron formations, specifically of banded iron, which was the richest possible form. The fairly pleasant, for a human, valley was perfect for mining development. Of course, as Cord's comment reminded him, for any scummies exiled to it, it would be a lesser ring of Hell.

"Oh, I don't know," he disagreed. "I like it here. I love mountains—they offer up the soul of a planet to you if you know what you're looking at."

"Pah." Cord snorted and spat. "What does a place like this hold for The People? No food, cold as death, dry as a fire. Pah!"

"Actually," Roger said, "there's a lot of good geology up here."

"What is this 'geology'?" the shaman asked, shaking his spear at the valley walls. "This 'spirit of stone'? What is it?"

It was Roger's turn to snort as he took off his helmet and ran a hand over his hair. He'd put it up in a bun, and the lake looked awfully inviting. He badly needed a shampoo, but the Mardukan's question intrigued him away from that thought.

"It's the study of rock. It's one of the things I found interesting when I was in college." Roger sighed and looked at the line of Marines hell-bent on protecting him from harm. "If I hadn't been a prince, I might have been a geologist. God knows I like it more than 'princing'!"

Cord considered him quietly for a moment.

"Those who are born to the chiefs cannot choose to be shamans. And those who are shamans cannot choose to be hunters."

"Why not?" Roger snapped, suddenly losing his temper

at the whole situation and waving his arms at the company as it trudged past. "I didn't ask for this! All I ever wanted to do was . . . well . . . I don't know what I would've done! But I sure as hell wouldn't have been His Royal Highness Prince Roger Ramius Sergei Alexander Chiang MacClintock!"

Cord looked down at the top of the young chieftain's head for several moments before he finally decided on the best approach and drew a knife from his harness. A half dozen rifles snapped around to train on him, but he ignored them as he tossed it up for a grip on the long iron blade . . . and thunked the prince smartly on top of the head with the leather wrapped hilt.

"*Ow!*" Roger grabbed the top of his head and looked at the Mardukan in consternation. "What did you do that for?"

"Quit acting like a child," the shaman said severely, still ignoring the readied rifles. "Some are born to greatness, others to nothing. But no one chooses which they are born to. Wailing about it is the action of a puling babe, not a Man of The People!" He flipped a knife in the air and resheathed it.

"So," Roger growled, rubbing the spot which had been hit, "basically what you're saying is that I should start acting like a MacClintock!" He fingered his scalp and pulled away slightly red stained fingers. "*Hey!* You drew blood!"

"So does a child whine at a skinned false-hand," the shaman said, snapping the "fingers" on one of his lower limbs. The hand on the end had a broad opposable pad and two dissimilar-sized fingers. It was obviously intended for heavy lifting rather than fine manipulation. "Grow up."

"Knowledge of geology is useful," Roger said sullenly.

"How? How is it useful to a chief? Should you not study the nature of your enemies? Of your allies?"

"Do you know what that is?" Roger demanded, gesturing at the coal seam, and Cord snapped his fingers again in a Mardukan sign of agreement.

"The rock that burns. Another reason to avoid these demon-spawn hills. Light a fire on that, and you'll have a hot time!"

"But it's a good material economically," Roger pointed out. "It can be mined and sold."

"Good for Farstok Shit-Sitters, I suppose," Cord said with another snort of laughter. "But not for The People."

"And you trade nothing with these 'Farstok Shit-Sitters'?" Roger asked, and Cord was silent for a moment.

"Some, yes. But The People don't need their trade. They don't require their goods or gold."

"Are you sure?" Roger looked up at the towering alien and cocked his head. There was something about the Mardukan's body language that spoke of doubt.

"Yes," Cord said definitely. "The People are free of all bonds. No tribe binds them, nor do they bind any tribe. We are whole." But he still seemed ambivalent to the human.

"Uh-huh." Roger put his helmet back on, carefully. That tap had hurt. "Physician, heal thyself."

CHAPTER NINETEEN

The jungle wore mist like a shroud. This was a cloud forest more than a rain forest—a condition of eternal damp and fog rather than a place of rain.

But it was also a transition zone. Soon the company would pass out of it into the enveloping green hell of the jungle below. Soon their vision would be blocked by lianas and underbrush, not mist. Soon they would be in the cloaking darkness of the rain forest understory, but for now there were only tall trees, very similar in many respects to the trees on the desert side of the mountains, and the omnipresent mist.

"This sucks," said Lance Corporal St. John, (M.). Sergeant Major Kosutic required him to respond that way—"St. John, M."—because he had an identical twin in Third Platoon, St. John, (J.) She also required each of them to have a distinguishing mark at all times. In St. John (M.)'s case, it was that one side of his head was shaved bald, and he reached up to scratch under his helmet as he looked around at the steamy twilight.

The temperature was over 46 degrees, 115 Fahrenheit,

and the fog was dense and hot, like being in a steam bath, and nearly impenetrable. Visibility was no more than ten meters, and the helmets' sensors were overwhelmed by the conditions. Even the sonics were defeated by the swirling, choking steam. St. John (M.) turned to bitch some more to the plasma gunner behind him . . . just in time to be hit by a high-pitched squeal in his right ear.

"Eyow!"

"What?" PFC Talbert asked as the lance yanked off his helmet. The two of them were covering the right flank of the company, slightly out of line with the point man and fifty meters back.

"Ow!" the grenadier said, banging the helmet into a convenient tree trunk. "Goddamn feedback! I think this damned steam blew out a circuit."

Talbert laughed and let her plasma rifle dangle on its sling as she slapped a stingfly on her neck and fished in her jacket with the other hand. She extracted a brown tube.

"Smoke?"

"Nah," St. John (M.) snarled. He put the helmet on his head and yanked it off again. "Shit." He reached into the depths and pulled a harness plug, then held it up to his ear again. "Ah, that got it. But I just lost half my sensors."

Talbert popped the brown tube into her mouth and tapped the end to light it, then paused and looked around at the mists.

"Did you hear something?" she asked, hitching up her plasma rifle cautiously.

"I can't hear shit," St. John (M.) said. The big lance corporal rubbed his ear. "Nothing but chirping crickets!"

"Doesn't matter," Talbert said around the nicstick. The mild derivative of tobacco had a low level of pseudo-nicotine and was otherwise harmless. It was, however, just about as addictive as regular tobacco. "Sensors can't do shit in this cra—"

St. John (M.) spun in place like a snake as the scream began behind him.

Talbert, shrieking like a soul in hell, was connected to one of the trees by a short, wiggling worm. The worm stretched down from perhaps a meter over head height and was connected to the curve where shoulder met neck. Even as the corporal watched, frozen, the juncture spurted bright red arterial blood, and the worm snatched Talbert up into the air.

St. John (M.) was shocked out of coherent thought, but he was also a veteran, and his hands jacked the belt of high explosive rounds out of his grenade launcher without any conscious order from his brain. They were reaching for a shotgun shell when Gunnery Sergeant Lai appeared out of the mist. The senior NCO paused for no more than a heartbeat to take in the situation, then blew the worm off the tree with her bead rifle.

The plasma gunner hit the ground like a sack of wet cement, then broke into convulsions. The ululating shrieks never stopped as her arms and legs spasmed on the ground, tearing up handfuls of dark, wet soil.

Lai dropped the bead rifle and ripped the first-aid kit off her combat harness. She threw herself onto the writhing plasma gunner and covered the spurting wound on her neck with a self-sealing bandage. But even as she did so, the wound erupted with red, streaming jelly. The smart bandage expanded to cover the bleeding areas, looking for clear undamaged tissue to bond to, but the damage spread faster than the bandage as flesh-eating poisons began dissolving the proteins under the skin that bound the private's flesh together.

Lai cut the gunner's camouflage jacket open with a combat knife as the subcutaneous hemorrhaging spread. She whipped out another bandage, but it was obviously useless as black-and-red pools of destruction crossed the private's tanned torso. The skin around the initial puncture broke, and a slit ripped open down Talbert's ribs as blood, fats, and dissolved muscle poured out onto the forest floor.

The plasma gunner went into fresh paroxysms as the blackness spread and both of her exercise-flattened breasts melted into pools and washed out through the slash in her chest.

Lai backed away in horror as the black blood spread up the Marine's neck and the skin and muscles of her face fell flaccid against the bones of her skull.

Final dissolution didn't take all that long. It only seemed like hours until the private stopped thrashing and screaming.

"What the fuck is this, a picnic?" Sergeant Major Kosutic snarled. She shoved one private towards the perimeter and looked the platoon sergeant in the eye. "We need a perimeter, not a cluster fuck!"

The group around the incident broke up, scattering towards guard positions, as she strode through them.

"Okay, what happened?" She looked down at the skeleton at her feet and blanched. "Satan! What did that? And who is it?"

"It was jus' . . . it was . . ." St. John (M.) said incoherently. He was swinging from side to side, training his grenade launcher up into the treetops of the surrounding forest. He was obviously still in shock, so Kosutic looked at Lai.

"Gunny?"

Lai hefted her bead rifle and looked around at the trees, wide-eyed.

"It was some sort of worm." She kicked what was left of the invertebrate where it had fallen at the base of the tree. "It bit her, or stung her, or something. When

I got here, it was pulling her up into the tree. I shot
it off of her, but she just . . . she just . . ." The sergeant
stopped and retched, still searching the enveloping mists
for more of the worms.

"She just . . . *that*," she finished, gesturing to but not
looking at the partial skeleton at her feet.

Kosutic pulled out her combat knife and prodded the
alien carcass. It was darkly patterned, with noticeable
blue patches along its back. All that was left after Lai's
bead rifle had blown it apart was ten centimeters or so
of the base. What appeared to be the back end had
several pod-feet with hooks. One of them still had a bit
of bark attached, indicating where it hung out. Literally. And the business end apparently . . . dissolved
people. She stood up, stuck the knife back into her
combat harness, and wiped her hands.

"Nasty."

Captain Pahner appeared out of the mist, trailed by
Prince Roger and his pet scummy. The captain padded
up and looked down at the casualty.

"Problems, Sergeant Major?"

"Well," she said grimly, pulling at an earlobe, "point's
not going to be a favorite spot."

Cord walked over to the group gathered around the
skeleton and snapped his lower fingers.

"*Yaden cuol*," he said, and Kosutic raised an eyebrow
at Roger.

"'Vampire' what, Your Highness?" Her toot had picked
up the "*yaden*," but the second word wasn't yet in its
vocabulary.

"Vampire . . . baby?" Roger suggested doubtfully. He
wore an odd, introspective expression, and the sergeant
major realized he was communing with the software. "I'm
beginning to think this language program is making too
many assumptions. I think it means larva of whatever the
vampires are."

"How do we fight it, Sir?" Gunny Lai was beginning to get over her shock, and she turned almost pleadingly to the prince. "Talbert was a good troop. St. John (M.), too. I doubt they were fucking off. And it's camouflaged to the max. How the fuck do you fight something like that? No motion, no heat, hardly any electrical field?"

Roger let loose with a stream of liquid syllables and clicks. The scummy knocked his lower hands together and let loose a string back. Then he looked around, knocked his hands together again, and shrugged his cape up to cover his head, shoulders, and neck.

"Well," the prince said doubtfully, "he says that you need to start paying attention. He says he's watched us walking, and we never look 'hard enough' or we look at the wrong things. He also says that these worm-things hang out in the trees and are hard to see, so if you put something up to cover your head and shoulders you're better off."

Cord produced another spurt of syllables and gestured around the woods. He pulled the cape back down and clapped his hands again, and Roger nodded and gave a grim snort.

"He also says that they're just about the most horrible things in the woods, but not the most dangerous. They can't move very fast, except to strike, so you can easily kill them with a spear. He said, 'Wait until you face an *atul-grack*,' whatever that is. And these . . . killer caterpillars . . . sometimes come in groups.

"He's pretty philosophical about it," Roger added. "That handclapping gesture is a shrug. Basically, 'Life's a bitch—'"

"'—and then you die,'" Kosutic finished with a nod. "Got it."

Eleanora's feet slid out from under her on the muddy hillside, and she landed flat on her rump. The jarring impact sent shooting pains all the way up her spine and into her skull, and she started to slip down the hill. She scrambled wildly for some sort of braking grip, but without success until a hand snapped out and caught the light rucksack on her back. She looked over her shoulder and smiled wearily at her savior.

"Thank you, Kostas," she said with a sigh.

She rolled over on her stomach and tried to struggle to her feet, but it was no use. She'd been barely staggering along as it was, and between the mud, and the heat, and the biting flies, and the screaming muscles in her back and legs from the last two days of exertion, it was just too much.

"Oh, God," she whispered. "I just want to die and get it over with."

A Mardukan insect, more from curiosity than malice, landed on her ear and started to investigate her ear canal. She summoned a burst of energy to shake her head violently and swat at it, but then she slumped back into the mud.

"Now, now, Ma'am," Matsugae said with a smile. "We're nearly to Cord's village. You can't give up now." The valet hooked a hand in her rucksack's straps and helped her claw her way to her feet.

She swayed in exhaustion and leaned on a tree . . . carefully. Her arm was covered in a welter of swollen bites from the defenders of a previous support, and since that incident she'd become much more careful where she put her hands. But this tree, at least, didn't seem to want to kill her, and she leaned into it gratefully.

They were below the clouds now, and into the fringe of the planet's all-encompassing jungle. They'd followed the river out of the valley as it grew larger and larger, until finally the ground around it became too marshy to continue along its banks. The company had turned off to the south, but continued to parallel the watercourse, although the gurgle of its passage could be barely distinguished through the background racket of the jungle.

The incessant hum of flying insects was everywhere. The Mardukan version was eight-legged and had a six-winged pattern, as opposed to the terrestrial six-limb/four-wing arrangement. The local bugs also used an aramid polymer, similar in some respects to Kevlar, as the hard core of their exoskeletons. Since it was both lighter and stronger than chitin, it allowed the existence of species which would be considered extremely large on Earth—or on most other planets, for that matter.

There were thousands of different kinds of beetle analogues, some of them huge. Most of them seemed to be turners of the detritus on the forest floor, while a few joined forces with the midge analogues to take turns biting the humans. Dozens of species swarmed on the human intruders, ranging from tiny creatures that looked so much like mosquitoes that the Marines simply named them skeeters, to a slow-flying beetle the size of a blue jay that had the troopers pulling out their multitools and swinging axes during its infrequent attacks. The chameleon suits were impervious to even the local insects' best efforts and could be sealed up completely, but while the chameleon cloth actively transpired carbon dioxide and oxygen, the rate was too low to support heavy activities. The Marines would occasionally close up their suits to escape the insects, but soon enough they were forced to open their helmets back up and take deep gasping breaths. Then spit out the midges they'd swallowed.

But the hum of the insects, as up-close and personal as it was, was overwhelmed by the rest of the bedlam.

The air rang with strange cries—here a shrill whistle, there a grunting roar, in the distance a banshee howl as some beast celebrated a victory or defended its territory, or perhaps simply called longingly for a mate.

Besides the sounds, the atmosphere was suffused with

weird smells. The odor of rot was a near universal on oxygen-nitrogen planets, and overpowering in any jungle, but here there were thousands, millions, of other scents.

Nor was vision left unassaulted. The entire jungle was a riot of bright colors in the oppressing gloom. The combination of the double layer of cloud cover and triple-canopy jungle made the understory tenebrous to a degree rarely found on Earth, but the depths of that overarching gloom offered beauty of its own.

A dangling liana near O'Casey's head was decorated with tiny carmine blossoms. The blossoms released a heavy perfume that had attracted dozens of similarly colored butterflies. That was the tag which came to the sociologist's mind, at least. The insectoids' covering was smooth, instead of the furry look of terrestrial butterflies, but they were just as brightly patterned. As she watched the swarm of fluttering beauties, a purple spider/beetle dropped from a branch into their midst and snagged one of their number. The flock of nectar eaters took off in a crimson cloud that briefly surrounded the chief of staff in a fall of gorgeous red, then dispersed.

O'Casey took a deep whiff of the glorious blossoms' perfume as the tiny predator finished off its tiny prey, then pried herself back off the tree. A good part of the company had stumbled past as she rested, and now she would have to hurry to catch up to her assigned position.

Pahner had put the "hangers-on," as he phrased it, just behind the command group. Beside Eleanora and Kostas, that included the pilots of the four shuttles. If they could retake the port, those pilots would be their only hope of capturing an interstellar ship and escaping the system, so it was nearly as important to keep them alive as it was to keep Roger that way.

Eleanora had realized, however, that neither she nor Matsugae were as high on Pahner's list. The Marine captain was determined to reach the port with as few casualties as possible, but if he had to lose the odd academic or valet along the way, then so be it.

She couldn't fault his logic, for there was no margin to spare on this operation, but she didn't have to like it. And she doubted that Roger had made the connection, for the prince would probably object if it ever came down to losing either member of his "staff."

The conclusion that the man responsible for keeping all of them alive had earmarked her as, regrettably, expendable was disturbing. Throughout her entire life, she'd always functioned under conditions where she could move at her own pace. Academically, that pace had been quite fast, and she remembered looking down on those who fell by the educational wayside, but even those unfortunates had simply found less satisfying and successful positions.

That wouldn't be the case here. Now she faced a physical challenge that was, literally, life or death, and she knew instinctively that if she asked for some respite, it would be denied. She was unimportant to the mission, and the safety of the entire company couldn't be jeopardized for her sake. So for her and Matsugae, it was "march or die."

She was fairly certain it was going to be both for her, but Matsugae seemed to be taking to the change in conditions fairly well. The fussy little valet carried a pack nearly as large as the armorer's, but he was keeping up with the company without complaint, and had helped her along the way several times. She was, frankly, astounded.

She straightened up and started along the muddy track which had been smashed through the undergrowth by the passage of most of the company. The Marines around her were paying as much attention to the back trail as to the sides, so she knew she was dangerously close to the tail of the company. As she picked up the pace to catch back up to the center of the force, she glanced up at the valet, still doggedly tailing her.

"You don't seem to be having any troubles with this march at all, Matsugae," she said quietly.

"Oh, I wouldn't say that, Ma'am," the valet answered, adjusting the straps of the internal frame rucksack which, along with the chameleon suits they both wore, had come out of the company's spare stores. He idly slapped a "skeeter" and winked at the academic. "I'm afraid I've spent rather a lot of time following Roger through places almost this bad on safari, although, to be fair, never under conditions quite so . . . resource-limited and extreme. But I think this is hard on everyone, even the Marines, whether they show it or not."

"At least you don't have any trouble keeping up," she said bitterly. The backs of her legs felt as if someone were sticking hot knives into them, and they'd just gotten to the bottom of the hillside. That meant crossing a shallow stream and climbing another hill that looked even taller. Slipping and sliding in the sweltering muck, not being able to hold onto the trees for fear of something eating you, constantly tired and constantly afraid.

"You just have to put one foot in front of the other, Ma'am," the valet said reasonably. He planted a foot on the worn path up the hill and offered the chief of staff his hand. "Alley-oop, Ma'am!"

O'Casey shook her head and took the offered hand. "Thank you, Kostas."

"Not much further, Ma'am," the valet said with a smile. "Not much further at all."

CHAPTER TWENTY

The village nestled on a hilltop, surrounded by a log and thorn wall.

The hill itself sat in an angle where a large stream intersected the river the company had been paralleling. Just upstream from the junction, the river thundered over a cataract, and downstream from the hill, the combined flows created a deep, wide river that was probably navigable by barges. As they'd gotten lower and lower in elevation, however, the signs of frequent floods had become obvious. Clearly, the village was situated atop its hill to avoid this recurring phenomenon, and it was likely that frequent flooding would also interfere with navigation.

It began to rain as they approached the hill. Not a slight, steady rain as a cloud parked itself and motheringly watered the parched soil. Not even the hard, firm rain of a powerful weather front. This was the pounding, drowning rain of a tropical thunderstorm—rain like a waterfall, hitting so hard that weaker members of the party were actually knocked off their feet by its first rush.

"Is this normal?" Roger yelled to Cord as the company struggled up the hill.

"What?" Cord asked, hitching his general-purpose cape up a little higher.

"This rain!" Roger yelled, gesturing at the sky.

"Oh," Cord said. "Of course. Several times a day. Why?"

"Joy," Pahner muttered, having monitored the conversation. Roger had fed the language kernel he'd collected during the day's walk to all of the party's toots, and the company's members were now capable of translating the local language on their own. It was expected that they would be able to pick up each dialect quickly as they progressed from area to area, now that they had a local kernel.

"I should go to the head of your group," Cord pointed out. "I'm sure I have been watched as we approached, but I should go to the head so that they're sure I'm not a prisoner or a *kractan*."

"Yeah," Roger said, and turned to look at Pahner. "Are you coming, Captain?"

"No," the Marine said, and triggered his communicator. "Company, hold up. Our local is going up to pass us through."

"I'll stay here," he continued to Roger, and raised one hand in a beckoning gesture. "Despreaux!"

"Yes, Sir!" the NCO snapped. She'd been scanning the bushes with a hand-held scanner, and she didn't like the fact that she'd kept getting twitches but hadn't been able to lock them down.

"Take your squad up front with the Prince and Cord."

"Roger, Sir." She gestured at the squad and pointed to the front. "Up and at 'em, Marines."

She put the scanner away and glanced off to the north one more time. There was something out there, she was sure, but what it was eluded her.

Cord and Roger moved up to the front of the company, surrounded by Despreaux's squad. The company had spread out in a standard cigar-shaped perimeter, and now most of the Marines were down in the prone, covering against any attack. There was no such thing as "safety" in a combat zone, but a unit temporarily at rest like this was in the worst possible situation. Unless an enemy has had time to prepare an ambush, a moving unit is a hard target to hit. Similarly, a unit which has had time to prepare defenses is a tough nut to crack, but a company which has just stopped can be hit at any moment and isn't prepared for the attack.

It makes soldiers who are well trained—like those of The Empress' Own—very nervous.

Cord followed a beaten track up to the single opening in the palisade. As he approached, another Mardukan of the same height and general demeanor appeared in the opening. At the sight of Cord, followed by the humans but clearly not threatened by them, the second Mardukan waved his upper arms in welcome.

"Cord," he called, "you bring unexpected guests!"

"Delkra!" the shaman shouted back, waving his spear. "As if you hadn't been shadowing us these last few hours!"

"Of course," the greeter agreed imperturbably as Cord and Roger's party reached the top of the hill.

The last portion of the path was so steep that steps had been cut and reinforced with logs and rocks. The top of the hill had been roughly leveled, and now Roger could glimpse the village through the palisade opening. It looked much like other villages on other planets. A large communal fire pit was at its center, surrounded by an open area which was currently deserted. Immediately inside the walls were rude, thatch and wattle huts, open to the inside of the palisaded area. The similarity to villages once found in the Amazon basin and other tropical areas on Earth would have amazed Roger if he hadn't spent enough time hunting on primitive planets to realize that there was only so much that could be done with mud and sticks.

"D'Net Delkra, my brother," Cord said, clapping the greeter on his upper shoulder, "I must introduce you to my new *asi-agun*." He turned to Roger. "Roger, Prince of the Empire, this is my brother, D'Net Delkra, Chief of The People."

The greeter, Delkra, hissed and clapped all four hands together in agitation.

"Ayee! *Asi-agun?* And at your age? Foul news, brother—foul news, indeed! And your quest?"

Cord clapped right true-hand to left false-hand in a gesture of negation.

"We met on the way. He saved my life from a *flar* beast without clear need, without threat to his life, and being not of my tribe."

"Ayee!" Delkra repeated. "*Asi* debt, indeed!"

The Mardukan, who was a bit taller than the shaman, turned to the prince, who'd doffed his helmet. The armor was more comfortable than the steamy heat of the jungle, but Roger felt it was more diplomatic to face this Delkra, who was presumably senior in the local hierarchy, without the obscuring head gear.

"I thank you for my brother's life," Delkra said. "But I cannot be happy for either his enslavement or the failure of his quest."

"Whoa!" Roger said sharply. "What's this 'enslavement' thing? All I did was shoot a . . . a *flar* beast!"

"*Asi* bond is the tightest of all bonds," the chief explained. "To save another's life, without fear or favor, binds him to you through this life and beyond."

"What?" Roger was trying to get over the "slave" concept. "You guys never help each other out?"

"Of course we do," Cord said, "but we are members of the same clan. To help another is to aid the clan, and the clan, in turn, aids us. But you had no such reason to kill the *flar* beast. For the life of me, I'm not sure that you should have."

"It could have attacked the Company," Roger pointed out. "That was the real reason I shot. I didn't even see you."

"Fate, then," Delkra said with a hand clap. "It wasn't threatening you or your . . ." he glanced over the Marines scattered down the hillside " . . . clan?"

"No," Roger admitted. "Not at the time. But I could tell it was dangerous."

"Karma," Cord said with a double hand clap. "We will complete the binding tonight," he continued with another gesture. "Delkra, I request shelter for the night. And shelter for my *asi's* clan."

"Oh, granted," the chief said, stepping out of the palisade opening and waving into the jungle. "Granted. Come in out of the rain!"

"We're getting sensor ghosts all along the perimeter," Lieutenant Sawato had just taken a tour of the company while Captain Pahner kept an eye on the negotiations of the top of the hill. Now she looked around at the curtaining rain and shook her head. "I've got that funny feeling. . . ."

"We're surrounded by the warriors of this tribe," Pahner said in a distant tone. "They're good. They move slow, so the motion sensors aren't sure if they're really there, and they're isothermal, so the heat sensors can't pick anything up. No power sources, no metal except a knife or spearhead, and we don't have the sensors dialed in for scummy nervous systems." He pulled out a pack of gum and absentmindedly extracted a stick and popped it into his mouth. He shook the pack a couple of times to get the water out, and put it away, all without looking. "Take a glance over to the left. There's a big tree with spreading roots. Halfway up, there's a limb covered in . . . stuff. Go out the limb five meters, just before a red patch. About a half a meter to the right of the red patch. Spear."

"Damn," Sawato said softly. The scummy was as hard to spot as any professional sniper she'd ever seen. He appeared to be covered with a blanket that broke up his outline. "So, what do we do about it, long-term?"

"Dial in the nervous system sensors. We'll have enough data after tonight to do that. After that, any scummy comes within fifty meters of us, we'll be able to detect them. And warn everybody that they're out there. We don't want any accidents."

"I'll pass that on then, shall I?" Sawato asked. Pahner seemed awfully detached about the whole thing, she thought.

"Yeah. Might as well. Looks like the negotiations are going all right after all. I was waiting to see if it dropped in the pot."

"You know," Julian said, "I've been shot, blown up, deep frozen, and vacuum dried. But this is the first time I ever worried about being washed away."

The rain had yet to let up, and the position the squad leader occupied—a slight depression behind a fallen and rotting tree—was rapidly filling. The combination of rising water and the weight of his combat armor meant he was slowly sinking in quickmud.

"Or drowned," he added.

"Ah, come on," Moseyev said as he gently moved aside a bit of fern with the barrel of his bead rifle, "it's just a little rain." He was sure there was something watching them, but he wasn't sure what it was.

"'A little rain,' he says." Julian shook his head. "That's

like saying Sirius is 'a little hot,' or that New Bangkok is 'a little decadent.'"

"It's not like it's gonna kill you," Moseyev said. "The armor has air for nearly two days." The fire team leader jerked his head to the side as his helmet highlighted another possible contact. But then it faded again. "Damn. I wonder what's causing that?"

"I'd say it was the wet," Julian said, lowering his own rifle. "But since we're all getting the same ghosts, I'd say it's something in the jungle."

"All hands." The radio crackled with Lieutenant Sawato's calm soprano. "Those sensor ghosts are the local tribesmen. Be calm, though; the natives are friendly. We're going to be going into the village soon, so they'll probably make themselves evident. No firing. I say again, no firing."

"Everybody get that?" Julian called, standing up to make sure he could see all the members of the squad. "Check fire for partisans."

"Got it, Sarge," Macek replied from the far end. "'The natives are friendly.' Riiight."

The private's position was the edge of the squad's area of responsibility, and Macek was the member with the least time in the unit. If he'd gotten the word, everyone else probably had, but Julian wasn't in The Empress' Own because he settled for "probably."

"Yeah, and 'The transfer's in the system,'" the sergeant responded with a laugh. "Give me a thumbs up on that check fire," he added more seriously, and made sure he saw a thumb from everyone before he resumed his position in the puddle. He might bitch about it, but the depression was still the best location for him. Even if it *was* turning into a lake.

"'I'm from the Imperium,'" Moseyev continued with a litany as old as government, "'I'm here to help you.'" He gave a thumbs up.

" 'Don't worry, it's a cold landing zone,' " Cathcart added from behind his plasma gun. Thumbs up.

" 'We're getting air-trucked to the barracks,' " Mutabi said in an evil tone. Middle finger up.

"Oh, man, you *would* have to say that one!" Julian chuckled. "My aching feet."

"Modderpocker," Poertena said. "Chus what we need. Surrounded by tee cannibals."

"Chill, Poertena," Sergeant Despreaux advised. "They're friendly."

"Sure they are," Poertena replied. "Why fight tee roc if you can get it to fly into tee pot."

Even as he spoke, his helmet registered another contact. Then another. It began popping up icons everywhere, and an entire line of Mardukans materialized magically out of the rain.

"Modderpocker," Poertena said again, quietly. "Neat trick."

CHAPTER TWENTY-ONE

The company barely fitted inside the walls of the village. The Marines and their equipment were packed into every nook and cranny as the women of the village, significantly smaller than the male warriors, came out with hoarded foodstuffs for what was shaping up as an evening of celebration. The company reciprocated in building the menu as best it could. Despite the critical importance of the food supplies they'd brought with them, some of the Marines' rations were never going to survive conditions on Marduk, and they brought those out to add to the various edibles being produced by the Mardukans.

Platters of grain, similar in texture to rice but tasting more like barley, were scattered about among the residents and visitors, along with carved wooden bowls of fruits. The predominant fruit species appeared to be a large, brown oval with a thick, inedible skin but a ripe red interior that tasted something like a kiwi fruit. Since it grew on palmlike trees, the humans promptly christened it a "kiwi-date" or "kate" fruit. In addition to the grain and fruit, there were steaming platters of unrecognizable charred things. Most of the humans passed those up.

There was also a sort of wine made from fruit juices, but it was obviously distilled and not just fermented. Like humans, the Mardukans metabolized alcohol for pleasure, and after one tentative sip of the potent beverage, the sergeant major growled at the platoon sergeants. Her growls then wandered down the chain of command until even the lowliest private was aware of the penalty for getting plastered in the middle of a potentially hostile jungle. There was also a heavy and bitter beer that some of the Marines relished and others found disgusting.

The Marines followed the custom of their hosts, reaching into the piles to extract handfuls of grain and fruit and brushing away gathering insects, livestock, and pets.

Pride of place was given to a large lizardlike creature roasting on a spit at the center of the camp. The head had been removed, but the bulky body was a meter and a quarter in length, with a longer tail dragging off into the fire. The spit was turned, with serious and dedicated attention to the responsibility, by a Mardukan child—one of several running about the stockaded village.

The Mardukans were viviparous and bore live young, but they had "litters" of four or more. Baby Mardukans were extremely small, barely the size of a Terran squirrel, and mostly stayed glued to their mothers' backs, mired into the mucous from which they also derived nutrition. Half-grown Mardukans were everywhere underfoot, inextricably mixed with livestock, pets, and, now, Marines.

O'Casey stopped tapping at her pad and shook her head.

"They must have an enormous infant mortality rate," she said with a yawn.

"Why?" Roger asked.

As one of the stars of the evening, he was seated in a place of honor under the awninglike front section of Delkra's hut. He took one of the charred things off the broad leaf that served as a platter and tossed it to a lizardlike creature which had been looking at him with begging eyes. It started to pounce on the morsel, but was pushed aside by a larger version. The larger beast, patterned red and brown with pebbly skin like the *flar* beast's, and with the ubiquitous six legs and a short, wide tail, came over to the prince, sniffing at his platter, but Roger shooed it away.

"I mean," he continued, still looking at the smaller beast, "what makes you say that?"

The little beast was interesting, he thought. The legs, instead of being splayed out like a lizard's, were directly under the body, like a terrestrial mammal's. And the eyes looked much more intelligent than any Terran lizard's.

But it still looked like a six-legged lizard.

"All these children," O'Casey said, snapping her pad closed. "There are six children below what I would guess to be reproductive age for every adult. Now compare that to humans, and you can see that they must have either a tremendous rate of population growth, or a high infant mortality rate. And there's no evidence of population growth. So—"

"What would cause it?" Roger asked absently, holding out another charred bit to the lizard. It shuffled forward hesitantly, sniffing at the tidbit and looking around cringingly. Reasonably sure that it was in the clear, it bared two-centimeter long fangs and hissed, then darted forward with the speed of a striking snake to take the offered treat out of Roger's fingers. It was a precise strike; Roger was left holding a tiny bit of the meat, which had been sheared off cleanly within a millimeter of his fingertips.

"Youch," he said, wiping off the carbon on his fingers.

"Oh, various things. I suppose barbarism is probably the biggest single factor." O'Casey leaned back on Matsugae's rucksack. The valet had left the overstuffed container in her "care" while he went around the camp, examining the cooking methods of the Mardukans. He was currently discussing something with a Mardukan female who'd emerged from one of the huts to lather a substance on the lizard being cooked in the center.

"People evolve to barbarism and usually stop there. Little civilizations rise and fall under the tide of barbarism." She yawned and thought about the history of Earth and some of the less well-prepared slow-boat colonies. "Sometimes, it seems that barbarism, for all its horrors—and they are many—is the natural state of a sentient species. So many, many times humanity has slid into barbarism in one area or another on one planet or another. In fact, we came within a centimeter of it on an interstellar scale during the Dagger Years; I think only your great-to-the-umpteenth grandmother prevented it. Not that that was what she was thinking about—"

She broke off as a yawn interrupted her, then winced as she stretched.

"God, I hurt," she observed, and lay back and closed her eyes. "Which, I might add, is a consequence of another mortality factor: living in a jungle ain't easy. It's a very competitive environment. Something is always trying to eat you, and finding things *you* can eat is hard."

She reopened her eyes looked up at Roger as the rain began to fall once more. The thunder of it on the thatch was lulling, and she yawned again.

"Roger, we're in a jungle," she said, and her tone was oddly ambiguous. "Jungles try so hard to kill you. They're always trying to." She stopped and smiled at him. "I've tried to get you to listen to me so often, but I'm going to try again. You have to check your tongue. You have to keep your temper. *Learn* from Pahner, don't piss him off, okay?"

He opened his mouth to protest, but she waved him quiet.

"Just . . . try to bite your tongue from time to time, all right? That's all I ask."

The last two days of strain had drained her, and she could feel herself drifting off despite every intention of staying awake. Not only was the social organization of the natives fascinating, but opportunities to catch Roger in a mood to learn anything but sports and hunting tricks were rare. Yet, despite that, she simply couldn't keep her eyes open.

"Jungles are beautiful," she continued in a mumble, "until you have to live in them."

Her eyes closed, and despite the heat, flies, and noise of festive preparation, she slept.

"You're making me proud, brother," Cord said, watching the gathering feast. Its lavishness would extract a price from the tribe, but it showed they were of good status. Something that would be important for this "Roger" to remember.

"It's the least I can do for my brother," Delkra replied. "Ayah! And for these odd strangers." He paused for a moment, then gave a grunting laugh. "They look like *basik*, you know."

Cord clacked his teeth sourly. "Thank you so much for pointing that out, brother. Yes, I'd made the same connection."

The small *basik* were often found around open areas in the jungle. Their mid-legs were foreshortened, and when they were frightened—which was virtually all the time—they ran on their hind legs with their upper limbs flopping loosely about. They were a beast of choice when it came to training young children to hunt, since they were small, harmless, cowardly, and stupid.

Very stupid.

"Get used to it, brother," Delkra said with another grunt. "Others will make the same connection."

"I suppose," Cord conceded. "And, demons know they're just about as stupid in the jungle. But although I've only seen those weapons of theirs used twice, I know to fear them. And rarely is the guard of a lord taken from among the most foolish. I don't underestimate them."

Delkra clapped his lower limbs together and changed the subject abruptly.

"*Asi*, at your age!"

"You keep saying that, brother," Cord observed. "You're not that much younger."

"Tell me a truth unknown," the chief replied somewhat sourly.

Cord understood, of course. Both of them would soon have to leave the Warrior Path, and although those who'd survived it enjoyed great status, few lived long thereafter. It was a thought neither enjoyed contemplating, and the shaman looked around, searching for a neutral change of subject. His gaze flitted about the familiar village which he soon would leave behind forever, and his eyes narrowed as he noticed a puzzling absence.

"Where is Deltan? Hunting?"

"One with the mists," Delkra said, rubbing his hands together to drive away bad luck. "An *atul*."

"What?" the shaman gasped. "How? He was surprised?"

"No," the chief snapped. "The spearhead broke."

"Ayah!" the shaman said, but he refused to show the emotion that threatened to overwhelm him. He'd never had children, not even daughters. A single paring as a youth had resulted in the death of the brood wife from an infection that was, unfortunately, all too common. Since then, he'd never taken another mate, and his brother's children had become as his own. Delkra certainly had enough to go around; half the females in the tribe had brooded a litter for him at some point. And he ran heavily to males in his broods.

But Deltan had been one of the special ones. He'd shown a flair for the learning of the shaman, and Cord had hoped that someday the fine young warrior might follow in his own footsteps. Now that was done, and it boded poorly for the tribe that he must leave with his *asi* and there would be no shaman to pass on the traditions. He'd hoped to pass on a few critical pieces of knowledge to Deltan before leaving, or perhaps to have him accompany them on the first leg of the humans' travels.

"Ayah," he repeated. "Evil times. The iron?"

"Bad," the chief spat. "Soft and rotten beneath a brittle exterior. It looked fine, but . . ."

"Aye," the shaman said, "but—"

"There's no other choice," the chieftain interrupted. "It must be war."

Cord clapped opposite hands in negation.

"If we war with Q'Nkok, the other tribes will pick our bones."

"And if we don't," the chief pointed out, "Q'Nkok will continue taking our lands and giving *feck* back! We must have the lands or the tribute. As it is, we have neither."

Cord clasped all four arms around his knees and rocked back and forth. His brother was correct; the tribe was in a lose/lose situation. They could neither survive a war with the local city-state nor permit the present intolerable trends to continue, yet war was the only way to stop it. There seemed no way out.

"Q'Nkok is to be our first stop," he observed after

a moment. "The humans want to trade for such things as only the shit-sitters can provide. We will discuss this with the humans."

"But—" his brother started to object.

"The humans aren't good in the jungle," Cord overrode the objection, "but they are very wise, nonetheless. I know they're shit-sitters, but they're smart and, I think, honorable shit-sitters. If I had my old master here, I would ask him for advice. But I don't. Far Voitan is fallen, and all its heroes with it. I can't ask my master; therefore, we will ask the humans."

"You're a stubborn *flar* beast," Delkra told him.

"But I'm also right," Cord retorted with a grunting laugh.

CHAPTER TWENTY-TWO

Eleanora awoke to a high-pitched, atonal chanting and a low-tempo, muffled drum beat. Her eyes flickered open, and she froze in adrenaline shock at the sight of a swaying vampire larva. The perspective was weird as the flickering firelight of full dark combined with the swaying dance of the creature to make it seem a strange hallucination. It seemed to shrink to the size of a caterpillar, and then swelled suddenly up to the size of a . . . Mardukan in a mask.

The dancer swayed in the firelight, and as Eleanora blinked at him the long, dripping fangs of the beast were revealed as a crown about his head, the camouflaged body as a painted wrap. Behind the shuffling figure were more dancers: a giant, pincer-armed beetle, a two-armed snake like the legendary Naga, and a low, writhing, six-armed beast whose maw was filled with sharklike teeth.

The fog of sleep and firelight, the swaying of the dancers, the singing and drumbeats were hypnotic. Eleanora lay in a spell, trapped by the symbolism of the animistic rite as the drumbeats increased and the singing shifted through patterns of atonality. The tempo increased, and the dancers' rhythm became more frenzied, until with a final burst of song, now perfectly blended with the drums in tone and pitch, there was a final crash, and the dancers froze.

The audience was left with a feeling of pleasant incompleteness as the dancers departed and conversation broke out among the Marines and Mardukans. Eleanora tried to shake off her fog and looked around for something to help with the attempt, only to find herself rather dreamily contemplating a boot.

She blinked, and her eyes moved upward. The female Marine to whom the boot was attached stood at parade rest by her head, one arm behind her back, plasma gun cocked forward. Eleanora looked around, and discovered another one—this one a grenadier—at her feet. How interesting.

She sat up and rubbed her eyes. It didn't help. She still felt like death warmed over, but at least her brain was a little clearer than before the nap. She looked up at the Marine at her head.

"How long was I out?" She hadn't checked the time at any point in the afternoon, so the current time, halfway through the local evening, told her nothing. Nor did her question communicate very much to the Marine. It came out mostly as a croak, so she cleared her throat and tried again.

"Corporal . . . Bosum, isn't it? How long was I sleep? And, thank you, but guarding me was probably unnecessary."

"Yes, Ma'am." The Marine looked down and smiled. "But His Highness told us to make sure no one bothered you." She thought about the other question. "I don't know how long you were asleep before we got here, but we've been on guard for three hours."

"Five or six, then," was Eleanora's mumbled guess.

"I should feel better than this after five hours' sleep," she muttered plaintively.

She stood up, and every joint in her body seemed to creak or pop. Her legs hurt so much that she felt light-headed and queasy, and she swayed for a moment until the Marine corporal steadied her.

"Take it easy, Ma'am," the plasma gunner said. "You'll get used to it after a few more days."

"Oh, sure," Eleanora said bitterly. "That's easy for you Marines to say. You've got so many nanites running around in you, you're practically cyborgs! And you're trained for this, too."

"But we don't start out that way," the male Marine put in. "They start us off systems-free in Basic."

"He's right," Bosum agreed with nasty cheerfulness. "We all go through this the first few days in Basic. It's just your turn," she added with an evil grin.

O'Casey twisted her torso and gasped as she felt her back crack in half a dozen places. Rotating her shoulders, arms, and legs extracted more crackling, and she decided that with a shower, a bath, another shower, a couple of tubes of heating gel, and two days' sleep, she'd be just fine. Barring that . . .

"Where is His Highness?" she asked, as she glanced around the clearing without seeing either Roger or Pahner, who was bound to be close by the prince.

"I'll lead you to him," the plasma gunner replied, and the male Marine fell in behind as they wove their way across the stockade.

Roger, Pahner, Kosutic, and the senior Mardukans were in a nearby hut, watching the festivities. Roger looked up from feeding the lizard he'd apparently adopted and smiled as Eleanora hobbled in.

"Ms. O'Casey," he said formally. "You're looking better for your nap."

The creature swarmed onto his lap at the chief of

staff's approach and hissed at her faintly. His Highness tapped it lightly on the head, and it ducked down and stretched out its neck to sniff at her. Apparently, it decided she was part of the pack, because it gave one last sniff, then twisted around and curled up on the prince's lap, exactly as if it belonged there.

"I feel like death warmed over," she answered. "If I'd known you were going to be taking me on adventure tours, I would have had the appropriate upgrades before we left."

She nodded at Matsugae as he handed her a plastic cup of water and two analgesic tablets.

"Thank you, Kostas." She took the tablets and a sip of the water, which was surprisingly cool. It had obviously been chilled by one of the bladders. "Thank you again."

She looked around the gathering. The Marines were scattered throughout the village, interacting much more fully with the Mardukans than they had been. Some of the humans were cleaning weapons, and some were quite obviously on alert, but most were socializing. Poertena had produced a pack of cards from somewhere and appeared to be teaching some of the younger Mardukan warriors poker while other Marines were demonstrating their entertainment pads or simply talking. Warrant Dobrescu had apparently set up an aid station and was doing a little "hearts and minds" work.

Dobrescu, it turned out, was a pearl beyond price in more ways than one. The chief warrant officer had gone to flight school as a second career track after spending sixteen years as a Marine Raider medic.

Normally, the Navy provided Marine units in combat environments with corpsmen, but the Raiders were the Empire's version of Saint special ops teams. They were designed to be out of contact with support for long periods of time, and thus needed specially trained medics

who could do more than slap on a bandage and decide
who went into the cryochambers and who didn't. The
training was intense, and included everything from
primitive methods of reducing gangrenous infection to
serving as the hands of a remote surgeon for thoracic
trauma surgery.

Since Prince Roger's company had never been
intended for detached duty, none of the Powers That
Were had ever considered the need to assign it an
integral, dedicated medic. Unfortunately, *DeGlopper's*
sickbay attendants had been needed to support the
transport's final battle, and somehow not even Eva
Kosutic had thought to point out that the company would
require medical services on the planet. All of which made
it extremely fortunate that Dobrescu was along.

At the moment, he was examining the Mardukans
who were willing to let him and doing his best to
repair the various wounds and infections that any jungle
inflicts on its inhabitants. As in other jungles, both on
Earth and other planets, surface lesions were the main
complaint. The Mardukans' mucus covering helped in
that regard, however, and only in spots where the coating
had been damaged did the sores break out.

Dobrescu had analyzed the lesions and determined
that they were primarily fungal in nature. A universal
antifungal cream seemed to work on them and didn't
cause negative side effects. Better yet, the cream was
produced by yeast in an auger jelly which could be
replaced with sterilized meat broth. That made it one
of the few regenerating systems that they had, which
meant he could be relatively spendthrift in its use. Since
some of the Marines already sported similar infections,
that was going to be a good thing.

With the cream and self-sealing bandages, he'd just
about fixed all the simple problems in the village. There
were a few advanced cases of infection that he was less

sanguine about, and a couple of other cases where something was attacking eyesight had him scratching his head. But in general, he'd done good service to the village that day.

"What did I miss?" O'Casey asked as she watched the slight warrant officer packing up his tools. He'd obviously worked through the celebrations that *she* had slept through, and the realization made her even less thrilled with her physical weakness.

"Oh, you would've loved it," Roger admitted in Standard English, scratching the lizard's head. It hissed with pleasure and rubbed its chin on his chest.

"We had a nice little ceremony. Very symbolic of all sorts of things, I'm sure. Cord forswore all previous allegiances in my favor, while I promised not to throw his life away pointlessly. Then we had all sorts of bonding oaths: the usual suspects. Last, but certainly not least, it involved eating a small bit of slime from Cord's back," he finished with a grimace.

Eleanora chuckled and seated herself carefully on the ground with the rest of them. The hut was walled on three sides by bundled branches with mud packed in the cracks between them. There was a rolled up covering for the open front, woven out of some sort of fibrous grass or leaves, and the sleeping areas arranged along the back and sides were also covered with the woven mats, which appeared to be designed to be staked down. It would be an awfully warm way to sleep in the muggy heat.

"I'm sorry I missed it," she said, and meant it. She'd initially taken her third doctorate in anthropology because it was a traditional complement to sociology and political science. But she'd quickly found that one developed a richer and fuller appreciation for the politics of a culture if one looked at its underlying premises, which was what anthropology was all about.

"I don't understand all the fuss." Roger pulled his hair up off his neck. "I can't believe they treat all visitors like this."

"Oh, I'm sure they don't," O'Casey said as her mind gradually cleared of fog. "You do understand the meaning of all this ritual, don't you?"

"I suppose I don't," Roger said. "I don't really understand most rituals, even the ones on Earth."

O'Casey decided that it would be more discreet to avoid agreeing overenthusiastically with him, and took another sip of her warming water while she considered how best to respond.

"Well," she said after a moment, "this was a sort of cross between a wedding and a funeral."

"Huh?" Roger sounded surprised.

"Did Cord maybe take something off or put it on? Or maybe give something to someone?"

"Yeah," Roger said. "They gave him a different cape to replace the one he was carrying. And he gave a spear and a staff to one of the other Mardukans."

"I talked a little to Cord on the way down from the plateau," Eleanora said. "This *asi* thing is a form of slavery or bondage—you realized that?"

"Today I did," Roger said angrily. "That's crazy! The Empire doesn't permit slavery or bondage of any form!"

"But this isn't an imperial world," she pointed out. "We've barely planted the flag, much less started on socialization. On the other hand, I think you misunderstand the situation. First of all, let's take a look at the definition of slavery."

She considered how to go about explaining slavery, marriage, and the similarities between them that had existed for thousands of Earth's years to a man of the thirty-fourth century.

"For most of history—" she began, and saw him glaze over immediately. Roger was always interested in the battles, but get onto the societal structures and faction struggles, and he completely lost interest.

"Listen to me, Roger," she said, meeting his eye. "You just married Cord."

"*What?*"

"That got your attention, didn't it?" she asked with a laugh. "But you did. And you also took him as your slave. For most of history, the rituals of marriage and slavery were practically identical. In this case, you performed an action that required that you 'marry' the person whom you'd saved."

"Oh, joy," Roger said.

"And you are now required to 'keep' that person, for the rest of his life and into the afterlife, most likely."

"Another mouth to feed," Roger joked.

"This is serious, Roger," his chief of staff admonished, but she couldn't help smiling. "By the same token, Cord must obey your wishes religiously. And to his family, it's as if he's dead. Which is probably the origin of the big festivities at weddings, by the way. In most primitive cultures, there are practically no rituals involved in marriage bindings, but elaborate rituals for funerals. There's a strong theory that the wedding rituals eventually evolve out of the funeral rites because the bride and groom are leaving their families . . . just as would have been the case if they'd died.

"Now, I used the term 'marriage' because I knew it would get your attention," she admitted. "But I could have said 'permanently binding oath of fealty,' 'slavery,' or 'indenture.' The rites and customs for all of them were practically identical in most early human societies, and we've found parallels for that in almost all of the primitive nonhuman societies we've studied. But any way you look at it, it's a very important sacrament for the Mardukans, and I'm really sorry I missed it," she concluded.

"Well, the dance of the forest animals was apparently the climax," Roger told her. He picked up one of the blackened bits of meat and popped it into his mouth, following it up with one for the tame lizard. Her explanation made quite a few little bits which had been confusing him fall into place. He would worry about the ones that hadn't at another time.

"But I'm glad you woke up," he went on. "If you hadn't, I would have had to send someone for you. Cord has just broached an interesting subject."

"Oh?" She picked a leftover bit of fruit off a plate . . . and set it back down hastily when she saw that several of the "seeds" were moving.

"Yes. It seems that his tribe is in need of some advice."

The hut was hot, dark, and close.

The party had gradually broken up, and as people left the square, the front covers of the huts had come down. They were, indeed, designed to be pegged down, and the Mardukans had also laced up the sides. Most of the Marines were packed into the huts, while a few were in tents, but at least the entire company was under cover, and most of its members were asleep.

But in Delkra's hut, the futures of both the company and Cord's tribe were under discussion as Cord explained why the interruption of his vision quest and his departure with Roger constituted such a bitter blow.

"In the days of my father's father's father, traders came up the Greater River to the joining of Our River and the Greater River. Traders had long come upriver, but this group made peace with my father's father's father and took up residence on a hill at the joining. We brought the skins of the *grack* and the *atul-grack*, the juice of the *yaden cuol* and the meat of the *flin*. In my father's day, I was sent to Far Voitan to study the ways of the sword and the spear.

"The traders brought with them new weapons, better metals. Cloths, grains, and wine. The tribe flourished with the wealth that was brought in.

"But since that time, the town has grown greater and greater, and the tribe has become weaker and weaker. During my father's time, we were at our greatest. We were more numerous and more fierce than the Dutak to the north or the Arnat to the south. But as the city has grown, its people have taken more and more of our hunting lands. Starvation has loomed more than once, and our reserves are always scanty."

The shaman paused and looked around, as if trying to avoid an awkward truth.

"My brother has been overgenerous in this celebration. The barleyrice is purchased from the city, Q'Nkok, at great price. And the other foods. . . . There will be hungry mothers in weeks to come.

"The problem is the city. It has extended its fields too far, yet that's hardly the worst of it. Their woodcutters are not to go beyond a certain stream, and even in that stretch where they are permitted, they are only to take certain trees. That is the treaty. For that, we are to be given certain goods—iron spears and knives, cooking pots, cloth. Yet these goods have become of worse and worse quality, while the woodcutters drive deeper and deeper into the forest. They do not restrict themselves to the proper trees, and their intrusion drives out the game or kills what remains."

He looked around again and clapped his hands.

"If we kill the woodcutters, even if they are beyond the line, it breaks the treaty. The Houses of Q'Nkok will gather their forces and attack." He ducked his head in shame. "And we will lose. Our warriors are able, but we would have to defend the town, and we would lose.

"But if we attack Q'Nkok, without warning, we can take it by surprise as the Kranolta took Far Voitan." He looked around the humans, and Roger was forced to recognize that a fierce look was nearly universal. "Then we feed on their hoarded grains, kill the men, enslave the women, and take the goods that are rightfully ours."

"There is, however, a problem with this," Delkra said, and leaned forward as he took over the thread. "We will lose many warriors even if the attack is successful, and then Dutak and Arnat will fall upon us like *flin* on a dead *flar* beast. We didn't know which way to go, so Cord went on a spirit quest in search of a vision of guidance. If he'd seen peace in the future, it would have been peace. If he'd seen war, it would have been war."

"What if he hadn't come back?" Pahner asked. "He nearly didn't."

"War," Delkra replied simply. "I'm in favor of it anyway. Without Cord to hold me back, we would have attacked last year. And, in all honesty, probably have been eaten by Dutak and Arnat."

"Make peace with Dutak and Arnat," Roger said, "and attack in concert."

He felt O'Casey's elbow connect with his ribs and realized what he'd just said. He supposed that advising the local barbarians to cooperate with one another in the destruction of this Q'Nkok would hardly advance the cause of civilization, and he remembered what his chief of staff had said about barbarism and infant mortality rates. On the other hand, *these* "barbarians" were his friends, and he didn't particularly care for either of the possible outcomes Cord had described.

He started to glower at her, then stopped and looked down at his hands, instead. His history teachers— including Eleanora, when she'd been his tutor—had harped incessantly and unpleasantly on a ruler's responsibility to weigh the possible impact of his decisions with exquisite care. He'd never cared for their apparent assumption that he wouldn't have weighed such matters carefully without their pointed prodding. But now he suddenly realized just how easy it was for purely personal considerations to shape a decision without the decider's even realizing it had happened.

He drew a deep breath, decided to keep his mouth shut, and went back to scratching his pet dog-lizard. He'd seen larger specimens around the camp, and if this one grew as large as some of the larger ones, it was going to be interesting. The biggest had been the size of a big German Shepherd, and the species seemed to fulfill the role of dogs in the camp.

Delkra, unaware of the prince's thoughts, clapped his hands in resigned negation.

"The chiefs of both tribes are crafty. They have seen us weaken. They feel that if they just let us wither a bit more, they can take our lands and squabble over the leftovers."

"So how can we help?" Captain Pahner asked. From his tone, Roger decided, it was pretty obvious that he knew at least one way they could help . . . and just as obvious that he was unwilling to do so.

"We don't know," Cord admitted. "But it's obvious from your tools and abilities that you have great knowledge. It was our hope that if we described our quandary to you you might see some solution which has eluded us."

Pahner and Roger turned as one to look at Eleanora.

"Oh great," she said. "Now you want my help."

She thought about what the two Mardukans said. And about city-state politics. And about Machiavelli.

"You have two apparently separate problems," she said after a moment. "One on the receiving side, and one on the giving side. They might be connected, but that's an assumption at this point."

She spoke slowly, almost distantly, as her mind ranged back and forth over the Mardukans' description of events, and she scratched the back of her neck while she thought.

"Have you been actively offered offense in your dealings with the rulers of the city-state?"

"No," Cord answered definitively. "I have been to Q'Nkok twice recently to discuss the problems with the quality of the tribute and the unlawful intrusions of the woodcutters. The King has been very gracious on both occasions. The common people of the city don't like us, nor we them, but the King has been very friendly."

"Is wood-cutting a monopoly?" Eleanora asked. "Does one house cut all the wood? And what are these houses? How many are there, and how are they organized?"

"There are sixteen Great Houses," Cord told her. "Plus the House of the King. There are also many smaller houses. The Great Houses sit on the Royal Council and . . . there are other rights attached to them. No single house has the right to cut wood, and the woodcutters who offend are not from a single house."

"And the tribute? Is it supplied by the Houses or by the King?"

"It is supplied by the King through taxes on the Houses, Greater and Lesser. But it is usually conveyed by one of the Great Houses."

"Expansion of the city-state is inevitable," she said after a moment's thought. "And as long as they need the wood as a resource, they'll encroach farther and farther on your lands. Wars are usually about resources— about economics—at the base. But your concerns are certainly justified.

"I can't know what's going on from here. As I understand it, we're traveling to this Q'Nkok next?" She made it a question and looked at Pahner, who gave a confirming nod and then looked at their hosts.

"I ask that you hold off on any attack until we visit the city," the Marine said. "I ask for two reasons. One is that we need to trade for goods and animals to make our journey; Q'Nkok is the closest and most accessible source of what we need. The second is that we might be able to come up with a third option that would avoid the needless bloodshed of a war. Let us do a reconnaissance of the town, then we'll send back word of what we find. As outsiders, we might be able to discern something that you can't."

Delkra and Cord looked at one another, and then the chief clapped his upper hands in agreement.

"Very well, we won't rush to attack. When you go to the town, I will send some of my sons with you. They'll aid you on the trip and act as messengers." He paused, and looked around at the gathered humans, and his body language was sober. "I hope for all our sakes that you are able to find a third way. My brother is *asi* now, and dead to his family, but it would grieve him if his family were dead in truth."

CHAPTER TWENTY-THREE

The city-state was a larger version of the village of The People and was obviously expanding. The company had followed the river from Cord's village downstream to its junction with a still larger river, and the city sat on a small ridge on the eastern side of the new one. The ridge was near the apex of the confluence of the two streams and more or less covered with structures. A wooden palisade surrounded the intersection, but the palisade was obviously a temporary expedience, and several sections of it had already been replaced with a high stone curtain wall. It was nearing evening as the travelers came to the cleared boundary of the city-state's lands, and the sky over the town was gray with the smoke of the evening's fires.

The jungle ended with knife-sharp abruptness at the border of the city-state's territory. The stream that marked the boundary was the fourth one they'd crossed, but this crossing had significant differences from any of the earlier ones.

On the west side of the stream—the "civilized" side—

there were large mounds every few hundred yards. They were surmounted by oddly constructed houses, and more mounds and houses were scattered throughout the valley of fields and orchards. The houses had no lower-floor doorways, and the upper floors extended out to over-hang the walls of the lower sections, which were very stoutly constructed. For the life of him, Roger couldn't figure out why they were designed that way, but from their placement, they were clearly intended to defend the fields.

Also scattered along the banks of the irrigation ditches and poor roads were very simple huts. Compared to them, the huts of Cord's village were masterpieces. These were more stacks of barleyrice straw than true dwellings, and Roger was fairly sure they were temporary shelter for the peasants who worked the land. No doubt they were expected to wash away with the regular seasonal floods, for they could certainly be "rebuilt"—if that wasn't too grand a term—easily enough.

The cultivation of barleyrice took up the majority of the several square kilometers of cleared land. Unlike Terran rice, it was dry farming, and Roger thought it might be a tradable grain in the Empire. It was as easy to prepare as rice but had more and better taste, and if it lacked some amino acids, so did rice. Combined with the proper terrestrial foods, it would provide a balanced diet.

It was clear that the single biggest difficulty in cultivating the grain around Q'Nkok wasn't the jungle, but rains and floods. Most of the fields, especially in the lower areas near the river, were surrounded by dikes intended to keep water out, not in. Lifting pumps, like a sort of reverse waterwheel, were everywhere, pulling water out of depressions cut into the corners of the fields. Some were driven by peasants pushing circle wheels, but most were attached to crude windmills.

What was not evident were reasonably sized domestic animals. As they emerged from the jungle, they'd seen a line of what Cord identified as pack beasts entering the distant city, and Roger, along with several of the Marines, had used his helmet to zoom in on the large creatures. They'd been surprised, for the beasts were apparently identical to the *flar* beast which had threatened Cord. When Roger commented on it, Cord had responded with a grunting laugh and indicated that although the pack beasts, which he called *flar-ta*, might look the same as the creature he called *flar-ke*, which Roger had killed, there were huge differences between the two obviously related species.

The peasants who worked the grain were scattered throughout the area, weeding and planting. Some were done for the day and were drifting back to their dwellings, whether those were the temporary huts, the blockhouses near the jungle, or the distant town, when they spotted the travelers' approach and slowed abruptly.

As the humans followed the twisting roads towards the town, the crowd of workers became thicker. Some who'd gone ahead turned and retraced their steps, and others looked up from the fields and began to flow towards the roadside. Pahner had started to get a feel for Mardukan body language, and he didn't care for the hostile looks and gestures thrown their way. Nor did he like the occasional, half-understood insults . . . or the way one or two of them waved agricultural implements.

The hostility seemed to be directed more towards Cord and Delkra's sons than at the humans, although the strangers came in for some heaped abuse, as well, and as the crowd grew larger, its mood got uglier. By the time they neared the city walls, a large mob had gathered, and more people flowed out from inside the walls to join it. Shouts and the local equivalent of catcalls grew louder and bolder, and Pahner recognized a building riot with the Marines as its object.

"Company, pull in. I want a coil perimeter around Roger. Standard riot procedure. Armor to the front, link arms. Second layer, fix bayonets and prepare to repel rioters."

The Marines responded with automatic precision, folding the spread-out formation in which they'd been moving into a circle around the command group. Julian's armored squad moved to the section of road facing the city and passed their weapons back. The ChromSten-clad powered armor was capable of lifting five times its own weight, and no known Mardukan weapon could damage it, so mere weapons would only have been in the way for riot work.

The poorly graded road was about ten meters wide and bordered by high dikes, which allowed the coil formation to block it like a cork. The group at the Marines' back was relatively small—no more than fifty or sixty individuals. For it to join with the larger group spilling from the city, it would have to trample the growing crops to either side of the road. That balked them, since farmers tended to care about such things. A few of them rushed the rear ranks instead, trying to break through, and they went over the line from crowding to attacking. The bayonets protruding over the wall of Marines in the rearmost rank drove them back despite their large size. One Marine was badly injured by a threshing flail that cracked his clavicle, but his companions beat the Mardukans back without being forced to open fire.

At the front, the armored squad stymied the movement of the mob from the city. The newcomers obviously weren't farmers, for they were far more ready to spread out over the fields, but they were also less aggressive than the group at the rear. They threw a few stones, but their main weapon was lumps of fecal matter. The armored Marines quickly learned to dodge the stinking projectiles after one of the first hit Poertena. His sulphurous comments were a clear violation of his orders from the sergeant major, but she forbore to point that out, and some of them were so accidentally accurate it was hilarious.

Unfortunately, the situation was a stalemate. The town-dwellers couldn't get past Julian's squad, but neither could the Marines get past *them* without employing a level of force guaranteed to cause serious Mardukan casualties. Pahner was tempted to do just that as the rain of stones and other matter became denser, but killing or crippling several dozen members of the local citizenry, whatever the provocation, would scarcely endear them to the Q'Nkokans with whom they'd come to trade.

On the other hand, the rioters or protesters or whatever the hell they were were creating sufficient bedlam that whoever was responsible for maintaining what passed for civil order in the city could hardly fail to figure out something was going on outside his front door. Which *ought* to mean that any minute now—

A group of Mardukan guards suddenly emerged from the city. They were the first Mardukans the Marines had seen wearing any clothing, and even Roger recognized it as armor.

The leather armor was worn like a long apron, open at the back, and doubled in critical spots over the chest and at the shoulders. It stretched from shoulder to knee, painted with a complex heraldic device, and each guard also carried a large, round shield with an iron boss.

Their weapons were long clubs, apparently designed for riot work, not swords or spears, and they waded in with abandon. They didn't maintain any sort of formation. Each simply found a rioter to attack and charged, and the mob scattered away from them like pigeons from hawks, running out into the fields and back around the knot of soldiers into the town.

The guards paid no attention to those who ran away, concentrating instead on any who stood and fought or didn't run away fast enough. Those laggards were brutally beaten down with the long, heavy-headed clubs, and the guards seemed to have no compunction about the use of deadly force. Their weapons might not be edged, but when they were done, at least one of the rioters was obviously dead. His head had been split like a melon, but the guards showed no particular concern as they dragged the corpse—and several other inert bodies, most of which were probably simply unconscious—off the road before they gathered back together between the Marines and the city gate.

Cord passed through the cordon of Marines to approach the regrouped guards, trailed by Roger and a couple of nephews. Pahner rolled his eyes as the prince followed the shaman, then signaled Despreaux to take a group with him. She snapped her fingers at Alpha Team, and the six Marines chased after the prince as Cord approached the apparent leader of the group of guards—or the one who had been shouting the most, at least—and nodded.

"I am D'Nal Cord of the Tribe. I come to speak to your king on matters of treaty."

"Yeah, yeah," the guard answered surlily. "We greet you and all that." He looked at the Marines following Cord and snorted. "Where'd you find the *basik*? You could feed a family on one of these!"

At those words, Roger stopped abruptly. It hadn't occurred to him that although the Mardukans were no more cannibalistic than humans, they might not put humans in the same category as "people." He'd intended to make his own announcement along with Cord, but the guard's suggestion made that seem . . . less attractive, somehow.

"I am *asi* to their leader," Cord said definitively. "Thus they are bonded to my tribe and should be accorded the same privileges as The People."

"Oh, I don't know," the guard leader argued. "They seem like regular visitors, so they should fall under trader's rules. Besides, no more than ten of you barbs are permitted in the city at the same time."

"Hey," another guard put in, "let's not be hasty, Banalk! If you consider them traders, does that mean we don't get to eat them after all?"

He meant it as a joke—probably—Roger thought, but Pahner had been monitoring the conversation through a feed off of Sergeant Despreaux and decided that it was time to nip this particular discussion in the bud. He looked around for something relatively useless and found it quickly. The hills that supported the town were igneous basoliths, ancient granite extrusions from a deep magma rift. Their surroundings had slowly worn away until the erosion reached the stony outcrops, but although the refractory granite was much more weather resistant than the soil around, it still tended to crack and fissure over time. That had produced large boulders that congregated at the base of the hill, which the locals had dragged away from the town's wooden palisade when it was erected. One such boulder was no more than a hundred meters from the road, in easy sight of the guards and the few bystanders who'd remained outside the walls.

"Despreaux." Pahner placed a targeting dot on the boulder. "Plasma rifle."

"Roger," the squad leader responded, spotting the dot in her own visor HUD, then waved her arms to get the attention of the arguing group.

"Excuse me," she said in a pleasant soprano. "We think this conversation has gone far enough."

She'd already relayed the targeting dot to Lance Corporal Kane, and now the slight blonde hefted her plasma rifle and triggered a single round.

The plasma bloom left a scorched track through the green corn of the field, but that was nothing compared to what it did to the boulder. It struck with an explosive whipcrack of sound, and the transmitted heat caused diffusive expansion through the meter and a half boulder that shattered it like an egg. Pieces flew in every direction, from head-sized lumps down to relatively fine gravel, some of which reached clear back to the roadway before it pattered to the ground.

As the last echo faded, the last bit of gravel plunked into silence, and Sergeant Nimashet Despreaux, Third Platoon, Bravo Company, turned back to a suddenly frozen and speechless group of guards and smiled.

"We don't care if you treat us as The People or as traders, but they won't find enough to bury of the next one who suggests eating us."

CHAPTER TWENTY-FOUR

The front hall of the king's castle was a vaulted arch in a gate bastion of the outer curtain wall. Unlike most of the city, the king's citadel was built of a combination of the local granite and limestone. The lower portions of the walls were the dark gray of the granite, but they were surmounted by the limestone in a pleasing duotone pattern. Although it was obviously intended for greeting and ceremony as much as for defense, the hall was unornamented aside from the pattern, and it was floored with simple paving stones. The far wall sported large, open windows, which revealed gardens in the bailey and an inner line of defenses.

The local ruler, along with a sizeable bodyguard of his own, greeted Roger's party in this public arena. Their passage uphill through the town had been much more muted than their reception, and Pahner had become increasingly suspicious that the mob scene had been staged.

"Welcome to Q'Nkok." The king, accompanied by a

much younger son, greeted them with grave courtesy and glanced at the humans curiously and a bit warily. Pahner smiled behind his flickering visor; clearly, the king had already been apprised of their demonstration at his gates.

"I am Xyia Kan, ruler of this place," the king continued, and gestured to the youth at his side. "This is Xyia Tam, my son and heir."

Roger nodded calmly in response. He had taken off his armor's helmet, both so that his face would be clear and as a gesture of respect. The ruler appeared old. He had the slightly flabby skin and patchy mucus that Roger had noted on Cord, although it was worse in Xyia Kan's case.

"I am Prince Roger Ramius Sergei Alexander Chiang MacClintock, of the House MacClintock, and Heir Tertiary to the Throne of Man," he said formally. "I greet you in the name of the Empire of Man and as the representative of my mother, Empress Alexandra."

He really hoped that the toot was getting these terms right. He was becoming increasingly convinced that the translation software was screwing up something major. Little glitches were appearing in translation left and right and this was too important a meeting to get things wrong.

The "repeat" of his translation which the software played back to him had his mother momentarily as a male, which was a hoot. It had actually formed an image of her as a guy, and she really wasn't all that bad looking. His lips twitched, fighting to smile as he visualized her response to the image, but then, in response to another repeat query, he got an image of himself dressed as a fairy-tale princess, which quashed all humor. This software was definitely buggy as hell.

"We are travelers from a far land who have been stranded in this one," he continued with the story which had been decided upon as easier than trying to explain the truth. "We are passing through your kingdom on our way to a place where we can obtain passage to our home.

"We bring you these gifts," he continued, and turned to O'Casey, who deftly handed him one of the Marine multitools.

"This device can change its form into any of several useful objects," Roger said. It wasn't the sort of thing one commonly gave to a ruler, but they didn't have anything else that was better, and Roger quickly demonstrated the settings to Xyia Kan. The king watched closely, then nodded gravely, accepted the gift, and handed it to his son. The younger Mardukan was no more than a child, judging from what Roger had seen in Cord's village, and looked much more interested in the multitool, but restrained his curiosity admirably.

"Estimable gifts," the king said diplomatically. "I offer you the hospitality of the visitors' quarters of my home." He looked at the line of Marines and clasped his hands together. "You should be able to fit your force in there."

Roger nodded his head again in thanks.

"We appreciate that kindness," he said, and the king nodded in return and gestured to a hovering guard.

"D'Nok Tay will lead you to the quarters, and we shall meet more formally in the morning. For now, take your rest. I will have food and servants sent to your quarters."

"Thank you again," Roger said.

"Until then," the king responded, and walked out of the bastion, trailed by his son. The younger Mardukan, unlike his father, kept looking over his shoulder at the Marines until they were out of sight.

Roger waited until the king was decently gone, and then turned to the guard.

"Lead on."

D'Nok Tay turned without a word and walked out of

the far door, but whereas the king had turned to the left on exiting, the guard turned to the right.

They proceeded across an open bailey and up a steep ramp. The ramp ran between the outer curtain wall and the base of the citadel proper, and the fairly narrow way was dark and dank. As they started to ascend it, the skies opened up in another monsoon-quality rainstorm and filled the narrow track with vertical water. The sound of pouring water and flying spray in the slotlike space was like the underside of a waterfall, but D'Nok Tay paid it no more attention than Cord or his nephews, and the humans did their best to emulate the natives. Fortunately, the ramp turned out to be well designed for the storms, and a slight outward slope carried the water to regular openings in the outer wall and thus out of the castle.

The whole town had obviously been designed to take advantage of the regular rains. The main road up which they'd traveled from the city gate had switched back and forth with very little rhyme or reason, but it, too, had been well designed to handle the water. Both sides had been lined with gutters which linked with others to carry the water around to the river side of the hill, where, presumably, it was dumped into the river.

The efficient storm water system also reduced, but did not eliminate, the problem of hygiene in the city. Clearly, the Mardukans had never heard of the concept, for the road had been strewn with feces from the Mardukans and their pack beasts. According to O'Casey, this was normal in lower technology cultures, but at least with the rains the majority would get washed away.

And it certainly explained The People's epithet for the townspeople.

The narrow ramp finally opened out to the level of the curtain wall's battlements, and the company was afforded a spectacular view of the surrounding countryside. The clouds had broken momentarily, the rain had stopped as abruptly as it had begun, and the larger moon, Hanish, was rising over the mountains to the east. They were about a hundred meters above the floodplain, and the valley of Q'Nkok spread out below them in the moonlight. The city was surprisingly dark to humans who were used to the streetlighting found in even small towns on the meanest worlds of the Empire, but the valley was a fairy-tale place under the primary moon.

The river glittered a silver tracery across the plain and the shimmer of water through the fields and irrigation ditches echoed it. The evening fires of farmers dotted the plain here and there, and the coughing roar of some beast from the jungle across the river could be heard even at their height.

Roger paused to take in the vista and found Despreaux beside him. Her squad had never been taken off "close protection," and she was still following him doggedly.

"You can probably drop back into the Company now," he said quietly, and raised one arm of his armor with a smile. "I don't think anything local is coming through this."

"Yes, Sir," she said. "You're probably right, but we haven't been relieved by our CO."

Roger started to open his mouth to object, but decided not to for two reasons. One was that scathing ass-chewing from Captain Pahner about interfering with the chain of command. The other was, frankly, that it was a pretty night and Despreaux was a pretty young woman, and he would be a fool to trade her for a random choice replacement. He looked back over the valley as the company passed, and smiled in the gathering darkness.

"When it's not awful, this can be a pretty place."

Despreaux sensed that the prince wanted more than a simple "yes, Sir; no, Sir," and nodded her head.

"I've seen worse, Your Highness." She thought about one assignment, in particular. The planet Diablo had the highest tectonic instability rating of any inhabited planet in the Empire, with air quality so low children were routinely kept inside until they were old enough to wear a breath pack properly. "Much worse," she said.

Roger nodded, and sensed that the tail of the company was catching up with them in the darkness of the ramp. He didn't want to break the spell, but it was time to move on again.

"We need to get moving, Your Highness," Despreaux said, as if she'd read his mind.

"Right," he said with a sigh. "Time to find out what new joy awaits us."

The "guest quarters" of the castle were odd. To reach them, the company passed through a doglegged tunnel sealed with two gates. At the far end, the tunnel led into a small open area, a bailey, and a single door into the building which was, effectively, a separate keep. The entryway was very low for a Mardukan—low enough that D'Nok Tay had to bend nearly double to lead the way—but about right for the humans.

The building beyond had three levels. There were no interior partitions on the first two levels, and no windows on the lowest one. The second level had small windows and a simple wooden floor that was accessible through a single trapdoor. The third level was also accessed through a single trapdoor, but was separated into six wooden-walled rooms grouped along a common corridor. All six of the rooms had large windows, with wooden shutters to seal them. On the ground floor was a simple latrine kept "flushed" by rainwater from the roof.

Roger stood in the largest of the rooms, looking out over the vista of the valley once again, with his hands on his hips.

"This is the strangest building I've ever seen," he commented to Pahner.

Matsugae had been laying out Roger's bedroll when the company commander entered the room. He looked up at the captain and winked, but Pahner just shook his head.

"Not really, Your Highness. It's a fort designed for visiting dignitaries. We can defend it even if the King turns on us, and he doesn't have to worry about us trying to take over from within. The gates in the tunnel may seal us in, but getting in here without our permission would be hard. For example, that door is offset so that you can't get a good run up with a ram. I'm happy with it."

Roger turned away from the view and looked at the Marine. The captain stood in the pool of shadow cast by the camp light in the corner, and his face was obscured. Not that Roger could have gotten anything from seeing it; except when he was really enraged, Pahner was very hard to read.

"Do you think Xyia Kan would turn on us?" the prince asked. The idea surprised him. The Q'Nkok monarch had seemed friendly enough to him.

"I didn't think there was a toombie onboard the *DeGlopper*, Your Highness," Pahner said bitterly, and Roger nodded.

"What are we going to do about it?" he asked reasonably.

"Get our stuff traded, get the supplies we need, and get out of town as fast as possible, Your Highness," Pahner said, and Roger nodded again and clasped his hands behind him.

He started to reply, then stopped himself. O'Casey's

little lecture had been perking at the back of his mind, and he decided that now was a good time to start biting his tongue. And he had no *specific* problems with what Pahner had just said, only vague reservations. Until and unless they became more specific, it would be much smarter to just let it ride.

"I suppose we'll see tomorrow," was all he said.

"I'll go see about the arrangements downstairs then, Your Highness," Matsugae said. He'd set up the prince's sleeping area and laid out a fresh uniform.

The sight of the uniform sent a fresh prickle through Roger from the itch down his back, and he felt a sudden overwhelming desire to get out of the armor. The equipment had a cooling unit, so he hadn't suffered from the heat and humidity as much as the rest of the company, but it was still uncomfortable to wear hour after hour.

"I'm going to get out of this damn armor and have a good rubdown with a cleaning cloth," he announced.

"Yes, Your Highness," the captain said, with a faint frown.

"What?" Roger asked, stripping off the uniform.

"Well, Your Highness," the captain said carefully. "You might see about your rifle first."

The officer chuckled and shook his head at the prince's frown. "Just thinking of an old service poem, Your Highness. It ends 'mind you keep your rifle and yourself just so.' "

Roger nodded. "I take your meaning, Captain." He glanced at the weapon and nodded again. "I know better than to go to bed with a fouled weapon; you never know if you'll wake up with a banshee in your tent. I'll take care of that first. But I'm not sure I'll be down for supper. I might just have a ration and go to bed."

"Yes, Sir," Pahner said. "If not tonight, I'll see you

in the morning. We should discuss the audience before-hand."

"Agreed. In the morning then."

"Goodnight, Your Highness," Pahner said, and vanished into the shadows.

CHAPTER TWENTY-FIVE

Roger bowed to the king and presented his documentation as a member of the Imperial Family. The piece of paper was in Standard English, utterly unintelligible to the locals, and he had no idea if it was a protocol that they observed. But the king looked it over, and it was certainly impressive enough with its gold lettering and vermillion seals. He handed it back after several moments, and Roger launched into his prepared speech.

"Your Majesty," he said, throwing back his head and interlacing his hands behind him. "We visit you from a distant land. In our land we have come far in the areas of technology, the knowledge of making things, yet we continue to seek more knowledge of all aspects of the world, and that search often takes us upon long journeys. We set out on such a voyage of discovery, but our ship was blown far off course, and we crashed on the eastern shores of this land."

Eleanora O'Casey stood back and watched the prince's performance. The toot seemed to be adequately translating the speech into the clicks and growls of the local dialect. It was impossible to be certain without any reliable native to return the translation, but Roger had tried most of it out on Cord, who had pronounced it fit, so it should be okay. At least so far there'd been none of the laughs or grimaces which were normal signs of a flop.

"The eastern shores are beyond the high mountains," Roger continued, gesturing out the windows which ringed the throne room. The room was near the pinnacle of the citadel, and had high windows on every side to catch the breezes. It was, for Marduk, remarkably cool and comfortable, with a temperature that couldn't have been much over thirty degrees Standard.

The throne itself was elevated and elaborately carved out of some lustrous wood. The room was paneled in carefully contrasting multihued and grained woods, and each panel was itself a work of art. The panels depicted scenes of everyday Mardukan life, alternating with images of the various gods and demons of the local pantheon. Given the monsters the local wildlife gave the natives as models, the demons were particularly good.

It was a beautiful and obviously expensive display, and, just as clearly, no expense was spared for the security of the king. The walls were lined with guards in the same leather apron armor as the ones who'd escorted the humans to the palace, but this armor was reinforced in strategic spots by plates of bronze. And instead of clubs, these guards carried spears that were nearly three meters long. Those spears were apparently designed not only for stabbing, but also for slashing, given the keen edges of their broad, meter-long heads.

"We traveled over those mountains," Roger was continuing, "for we do not share your form or your desire for damp and heat, and met upon the edge of them with my good friend and companion, D'Nal Cord. He has since guided us to your beautiful kingdom, where it is our desire to trade and prepare for a great journey."

The prince had a deep, rich baritone which had been trained (often over his strenuous objections) as an oratorical instrument, and it seemed the Mardukans responded to oratory in many of the same ways humans did. O'Casey had begun to develop a feel for Mardukan body language, and the speech had so far evoked a positive response. Which was good, because Roger was about to shock them.

"We know little of your lands, but we do know a place where a trading mission from our own land exists. It is a long journey from here, which will take many, many months. And it will take us through the lands of the Kranolta."

The group of Mardukan nobles gathered at the audience began to buzz with conversation, and there were occasional grunting laughs, but the king simply looked grim.

"This is sad news," he said, leaning forward in the throne. His son, sitting on a stool at his feet, on the other hand, looked very excited at the pronouncement. But he was young. "You know that the Kranolta are a vast and fierce tribe?"

"Yes, Your Majesty." Roger nodded gravely. "Nonetheless, we must pass through that region. Far to the northwest lies an ocean we must reach. I have spoken with Cord, and he tells me that most of your trade goes to the south. As you know, the ocean in that direction lies several months' journey further away. We . . . don't have that much time."

"But the Kranolta are fierce and numerous," Xyia Kan's son put in. He glanced at the team of armored Marines, and tapped his half-hand fingers nervously.

Roger had been surprised by the amount of backstage negotiations which had gone on to set up this meeting.

Pahner and O'Casey had been up half the night negotiating with the local equivalent of the palace chamberlain about who was going to be allowed into the king's presence.

The problem was the guards.

Pahner wasn't about to let Roger wander into the king's presence without at least a squad of guards. First of all, it wasn't done. A member of the Imperial Family didn't meet with a barbarian king without *some* retainers. But even more to the point, there was no reason at all to trust the monarch, so both protocol and sense dictated having guards in attendance. But the locals were no dummies. It was clear that the town was highly factionalized, and the king had long since mandated specific limits on the number of guards permitted in his presence.

Commoners and merchants weren't allowed to bring guards or weapons of any form into the royal presence. Nor were members of the lesser houses of the city-state. The heads of the Great Houses who made up the town council could each bring up to three guards, but no more than fifteen total as a group. Since the council numbered fifteen, it had become the custom for each counselor to bring a single guard as a token of his status. Which meant that Pahner's insistence that it was impossible for the prince to travel with less than eight guards was a major sticking point.

The number finally settled on was five, and despite the stubbornness with which he'd held out for eight, Pahner had to admit that Roger in armor and Julian with his Bravo Team, also fully armored up, probably had the king's guard outnumbered.

Hell, they probably had all of *Q'Nkok* outnumbered!

"Even with your fierce guardians and your powerful weapons, you will surely be overwhelmed," the king commented now, in apparent agreement with his son.

"Nonetheless," Roger said grimly, "it is to the north we must go. We will try to make peace with the Kranolta." He shook his head and clapped his hands by his waist in an attempt to replicate the Mardukan version of a shrug. "But if they will not have peace, then we will give them war to the knife."

The king clapped his upper arms and grunted in agreement.

"I wish you luck. Well it would be to be rid of the Kranolta. They have never attacked this side of the mountains. Indeed, they have been much weaker in my generation than in my father's. But the mere fear of them keeps many traders from coming up the river. Any aid we can give you will be proffered."

He looked around the throne room and grunted again.

"And speaking of war to the knife, I fear that I know why D'Nal Cord is back so soon." The words were strong, but the intent appeared to be friendly. "Come forward, counselor and brother of my friend Delkra, and tell me what transgression has brought you from your beloved forest hell this time."

Cord strode forward gravely, and raised his hands towards the monarch.

"Xyia Kan, I greet you in the name of The People and the name of my sibling D'Net Delkra. I bring sad tidings of continued cutting beyond the Treeline. Further, much of the last shipments of spears and javelin heads have been of unacceptable quality. I am deeply grieved to inform you that my nephew and apprentice D'Net Deltan was killed when the spear he was using snapped. It was of inferior quality, or he would still be alive."

The shaman stepped forward and carefully withdrew a reversed spearhead from his cloak. He handed it to the king, who examined it with care. On the surface, it appeared to be good iron, but one tap on the arm of the throne revealed the rotten tone of poorly smelted material, and Xyia Kan's expression was grim as he set it down and gestured for Cord to continue.

"This has gone beyond the pale." The shaman clapped his hands emphatically. "There is now a blood debt." He clasped his hands gravely and looked at the floor.

"I am now . . . *asi* to this young prince. I go with him on his quest to reach Far Voitan and the fabled lands beyond. I shall not be here to see the results if this is not resolved quickly and clearly." He looked up again and clacked his teeth in anger. "But, yes, I would think that if the words sent back are once again simple platitudes and promises that it will indeed be war to the knife.

"And the burning of Q'Nkok will rise to the sky to mingle with fallen Voitan's."

CHAPTER TWENTY-SIX

Xyia Kan entered the audience chamber and ascended his throne. The Council had been summoned immediately at his insistence. And, also at his insistence, the single traditional armed retainer of each councilor had been stopped at the chamber door. The only visibly armed Mardukans present were his guards, lining either side of the room, where, at a single gesture from him, they could stop the intrigues that were plaguing him in their tracks forever.

And insure the end of his dynasty.

Once he was settled, he simply sat and looked at them. Just . . . sat. He let seconds tick by, then a full minute. Two minutes. Even the hardiest of his councilors looked away, confused and perplexed or confused and angry, depending upon their personalities and exactly how much they understood about the stakes for which they played, under the insulting weight of his baleful gaze. He felt the tension singing about him, but he made no move to break it until, finally and somewhat predictably, W'hild Doma burst with fury.

"Xyia Kan, I have a House to manage!" he snapped. "I don't have time for games. What is the meaning of this?"

Since Kan was particularly furious with the W'hild, he almost cracked. He wasn't furious because the house-leader had switched out good weapons in the tribute for bad. Among other things, if that had been done in the House W'hild, the monarch was virtually certain Doma was unaware of it. No, he was furious because Doma, whom he trusted to be both capable and loyal, had let someone sucker his House so thoroughly.

But he managed to not even flinch, simply looked at the fulminating W'hild and stared him down. Doma was hardly the sort to cower, but even his angry eyes finally fell under the unrelenting weight of Xyia Kan's, and the heavy silence returned until, finally, the king relented.

He leaned sideways and spat on the audience chamber floor.

"*Women!*" he snarled. His councilors, already simultaneously uncertain and angry, looked at one another in confusion, and he spat on the floor again.

"Women," he repeated. "All I see before me are stupid women!"

This time, there was no confusion. Fury at the carefully chosen insult overwhelmed any other emotion, and three or four of the councilors actually came to their feet. Fortunately, Xyia Kan had warned his guard captain, and his warriors' spears remained at their sides, but his own hands slammed down on the arms of his chair.

"*Silence!*" The pure venom of his wrath sliced through the shouted posturing of their outrage like a whetted spearhead. "Be seated!"

They sank back into their chairs, and he glowered at them.

"I've had another visit from D'Nal Cord. He will be

leaving for good when the humans leave, for he is now *asi* to the human leader."

"Good!" W'hild shot back. "Maybe with Cord gone, Delkra will understand that we cannot control every peasant who sneaks into the forest!"

"Delkra will have our heads!" Kan snapped. "It has been Cord restraining his brother all along, you fools! Without him, the X'Intai will roll over us in a day! Either I must have more guards, or I must have command of the household guards in the event of an attack!"

"Never!" P'grid shouted. "If the barbarians attack, however unlikely that is, the Houses will provide for their own defense, as always. It is the duty of the King to protect the town as it is the duty of the House to protect itself. This is as it has always been!"

"In the past, we weren't looking at being overrun by the X'Intai! And if you think that after having a spearhead break and kill the son of Delkra, the protégé of Cord, that they are *not* going to attack, you are a greater fool than even I believe you can be!"

"Spearheads break," P'grid said with a grunt of laughter. "One less barbarian for you to lose sleep over."

"Especially spearheads like *this*!" the monarch snarled. He whipped out the offending weapon and hurled it at the floor, and it shattered, scattering splinters of iron among the councilors.

"Where did that come from?" Doma demanded sharply. "Not out of the last shipment!"

"Yes, Doma," the king retorted. "Out of the demon-cursed shipment. *Your* demon-cursed shipment. That you were responsible for! I ought to send the X'Intai your head!"

"I am *not* responsible for this!" the councilor shouted. "I shipped only the finest wrought iron spearheads. *I* took a loss!"

"Nevertheless," the king said flatly, "this is what the

X'Intai received. And what killed Deltan. So if anyone has anything to say about this, now would be a good time!"

Again there was much glancing around, but none of the eye contact seemed to mean much. And not many of the eyes were willing to meet Kan's. Finally, Kesselotte J'ral clapped his false hands.

"What would you have us say, O King?" he asked. "Would any of us jeopardize this fair city? The city that is our home, as well as yours? What purpose would it serve?"

"Most of you would sell your mothers for a hunk of scrap bronze," the monarch hissed. "Get out of my sight. I doubt that we'll have another council meeting before the X'Intai come over the wall. And woe betide you then, for the gates of this citadel shall be shut against you!"

"—shall be shut against you!"

"Interesting," Pahner said. The video from the nanitter bug was extremely grainy. There was only so much any system can do with a nanometer of visual receiver, but the audio enhancement at the receiving end did a much better job with the sound. "Hmmm. 'It was an August evening and, in snowy garments clad . . . .' "

The nanite transmitter resembled, in many respects, a very small insect. It could move itself, not just stay in one place, and this one had jumped from the spearhead Cord had given Xyia Kan to the king's ear. From there, it was party to every conversation the king had, and it had made it evident that the king was either on the level or a very good actor.

"I think he's serious." O'Casey wiped her face with a cloth that came away sopping with sweat. "I can think of a double-blind situation where he might be trying to crack the Great Houses through the threat of Cord's tribe, but I don't believe that's what he's trying for two reasons. First, he sounds *awfully* angry, and I don't think he's that good an actor. And second, even if he was, any attempt like that would be terribly risky. He'd have to have a second force available to act as the cavalry. Where is it?"

It was a particularly hot and muggy day and the room had both windows open to catch the breeze. One of Marduk's gully washers had just finished, and even the skeeters seemed to be sluggish as they struggled through the incredibly humid air.

"He could be collaborating with Cord's enemies," Kosutic suggested, tugging at an earlobe. "The other two tribes. The . . ." She paused to consult her toot and slapped at a bug. Her hand came away red. "Hah!"

"Dutak and Arnat," Roger said offhandedly. He was holding a bit of meat up, trying to teach the dog-lizard simple obedience. "Sit!"

It wasn't working. The dog-lizard measured the distance to the meat, the gravitational forces, and Roger's own reactions, and flashed out like a snake.

"Damn," Kosutic said with a laugh, wiping her hand on the tabletop. "Down another morsel, Your Highness?"

"Yeah," Roger said sourly. The animal was friendly enough, and seemed to be intelligent, but it was completely uninterested in learning tricks. It came when called, but not if too much time elapsed between treats. Although, even when it wasn't called, it followed Roger around most of the time now. When he went to the audience, it had been closed up in one of the smaller rooms and, from reports, none too happy about it. It had two vocalizations: a sort of hissing purr that it made when it was happy, and a battle-roar. The dog-lizard was still young, but its roar was already rather loud.

"You should name it," Kosutic told him. "Call it 'Bullseye.' "

"'Cause it's so accurate at taking bits from my hand?" Roger sounded testy.

"No, because one of these days you're gonna shoot it!"

"If we can get back to business?" Pahner suggested. "Sergeant Major, do you actually find it likely that Xyia Kan is collaborating with the other tribes?"

"Nope. That was more in the nature of brainstorming, Sir. I'm fairly sure that Cord or his brother has some intelligence on those tribes, and we should check that out with Cord. If they do, they'd be bound to know about something that large."

"Agreed." O'Casey said. "Cultures at that level usually know, in a broad sense, what's going on with surrounding tribes. If one of the tribes were preparing for a full-scale assault, it would be known."

"And these people don't seem to have roving mercenaries," Pahner observed. He pulled out his pack of gum and counted the slices, then carefully put it back away in its sealed container. "What's the upside for one of the other Houses?"

"Unknown." O'Casey consulted a pad and snorted. "What I wouldn't give for a copy of *The Prince* right about now! Fortunately, I've got most of it memorized, but we need more information."

"Right." Pahner scratched his chin. "I think we need to bug the Great Houses."

"What pretense could we use?" Kosutic asked. "Why do they let us in?"

"Well," O'Casey mopped her brow again, "we're going to have to buy equipment and supplies anyway. Why don't we send a squad and one of the officers around with a list of bids?"

"That could work." Pahner started to fish out his gum again, and stopped. "We'll just send Julian along."

"Why do we care?" Roger asked. He had, with difficulty, placed a morsel of meat on the dog-lizard's nose. Now he slowly withdrew his hand, planning on stepping back before giving the dog-lizard the word that she could have the choice bit.

The dog-lizard had other ideas. The instant the pressure of his hand on her snout was relieved, she flashed her muzzle in two directions with an intervening "Clop."

"Damn." Roger gave up for the time being and looked up with a shrug. "I mean, why should we care if these barbs beat each other bloody? We just need to get our supplies and get out of the way. Let The People overrun them. Or not."

He looked around at the staring faces, and gave another shrug.

"What? We're not here to save the world; we're here to get off it. Isn't that what you've been telling me, Captain Pahner?"

"We're going to be here for a few days at least, Your Highness," O'Casey pointed out carefully. "We need a fairly stable area to prepare in before we head out."

"And we need the local boss backing us," Kosutic said, without meeting the prince's eye. "Having strong backing is a whole different thing from just having him say 'ain't that nice.' If the King is really backing us, we'll have a much easier time. The troops will have an easier time."

"Correct, Sergeant Major," Pahner said formally. "I strongly recommend, Colonel, that we obtain more intelligence before we fail from either action or inaction."

"Oh, very well," Roger said. "But I hate the thought of staying in one place any longer than necessary." He looked out the window towards the distant jungle. "Maybe Cord and I can see what sort of game there is in the jungle."

"If you do, Your Highness," Pahner said in a painfully expressionless tone, "might I ask that you take a significant force with you. Also, we won't be able to spare the armor. We seriously drained the power systems on the march here; we'll need to pack the gear from here on out."

"And that means we need some of those big pack beasts, Sir," Kosutic said. "And handlers for them."

"And we need local weapons," Pahner agreed. "We have to have the advanced equipment to take the port and for emergencies, but we need to obtain local weaponry and start training with it as soon as possible."

"And all of that will take money and time," O'Casey said. "And *that* will require a stable base."

"I got it." Roger sounded even testier than he'd intended, but the heat and humidity were starting to get to him. "I'll talk to Cord about the training. He's been wanting to teach me the spear already. I'd prefer a sword, though."

"Be hard to make a good sword with this rotten metal they've got." Kosutic looked around as the others regarded her with surprise and shrugged. "It's not a big deal; I know that much about swords. Good ones are made out of fine steel, and I don't see much steel around here."

"We'll have to see what we can find," Pahner said. "Sergeant Major, I want you to get with the platoon sergeants. We don't let the troops out until we get the lay of the land. I'll assign that to you, initially. Move out with a group and get a feel for what we're dealing with and what sorts of trade we can get for our items. And when the troops *do* go out, I want them moving in groups. Understood?"

"Understood, Sir. What are we going to do for pay?"

"Is that a problem?" Roger was surprised. "We're feeding and clothing them, and they are getting paid. We just don't have access to it."

"It will be, eventually, Your Highness," Pahner told him. "The troops will want to buy souvenirs, local food . . ."

"Alcohol," Kosutic grunted.

"That, too," Pahner admitted with a grin. "And that takes pay. We'll need to factor that into our budget."

"Arrgh!" Roger clasped his head in his hands. "I don't care *what* we get for those shovels and lighters. It won't be enough!"

"All the more reason to have a friend at court, Your Highness," Pahner pointed out, then glanced at the others. "I think that wraps it up. I'll pass on the relevant sections to the lieutenants, including the intel pass. Sergeant Major, tomorrow I want you find the local market and check it out. Take a squad and a couple of the headquarters people with you."

"Yes, Sir," Kosutic said. She already had the relevant group in mind.

"Your Highness," Pahner said, "I know you feel cooped up here. But I'd really prefer that you not go hunting in that jungle."

"I understand," Roger sighed. Maybe the heat was sapping him, but he just didn't feel like getting into an argument. "But I can circulate in the city?"

"With sufficient security," Pahner conceded with a thankful nod. "At least a squad and fully armed."

"But not armor," Roger argued.

"Fine," Pahner said with a slight smile, then nodded briskly. "I think we've got us a plan, people."

CHAPTER TWENTY-SEVEN

Lieutenant Gulyas looked elsewhere as Julian dealt with the guards.

"My officer has come upon matters of trade," the sergeant said grandly. "He wishes to speak to the Kl'ke." The Mardukan guard might overtop him by a meter and a half, but a Marine could out hauteur any old barb. "We are expected," he concluded with a slight sniff of derision.

The guard looked down his nose at the diminutive human, but turned and banged on the door.

The House of Kl'ke was of a piece with the other Great Houses the squad had visited. The walls were granite, unlike the wood of the rest of the town, and coated in highly decorated plaster. The walls of the Great Houses were covered in bas reliefs and decorative arches, and the dominant theme of each House's art was its primary trade. In the case of Kl'ke, the bas reliefs depicted a variety of forest prey, for the House had been founded on the skin and leather trade. There were no windows on the first floor, and, as in the citadel visitors' quarters, the narrow openings in the second-story walls were more like arrow slits than windows.

As with all the other Houses, the front door was massive—over two stories high and constructed like a castle gate. The heavy wood was a Mardukan equivalent of ironwood that was virtually impervious to fire, and the door was banded and studded with bronze. Knocking it down would require time and a good battering ram.

Set into it, again, was another of those odd doors like the entrance to their visitors' quarters. Low enough to require a Mardukan to duck to enter it, it not only put a visitor's head in position to be opened up like an egg, but also symbolically caused him to bow to the holder of the House.

The lower portal opened to reveal another impassive guard. This worthy waved them in, and they entered one by one. Unlike Mardukans, the humans could walk through standing up.

The interior was similar to a series of concentric Roman villas. The outer wall held inward-facing rooms on all levels, but there was also an "inner" building of wood which was where the majority of the House's business was conducted. The area immediately behind the gate was a vaulted entranceway, with several doors to either side. It was open on the inner side, revealing the gardens that surrounded the inner sanctum.

The guard led them through the gardens and from there into the inner house. This was also open at the center, and surrounded yet another garden. Passing around the edge of this garden, they entered the back of the house, where Gulyas and Julian were separated from their squad of guards and led to a small, high-ceilinged room. The room was open on both sides to let in the air, and the walls were of multiple woods, cunningly crafted to give an impression of rolling waves.

It held a high table, behind which the Kl'ke stood making notes in a ledger.

Gulyas had the spiel down pat now and nodded to Julian, who began laying out samples.

"As you know, Sir," the lieutenant began, "we are visitors from a far land. The items that we carry are very few, but of such surpassing workmanship that each is, in itself, a jewel of craftsmanship."

Julian had laid out the chameleon cloth, and now began demonstrating the utility of the multitool. The part that got to the Kl'ke was the same as the one which had so intrigued all the house-leaders: the final "blade" function which cut cleanly and easily through one of the soft iron spearheads.

"There are only a limited number of each of these items, and when they're gone, they're gone. We'll be holding an auction for each of them," the lieutenant continued as Julian demonstrated Eterna-lights and fuelless lighters.

"The auction is to be held in the public square on the fifth of T'Nuh." That was six days from now; time enough for the Houses to conspire to cheat them if they so chose. Of course, the humans would be listening to every word if they did.

"In conclusion," Gulyas said, stepping forward, "let me offer you this lighter. It is useful for starting any type of fire, and is impervious to wind."

The lieutenant demonstrated this time, ensuring that the bug was well and truly planted on the alien. He'd let Julian plant the others, but he wanted to do at least one himself.

"Does the Kl'ke have any questions?"

The Mardukan thumbed the lighter and held it to a piece of the local paper until it flamed. He put the small fire out quickly, and cocked his head at the humans.

"You say 'not many' of these devices," he said,

gesturing with the technological artifact. "How many is 'not many'?"

"That hasn't yet been determined," Gulyas admitted. "For the multitools, somewhere between seven and twelve."

"Ah." The house-leader made a Mardukan gesture of agreement. "Not many, indeed. Very well, I shall ensure that a factor is present to bid and has full instructions."

"Thank you, Sir," Gulyas said. "And, of course, most of the money will be coming back to Q'Nkok. We'll be purchasing food, equipment, and pack beasts for our long journey."

"Ah, yes." The Mardukan lord grunted a laugh. "Your quest for fabled Voitan."

"It isn't actually Voitan we seek, Sir," Gulyas corrected tactfully. "But from Voitan there are routes to the northeast. Thus we must pass near Voitan."

"Well, it's still a waste of good transport," the Mardukan said with another grunt. He seemed undisturbed by their probable death. "But I have a full stable of the beasts. The best in the city."

"We'll keep that in mind," the lieutenant said, bowing his way out of the room.

"See that you do," the house-leader snapped as he went back to his ledger.

Roger looked into the distorted mirror and turned his head to the side. The ponytail left hair dangling everywhere, especially in this damp heat. What he really needed was a braid but there was a problem with that. Finally, he took two more leather ties and wrapped the ponytail in the middle and at the bottom. Now if they'd just stay in place, his damned hair would stay out of his face.

The knock on the door was followed by its opening so quickly that the two blended. He spun in place to scorch whoever it was, but paused when he saw that it was Despreaux. Just because he was having a bad hair day didn't mean the sergeant should be blasted.

"What?" Unfortunately, the question came out before he could control his irritated tone. So even *without* meaning to, he managed to sound like a jerk.

"Captain Pahner has called a meeting for 14:30," the sergeant replied blandly.

"Thank you, Sergeant!" the prince snapped, then sighed. "Let me try that again, if you don't mind. Thank you, Sergeant."

"You're welcome, Your Highness," the Marine said as she closed the door.

"Sergeant?" the prince called hesitantly. They were going to be on this planet for a long time, and he might as well bite the bullet on this one.

"Yes, Your Highness?" Despreaux replied, opening the door again.

"Could I have a moment of your time?" Roger asked, quite sweetly.

"Yes, Your Highness?" the sergeant repeated rather more warily as she stepped into the room.

"If you don't mind," Roger said, clearing his throat, "this is somewhat private. Could you close the door?"

Despreaux did, then crossed her arms.

"Yes, Your Highness?" she said for a third time.

"I know you're not a servant," the prince said, fiddling with his hair, "but I have a little problem." He took a deep breath and went on despite the hammerlike look on the sergeant's face. "It's something I can't do for myself: Could you possibly braid my hair for me?"

"There's no reason for them to notice the plant, Sir," Julian said as they walked away from the building.

"So why am I drenched in sweat?" Gulyas asked.

"Because . . . it's hot?" Julian suggested with a smile. "Sir?"

Gulyas smiled at the NCO's quip and stopped to look back at the building.

"What do you think?" he asked quietly. As long as they used Standard, no one was going to be able to know what they were talking about. But it never hurt to be careful.

"Like shooting fish in a barrel, Sir," Julian responded. "Two exits. Complex interior, but not bad. All the guard rooms at the front, servants at the back, family in the middle. If we need to take one, or even two or three, it won't be much of an op." He paused and then continued ruminatively. "Of course, it would use up ammo."

"Not much," Gulyas responded. "Okay, only three more to go. You can plant those; that was too much fun for me."

"Ah, that's nothing, Sir. Did I ever tell you about the time I stole a space limo?"

"You never learned how to braid your own hair?" Despreaux asked. The prince had the best hair she'd ever run across, solid without being too coarse, and long as a Mardukan day. "This is gorgeous stuff."

"Thanks," Roger said calmly. He wasn't about to tell the sergeant how sensuous it felt to have her brushing it. "Just another legacy of illegal gene engineering."

"Really? Are you sure?"

"Oh, yeah," Roger said ruefully. "No question. I've got the twitch muscles of a shark, the reactions of a snake, and *way* more endurance than I ought to have. Somebody on either Mommy or Daddy's side, or both, did a lot of engineering back in the Dagger Years, but I guess anyone who had the cash would have done the same thing then, rules or no rules. I even got enhanced night vision out of it."

"And Lady Godiva's hair. But you'd better learn how to do this yourself."

"I will," Roger promised. "If you'll show me. I've always had *someone* to do it for me, but I think servants are going to be in short supply on Marduk, and Matsugae didn't know how, either."

"I'll show you how. And it can be our little secret."

"Thanks, Despreaux. I really appreciate it. Maybe you can get a medal for it," he added with a laugh.

"The Order of the Golden Braid?"

"Whatever you want. As soon as we get back to Earth, I'm rich again."

"Rich city," Kosutic said.

This was the third bazaar the team had found, and it was of a piece with the others. The majority of the market was permanent, wooden stalls set side-by-side on narrow alleyways. There were also occasional open areas where temporary carts were set up, selling everything imaginable, but most of the trade was in the back alleys.

Kosutic had initially entered those with care. She'd been on enough planets and around enough alleys to know that they contained both the best and the worst available on worlds like this. The Marines had dispensed with armor, and if she gave them the chance, these Mardukans could be a nasty proposition at close quarters. So she was slow. And careful.

As it turned out, the alleys were generally the best part of the market. The small shops were very old and established, and had not only the best items, but better prices. Unfortunately, the products weren't what they wanted.

The region was a supplier of raw material and gems. There was more than sufficient food and leather goods available for their purposes, but what they really needed—pack beasts and weapons—were expensive and hard to find.

She stopped at one of the small booths selling weapons as a sword on its back wall caught her eye. The Mardukan running the booth squatted on a stool, and still overtopped her. Even by Mardukan standards he was a giant, and it appeared that he might not always have been a merchant. His left true-arm ended in a stump at the elbow, and his chest was an Escher painting of scars. Both horns had been capped with bronze points that were wickedly sharp, and a hook depended from the arm stump.

He looked up at what she was staring at, and slapped his hook with his remaining true-hand.

"You know that?" he asked.

"I've seen it before," she said carefully. "Or something similar."

The weapon was unlike the others she'd seen in the bazaar, for the steel was damascene. The black and silver water pattern was clear as day. The blade was long for a human, short for a Mardukan, and curved to a slightly widened end. It was neither precisely a katana nor a scimitar, but something in between.

And it was flat out beautiful.

She'd seen swords of that type on several worlds, but all of them were much more advanced than this one's tech level. Or than the local tech level, at least.

"Where is it from?" she asked.

"Ah," the merchant said, clapping his cross hands. "That's the sad part. This is a relic of Voitan. I have heard of you visitors, you 'humans.' You are from a far land, so do you know the story of Voitan?"

"Some of it," Kosutic admitted. "But why don't you tell it to me from the beginning?"

"Have a seat," the local invited, and reached into a bag to extract a clay jug. "Drink?"

"Don't mind if I do." Kosutic looked over her shoulder at the small group which had been following her around. Besides Koberda's squad, it consisted of Poertena and three of Cord's nephews. "You guys go circulate." They'd each been given an Eterna-light and a lighter. "Do a little trading. See what they bring. I'll be here."

"Do you want someone to stay with you, Sergeant Major?" Sergeant Koberda asked. His tone was mild, but the orders had been fairly strict.

Kosutic raised an eyebrow at the merchant, who grunted in reply.

"No," she said with a headshake. "I'm just gonna sit here and shoot the shit for a while. I'll give a holler when I'm ready to head back, and we can link up."

"Aye." Koberda gestured at his squad; he'd seen a place that looked a lot like a bar a few alleys back. "We'll be circulating."

Poertena followed Denat down the alleyway. He figured that three of Cord's nephews counted as "a group," and the Mardukan swore he knew the best pawn shop in the city.

The shopkeepers and artisans to either side of the narrow way looked up with interest as he passed. Word of the humans' arrival had spread through the grapevine, but he was surprised that there wasn't more overt curiosity. On most human planets, there would at least have been a group of children following him around, but not here. For that matter, he didn't see any children or women, and hadn't since they arrived in the area.

"Where are tee women?" he asked Denat as the Mardukan took another turn. Poertena decided that if they got separated he would be in trouble finding his way back.

"The shit-sitters lock them away," the tribesman said

with a grunt of laughter. "And the children. A stupid custom."

"Well, I'm glad you got pocking respect for tee locals," Poertena said with a bark of laughter of his own.

"Pah!" Denat spat and made a derisive hand gesture. "Shit-sitters are for killing. But if we kill one, it's the knife for us, as well."

"Yah." Poertena nodded. "I guess they probably give a fair trial and slit your throat."

"No." Denat stopped for a moment to get his bearings. "The town law doesn't apply to us. If we violate a town law, we're turned over to the tribe. But for a killing, the tribe will give us the knife as quickly as the town. And any townsman found violating our laws is turned over to the town. Just as our tribe judges us more harshly than the town would, the town judges its people very harshly.

"Ah." He'd obviously located the landmark he sought. "This way. It's close now."

"Put why do tee town kill t'eir folk for breaking your laws?" Poertena was confused.

"Because if they don't," Tratan said from behind him, "we'll burn their abortion of a shit-city to the ground."

Denat grunted in laughter but clapped his hands in agreement.

"They dare not offend us too greatly, or we'll attack them. Or camp outside Q'Nkok and pick them off in the open until they don't dare step outside their gates to relieve themselves. But they can also attack us, attack our towns. We had a war soon after this city started to grow, and it was terrible on both sides. So we keep the peace."

"For now," Tratan said with a hiss.

"For now," Denat agreed. "And here we are."

The shop was similar to all the others, if a bit smaller. Made of some hardwood, it was abutted on both sides

by other shops and looked to be about five meters deep,
but the opening was half covered with a leather curtain
that shadowed its interior. Inside, dim shapes of piled
skins and containers could be barely discerned, but there
were more goods piled outside on a leather ground cover
spread out into the narrow alley.

The products were a magpie's nest of gewgaws.
There were a few spearheads, some jewelry (ranging
from decent to quite bad), tools for wood- and metalworking, cups and platters, candle holders of ruddy
brass, leather and wood boxes (some elaborately decorated), spice containers, and a myriad of other items
piled haphazardly.

Squatting in the midst of this disorder was an old
scummy. His right horn was broken at the tip, and the
mucous covering his body was patched and dry, but for
all that, his eyes were bright and interested.

"Denat!" The merchant got creakily to his feet. "You
always bring such interesting things!" he continued,
eyeing Poertena.

"Time to do a little trading, Pratol," Denat laughed.
"I brought a few things, and my friend here wants to
show you some others."

"Of course." The merchant pulled a bottle and some
cups out of one of the boxes. "Let's see what you
brought. I know you'll cheat me, as you always do, but
if you promise not to take too much of my money,
perhaps we can bargain!"

"T'at sounds like we goin' to tee cleaners," Poertena
observed with a chuckle of his own. It felt like home.

CHAPTER TWENTY-EIGHT

The "tavern" was a large tent, open on all sides and located on one side of the square that defined the beginning of the bazaar. A series of upended barrels at one end served as the bar, and behind the barrels the carcass of some unknown beast turned slowly over a large brazier.

There were several long tables scattered throughout the tent, and the Mardukans gathered at them shoveled in the barleyrice, meat, and vegetables being served with gusto.

The square was a bazaar in its own right, with temporary booths scattered around its periphery. It wasn't a planned opening—simply a space between one of the Great Houses, a warehouse, the bazaar, and a drop off. Two roads led out of it: one down past the warehouse, and the other up past the Great House. The square was also, clearly, a hangout for the guards from the House. They strode around in their leather armor and carrying their broad headed spears as if they owned the area, which in a way, they did. The merchant eyed them warily, and Koberda doubted that they paid for most of their trifles.

The NCO looked up from his heavily spiced stew and waved to Poertena. The armorer had picked up another scummy, this one an old guy, and he looked pleased with himself.

"Hey, Corp," the Pinopan said. The tables everyone else was standing at came nearly to his head, so he found an empty barrel, rolled it over, and upended it to provide himself with a highchair. "Watcha eating?"

"Some *hot* shit," Andras said, taking a pull on his beer and waving at his mouth. "I don't know what they're putting on that damn stew, but it is hot, hot, *hot*."

"Sounds good!" Poertena headed for the bar.

"I made a deal with the guy," Koberda said. "We all eat free for one of those Eterna-lights."

"Ayah!" The new scummy clutched his head. "That I didn't need to hear! I'll go see if I can negotiate being included in it!"

Denat laughed and picked up the jug in the middle of the table. He shook it, took a sip, and grimaced.

"Pah! Shit-sitter piss!"

"Better than that rotgut you served," PFC Ellers said with a laugh. The grenadier took another bite of meat and sipped more beer. "At least you can taste something of the beer."

"Hey," Cranla, the third of Cord's nephews, protested. "We just expect some taste in our drinks."

"Taste, sure," Ellers agreed. "But did you have to add the turpentine?"

Poertena turned back up with a large platter and put it on the table. The table was long, constructed of a thick slab of almost black wood taken from a single trunk. The humans had occupied one end, and the tribesmen gathered around them, snatching at the hot slices of meat on the platter. There were also slices of fruit, and a sliced root the humans didn't recognize. It was good, though—somewhere between a sweet potato and a white potato.

"Smells good," Denat said, popping a piece of the highly spiced meat into his mouth, then choked. "Ayeeeeii! Peruz!" He grabbed for the beer jug as the spice kicked in.

"Pock!" He took a huge gulp of beer and gasped. "Whai-ee! I guess that beer's not so bad after all!" he wheezed.

"Where are you, Koberda?" Kosutic asked over the communicator.

"Ah, my squad is just finishing up lunch, Sergeant Major," the NCO replied, putting down his cards and looking around.

The squad was sprawled around the tables, taking it easy. The heat of the day had been building, and most of the Mardukans had beat it for cooler climates. But it wasn't really all that bad under the tent: no more than 43 Standard, or 110 on the old Fahrenheit scale.

Poertena had started up a poker game. He'd apparently taken the old Mardukan merchant for a ride dickering over a couple of Eterna-lights and lighters. Now the old guy was trying to get his own back . . . in a game he'd never played before.

Koberda picked his cards back up and looked at them in disgust. Poertena had let him exchange some of his imperial credits for a few pieces of the local silver and copper. He knew he should've kept them in his pocket. "Fold."

Poertena looked over his cards at the old Mardukan. The merchant looked at his cards, then at the pot.

"I raise you," the Mardukan said. He thought about it, then tossed one of the Eterna-lights into the pot. "That should be worth more than that pile."

"Yeah," Poertena agreed with a smile. "Or lunch for twelve."

"Ayah! Don't remind me!" Pratol snapped.

"Pace it," the Pinopan said. "Koberda got taken!"

"Well," the squad leader said, wondering just how much the little Pinopan had squeezed out of the obviously experienced pawnbroker, "somebody did."

Poertena gave his cards another glance and shook his head.

"Fold."

"I like this game!" Pratol gave a couple of grunts and reached out with all four arms to scoop in the pot.

"Yeah, yeah," Poertena said as he dealt the next hand. "Just you wait."

"Hah!" Tratan said suddenly. He had gotten sense and dropped out while he still owned his weapons. "Look at those shit-sitter pussies!"

A group of five armed scummies was passing the eatery. The Mardukans were armed with swords, which they carried in the open, rather than scabbarded. The swords were long, straight, and broad; they would have been two-handed weapons—at least—for any of the humans.

Unlike other guards the humans had seen, these wore full coverage leather armor, with plate patches on the shoulders and breast. They were obviously guarding the lone unarmored scummy in the middle of their formation, who carried a small leather purse slung on a strap around his neck. Apparently, he had less than total confidence in the stout-looking strap, since he also clutched the purse in both true-hands.

"What's t'at?" Poertena asked. He picked up his cards and stayed very, very calm.

"Gem guards," Pratol replied. He tossed in two for draw.

"Pussies," Tratan repeated. "They think all that fancy leather makes them immortal."

"I wouldn't mind some armor." Koberda picked up the beer jugs and shook them, looking for one that wasn't empty. "If Talbert'd had some armor, she'd still be here."

"Yeah," Poertena agreed as he drew two cards. It was down to three players, and that was too few for a good poker game. Denat was still hanging in, though. He'd traded a couple of nice gems to Pratol for some silver and credit on goods. Now he was trading on some of Tratan's silver and the edge of his credit. Poertena glanced up at him as he looked at his draw, then set his cards down in disgust.

"Fold."

Poertena looked at his own cards and didn't smile. Fortune favored the foolish.

"Raise you." He looked at his pile, and flicked over a tiny lapis lazuli. It was an exquisite royal blue, shot through with lines of raw copper.

"Hmmm." Pratol pushed over a pile of silver and added his own lapis, slightly larger and polished into a large oval. "See you and raise."

Poertena looked at the pile and rolled over a ruby.

"See you an' raise, ag'in."

Pratol tilted his head to the side suspiciously, then pulled out a tiny sapphire like a flick of blue fire, and placed it carefully atop the pile. The blue and red gems were of a piece, dark but translucent. The gems of the region were its greatest treasure, and watching them glow in the center of the table made it abundantly clear why that was true.

Poertena picked up the sapphire and the ruby and put them side-by-side. Then he looked at the rest of the items.

"I t'ink the pot's light," he said.

"Okay." Pratol tossed a few pieces of silver and a small citrine onto the table. "Now it's not."

"Call," Poertena said. "Four sevens."

"Crap!" The merchant slammed down his cards. "I still like this game."

"I'm out," Denat said. "I want to keep my weapons."

"Why, young tribesman?" a new voice asked. "I'd be happy to sell you more."

Kosutic and the merchant she'd stopped to talk with were both smiling as they watched everyone else jump. They'd approached the group so silently that no one had noticed them coming, and Koberda cleared his throat.

"Ah, Sergeant Major, we were just . . . uh . . ."

"Gathering energy for the coming march?" she asked. "Don't sweat it, Koberda. But you need to keep at least one person alert at all times. We're still not out of the woods here. Clear?"

"Clear, Sergeant Major," he said, and then an eyebrow crooked as he noticed the oddity sticking up over her shoulder. "Is that what I think it is?"

"Yep." Kosutic drew the sword over her shoulder. The ripples of silver and black were muted in the overcast gray sunlight, but it was clearly a work of art. "I like it, but I actually got it for the prince. It was designed for the child of a king, so it's human-sized."

"Yeah." Koberda nodded. "I can understand that. But what about other weapons?"

"Alas," the hook-handed merchant replied, "this isn't a good area in which to look for large supplies of weapons or armor. The weapons available here have mostly been made elsewhere. They're from T'Kunzi, or even relics from Voitan, as is this one."

"Folks, meet T'Leen. He used to be a trooper until he lost the arm. Now he sells swords."

"Spears and knives also. Anything with a blade. Mostly to the guards of the gem merchants and the occasional group of mercenaries," T'Leen said, fingering one bronze-capped horn. "Or the House guards, occasionally. There are both independent gem merchants and those of the Houses in the town. Although," he added, "the House merchants sometimes make it . . . hard on the independents."

"Pah!" Pratol said, looking up from his examination of the poker deck. He really liked this game. It was better than knucklebones because it included elements of bargaining and skill as well as luck. Very interesting.

"The Houses are all peopled by bastards!" he went on. "They squeeze us until we're dry, then have their bully boys come around to wreck us so that we leave town!"

"That has, admittedly, happened more often than one would like," T'Leen agreed soberly. "This is a piss-hole of a town."

As if to punctuate his remark, there was a crash of metal across the square.

Two groups, one a cluster of toughs from the local House, and five fighters from a rival, had clashed near the edge of the square. The home team far outnumbered their rivals, but they didn't use their superior numbers to overwhelm the invaders. Indeed, the invaders seemed to be far more proficient as individuals, particularly two who were each using a long dagger or short sword in a lower false-hand. The additional weapon was used almost purely for blocking, and Kosutic wondered why they didn't use something like a small buckler shield. Since the local fighters persisted in taking on their more skilled opponents one-on-one as scummy military tradition appeared to require, they were also taking heavy casualties despite their numerical advantage.

The spears were used somewhat like bayoneted rifles, Kosutic noticed. Their technique emphasized blocking and thrusting, but also parries and ripostes which humans weren't normally taught with bayonets. There was very little contact, but what there was was bloody, for the broad spearheads caused wide and deep wounds.

The injuries being suffered were serious, but clearly not life-threatening. If one of the local fighters felt he was getting ready to lose, he simply withdrew, and someone else took his place.

The rival house's fighters had so far not faced anyone who was their equal, but just as it seemed that the locals were going to lose totally, the doors of the House opened, and a group of guards in heavier armor emerged.

"Ah, now you'll see something," T'Leen said. "The guards from Crita were chosen from among their elite. They came here to see what the new N'Jaa guards are like, and now they will. The newcomers are N'Jaa's elite—they're considered the best in the city."

"Are they?" Kosutic asked.

"Possibly," the weapons merchant snorted. "But that's not saying much. The local bully boys aren't up to any but local standards. They should go collect debts for the House Tan."

The two groups squared off, and the battle began. The local elite was both more heavily armored and unwinded, so it was short and furious. When the two groups parted, two of the Crita fighters were laid out, apparently dead, and so was a N'Jaa. The surviving Crita had beaten a hasty retreat, chased by jeers from their N'Jaa opponents.

"There!" T'Leen said. "Did you see that riposte in *secundus* K'Katal made?"

"I don't even understand what you just said," Kosutic replied, tapping her mastoid bone to get the toot to translate into Standard. "What's *secundus*?"

"Down here." T'Leen gestured with a false-hand. "Great move! I've only seen it once before, in Pa'alot. Very difficult to execute—you have to have your feet positioned just so. But if you perfect it, it's very difficult to defeat." He pantomimed the move and grimaced when the necessary contortion drew a twinge from some scar tissue. "Ouch."

"Where'd you learn all this?" Koberda asked. "I mean, what? Were you a guard?"

"Yes," T'Leen said, abruptly losing the animation he'd drawn from his explanation. "But not for a long time. My fighting days are over."

"He was from Voitan," Kosutic said quietly.

"I was an apprentice weapons maker," the old merchant explained. "I'd traveled with a caravan to T'an K'tass when word came back that the Kranolta had swept down and taken all of the outlying cities. Gone was S'Lenna, shining city of lapis and copper. Gone was fair H'nar, perhaps the most beautiful city I've ever seen in all my travels. Gone were all the other sister cities of far Voitan.

"Voitan held, though. We had word through the few who could trade with the Kranolta without losing their horns. The barbarians attacked her repeatedly, but the walls of Voitan were high, and they not only had great stores of food, but could still trade across the ranges to the cities on the far side.

"T'an K'tass knew the worth of Voitan. No one in all the lands knew the making of weapons as did the Steel Guild of Voitan. No one else knew the secrets of the Water Blade. And Voitan and the region around it were the source of most of the metals that T'an K'tass and the other southern city-states depended upon.

"The Council of T'an K'tass called upon the other cities to send a force against the Kranolta, to drive through to the aid of Voitan. But no such thing had ever been done, and the other cities didn't see the need. They saw only the wealth of Voitan, as the Kranolta had, and laughed at the fall of all that fair land."

His face turned very bitter, and he became quiet, looking back over the years at that memory.

"The King of Pa'alot and the Houses of this stinking Q'Nkok both repudiated us. That was before the House of Xyia arose to the kingship. I will admit that Xyia spoke for us, or so I have heard.

"I was on the delegation from T'an K'tass that went to Pa'alot to plead our case, but they said that each state must survive or fall on its own. They asked what they had gotten from Voitan that they should risk their money and goods, and to that question I could make no answer." He clapped his false-hands in sadness. "I could not answer for my lords of Voitan.

"So T'an K'tass sent out a force by herself. And we met the Kranolta in the Dantar Hills." He clapped his false-hands again, softly. "We were defeated. The Kranolta were as numerous as the stars in the sky, as the trees in the forest! And fierce, fierce!

"We fought through the day and into the next, but we were defeated. Finally, we could fight no more and retreated in good order. But the Kranolta pursued us to T'an K'tass." He clapped his false-hands once more. "They followed us wherever we went."

"And they took that city," Kosutic concluded grimly. "And two others in the area. And that was the last news of Voitan that anyone has heard."

"Some few of us remain," T'Leen said sadly. "A few of the House Tan escaped with the force. They're doing well financially; they got out most of T'an K'tass' specie and went into the banking business. We talk from time to time.

"And there are a few left of Voitan. Such as myself. A few." The Mardukan shook his head. "So very few."

"How long ago was this?" Koberda asked.

"I was a youth," T'Leen admitted. "Long, long ago."

"No seasons," Kosutic pointed out with a shrug. "No sun. They don't count time like we do, and your guess is as good as mine how old any of these guys are."

"Hang on a second," Bosum said, setting down a glass of water. "This is the place we've got to go next?"

"You betcha," Kosutic said with a grim smile. "Or at least the *way* we have to go. Right through them Kra... Kra..."

"Kranolta," Poertena said helpfully.

"Yeah. Them bastards," Kosutic said with a laugh. "I'd suggest you make sure your plasma rifle's in good shape, Marine."

"Yeah," the newly arrived corporal agreed. "No shit."

CHAPTER TWENTY-NINE

Roger moved the blade across slowly, trying to remember the way the move felt.

"What is that?" Cord asked. The shaman had begun teaching the human his own half-remembered lessons in the sword, but this move had a look he didn't recognize.

"I took a semester of something called 'kendo' when I was in school," Roger replied, frowning in concentration. His feet were wrong, and he knew it. "But I can't remember the moves!"

He made a small adjustment, but it was still wrong, and he growled inwardly in frustration as the ghost of Roger III and all those generations of MacClintock history fanatics enjoyed a hearty horselaugh at his expense. He'd fought tooth and nail to avoid his *kendo* classes. Officially, he had objected to them because they took time away from his other martial arts classes; in fact, as he'd made certain his mother knew, he had simply refused to embrace their stupid traditions. It had been a petty triumph, perhaps, yet one he had treasured at the time when she finally gave up and let him drop out.

Of course, that had been then, and this was now. . . .

Cord cocked his head and examined the stance. The four arms of the Mardukans meant that many of the methods of the humans, and not just weapons craft alone, were different in detail. But despite both the inevitable differences and the partial nature of what Roger recalled, Cord recognized a more advanced technique when he saw one.

The two had been working out with the sword Kosutic had procured for the past two days while the company rested and the commanders waited for better information. Pahner had joined them from time to time to watch Cord at work, and generally approved. The old scummy had been imparting far more than just weapons instruction; maybe what Roger had truly needed all along was a coach.

"It is always about balance, young prince," the Mardukan said, walking around Roger as the human moved through his *kata*. "You're off your center."

Roger stopped, and the Mardukan looked at his foot placement, then grunted. He tapped one foot with the butt of his spear.

"Try from there," he commanded, and Roger took the steps of the *kata* again, and smiled.

"You did it again, you old sorcerer."

"You need to learn to find your balance better," the Mardukan said, with a clop of teeth. "If you don't have your balance, *everything* is harder. If you have your balance it is not necessarily easy. But it is far easier than otherwise."

He looked up as PFC Kraft entered the salle. The training room was in a part of the castle distant from the visitors' quarters, so there was a squad of Marines outside the door, and the rifleman tapped his helmet to indicate that he'd received a transmission.

"Captain Pahner says he'd like to see you, Your Highness. At your earliest convenience."

Roger opened his mouth to retort angrily at the interruption of his session, then closed it again as Cord laid a hand on his arm.

"We'll be there in a moment," the Mardukan said. "Please send the Captain the Prince's regards."

Kraft nodded and withdrew, and, as the door closed, Cord grunted in laughter.

"Center, young prince. The wise monarch listens to his generals in matters of war, to his ministers in matters of state, and to his people in matters of morality."

"Ha!" Roger laughed. "Where did you hear that one?"

"It was in the writings of the Sage of K'land," the barbarian shaman admitted with a shrug.

"Why in the hell did you go back to the jungle?" Roger asked as he picked up a cleaner cloth to wipe down from the workout. He'd discovered that the shaman was as well read as any sage in the city, one of the reasons Xyia Kan listened to his pronouncements with such care. He was far more than just a "dumb barbarian," and now he clapped his false-hands in a Mardukan shrug.

"I had duties to discharge to my tribe. It needed a shaman; I was the shaman."

"I hope Teltan can fulfill the trust you placed in him."

Roger shook the cloth to clear the majority of the filth it had picked up. The cleaner cloths actively removed dirt and grime from any surface and were easily cleaned for reuse. Unfortunately, they eventually wore out, and soon the company would have to find a substitute, which wouldn't be easy. The Mardukans didn't bathe. They didn't need to, and their mucus coverings would have prevented the use of anything like soaps. They did have some cleaners designed for equipment, but they were unbelievably harsh. It would be an . . . experience to take a bath in them. Rather like lathering up with bathroom cleaner, Roger suspected.

There were many similar problems. Equipment had already started to break down in the oppressive heat and humidity. Several Marines were already without functioning helmets, and two plasma rifles had been deadlined by Poertena. As the journey went on, it would only get worse, and Roger wondered idly what they would look like at the end of the trip. Would they be covered in skins and swinging swords like the one he was putting away? It was an unpleasant thought when he considered that their ultimate objective was a fortified spaceport.

"We all have challenges to face," Cord said, and Roger had a sudden sense that the old Mardukan was responding to much more than the prince's comment about Teltan, as if he could read the other thoughts flowing through his *asi's* mind.

"It is each man's life to rise or fall to *his* challenges," the shaman went on gently. "Thus are we judged."

The command group sat on pillows on the floor of the room which had been designated as the headquarters. It was the first time since they'd left the shuttles that they'd all been gathered in a single place, and Roger gave a silent snort as he thought about what one grenade in the room would do. However, the only grenades were in the hands of the Marines, and they, so far, were supporting the chain of command. Or Pahner, at least.

The captain stood at the end of the room at parade rest as Lieutenant Jasco, the last member of the command group, came in and grabbed a seat. Pahner waited to be certain all of them had their pads out, then cleared his throat.

"Lieutenant Gulyas and Sergeant Julian have finished analyzing the take from their listening devices, and they're prepared to report on just what we're facing here.

Lieutenant Gulyas has suggested that Julian present the data. Julian?" he concluded, glancing at the noncom who'd been trying to stay inconspicuous in the corner.

The normally irrepressible sergeant was clearly ill at ease as he got to his feet and took Pahner's place, looked around the room at the assembled officers, and activated his own pad.

"Ladies and gentlemen," he began, glancing at Cord, squatting behind Roger, "this report has been developed from several sources besides our monitoring devices. However, *all* sources clearly point to one conclusion: we're in a snake-pit.

"There are several factions in this town, most of them working at one or another plot, and mostly to cross purposes. If any of the locals, including the King, have any idea of just how many of these plots and counterplots there truly are, I would be very surprised.

"The single plot that's of particular interest to us, however, is the one which focuses on the issue of woodcutting, and why the woodcutters continue to violate treaty provisions, despite repeated threats from Cord's tribe." He looked at Lieutenant Gulyas as if in question, but the officer only nodded and made a "go on" gesture with one hand.

"As it happens," Julian said, turning back to the rest of his audience, "the Lieutenant and I see a clear opportunity in this situation for us. What we need is to . . ."

"Would you mind explaining that to me again?" the king said carefully.

Cutting through protocol to arrange the meeting, especially quickly, had been difficult. In the end, the "guest list" had come down to Xyia Kan, Roger, O'Casey, Pahner, H'Nall Grak, the commander of the king's guards (and the only one in the room with a visible weapon), and Sergeant Julian. The choice for the final human

member had been between Julian or the intelligence
lieutenant, but Gulyas had recommended that they take
the NCO. It turned out that most of the plan had been
Julian's from the first.

"You're in what we call *rok-toi*, Your Majesty," he
responded now. "That's a complicated and nasty food in
our . . . land . . . that smells to high heaven.

"There are three Houses involved in a complex plot
against your House. They've been sending the woodcutters and hunters, managed through intermediaries,
into the woods to stir up The People. They've also
switched out the high-quality goods in the last two
shipments for those of lesser quality, also to enrage
Cord's people.

"At the same time, they've been resisting your calls
for increased defense, because they plan on taking over
the town, using a group of Kranolta."

"That's the part I'm afraid I don't understand," the
king admitted. "Not even the C'Rtena could be stupid
enough to believe they could control the Kranolta
inside the city walls! Could they?"

"Frankly, Your Majesty," O'Casey replied, "that's
exactly what they believe. The group of Kranolta they've
hired is fairly small, only a few hundred, and most of
them will be fighting The People outside the walls. But
they've been promised that after the fighting they can
sack portions of the city: specifically, the bazaars where
the independent tradesmen are based. The conspirators
are of the opinion that they can limit the depredations
of the Kranolta to the bazaars and the lesser houses.
Perhaps one or two of the great Houses who aren't part
of their plot. But any damage to those groups would only
leave them in a better position at the end."

"They're mad!" Grak snarled. The scarred old soldier
grunted in grim humor at the thought. "If the Kranolta
leave one stone standing on another, it will only be so

that there's something left for the rest of their tribe to pick over!"

"Well, yes and no," Julian said. "Our . . . information includes data on the Kranolta which is apparently new. It appears Voitan did fall, finally, but the Kranolta were significantly reduced in number in the process. The tribe remains smaller than it was, and it's more or less stagnated since the fall of Voitan." The intel NCO shrugged. "Of course, even granting all of that, I still think the correlation of forces is adverse."

Grak translated the translation and laughed again. "Adverse. Yes. And what do they think we shall be doing, hmmm? When they let the Kranolta in through the gates?"

"What they think, General," Pahner answered, "is that most of you will be dead. The Royal Guard is responsible for the defense of the city, and you'll spend yourselves fighting The People. Then the Kranolta will come in, wipe out the remnants of both forces, destroy the competitor minor Houses, and sack the independents in the bazaars. The King, who enjoys support among both groups, will be left without either a support base or a guard. He may keep the castle, but it's more likely he'll be deposed by the remaining guards."

"I'm fascinated to hear this," the king said. "But I would be even more fascinated to know where *you* heard it."

The humans had discussed how to answer that question when it inevitably arose, and had come to the conclusion that there was no good response. Pahner had originally wanted to avoid telling the locals anything which might reveal their intelligence-gathering capabilities or, even more importantly, limitations. Then there'd been the ticklish point that admitting that they'd spied on the Great Houses—and how—would probably start the king wondering whether or not they'd spied on *him*.

It was O'Casey, backed by Kosutic, who'd put forth the counter argument. By imperial standards, Q'Nkok and its monarch were primitive, but that certainly didn't mean Xyia Kan was unsophisticated. The likelihood that they'd spied upon him was going to occur to him whatever they said, so there was little point trying to hide the fact that they could. On the other hand, the king's confidence in them required that they at least make an attempt to convince him that they could gather otherwise unobtainable information reliably, and Julian faced the monarch squarely.

"Your Majesty," he said, "the information was gathered through what we would call 'technical means.'"

The king considered the sergeant's toot's translation effort for a moment, then grunted.

"'The way of pumps'? What in the Nine Halls of Kratchu does *that* mean?"

"I'm afraid our translations aren't quite up to explaining that, Your Majesty," Roger told him, and Pahner hid a smile at his unwontedly diplomatic tone. "Your irrigation systems and their pumps require the services of highly skilled mechanics, so the device which translates for us chose that term to substitute for one of our language's terms which refers to something which also requires great skill and long training. With all respect, you've seen our multitools and other devices. Could your artisans duplicate them? Or explain to another how they function?"

"No." The king didn't appear excessively pleased at making the concession, but he made it promptly.

"That's because *our* artisans have learned things yours have not yet discovered, Your Majesty," O'Casey stepped in, once again wearing her diplomat's hat. "And those same artisans have constructed devices which may be used to . . . observe and listen unobtrusively at a distance."

"You have mechanical *spies*?" The king glanced around the meeting room with a suddenly speculative expression, then returned to his attention to O'Casey.

"Ah, yes. That is to say, in a manner of speaking—"

"That must be a marvelous advantage . . . assuming that it's true. And that your description of what they've reported to you is accurate."

"You're wise to consider whether or not we might have motives of our own to deceive you, Your Majesty," Pahner said calmly. "But would it be possible, now that we've brought this information together for you, for you to confirm it by other means without allowing any of your enemies to realize you have?"

The king thought about that for a moment, and looked at Grak. The old soldier fluttered his hands, and then, finally, clapped them in agreement and turned to the humans himself.

"Yes," he answered.

"And if we do confirm it, the method by which you obtained it will be beside the point," the king told Pahner. "The question is, what shall we do about it if your reports prove accurate?"

"Actually," Pahner replied with a grim smile, "that's the easy part, Your Majesty."

"We kill them all," Julian said.

"And let the gods sort them out." Grak snorted. "Yes, I've heard that one. But how? Three Houses against the Royal Guard is still a . . . What was that term you used?"

" 'An adverse correlation of forces,' " the sergeant answered. "Actually, you'd be at just about at parity, with the advantage of a single unified command against a bunch of conspirators who don't trust anybody— including each other—as far as they can throw them. Of course, they've been planning this for quite a while, so at best, you'd have about a fifty-fifty chance of kicking their butts. However, Your Majesty, General Grak, there's an intersection of needs here. We need equipment, supplies, and transportation across this continent. Frankly, we need funding."

"And *you* need a force to crack this conspiracy," O'Casey cut in, smoothly maintaining the double-team approach. "Our company can supply that force. We'll break the conspiracy, uncover all the evidence you need to prove the conspirators' intent to bring in the Kranolta, point out the other Houses that were aware of the woodcutting part of the plot, and force concessions from all of them in your favor. In return, we'll retain a portion of the seizure and fines, and you'll lend your weight to the filling of our needs so that we obtain the quality of goods and services we need."

"Mutual benefit, indeed," the king murmured. He rubbed his horns. "If, of course, there is such a conspiracy."

"There is," Pahner said. "But confirm it, by all means. Please. In the meantime, we'd like to begin cross-training our people in local weaponry with your guard. That will make a good cover for getting integrated with them.

"But we would greatly appreciate it if you could make your inquiries quickly, Your Majesty. We've discovered that we have a particular need to strike before the auction we've arranged for our goods. It turns out that the Great Houses have also conspired to fix the bidding," the captain finished sourly.

"Yes, they would." Xyia Kan gave a grunting chuckle. "Have no fear. I shall make inquiries quickly, and if they are, in fact, conspiring to release the Kranolta upon the city, then we shall act even more quickly."

"But beyond this," Roger said, "there's still the problem of wood. The crisis which the conspirators are busy exploiting isn't entirely artificial."

Pahner was a highly trained, superbly disciplined professional. Which explained why he didn't wheel around to glare at the prince. Roger had done quite well in helping to explain why they couldn't explain how their "mechanical spies" worked, but that contribution to the meeting had been discussed and agreed upon ahead of time. Given his rank among the human visitors, it had been all but imperative to put the weight of his princely status behind that explanation, and the fact that he had a flair for the local language had also been a factor.

No one, however, had suggested that His Highness had anything else to add. Certainly no one had *discussed* anything else he might contribute, which meant that whatever he was up to now was going to be ad-lib. So the captain gritted his teeth and reminded himself that he couldn't rip his royal charge's head off. At least, not in front of outsiders. All he could do was pray that whatever harebrained idea the young idiot was going to concoct this time wouldn't queer the deal just when things had been going so satisfactorily.

"No," Xyia Kan agreed with a hiss of dissatisfaction. "It isn't artificial. If it were, they wouldn't be able to use it so effectively. We must have a new source of wood if Q'Nkok is to survive, but we've exhausted our supply in the area the X'Intai permit us to cut, and the Kranolta hold the other side of the river. Woodcutters who cross to their side of the river do not return. Some solution to this must be found, for it would be pointless to stop the conspiracy and *still* have the X'Intai attack."

"As I understand it," Roger said, nodding in agreement, "besides building, the majority of the wood cut for Q'Nkok is used for cooking and metalworking. Mostly as charcoal. Is that right?"

"Yes," Grak answered. "The majority is used in cooking fires."

"For which coal would work just as well, wouldn't it?" Roger asked, tugging on his braid.

"Coal?" Xyia Kan produced a Mardukan frown. "Perhaps. It's used in some other cities, at any rate. But there's no coal source anywhere nearby."

"Actually," Roger said with a grin, "there's one on the other side of The People's territory. Just upriver from Cord's village, in the mountains. In fact, I saw indications of several unmined minerals up there, and just down the mountain from the coal, at Cord's village, the river becomes navigable."

"So the coal could be packed to the village on *flarta*," the king said with a pensive expression, "then transferred to boats for the trip to the city. But I've heard of this valley. It is filled with *yaden*. Who would be so foolish as to go there to dig mines?"

"Well," Roger said with a thin, cold smile, "I was thinking that you might *start* with the members of the deposed families and their guards."

This time Pahner did glance at the prince—not in irritation, but in surprise. He hadn't heard that particular tone of voice from Roger before, and he suspected that the ruthless side the prince had just revealed would have surprised any of his old acquaintances. His tone wasn't cruel, just very, very cold, and the captain suddenly realized that when the kid had delivered that suggestion he'd looked a good bit like his umpteenth-something grandmother, Miranda I. She'd been famous for a certain lack of pity where enemies were concerned. Of course, such things could be taken too far, but it also might be the first symptom of a spine.

Now if only it could be moderated into decency.

The king, on the other hand, only grunted in laughter and glanced at his general before he looked back at Roger with a handclap of agreement.

"An elegant solution, young prince. You would make an excellent monarch someday. I've noticed that if you have only one problem, it is often insoluble, but that if you have many problems, they solve each other. We have a conspiracy to break, a need to fulfill, and hands to fulfill it. Excellent."

"In order to pull all of this together, we need some of my officers," Pahner said. "And we need to get down to planning quickly."

"Agreed," the king replied. "But we don't move until I've confirmed this."

"As you say, Your Majesty," Roger replied for the group. "We exist but to serve," he finished sardonically.

On the way back to their quarters, Roger found himself nearly alone with Captain Pahner. He glanced around to ensure that no one besides Marines were in the area, then sighed.

"At least Mom doesn't have to put up with conspiracies like this," he said. "I'd hate to deal with backstabbing bastards like N'Jaa and Kesselotte all day long."

Pahner stopped as abruptly as if he'd just taken a round from a bead rifle and stared at the prince, who continued for another step and a half before he realized the Marine was no longer beside him. He turned to the captain.

"What? What did I say this time?" He could tell he'd upset the officer, but for the life of him, he didn't have a clue how.

Pahner felt breathless. For a moment, he could only shake his head, speechless at the naïveté of the statement while he tried to figure out if the prince was trying to feel him out or if the young idiot really was that blind. He finally decided that it could be either, as impossible as that seemed. Which meant the truth was the best answer.

"You—" He stopped himself just before he called the prince an idiot and cleared his throat.

"Your Highness," he continued then, in a calm and

deadly voice, "your Lady Mother deals with plots ten times as Byzantine as this every day of the week, and twice on Sunday. And she comes up with, I guaran-damn-tee you, better answers than this one. *She* would figure out a way to have all the Houses continue under current leadership on a completely different political track, and I wish to hell that we could do the same.

"However hard we try not to, we *are* going to kill innocents with this 'bigger-hammer' approach, and that doesn't make me a bit happy. Unfortunately, none of us are as smart as the Empress, so we'll just have to muddle through and hope she manages to survive all the crap headed her way while we're trying to get home!"

Roger stared at him, eyes wide, and the Marine snorted bitterly. Whatever the prince might think, Pahner knew only too well just how false the surface serenity of the Empire of Man was, for he'd had access to intelligence reports very few mere captains would ever see.

"You think I'm exaggerating, Your Majesty?" he demanded. "Well I'm not, so for God's sake wake up and smell the coffee! You think, perhaps, that all of us are here on sunny Marduk because we *want* to be? You think that *DeGlopper* just happened to have a few minor technical problems which had nothing at all to do with your presence? *Somebody* slipped a toombie onto your goddamned ship and marooned us on this God forsaken planet, and I guarantee you it wasn't N'Jaa!"

CHAPTER THIRTY

Julian looked around the rainy midnight square.

His armor's light-enhancement system made the details as clear as day . . . not that there was a great deal to see at the moment. The tavern had been taken down, and the food vendors had packed up for the evening. Which was normal. The city always more or less rolled up its streets at dusk, but this was still eerie. No people at all were moving on the streets, and the shutters on every house had been closed almost before the square emptied. Clearly, the common folk knew something was going down.

It had taken barely a day for the king to confirm the broad details of the humans' intelligence. The clincher had been a scouting foray by some of the city's few skilled woodsmen, who'd found the Kranolta force awaiting word to move on the city exactly where the humans had told them to look. That had been more than sufficient for the king to give his go-ahead.

The Council had been summoned once again, this time at night. Its members were currently at dinner, or so said the latest situation report. Now all three platoons were in position and ready to move.

Julian's own squad of armor had been spread throughout the company. Since the chameleon suits were going to be effectively useless against the low-speed impacts of swords and spears, Captain Pahner wanted the virtually impregnable armor on point for the entry. Which was why Julian found himself standing in front of the door to House N'Jaa, scanning the surroundings, checking his paltry power levels, and wondering if there was something that could penetrate ChromSten armor on this planet after all.

"Teams check in," the communicator said. Lieutenant Sawato had that remote, robotic tone down cold; she sounded like a bad AI answering machine.

"N'Jaa team in position," Sergeant Jin announced. Third Platoon had gotten N'Jaa, since it was the largest and toughest House. Lucky them. They might be the more experienced platoon, but they were also short a squad.

"Kesselotte team, in position," came the next check, and Julian wondered if the Old Man were listening. God knew that very shortly he was going to be busy enough his own self.

"C'Rtena team, in position." Lieutenant Jasco's response was late, and Julian called up the remote plot on his helmet HUD and grimaced. The remote reported that C'Rtena's backdoor still didn't have anyone covering it, but just as he thought that, the last few troopers got into position.

Each mansion, unbeknownst to its inhabitants, now had two-thirds of a platoon parked outside its front door under cover. Even worse, two troopers in powered armor were poised to lead the entry, with the rest of the force in support. In Julian's case, the backup was across the square, ready to jump off instantly when the word came.

The unit had moved up in nearly complete silence, which, coupled with the chameleon systems of their uniforms and armor, made it extremely unlikely that anyone had even noticed their passage, despite the narrow, twisting streets.

The third squad of each platoon was on the backdoor of that platoon's objective, ready to plug the bolt-hole, and each detachment was also accompanied by a squad of Royal Guards. The remainder of the armored suits were at the castle, ready to move as reinforcements if they were needed.

Which they shouldn't be.

"All right," the XO said finally. "All the pieces are in position, and the dinner is underway. All teams: *Execute*."

Julian drew a deep breath. He shouldn't be nervous; there ought to be zero danger in this for him. And worrying didn't help matters, anyway. It was time to do the deal, and he raised a hand and knocked on the door, hard.

K'Luss By paused just as he was about to throw the knucklebones. He'd heard that there was some new game going around, one that used pieces of paper, but he was a traditionalist. Knucklebones had been good enough for his father, and they were good enough for him.

"Who the hell is that?" he asked rhetorically, looking around at the other guards in the front room, and T'Sell Cob clapped his false hands and shrugged, then picked up his favored ax as the door boomed again.

"I don't know. But he's about to be in pieces."

"*Open in the name of King Xyia Kan!*" a voice boomed through the hallway.

"Ah," By said as he picked up his own spear, "maybe we ought to wait for the others to join us?"

❖   ❖   ❖

It had always bothered Julian that there was no way to fidget effectively in armor. He wanted to pick at a finger, or bite fingernails. Nope. Pull hair? Nope. The best he could do was to fiddle with his bead cannon as the sensors indicated more and more guards gathering in the front area. A loud boom suddenly racketed through the night like a rogue thunderclap, and his sensors processed the sonics and electromagnetic flux and then announced that a full powered charge from a plasma cannon had just struck something at the facility the HUD designated "House C'Rtena."

Nice to know the sensors were working.

He nodded at PFC Stickles and stepped to the side of the vast door.

"Gunny, I'd say we've got about max participation here," he said, keying his helmet to darken. It was supposed to do that automatically, but it never hurt to make sure. Regrowing eyeballs would suck on this rock. "Stickles, darken your helmet."

"Yes, Sergeant," the PFC shot back just a tad testily. "Already done."

He was the junior guy in the squad, which was why Julian had picked him as his own backup. Better that Julian be stuck with the rookie, although, to be fair, a "rookie" in the Regiment was hardly the same thing as a rookie in a regular unit.

"We're ready here, Gunny," Julian said, and leaned into the wall and pointed his bead-cannon to the vertical as he took it off safe. Time to party.

"What was that?" N'Jaa Ide demanded. The booming echo was similar to thunder, but not identical. "It sounded like one of the weapons of these visitors, these humans," the house-leader went on with an ill-pleased glare.

Mardukan state dinners, in Q'Nkok, at least, were conducted on platters and covers on the floor. This one was no exception, and by careful manipulation of the seating arrangements, the human guests had been placed opposite the house-leaders considered particularly dangerous. And, just coincidentally, all of those humans were accompanied by Marines in armor.

"What was what?" Xyia Kan asked innocently. The monarch's power had been systematically hamstrung and undercut by the Houses for a generation, the very Houses which were about to be removed, and his dinner had been deliciously flavored with anticipation all evening.

"That noise," Kesselotte said in support of N'Jaa, sounding even more suspicious than his fellow house-leader. After the last acrimonious meeting, he'd insisted on bringing his full complement of guards to this one. Indeed, there were over twenty house guards present, far more than should have been allowed into the king's presence. Perhaps it was time to act. Sometimes even the deepest plots were improved by a willingness to take advantage of opportunities, and one such as this was unlikely to come again. He glanced at N'Jaa to see if the other leader was in agreement, but saw only worry.

Kesselotte was still considering the significance of the human weapon when two more booms echoed across the city. They were just as loud as the first one, and his eyes flew wide as other strange crackling noises followed them.

"Brothers!" He leapt to his feet. "It is an attack by the faithless Xyia Kan! We must—"

Before he could finish the sentence, two of the human leaders came to their own feet and drew weapons.

Pahner had been infuriated by Roger's insistence, but in the end, he could only accede to his demands. At least this time the prince had made them in private! So when the captain stood and drew his bead pistol, Roger stood up right alongside him. O'Casey, at least, had the intelligence to scuttle behind the armored trooper at her back, then out the door.

Each of the Houses involved in "The Woodcutters Plot" had brought its maximum of three guards. In addition, two other Houses which were fully aware of that plot and were involved in others of their own against the king, had brought their maximum, as well. It was up to the humans to ensure that none of those extra guards did anything unpleasant.

Two of Xyia Kan's bodyguards picked the king up and interposed their armored bulk between him and danger as the humans opened fire. Since each guest's guards were placed to watch his back, and since the prince and the captain been seated facing the plot leaders, all their targets were lined up in a neat, formal row down the opposite wall.

It was Hell's shooting gallery.

Armand Pahner had been shooting one weapon or another for the better part of his seventy-two years. The M-9 bead pistol was an old and dear friend, so as he began servicing targets, his hand moved as steadily as a metronome. The small bead pistols had tremendous recoil, which meant the maximum rate of accurate fire depended primarily on how fast the shooter could get the weapon back on target. Armand Pahner had plenty of bulk and plenty of forearm strength, so in the first four seconds, eight guards were slammed back against the far wall, staining the pale wood with huge splashes of blood before they slumped to the floor.

At which point, it was all over.

Sixteen of the guards had been designated as threats, and it had been decided that the bead-cannon of the armored Marines were a bit too overpowering for an enclosed space . . . particularly since the idea was for all the "lords" to survive. So it was up to the pistol-armed "officers."

Pahner had moved from right to left, concentrating on picking off the guards that were quickest to respond. The first to react were a couple of N'Jaa elite, but before either of them could draw a sword or hurl a javelin, they were both bloodstains. The rest went down nearly as quickly, but by the time he'd cleared "his" zone, the prince's zone was already empty.

He looked at the eight blood splotches, all high on the wall where Roger's assigned targets had stood, then at eight headless bodies, and turned to his charge.

"*Head shots?!*" he demanded incredulously.

Roger shrugged and then smoothed his hair as the house-leaders erupted in consternation, some wailing at the blood that covered everything—the people, the floor, the wall, the ceiling, the food.

"My toot has a *very* good assassin program, Captain," he said.

"Assassin program?" Pahner repeated. "There was no mention of any 'assassin program' in *my* brief, Your Highness!"

"I suppose that's because a secret weapon isn't very effective when it's not a secret," Roger said with a slight smile, then shook his head as the Marine's eyes narrowed. "I didn't mean to sound sarcastic, Captain. I didn't know you hadn't been told, and that's the only reason I can think of for your briefer, presumably Colonel Rutherford, *not* to tell you."

"Um." Pahner glanced at the bodies again. The pistol beads' damage was too extreme to be certain, but it looked as if every one of those shots had been dead center, and it happened that the Imperial Marines in general and The Empress' Own in particular knew quite a lot about combat enhancing toot software.

Pahner had several of the same sorts of packages tucked away in his own toot, for example. And because he was familiar with them, he knew that there were limits in all things. A package like the one the prince was suggesting was basically a shortcut for training, probably with some fairly impressive sight enhancing overlays to boost accuracy. But it was only a *training* device, one which had to have a human interlock if its possessor wasn't going to go around mowing down innocent bystanders in job lots, and no one knew better than a combat veteran how completely training could desert a man the first time it truly dropped into the pot.

That obviously hadn't happened here. Armand Pahner had a very clear notion of the sort of intestinal fortitude required for a combat newbie to stay focused— and confident—enough to take a single head shot, much less *eight* of them, rather than blazing away at center of mass.

"Head shots," he repeated, shaking his head, and the prince shrugged again. "Not even a samadh in your honor."

"Well, I didn't want anybody getting hit by accident," Roger said. "Safety first!"

"Now let's think safe here, okay people?" Gunnery Sergeant Jin admonished as First Squad entered the building. He was in the middle, watching everyone else's actions as the squad's troopers executed their dynamic entry. The most dangerous part of an entry like this was friendly fire. They had overwhelming firepower and good technique, but it was just as easy as ever to be shot by your own side.

He kept a careful eye on the squad's weapons. Each member had a zone to cover, including straight up, and the team leaders and Despreaux were ensuring that every-one covered his own area and not some random other.

"Julian," the gunny said over the com, scanning the upper stories as they came into the gardens around the inner house, "we're in the open. Be careful where you shoot."

The rounds from the powered armor's bead-cannons would go through the flimsy wooden walls as if they were tissue. There was plenty of evidence that the armored troopers had already been through; the swath of destruction looked like one of those pack beasts had gone on a rampage.

"No problem," Julian replied. "We're not firing much anymore. Most of them are being driven to the back. Make sure Third Squad is ready for them."

"Movement!" Liszez announced. "Balcony."

Jin saw two or three weapons twitch in that direc-tion, then settle down on their own sectors, as he looked up. A single Mardukan, probably panicked by the fire, was running down the balcony to the right. It looked like one of the small females.

"Check fire. No threat."

"Check," Liszez responded. If the target had been clearly hostile, it would already have been an ink blot pattern. "Clear." She disappeared around a corner.

"Target!" It was Eijken, and the grenadier triggered a round as the Mardukan who'd charged into view drew back his arm to throw a javelin. The forty-millimeter grenade hit just to the left of the native and tossed him sideways like a mangled doll. "Clear."

"Center building clear," Julian reported. "Entering back rooms."

"Don't get too far ahead," Jin told him. He paused and looked around. "Time to split. Despreaux, take Alpha Team into the left wing. I'll take Bravo to the right. Clear front to back."

"Roger," Despreaux acknowledged, and jerked her head at Beckley to lead her team out. "Alpha, echelon left. Move."

The team leader nodded acknowledgment of the order. She'd already spotted a downstairs doorway, and now she spotlighted it with an infrared laser designator. "Through there. Kane, take the door. Go."

The reconfigured team trotted towards the door with the plasma gunner in the lead. When she was fifteen meters away, the gunner triggered a single round into the heavy wooden door, which disintegrated in a roar of flame.

Kyrou and Beckley performed the primary entry. Kyrou went through and to the right and dropped to a knee. No more than five meters away a scummy was already starting to hurl the spear in his hand. Unfortunately for him, Kyrou reacted from thousands of hours of training, and the spearman was hurled backward by the hypervelocity beads punching into his chest. Another burst cleared a group further down before it could decide whether or not to attack.

"Right clear."

There was a burst from behind the private.

"Left clear," Beckley called. Another burst. "Really clear."

Despreaux set a cracker charge against the door opposite their entry point, and the thin, high expansion-rate charge shattered the simple bolts on the other side and scattered splinters of the door throughout the area.

She blasted the scummy on the other side of the doorway before she realized it was one of the females. Not only were they entirely untrained for combat, but this society sequestered them. This might have been the first time in this one's life that anything more exciting than sex had occurred. And it had been brief.

The sergeant gazed at the pathetic, shredded body, then inhaled sharply and looked around.

"Stairs," she called sharply. "Ground floor clear."

She stepped back out into the hallway, wiping at a line of blood from a flying splinter, and looked around. She pointed down the corridor.

"Kyrou, Kane," she said, then gestured at the stairs. "Beck, Lizzie." The team leader lead the way, and Despreaux followed. She carefully didn't look back at the pitiful shape sprawled in the shadows of the stairs.

Later for that. Later.

CHAPTER THIRTY-ONE

"Clear," Pahner said, nodding his head at the report over the helmet radio. It had nearly killed him to let Lieutenant Sawato take point on managing the company, but he'd had to be at the dinner. And better him on the line than anyone else in the company when that particular bucket of shit hit the rotary air impeller. Except, maybe, Roger. Which still had him floored.

Pahner was not the type to judge anyone by his ability to shoot. He'd known too many consummate bastards who happened to be good combat shooters to do that. But between Roger's surprising ability with weapons and the occasional depths he revealed, the captain was feeling distinctly whipsawed. Ninety percent of the time, he wanted to throttle the spoiled brat, but, lately, there'd been times when he was almost impressed. Almost.

He checked the maps and grunted at the report from Jin.

"Okay, I'll take it up with His Majesty. Make sure you hold the treasury, but don't get involved otherwise."

He looked over to where Xyia Kan was sitting. Most

of the blood had been washed off, but the king was still a sight. Bits of dried blood clung to the decorations on his horns and on his face, but he looked up alertly at Pahner's motion.

"Yes? It goes well?"

It had, in fact, gone perfectly in the castle. The ring leaders had been seized, and their crimes had been detailed to the other house-leaders. Those leaders had then been instructed to send orders to their own Houses to stand down their guards on pain of the same sort of assault. Pending the delivery of proof of their crimes, the leaders of N'Jaa, Kesselotte, and C'Rtena had been separated and imprisoned. Those who apparently hadn't had any knowledge of the plot had been released to return to their homes; the others were still being held in the dining room, surrounded by the now rotting blood of the dead guards. The psychological effect was salutary.

"It goes okay," Pahner said. "We took casualties at C'Rtena, which I didn't expect. No one got hurt bad, though, and other than that, we got off clean. But we have fires at C'Rtena and Kesselotte, and the troops need somebody to come put out the flames. And your guards are looting. My people can't get them under control."

"They will," Grak said with a resigned handclap. "How do you stop soldiers from looting?"

Well, you can, for example, kill them until the survivors figure out it's not permitted, Pahner thought with a mental snarl.

"I don't suppose you can," he said aloud, calmly. That shrug-your-shoulders, what-the-hell attitude was the sort of thing he had to ensure didn't happen with Roger, he told himself. There was a fine line between ruthless and evil . . . and another between sloppy and barbaric. At the back of his mind, though, the song called. "I suppose that's what makes the boys get up and shoot."

"I'll send servants to put the fires out," the king said. "And soldiers whose job it will be to make sure they do so," he said pointedly to Grak. "And to *prevent* them from looting. Is that clear?"

"I'll go myself." Grak hoisted his broad-headed spear and grunted in laughter. "Maybe I can pick up a few pretties myself."

After the general left, Pahner found himself alone with the king. Roger had gone to wash, and the various guards had been dismissed. The situation was irregular, but the captain ignored that as he followed the movement and condition of the company on his pad.

The monarch, for his part, watched the human officer. So somber and serious. So precise.

"You see no difference between us and the barbarians of Cord's tribe, do you?" he asked, wondering what answer he would hear.

Pahner looked up at the king, then tapped a command, sending half the reserve to reinforce First Platoon while he considered the remark.

"Well, Sir, I wouldn't say that. Overall, I think it's better to support civilization. Barbarism's just barbarism. At its best, it's pretty awful. At its worst, it's truly awful. Eventually, civilizations have the ability to pull themselves up to a condition which is better for everyone."

"Would you have assisted me if you didn't need supplies for your journey?" the monarch asked, fingering the decorations on his horns and flicking off a bit of dried blood.

"No, Your Majesty," Pahner shook his head, "we wouldn't have. We have a mission: get Roger to the port. If this operation hadn't advanced that, we wouldn't have done it."

"So," the monarch observed with a grunt of laughter. "Your support for civilization isn't so deep as all that."

"Your Majesty," Pahner said, pulling at a stick of gum and carefully unwrapping it. "I have a mission to complete. I will continue trying to perform that mission, whatever it takes. And so will my Marines. That mission has damned little to do with our individual survival and *everything* to do with maintaining a degree of continuity in our political environment." Pahner popped in the gum and smiled grimly. "Your Majesty, that *is* civilization."

Roger watched the Mardukan mahout securing his armor on the giant pack beast. The creature looked very much like the one which had been chasing Cord, but the native insisted they were different. Roger thought Cord was probably right. The Cape buffalo looked very much like the docile water buffalo, and there was no more dangerous beast on Earth. Of course, these looked like giant horned toads, not buffalo. Capetoad. He wondered if he could get the translation system to start substituting the term.

He also wondered, not without some trepidation, if he could master the local mahouts' skills himself. He'd always had a way with animals, and he'd been in the saddle of his first pony almost literally before he could talk and his first polo pony before he was ten, so it seemed possible. Despite that, he found the elephant-sized *flar-ta* daunting, and he didn't even want to consider how the rest of the company felt about them.

Still, they'd best get over it and learn. They'd been far luckier than they deserved when Portena and Julian turned up with D'Len Pah in tow, and Roger knew it even if the Marines as a whole seemed unaware of their good fortune. Of course, for all their survival training, they were much less accustomed to using

animal transport in inhospitable regions than Roger was
thanks to his taste for safaris, but the prince had been
shocked by Pahner's apparent blithe assumption that
they could simply buy their own animals and handle
the beasts themselves.

Fortunately, D'Len Pah had made the company a better offer. *Flar-ta* were scarce in Q'Nkok, and even with
the king's strong support, the prices being demanded had
been astronomical. Just buying the necessary pack beasts
would have come close to bankrupting the humans,
despite the hefty slice of Xyia Kan's fines and confis-
cations which had come their way. They certainly
wouldn't have had enough left for the other supplies they
needed.

But D'Len Pah had turned up in the nick of time.
He and his clan were something like a cross between
Old Earth's gypsies and professional caravaneers—
semi-nomadic freight carriers who owned and managed
their own string of *flar-ta*. Roger had been astounded
when he arrived at the citadel with Julian and Portena
to offer his clan's services to the humans, since no one
else in Q'Nkok had wanted to go anywhere near the
lunatics who thought they could actually get through to
Voitan. But D'Len Pah had gone by the Houses the
Marines had taken down to make a personal examination of the wreckage, and he'd also talked to survivors
who'd seen the humans' weapons in action. Clearly, he
calculated that if anyone could get through and reopen
the long-closed (and highly profitable) trading routes
through Voitan, Bravo Company was that anyone.

Roger had come to suspect that there were other fac-
tors at work, as well. For one thing, he was pretty certain
Xiya Kan had strongly "suggested" to D'Len Pah that
it would be in his best interests to make the offer. For
another, the chief mahout clearly hoped to pick up some
of the offworlders' marvelous devices and knowledge for

himself. And, finally, the scummy had insisted on receiving two-thirds of his payment up front, before leaving Q'Nkok . . . and extracted a promise that he would not be required to hand it back over if—or when—the humans actually encountered the Kranolta and realized they had no choice but to turn back or die.

For all that, though, D'Len Pah and his clansmen looked like tough customers in their own right. They were well armed, by Mardukan standards, and clearly accustomed to looking after themselves. No doubt they had to be, since their entire families, including women and children, traveled with them. They were likely to prove a worthwhile addition to the humans' forces in a great many ways . . . and whatever else, they would at least keep Pahner from losing a dozen or so of his Marines finding out that driving a *flar-ta* was just a *bit* more complicated than handling an air lorry!

Roger grinned at the thought and looked around as the company made its final preparations to leave. It was early, barely past dawn, and the heat wasn't really on the day yet. It would be soon—turning the humidity up into the customary steam bath—but for now, it seemed relatively cool.

Everyone was checking his personal gear, making sure that it was just right. A strap out of place would make for a sore day, so it made sense to check ahead of time. Weapons were being serviced, and ports sealed against the conditions. They were down another plasma rifle, and the Old Man had indicated that they might have to put them all away in sealable bags. Roger intended to have a few choice words with whoever had approved the weapons for deployment; they'd only been on the planet for a couple of weeks, and the complicated weapons were failing left and right.

He saw the captain coming up the line of pack beasts, checking the gear. Since the *flar-ta* were carrying so many items that were absolutely vital, not to mention valuable, the Marine officer had placed a small explosive charge on each of them . . . and demonstrated the devices to the mahouts. If one of the beasts tried, for whatever reason, to run away with the company's gear it wasn't going to get far.

Pahner hadn't even bothered to mention the tracker planted on each of them.

Nor was that the only "precaution" the human castaways had taken. Somewhat against his own better judgment, Pahner had given in to O'Casey's argument and agreed that the chief of staff could brief both Xyia Kan and D'Net Delkra on the true reason for their visit to Marduk. The captain was unhappy at the thought of telling anyone anything he didn't have to, but he'd had to admit that O'Casey had logic on her side when she pointed out that both The People and Q'Nkok already knew they were effectively shipwrecked. Telling their leaders and rulers how and why couldn't increase the risk that one or both of them might have designs upon them, but—like Pahner's radio listening watch—alerting people with reason to wish them well to the fact that their trail might need covering couldn't hurt.

"Your Highness," the captain said as he reached the pack beast Roger was examining. He looked up at the prince's armor, then back at the prince himself, and smiled. "Try not to get yourself killed, Your Highness."

Roger smiled back and hefted his rifle.

"I'll try, Captain. But it's going to be a long march."

"It will that, Your Highness." Pahner fingered his breast pocket, but decided to forego a stick. "A long march." He raised an eyebrow at the item at Roger's feet. "That looks . . ."

"Fairly full?" Roger hefted the rucksack and swung it into place. "Well, I couldn't let Matsugae carry it all, could I?"

"No, I suppose not," and Pahner said, then looked up as Kosutic caught his eye and made the circular hand motion that signaled everything was in order. In the years they'd been together, he'd never had reason to doubt her, and he didn't this time.

"Well, Your Highness, it looks like it's time," he said, looking up and down the line of pack beasts and the last-minute goings-on. O'Casey, still spouting Machiavellianisms from the top of her pack beast as the king said goodbye. Cord, having a last word with the delegation from The People which had arrived to negotiate the mining arrangements. Julian, making motions of kicking down doors to one of the female privates in First Platoon. Poertena, bickering with one last merchant. But, really, they were ready to go.

"Agreed, Captain," the prince said, looking at the hills across the river and shifting a strap of his bulging pack. The bridge had been lowered to let their caravan cross, now all they had to do was find a way through trackless jungles filled with vicious enemies to a fabled lost city. And from there, on into the true unknown. He looked to the northwest and tied the braid dangling from under his helmet into a knot.

"Time to head upcountry," he said.

CHAPTER THIRTY-TWO

Roger leaned over the big kettle and sniffed.

"Is that what I think it is?"

The company had waged an exhausting battle against nature across the brutal hills. Whatever paths had once existed had been erased over the years, and they were forced to create new ones. Driving a way through the choking undergrowth for the big pack beasts would have been bad enough under any circumstances, but the hills' vicious carnivores had made it nightmarish.

They had lost Sergeant Koberda to the carnivore Cord called an *atul* and the company just called a damnbeast. It was low, fast, and hungry. About two hundred kilos, it had a triangular head filled with sharklike teeth, and a rubbery, mucus-covered skin similar to that of the Mardukans.

A burst of bead fire had torn the beast apart, but not before it had savaged the sergeant. The tough old NCO had held on for a day, riding on one of the *flar-ta*, but he'd finally succumbed. Even the nanites and Doc Dobrescu's Magic Black Bag hadn't been able to heal all the damage, so they'd bagged the popular squad leader and fired him up. Captain Pahner had said a few words, and they'd moved on. Marching upcountry.

Along the way, they'd become accustomed to the constant danger. Roger saw it all around him, and even in himself. Everyone was getting better at reading the jungle, at anticipating the dangers. The Marines on the perimeter now made a game of spotting the killerpillars in the trees, and the ones that were on the path were harvested. The fangs of the horrible worms contained two poisons, both of which were considered valuable by the Mardukans.

The whole company was changing, getting a little wilder, a little wilier. They were learning about "waste not, want not," and that if something is attacking you, it's probably edible itself. Which brought Roger back to the stewpot.

Matsugae smiled, stirred, and shrugged.

"Damnbeast, Your Highness. The one you killed. Clean shot as well, which I appreciated. Not too torn up but well bled by the time I got it."

"I can't believe we're having *damnbeast* for supper," Roger said, and brushed a recalcitrant strand of hair out of his eyes.

"Well, the troops are having damnbeast stew," Matsugae said with another grin. "Just wait until you see what the *officers* are having."

"I still can't believe that was damnbeast," Roger said, leaning back and setting down his fork.

Matsugae had somehow secured not only a large quantity of a really good wine, but a variety of local spices. The troops had seen him at various times throughout Q'Nkok, talking to restaurant and tavern owners, and when the company started out on its journey, he had immediately established himself as a cross between chief cook and caravan-master.

The result was a smoothly functioning caravan. D'Len Pah's mahouts had experience of this sort of thing, and Matsugae hadn't hesitated to pick their brains. It was the mahouts who'd suggested unloading one beast and letting it break trail, for instance, thus lightening the load on the Marines. It was also the mahouts who'd pointed out that it was silly to waste good protein just because it was trying to eat you. And that there was nothing wrong with shooting for the pot.

That last point had nearly caused Pahner to go ballistic. Hunting on the move went against every bit of his training. Modern ground warfare required that troops move through the woods as if they weren't even there, since anything that could be seen could be killed. That a unit was "made out of mist" was a high compliment, and shooting at everything that moved and looked vaguely edible was noisy anathema to his dearest principles.

But in the end he'd been forced to concede that their situation was . . . unusual. After looking at their consumption rates and how far they'd traveled, he'd agreed—not without one last, severe tussle with his military professionalism—that they needed the supplement. Once he'd conceded the point, however, he'd implemented it with his customary thoroughness, and thereafter a member of the company who was a superior marksman was routinely put up front with the point specifically to look for game.

More often than not, and over Pahner's fuming protests, Roger could be found in the same area for the same reason. He usually rode the unencumbered *flar-ta*, like some latter-day raja on an extraterrestrial elephant. It should have been faintly ludicrous, but the elevation and the fact that the pack beast wasn't recognized as a threat by the local wildlife often gave him shots well before the "official" company hunter. And he rarely missed.

This day, the only thing he'd seen on the route hadn't been, to him, food game. The crouching damnbeast would have been invisible to the point until she reached attack distance. Given their increased awareness, and the guns pushed to the front of the formation, the point might have survived the encounter. And, then again, maybe not. The question was moot, however, for Roger had shot the beast while the lance corporal was still seventy meters distant.

Now he picked at a bit of the lightly spiced meat and shook his head.

"This was good! The last time you tried it, it was . . . well . . ."

"Rubbery," Matsugae said with a laugh. "Right?"

"Yes," O'Casey said. The academic was coming to her own terms with this world. She still resented the heat, the humidity, and the bugs, but they all did that, and at least she no longer had to slip and slide in the mud. Instead, she got to ride on one of the great pack beasts, and she thought she might live, after all. She'd felt bad about being "pampered" for a while, but one of the Marines had finally remarked that O'Casey had never volunteered for this, and she'd decided not to worry about it.

She wiped at her brow and drew a breath. The tent was hot and close, but it kept out the bugs and the *yaden*. The latter never seemed to attack when people were up and about, but better safe than sorry. And since the troops had taken to zipping their one-man tents closed at night, they hadn't lost anyone else, even if it did make for hot, fetid sleeping environments.

"But this is actually quite nice," she continued, taking another bite. "It reminds me of a light-tasting beef."

Fortunately, it was also leaner than beef. A heavy meal in this climate would be devastating.

"Emu," Lieutenant Jasco said, taking another helping of barleyrice and meat. "It tastes a lot like emu."

"Emu?" Cord repeated. "I don't know what that is." The shaman rolled a ball of barleyrice and popped it into his mouth. He had pulled it from the communal bowl, as was his people's custom. Not for him these bizarre human notions of forks and such!

"Flightless bird," Roger said offhandedly. He pulled a bit of his portion of damnbeast off his plate and fed it to Dogzard, who'd been patiently waiting by his chair. "Originally from the South American pampas. It's distributed all over now. Fairly easy to raise."

"We raised 'em on Larsen," Jasco said nostalgically. "Almost tastes like home. Now, if you'd just chop up the leftovers and put them in a hotdish, I'd have to marry you," he told the valet with a grin, and Matsugae laughed with the others as he poured Roger another glass of wine.

"Sorry, Lieutenant. I already had one spouse. Once was enough."

"How'd you get it so tender?" Kosutic asked. She took a sip of wine and picked up one of the barbecued vegetables. The squashlike plant had been christened yuckini because, unlike zucchini, it had a bitter taste in its uncooked state. However, a combination of one of Matsugae's marinades and cooking over a slow fire resulted in a surprisingly delectable vegetable course. The cooking, or perhaps the marinade, left the slices with a sugary coating somewhat like a honey glaze.

"Ah," Matsugae said with another smile. "That's a chef's secret." He put his finger against his nose and smiled again, then, with a slight bow and a spatter of applause, he let himself out of the tent.

"All right," Pahner said. "I want to make sure

everyone is clear on tomorrow's march. Gulyas wants to have a word."

"I've been talking with Cord and his nephews," the lieutenant said, swallowing a bite of barleyrice and clearing his throat with a sip of wine. The vintage was fairly heavy for the conditions, almost like a sherry. But wine was wine. "As everyone knows," he went on, "we're in Kranolta territory. So why haven't we been hit?"

"Yeah." Jasco nodded. "We must have passed right by that group that was waiting to attack Q'Nkok."

"They couldn't have stayed in one place for too long," Cord said. "The strip of flatland along the river is too narrow for good hunting. That's why The People have never taken it for their own."

"Apparently," Gulyas nodded at the shaman, "hunting parties go over there when game is sparse on their side of the river. The Kranolta hunt there also, but only occasionally. For the raiding party to stay there, they had to be broken up."

"Foraging." Kosutic nodded tugging at an earlobe. "Of course."

"So we might have brushed some of them," Gulyas said. "And, conceivably, they could be on our back trail, catching up fast."

"Do you rate that as likely?" Pahner asked. He and Gulyas had already discussed this, but he wanted the entire group to hear the whole story.

"No, Sir," the lieutenant answered. "At least, not quickly. They'd still be waiting for word from the conspirators in the city. Even if a messenger preceded us, they'd have to assemble before taking us on. Even the Kranolta are going to recognize that we're a serious military threat."

"However," Cord said, scratching at the tent floor with his knife, "that was a raiding party outside its traditional territory. They wouldn't attack unless they had all the warriors necessary to destroy us. Once we enter the home territory of the tribes, they'll attack at every turn. The deeper we enter, the bolder they will become, and the more they will attack."

"So," Pahner said, "we need to begin being extra alert. The tribes don't hunt the hills we just passed through, but they do hunt the lowlands. Whether there's a big force on our back trail or not, we now face the probability of regular attacks. And we haven't the time to teach them the price of an Earthman slain."

"The troops are going to have a problem with that," Kosutic admitted. "I'm worried that they're getting sloppy. We told them to expect regular attacks through the last two weeks in the hills, and no Kranolta materialized: just big nasties. We'll need more than the Lieutenant's read on it for them to take it seriously."

Pahner nodded.

"Get with the chain of command," he told the lieutenants. "Make sure that they, at least, are aware of the likelihood. We need to make sure the troops are as alert as possible. These aren't half made recruits. Remind them of that."

Julian leaned on his rucksack and listened to the quiet of the sleeping camp. The clouds often seemed to break for just a bit after sunset, and tonight was no exception. The smaller moon, Sharma, cast a faint, ruddy light over the scene. Dim as it was, it would have been more than sufficient for his light enhancers, but he'd switched them off. The jungle seemed placid tonight, with hardly any animals stirring. Even the roars and gurgles of the normal night were muted.

That was just as well. He had two more hours as sergeant of the guard, and then he could get some sleep. Tomorrow would be another long march through the jungle, and being stuck as sergeant of the guard meant damned little rest, but for the time being, he could chill out. All the posts were placed, and he'd done a walk-around a half hour ago. Everybody was staying awake and alert, per normal.

He leaned on the rucksack a little harder and sniffed. You could still smell the stew Kostas had cooked up, and Julian shook his head. Who would have thought that the fussy little valet could have become such a tower of strength? Or turn out to be such a good cook? The actual work was done by a couple of the scummy beast drivers, but Matsugae made sure it was done right and no one was about to complain about the result. The company definitely wasn't starving, although what might happen when they ran out of barleyrice and dried fruits and vegetables was another story. Hopefully, their supply would hold out to the next city-state—

He froze at the tiniest whisper of a scrape somewhere in front of him. The sound had been almost below the level of audibility, but the Marine had unusually sharp hearing. He considered turning on his helmet enhancers, but that scrape had sounded like it was right in front of him, and the helmet would take a second or to come fully online.

He reached up and flicked on the flash clipped to his combat harness.

The low-power red light blinked on instantly . . . and revealed five forms, crawling towards him. The creatures were shaped vaguely like moths, mostly black but with a spotted pattern that turned pale pink in the red light. A score of glittering red eyes gazed back at him, and ten poisoned fangs glistened. . . .

Roger was up, out of the tent, and halfway across the encampment before he realized he'd moved. He looked down, and discovered that he had his rifle in one hand, his bead pistol in the other, and nothing on but a singlet.

The discovery slowed him just long enough for Sergeant Angell to overtake and jerk him to a halt as his tent guards got in front of him.

"At least let us get there first, Sir," the NCO said with a laugh, and handed the prince his combat harness. "And always remember to grab ammo, too. It makes it easier on us."

Roger threw on the harness and resumed his progress more sedately, surrounded by his hovering bodyguards as he crossed to a cluster of troopers gathered in Third Platoon's area. Julian sat on the ground at the center of the small group, cradling a jug of the local wine and shaking his head.

" . . . low-crawling up on me," he said. The normally upbeat NCO was obviously shaken. "No wonder we lost Wilbur."

Roger looked at the shape on the ground while he pulled his hair up into a quick bun. It looked like a giant, six-winged moth, incongruously pinned down with a combat knife, and the area around it was torn up from its death throes.

Warrant Dobrescu ran a sensor over it and tapped the knife. The thing gave a few weak flaps of its wings, and the fangs quivered, but other than that it was quiescent. The warrant officer pulled the knife out and used it to expertly flip the thing over.

"Hmmm," he murmured and raised an eyebrow. "Fascinating."

"What happened, Julian?" Pahner asked. How long the big captain had been standing there nobody knew, but Julian shook his head again and capped the clay jug of wine.

"I was maintaining my post, Sir. I'd checked the posts a half-hour before, and I was just . . . sitting and listening. And I heard a scraping sound. So I turned on my flashlight, and—" He gulped and pointed the "moth" on the ground. "And five of those things were low-crawling up on me. Just like a fire team."

"I'd say that this is the species that got Wilbur the first night," Dobrescu confirmed. The warrant officer had a Marine shining a white-light flash over his shoulder and was examining the fangs of the still twitching moth with a field-scope. "These are clearly evolved for drawing liquids," he said, and looked up with a black chuckle. "I don't think these are nectar-drinkers, either."

"Okay," Pahner said. "We know the enemy now. Break it up and get back to sleep, people. We've got a long day ahead."

He watched the gaggle break up, the Marines heading back to their shelters and zipping them tight, and then turned to Julian.

"You gonna be okay?"

"Sure, Captain. I'll be fine. I was just shook. They're so . . ."

"Horrible," Dobrescu offered, and looked at Pahner. "What do you want me to do with the specimen?"

"Move it closer to the center of camp. We'll burn it with our garbage in the morning."

"Aye," the warrant officer said. "I wonder if this is a foretaste of things to come?"

Roger rocked with the movement of the pack beast, his eyes half-closed in the dim morning light. It had taken a while for the camp to get back to sleep, and everyone seemed quiet and subdued.

He watched the point chopping away a large liana. A multitool's monomolecular edge could cut through even the thickest vines like a laser through paper, but the company's point Marines usually tried to move through the brush without cutting. The pack beast immediately behind them would clear the way through most obstructions, so additional clearance would only have been extra effort. Even pack beasts had problems with some of the jungle's lianas, however, so the Marines generally cut a few heavy obstacles.

In this case, Roger's mount lent its strength to the female private who had point today, lifting away the upper section of the liana as the Marine cut through it closer to the ground. While she worked, Roger and the point-guard maintained an overwatch. It was when they stopped like this that Roger always felt the most vulnerable, whether they actually were or not.

Dogzard sat up and stretched from where she'd been sleeping, leaning on Roger's back. She sniffed the air, turned around, and lay back down. Nothing happening, no threats, time to sleep.

Patricia McCoy slung her bead rifle and stepped over the severed base of the liana. She could have cut it a little closer to the ground, but there was no need, since the *flar-ta's* broad, hard pads would pound the stump to splinters as they passed. Besides, she had other things to think about.

McCoy always felt vulnerable with only a mono-machete in her hand, but Pohm was right behind her, guarding her back. And, to give the devil his due, the prince was pretty good backup, too.

She stepped through a circle of smaller vines and looked around. The ground was getting wetter, and the vegetation even lusher, if that was possible. It looked like they were moving into a marsh, but it was all light brush. The beasts could clear all of this without her assistance.

She took another step . . . and dropped in her tracks, choking on blood, as the javelin appeared in her neck.

Roger's eyes widened as the flight of javelins erupted out of the jungle, but he reacted automatically. He kicked one leg over the back of the pack beast, rolled off and away from the javelins' source, twisted in midair with a contortion fit to shame a cat, and landed on his feet. He didn't stay there. Instead, he dropped to his stomach as two-tons of *flar-ta* tail whistled over his head.

The beast's driver was dead, with a javelin through him, and her own sides had been abruptly and impolitely feathered with light, iron-headed spears. She was not, to put it mildly, pleased, and she turned on her tail, snapping at whatever was biting her. But there was no enemy in biting range, so she turned her attention in the direction from which the bites had come. The little creature which had been intermittently riding on her was already pounding in that direction, and she saw movement that shouldn't have been there.

It looked like she'd found her enemy.

Roger scanned the brush for targets as the *flar-ta* gave a roaring bugle. He stayed prone as it charged off in Dogzard's wake and was rewarded with the sight of a scummy, scrambling to get out of the beast's way. There was heavy firing off to his right, from the main body of the company, but he had his own sector to cover.

Another scummy erupted into sight with Dogzard firmly attached to his arm. Roger removed him from view and dispatched the friend who'd been coming to his aid, then checked fire as Marines rushed into view.

It was time to follow his dog.

Pahner took one look at the flight of spears and snapped: "Ambush. Close."

There were two kinds of ambushes in the Marines' lexicon—close and far—and deciding which was which was the responsibility of the unit commander. The ability to tell the difference was one way to separate the schoolbook soldier from the true field tactician.

The difference was crucial because the reactions to each were diametrically opposed. In the case of a long-range ambush, the drilled reaction was for the company to take cover and use fire and maneuver to assault the ambushing force. It was massively more chaotic than that, of course, but that was the overall plan.

In the case of a close-range ambush, however, the doctrine was simply to turn into the ambush and charge. Even with the inevitable mines and booby traps, there was no percentage in taking cover if the enemy had you dead to rights where you were.

Kosutic was already in the brush and accelerating towards the concealed foes. Her bead rifle was on "automatic," and she was firing regular bursts from the hip, laying down a path of destruction to her front, "plowing the road." Again, with no enemy in sight and only ephemeral ghosts on the helmet sensors, there was no point in trying for aimed fire. Laying down massive firepower in the general area of the enemy was the best bet, and the hypervelocity beads chewed through lianas and tree trunks in a spectacular spray of sap, chlorophyll, and muck.

She burst through a curtain of undergrowth and saw a scummy rear up to hurl a spear. One burst spread him across the vegetation, and she spun in place, checking her surroundings. Nothing else was in sight, but that didn't mean anything. She knew she was ahead of the mass of the company; her helmet visor had blue "friendly" icons all over it when she looked behind her, but there weren't any in front of her. They were coming, though. The rest would be here any moment, and the only question was whether to go on or wait for support.

She paused indecisively, then hit the ground as the area to her left erupted in plasma fire. Somebody wasn't checking her helmet sensors.

❖   ❖   ❖

Nassina Bosum swore as she realized she'd almost torched the sergeant major. She'd paused to lay down covering fire for her team, and the blast had nearly converted the company's top NCO to charcoal. A corner of Bosum's mind told her that Kosutic would have a little something to say to her about that later, but there was no time to worry about that now.

She walked her fire away from the sergeant major, across the line of cover that had produced the javelins, and smiled as a flaming native tumbled into view and was cut down by the bead rifle of her team leader.

The charge exhaustion warning tone sounded insistently, and she ejected the ammo clip and slapped in another. The magazine contained lithium-deuteride pellets and a power source to feed the laser compressors and initiate the fusion reaction that drove the weapon. The system was relatively simple for imperial technology, but to ensure that everything worked properly, the ammunition manufacturer's quality control had to be precise, or the condition of the weapon firing it had to be perfect.

In this instance, neither was the case. The pellet that dropped into the firing chamber was partially contaminated by carbon. The contamination level was low, barely a tenth of one percent of the mass of material, but the results were catastrophic.

When the packet of lithium-deuteride was lased, the carbon reacted chaotically, causing a "flare" in the fusion reaction. The flare, in turn, exceeded the design parameters of the magnetic containment field, but even that would have been survivable under other circumstances. There was a backup containment system, designed specifically to prevent uncontrolled discharge in situations just like this one.

Unfortunately, Marduk's climate had had its way with

the capacitor ring managing the critical feature. When the containment spike hit the capacitor, it exploded.

The result was a small nuclear detonation in the lance corporal's hands.

Pahner cursed as the detonation's blast front punched outward through the jungle. Whether it was a string of grenades or a plasma gun hardly mattered. The general roar of combat had already begun to panic the pack beasts; now the explosion accelerated that process, and the hail of javelins continued unabated.

He called for reinforcements to fill in the sudden hole in the line in First Platoon's sector as he followed the Second Platoon squad which had been covering the headquarters section towards the concealing cover from which those javelins came. His helmet HUD was a welter of icons and images, but he'd had years of experience in deciphering them at an almost subconscious level, and the density of the spears and the width of the attack made it clear that they faced a large group of hostiles.

That was when he noticed a single gold icon on one end of the line.

"Roger! Your Highness! Damn it, get to cover! You're not supposed to be leading the damned assault elements!"

The grenade launcher appropriated from the late point-guard wasn't exactly familiar, but his helmet systems managed the conversion easily. Roger replaced the empty box of ammunition and hung the dead Marine's spares over his shoulder. The area had been cleared by the *flar-ta*, which was now headed into the distance, and cleared again by "His Royal Highness."

I really have to have a talk with Pahner about how I keep ending up on my own.

The com net was filled with chatter, and, as usual, it was impossible for him to sort out the conflicting calls. On the other hand, his visor HUD made it clear that he was behind the majority of the Mardukan ambushers and well in the lead of most of the company. He thought about that for just a moment, then smiled and looked down and shook his head as Dogzard trotted up to him.

"Am I crazy, Dogzard? Or just evil?"

Kosutic pulled her knife out of the scummy's head and looked around. She was deep in the brush now, and the damned assault elements had bogged up in the middle of the ambush. No matter how many times you told them, no matter how many times they practiced it, the unit always seemed to stop on the objective instead of going *through* the damn thing. Now the surviving scummies and the Marines were inextricably intertwined. It was practically down to hand to hand, since to fire in any direction was just as likely to hit a friend as a foe.

She was just about to charge back into the fray when she was assaulted by friendly fire.

Again.

Pahner ducked as the scummy's spear whistled overhead and struck another Marine with a meaty "Thunk!" He triggered a single round into the center of mass of the spearman, following the targeting caret of the helmet systems automatically, and looked around. Undergrowth restricted his line of sight, but everywhere he could see the Marines were locked in hand-to-hand combat with the larger Mardukans. He saw one private picked up and hurled away by a native who was nearly three meters tall, and shook his head angrily.

"Move through the ambush!" he bellowed over the com, and sprinted forward just as the trees around him started to come apart under the hammer of grenade rounds.

Roger laughed like a child. He'd figured out how to use the helmet systems to aim, and he was dropping grenades to the side of and above all the blue icons. Since the grenades threw out high-velocity shrapnel which, unlike javelins and swords, was stopped by the chameleon suits, theoretically the fire should be doing more damage to the enemy than to the Marines.

Theoretically.

Julian had just discovered that grappling with something with four arms and the size and disposition of a wounded Terran grizzly was a losing proposition. The Mardukan had him in a bear hug, and the knife was inching closer and closer to his throat when the world seemed to explode.

He and the native were thrown sideways into a tree, but the chameleon suit reacted to the strike, hardening to take the damage and puffing to pad the impact point.

The native wasn't so lucky. The explosion of the grenade tore off its head and one shoulder.

Julian stumbled to his feet, favoring his left hand, and looked around for his weapon. He finally found it under a pile of leaves thrown up by the explosion, then tried to get his bearings.

Throughout the ambush site, other Marines were doing much the same thing. Whoever had been firing the grenade launcher had apparently walked the things all the way down the ambush, and there were bruised Marines and dead scummies everywhere.

❖   ❖   ❖

Pahner saw Julian and walked over to him.

"Sergeant, assemble your squad and sweep this area. Then move out another twenty meters and establish a perimeter." He started to move on, then stopped when Julian didn't start moving. "Sergeant?"

Julian shook his head and took a breath. "Roger, Sir. Will do."

Pahner nodded and moved on down the line, shaking the occasional Marine into coherence or calling for a medic. Most of the injuries were the result of the fighting with the Mardukans, not the grenades from whatever maniac had peppered the fight. Whoever *that* had been was not going to enjoy the ass-chewing he had coming.

As the captain reached the end of the line of impacts, he saw the prince striding towards him, appropriated grenade launcher propped on his hip like a big game hunter surveying his kill.

"Did it work?" Roger asked with a grin.

Kosutic eeled out of the brush and looked around. The firing had died to nothing, and she'd found no sign of the scummies in the area beyond the ambush. It looked like the company had reacted so quickly that it had gotten every one of its attackers.

She walked over to Captain Pahner and was just opening her mouth when she realized he was rigid and shaking. She'd occasionally seen him perturbed, even angry, but she'd always wondered what he would look like if he was *furious*. Now she knew.

"What happened?" she asked.

"That arrogant, intolerable, insufferable little *snot* was the one with the grenade launcher!" Pahner said tightly.

"Oh," Kosutic said. Then: "Oh. So, was he an idiot or a genius?"

"Idiot," Pahner said, calming just enough to make a

rational judgment. "We'd already taken most of the casualties we were going to take. The Mardukans were either going to run away or stay in place as we passed through. Either way, we could have taken them with aimed fire. Now we've got half a dozen broken wrists and cracked ribs, not to mention shrapnel wounds."

"So what now?" Kosutic asked. She had her own opinion of the prince's actions. And she suspected that the captain's might, eventually, moderate.

"Reassemble on the trail." The captain ground his teeth. "Move back to drier ground to make camp, send out parties to recover the pack beasts, and dig in. I think this was the group that was going to hit Q'Nkok, but that doesn't mean that we're out of the woods."

"Nope," Kosutic agreed, looking around at the vegetation flailed by the grenade launcher and the scattered bodies of the Kranolta attackers, "it sure don't."

CHAPTER THIRTY-THREE

Cord examined the blade in the firelight.

The weapon was a Mardukan two-handed sword. At nearly three meters in length, it would have been ridiculously oversized for a human, but its proportions were lean, lethal, and graceful, and its silver-and-black patterning and elaborate engravings reflected red in the flickering light.

"Beautiful craftsmanship," Cord whispered. "Definitely Voitan work."

Much of the pattern was covered in a patina of rust which had been inexpertly scrubbed in places, damaging the very artistry the scrubber had meant to reveal.

"Damned Kranolta," the shaman added.

"Yeah, but it's useless for us," Lieutenant Jasco said, shaking his head. His arm was cradled in a sling with a broken ulna as a result of the ambush. Fortunately, his quick-heal nanites were on the job and he'd be out of it in a day or two, none the worse for wear.

Others hadn't been as lucky.

Captain Pahner appeared out of the darkness. He

332

tossed a short sword or long knife point-first into the ground beside the shaman and nodded to the lieutenant.

"True," he agreed. "But this will work just fine, and most of them were carrying at least one of them." He paused, looking speculatively at Cord, and then cleared his throat. "And a bunch of them were carrying something else, too. Horns that looked . . . sort of familiar."

The shaman clapped his true-hands in agreement with a shiver of disgust.

"The Kranolta take the horns of kills as souvenirs. They prefer the horns of champions, but in fact, any will do. The souvenirs of lesser enemies are made into musical instruments," he added, examining the knife before he tossed it down dismissively. "Well crafted, but it's only a dagger."

"Maybe for you Mardukans," Pahner replied, taking a seat by the fire. "But for us, that's a short sword. Combine it with large shields and a javelin, and I think we'll show you a thing or two."

"You're planning on using the Roman model?" Jasco asked. The need to use local equipment was a foregone conclusion. The ambush they'd just survived had depleted nearly ten percent of their plasma rifle rounds. At that rate, they would be "fired dry" before they made it to the next city-state, and that didn't even consider what had happened to Corporal Bosum. They had to start training on local equipment as soon as it could be obtained, but Q'Nkok, unfortunately, hadn't had sufficient supplies of human-sized weaponry to outfit the company.

Jasco had been arguing in favor of a technique using longer swords and smaller shields: the "Scottish model." He felt that the longer swords would be more effective against the reach of the Mardukans. Of course, against a weapon like the one the shaman was examining, any possible human reach with a sword wouldn't matter.

"I think the Roman model will be easier to learn," Lieutenant Gulyas put in. The Second Platoon leader joined the group gathered around the fire and took a seat as well. He slapped a bug on his neck and shook his head. "Not that it will help worth a damn, if today is any example."

The company had taken heavy casualties, particularly in First and Second Platoons. And while the majority of the deaths were from the spears and swords of the attacking Mardukans, there were numerous minor injuries from the grenades of the prince's bombardment. Reactions to Roger's actions were mixed. It came down to those who'd been saved by his intervention being in favor of it, and those who'd been injured by it being against. The only undecided were those like Sergeant Julian, who'd been saved while being injured. He said he would make up his mind after the ribs healed.

"We survived it," Pahner said stoically. The company had been devastated by the ambush, and had lost Lieutenant Sawato, a platoon sergeant, and two squad leaders. But that didn't mean the mission was a failure. Or impossible. "We need to move smarter. From now on, we're going to put a squad out front on a three-pronged point. That should spring any ambushes before we get to them."

"It's not doctrine, Sir," Jasco pointed out, fingering his sling. "It won't spring a long-range ambush, and you're effectively offering a squad as a sacrifice instead of one Marine."

The captain shook his head angrily.

"We keep forgetting that the Mardukans are range-limited. Or these Mardukans are, at least—that may change when we finally hit some of them with gunpowder. But as long as we keep flankers out at thrown-weapon range to the front, the Kranolta can't ambush the main body. They don't have the range. So we change the doctrine."

"And pack up the goddamned plasma guns," Gulyas said with a grimace. Bosum's death had been spectacular, and most of the plasma gunners had already unloaded their weapons as a precaution. No one knew what had gone wrong, and no one wanted to be the next person to find out.

"Yeah," Jasco snapped. "No shit."

He was out half a squad and a team leader from the malfunction. Between Koberda's death and the loss of most of the squad's Alpha Team to the plasma rifle malfunction, Gunnery Sergeant Lai had been forced to roll what was left of Second and Third Squads together under the Third Squad leader.

"Well, like the King said in Q'Nkok," Pahner pointed out, "if you have one problem, it's sometimes insoluble. But if you have several, they sometimes solve each other. We took enough casualties that there are spare weapons for all the plasma gunners to switch over to something else. I'll have Poertena and Julian start going over the plasmas in the morning, but in the meantime, we'll limit ourselves to grenades and bead guns."

"As long as the ammo holds out, Sir," Jasco said.

"That too," the company commander admitted with a grim smile. "That too. Which brings this conversation full circle."

Roger knew that doing *kata* while angry was pointless. No matter how many times he tried to find his balance, he could never quite manage it, yet he couldn't stop, either. He spun in the darkness behind his tent, hair windmilling out in a golden halo, away from the eyes of most of the company while he tried to work out his frustration, anger, and fear.

He was shocked by the casualties the company had taken. Despite everything, it had never truly occurred to him that the Marines might be wiped out by this march. Oh, intellectually he'd acknowledged the possibility, but not emotionally. Not at the heart of him. Surely modern troops, armed with Imperial weapons, would be able to slash their way through an enemy armed only with spears and swords or the crudest of firearms.

But that presumed the enemy was unwilling to take casualties. And it also presumed that the Marines could *see* the enemy in time to kill him before he reached such close quarters that all of their advantages in range and firepower were negated. The failure of the automated sensors to detect the attackers before they struck boded ill for the rest of the journey.

Although the tactical sensors were, theoretically, designed to detect a broad range of possible "traces," it was now clear that the software depended heavily on infrared and power source input. If it had a possible contact, but the contact was "anomalous," it filtered by infrared tracing and power emissions, which made perfectly good sense against high-tech opponents who would be emitting in those bands.

But the Mardukans emitted in neither of them, so the sensors were throwing out most detections as ghosts. In some cases during the battle, the helmet HUDs had flatly refused to "caret" the enemy at all, which had thrown off the Marines, who were trained to depend primarily on their helmet sensors precisely because those sensors were so much better than the ones evolution had provided. Except that now they weren't.

Roger had dealt with that problem by ignoring the targeting carets—first by using the simple holographic sights on his rifle, and then by firing into a melee where he knew the Marines *weren't* on the theory that that was where the enemy had to be. Of course, the burst radius of the grenades had caused a few problems, but still . . .

He spun on the ball of one foot, carrying the heavy sword through a vicious butterfly maneuver. It wasn't fair. He'd personally broken the back of the ambush. So the method was a little drastic. It had worked, and whatever Pahner might think, his actions had stemmed from neither panic nor stupidity nor arrogant carelessness.

Now if someone besides the ever-worshiping Dogzard would just *realize* that, he might even—

He froze at the sound of a cleared throat and turned gracefully to face the interruption. His face settled into a practiced, invulnerable mask of hauteur as he placed the point of the sword on the toe of his boot. It was an incredibly arrogant pose, and he knew it, but he didn't really care just at the moment. Screw 'em if they didn't like it.

"Yes?" he asked Despreaux. He hadn't heard the soft-footed squad leader approach, and he wondered what she wanted.

The NCO regarded him carefully for a moment, taking in both the attitude and the picture. The prince had changed into a pair of shorts to work out, and the heat and activity had raised a heavy sweat. The greater moon, Hanish, was breaking through the clouds, and the reflected fire and moonlight dappled the sweat on his body like patina on a bronze statue. The image sent a stab of fire through the NCO's abdomen which she firmly suppressed.

"I just wanted to say thank you, Your Highness. We probably would have cut our way through the ambush, but we were in the tight, no question. Sometimes you have to do things that seem crazy when it drops that far in the pot. Blowing the shit out of the Company isn't the dumbest thing I can think of, and it worked. So, from me, thanks."

She didn't add that the Mardukan who'd been blown all over her by one of the grenades had had her dead to rights when it hit. Another second, and the big bastard would've taken her head off before she could reload.

Since it was exactly what he'd wanted to hear, Roger couldn't understand why the statement caused him to flare with rage. But it did. He knew it shouldn't have, but it did. He tried hard—really tried—to swallow his contrarian reaction, but his inner anger leaked through his control.

"Thank you for your input, Sergeant," he replied tightly. "In the future, however, I'll try to think of a more . . . elegant solution."

Despreaux didn't have a clue what it was about her comment that had pissed the prince off so badly, but she was smart enough to back off.

"Well, thanks anyway, Your Highness," she said quietly. "Good night."

"Good night, Sergeant," Roger said more naturally. His intense flare of anger was already fading, and he wanted to apologize for his earlier tone, but he couldn't find the words. Which only made it worse, of course.

The rebuffed NCO nodded calmly to him in the moonlight and headed back into camp, leaving him to swing his sword and rage . . . now at both the world and his own stupidity.

CHAPTER THIRTY-FOUR

"I brought everyt'ing I could pocking pack," Poertena snapped. "How tee pock was I gonna pack a pocking plasma cradle?"

Captain Pahner had decided the company needed a day or two to repair and reconsolidate. His initial reaction had been to push on, trying to deprive the Kranolta of time to concentrate more warriors on their position. But although all the pack beasts had been recovered, many of them were injured, and the mahouts insisted that some of them needed a few days rest. Pahner had to admit that it would help the Marines as well, so the company had spent the next day improving the camp's defenses and recovering from the contact.

Well, most of them had. Julian and Poertena had a different mission.

The sides of the hide tent which had been turned into an *ad hoc* armory were rolled up, but they were still unpleasantly hot under it. Not as hot as the Marines digging stake-pits, perhaps, but at least the diggers didn't have to make bricks without straw.

"Tee pocking high-capacity tester for tee M-98 is a pocking tabletop pocking unit," Poertena went on sharply. "How tee pock was I gonna carry it? Huh?"

"Tell me something I don't know, Poertena!" Julian shot back. The two experienced armorers had already stripped down and inspected twelve plasma rifles, front to back. None of them had exhibited any sign that they would detonate like the late Nanni Bosum's, but they'd pretty clearly deduced what must have happened to Bosum, and they had no way to test the high flux capacitor systems. The machine that did that was, as Poertena had pointed out, a tabletop model which had become an expanding ball of plasma along with the rest of the *DeGlopper*.

Pahner walked into the tent and glanced at the disassembled rifles and parts strewn across its interior.

"Any luck?"

"No, Sir," Julian admitted tiredly. "Other than expected faults, we can't find anything. There's nothing to indicate a malfunction that would cause a blowout," he went on, and Pahner nodded.

"I heard you talking about capacitors. Nothing there?"

"No," Julian said. "Bad capacitors are the most common cause of breech detonations, but—"

"But we don't have tee pock . . . I mean, I couldn't hump tee test module, Cap'n," Poertena put in. "It was too po— It was too big."

"Oh." Pahner smiled. "Is that the only problem?"

"Yes, Sir." Julian gestured at the torn down weapons. "We've got a general meter, but we can't stress charge the capacitors. The charge exceeds the meter's capacity."

"Okay." Pahner turned to the Pinopan. "Poertena, go rip the system pack out of a suit of armor. Better make it Russell's." The grenadier had been one of Third

Platoon's few casualties in the ambush, and would no longer require her powered armor.

"Roger, Captain."

The small armorer trotted off towards where the armor had been stored, and Pahner turned his attention back to Julian as he extracted a precious stick of gum and popped it absentmindedly into his mouth.

"Julian. Go get me a plasma rifle that's been positively deadlined, a section of twelve-gauge superconductor, and a cyber-pad."

"Yes, Sir." Julian stepped into the bowels of the tent to find the required items. He wasn't sure what the captain was up to, but he knew it was going to be interesting.

Pahner held the charge-couple ring steady in one hand and applied the edge of his combat knife to the base of the contact points.

"Essentially, the tabletop tester for these things is identical to the built-in system in the armor." He sheared the contact off cleanly and caught it in midair. "But the contact points are different. The old Mark Thirty-Eight used different contacts, too, but it had a field service kit. You should have heard the bitching and moaning about not having a portable tester when these Mark Ninety-Eights came out! But this trick had been around for a long time, so we just kept using it."

"Why didn't they specify the same design?" Julian asked. "Or a field tester?"

"You don't know much about procurement systems, do you, Julian?" Pahner smiled crookedly and wiped a trickle of forehead sweat off on the shoulder of his uniform while he concentrated on lining up the superconductor and the contact.

"The same company that supplies the plasma rifles supplies testing equipment. Naturally, they want to sell the equipment with the rifles. If they say 'Hey, you can use the same testers as you use on your armor,' there goes the sale. Not to mention the fact that the table-top model is about three times as expensive as the field tester. I never have figured out why; it does exactly the same thing."

The captain shook his head, and this time there was very little humor in his smile.

"The Mark Ninety-Eight is about twice as powerful as the Thirty-Eight, but I think Kruplon Armaments just overcharged a Thirty-Eight and put on a new cover. The interior modules are practically identical. I'd heard the rumor that the Ninety-Eight had a tendency to blow, but this is the first time I've personally seen any evidence of it."

"But why doesn't somebody call them on it?" Julian demanded, then shook his head. "Never mind."

"Yeah," Poertena laughed. "You got any pocking idea how much pocking money 'e's talking about?"

"If they lose the sale, there goes the money for the senator's reelection campaign," Pahner agreed quietly. "Or the big dinners for the procurement officers. Or the high-paying jobs for the retired admirals."

He didn't bother to mention that the Imperial Bureau of Investigation had enough to do lately tracking down various conspirators against the throne without worrying about such minor matters as exploding weapons that killed the people using them. It was, frankly, a bad time to be a Marine.

He took the mated contact and superconducting wire and wrapped them with a piece of gum the size of a pea.

"The gum will harden when the current hits it," he said with a smile as he pressed the joint tight. "And you thought it was just a habit," he added, blowing a tiny bubble.

✧ ✧ ✧

Out of two dozen plasma chamber capacitors, they found a distinct drop in current management on half a dozen. As the current flow increased, they faltered. In a spike situation, the capacitors would fail catastrophically, with predictable results.

And all of them carried similar lot numbers from the same manufacturer.

"Fuck." Captain Pahner popped another tiny bubble and smiled grimly.

"There's microscopic cracking in tee capacitor wall," Poertena said, examining one with a field-scope. A tiny pseudo beetle wandered across the field of view, but he didn't even notice. "They probably let tee moisture get in. Especially when they been used and tee capacitor is swell. T'at's death on these dry capacitors."

"So if you don't have a spike, everything is fine." Julian shook his head. "And if you do, but don't have a bum capacitor, everything is fine. But not both."

"Right," Pahner said. "Okay. Toss these crap capacitors into the fucking jungle, except for a couple of samples. When we get back, I think Her Majesty is probably going to hang a couple of subcontractors. Given how annoyed she's going to be over this entire little adventure of ours, I think that may be a literal statement. And I'll tie the rope for her.

"After you get rid of them, put together the best plasma guns you can, as many as you can. Check every component, every piece and connection. Go over all of them with a field-scope. Then put them in zipbags with something to keep them dry."

Julian grimaced.

"Losing the plasma guns is really gonna *suck*, Boss." The weapons were almost a security blanket for the ground-pounders.

"Can't be helped. I'm not losing another squad to a

breech blow. We'll hold them in reserve until it really
has dropped in the pot. If it turns out we can't survive
without them, we'll bring them out."

"It'll take us a while to put them together," Julian said.

"I'll get you some help. You've got today and
tomorrow."

"Okeedokee," Poertena acknowledged with a resigned
headshake. "Nice pocking trick," he added. "Where'd you
learn it?"

"Son, I'm seventy-two," the captain said. "I joined up
when I was seventeen. After fifty-five years of being on
the ass-end of the supply chain, you learn to make do."

Kostas Matsugae had always enjoyed cooking on a
small scale, but preparing dinner for a wider audience
was a challenge. That was especially true with completely
unknown spices and foods, but he was learning to make
do.

With the company stopped, he finally had some
leisure to experiment. He knew the troops had started
complaining about the sameness of the menu, and he
didn't really blame them. With very little time each
evening and a large number of meals to prepare, he'd
been forced to fall back on stew almost every night. The
running joke was that they'd have a different meal every
day—today it was stew and barleyrice; tomorrow it was
barleyrice and stew.

The valet might not be a Marine, but he recognized
the importance of food to morale, and he meant to do
something about it. Although he intended to stay with
the basic "lots of stuff in a big pot" meal plan, those
parameters permitted a variety of dishes, and he was
working on a new one now.

The Mardukans grew a little-used fruit that was
vaguely similar to a tomato. He'd purchased a large
quantity of it, and now he was simmering it in a pot

spiced with the blowtorch herb *peruz* and filled with a brown legume which filled much the same culinary niche as lentils in Q'Nkok. With any luck—and it was certainly smelling good—he had a Mardukan chili in the pot. Or, it might turn out to be inedible. In which case, the company would be having . . . barleyrice and stew. It was Wednesday, after all.

He smiled as Sergeant Despreaux leaned over the pot and sniffed.

"My," she said, "that smells heavenly."

"Thank you." Kostas stirred at the top of the large kettle with a wooden spoon and took a taste. Then he waved at his mouth and took a hasty drink of water. "A bit too much *peruz*," he said in a strangled voice.

Dogzard had been sleeping in a patch of sun that penetrated the enveloping canopy. But at the sound of a spoon hitting the side of the pot, the lizard flipped to all six feet and padded rapidly over to the cooking area, and Kostas picked a small bit of meat out of the ersatz chili and tossed it to the begging lizard. The dog-lizard had become a general company mascot, emptying bowls and cleaning up messes with indiscriminate zeal. Since leaving the village of The People she'd started to grow, and was already a fairly large example of the species. If she didn't stop growing soon, she was going to end up a veritable giant.

"It'll remind us to drink," Despreaux said. She looked around for a moment, then lowered her voice. "Can I ask you a personal question?" she asked seriously.

Kostas cocked his head to the side and nodded.

"I would never betray the confidence of a lady," he said, and Despreaux snorted a laugh.

"La, sir! Seriously, no lady I. Being a lady and a grunt are sort of contradictions in terms."

"No," Kostas said. "They're not. But ask your question."

Despreaux looked around again, then looked at the pot rather than meet the valet's eye.

"You've known the Prince for a long time, right?"

"I've been his valet since he was twelve," Kostas said. "And I was a general servant in the Imperial Household before that. So, yes, I've known him for quite some time."

"Is he gay?"

Kostas stifled a snort. Not because the question was unexpected—he'd almost answered it for her before she asked—but because it was such an incredibly normal question out of this enormously capable Amazon.

"No." He was unable to keep his amusement entirely out of his tone. "No, he's not gay."

"What's so funny?" Despreaux asked. Of all the reactions she'd anticipated, amusement hadn't been one.

"You have no idea, nor will I try to give you one, how many times I've heard that question," Kostas replied with a smile. "Or heard the suggestion. Or noted the rumor. On the other hand, I've heard the opposite question just as often. There are just as many—perhaps more—gay young men as straight young ladies who have hit Roger's armor and bounced."

"So it's not just me?" she said quietly.

"No, my dear." This time, there was a note of sympathy in the valet's voice. "It has nothing to do with you. Indeed, if it makes you feel any better, I would guess that Roger finds you attractive. But that's only a guess, you understand. The Imperial Family follows the core world aristocratic tradition of providing its children with first-class sexual education and instruction, and Roger was no exception. I also know that he's inclined to prefer women; he's had at least one sexual encounter I'm aware of, and it was with a young lady. But he's also rebuffed virtually every other advance that I'm aware of." He chuckled. "And I'm aware of quite a lot of them. Frankly, if Roger were interested, he could have more 'action' than a company of Marines, pardon the expression."

"No problem." The Marine sergeant smiled. "I've heard it before. So what's with him? He's . . . what's the term? Asexual?"

"Not . . . that, either." Kostis shook his head, and there was a thoughtful, almost sad, look in his eyes. "I haven't discussed it with him, and I don't know anyone who has. But if you want the opinion of someone who probably knows him better than most, I would say it's a matter of control, not disinterest. Precisely why he should choose to exercise that control, I don't know, but that in itself tells me quite a bit." The valet shook his head. "There are many things Roger won't discuss with most people; I think there are very few he won't discuss with me, but this is one of them."

"This is . . . weird," the Marine said. Her own lovers hadn't exactly been as numerous as the stars in the sky, but she wasn't counting them on the thumbs of one hand, either.

"That's my Roger," Kostas told her with a smile.

CHAPTER THIRTY-FIVE

"Looks like it's just you and me again, Pat," Roger said, patting the pack beast just below the bandages swathing its side.

Pahner had the three most heavily injured *flar-ta*, shorn of the company's supplies, breaking trail. The pack beasts' individual reactions to the ambush had been remarkably variable. Most of them had run away from the fire and confusion of the attack, but two of them—the one Roger had coincidentally been riding and one in Third Platoon's sector—had charged the attacking Kranolta. For obvious reasons, these particularly aggressive beasts were two of the three breaking trail.

Roger, who'd decided that near a *flar-ta* was the place to be in an ambush, was walking beside "his." She reminded him of a "Patricia" he'd known in boarding school, and the name the mahouts gave her was nearly unpronounceable, toot or no toot. So "Pat" it was.

The company had been hit three more times, but not only had the additional ambushes been on a smaller scale, the wider path being forged by the trio of pack beasts had prevented the Mardukans from surprising them at such close quarters. Coupled with Pahner's decision to beef up his point team and push it further forward, the humans had escaped the attacks unscathed.

It would be nice if anyone had expected that to remain the case.

According to Cord, they were nearing the region Voitan had dominated in his father's day. Thus far they'd seen no sign of civilization, but neither had there been any sign of a Kranolta concentration against them, and the company was inclined to take the good with the bad.

Roger saw one of the point-guards raise a hand and drop to one knee. The mahouts drew the pack beasts to a stop instantly in response, and the prince trotted forward as the column accordioned behind them.

Dogzard looked up from where she'd been riding on Patty's rump. The dog-lizard raised her striped head as she sniffed the air and hissed. Matsugae wasn't cooking, and nothing was trying to eat anyone, so she jumped off her perch and followed Roger.

The point, Lance Corporal Kane from Third Platoon, was stopped at the lip of a marsh. The bank was short, barely a quarter of a meter of bare dirt, and then there was only water, covered with weeds.

The vista stretching into the distance wasn't encouraging. The swamp was choked with fallen trees and dead vines, and the live vegetation was gray and weirdly shaped, clearly different from the normal jungle foliage. Roger looked around, then walked over to a sapling and lopped it off with the sword he'd taken to carrying slung over his back.

He was probing the marsh with his stick while Dogzard sniffed at the water disdainfully when Pahner walked up behind him.

"You know, Your Highness," the captain said dryly, "sometimes there are things that *eat* people at the fringe of water like this." The Marine seemed to have at least partially forgiven Roger for blasting the company with a stick of grenades, but the prince was still inclined to watch his tongue with rather more care than usual.

"Yes, there are," he agreed. "And I've hunted most of them. This isn't exactly shallow," he continued, withdrawing the chopped off sapling and examining the sticky mud which coated the first meter of its length. A bubble of foul-smelling gas followed the probe to the surface.

"Or solid," he observed with a choking cough.

The company had spread out in a perimeter, and seeing that there was no immediate threat, Kosutic had wandered up behind Pahner. She looked at the black, tarry goo clinging to the stick, then at the swamp, and laughed.

"It looks like . . . the Mohinga," she announced in hushed, hollow tones which would have done a professional teller of horror stories proud.

"Oh, no!" Pahner said, with an uncharacteristic belly laugh. "Not . . . the Mohiiinga!"

"What?" Roger tossed the sapling into the swamp. "I don't get the joke."

Dogzard watched the stick land and considered going after it. But only briefly. She sniffed at the water, hissed at the smell, and decided that discretion was the better part of getting in there. Balked of any possibility of "fetch the stick," she looked up at the humans speculatively. None of them seemed to be up to anything interesting, though, so she trundled back to the *flar-ta* with her thickening tail waggling behind her.

"It's a Marine joke," Kosutic told the prince with a smile. "There's a training area in the Centralia Provinces on Earth, a jungle training center. It has a swamp that I swear the Incas must have used to kill their sacrifices. It's been drained a couple of times in the last few thousand years, but it always ends up back in the military's hands. It's called—"

"The Mohiiinga. I got that much."

"It's a real ball-buster, Your Highness," Pahner said with a faint smile. "When we'd get Raider units that were, shall we say . . . a little more arrogant than they should have been, we'd set up a land navigation course through the Mohinga. Without electronic aids." His smile grew, and his chuckle sounded positively evil. "They quite often ended up calling for a shuttle lift out after a couple of days of wandering around in circles."

"You were a JTC instructor, Sir?" Kosutic sounded surprised.

"Sergeant Major, the only thing I haven't instructed in this man's Marine Corps is Basic Rifle Marksmanship, and *that* was only because I skated out of it." Pahner grinned at the NCO. Although the marksmanship course was critical to developing Marines, it was also one of the most boring and repetitive training posts in the Corps.

"All paths lead into the Mohiiinga," Kosutic quoted with horrified, quavering relish, "but . . . none lead ooout!"

"I won't say I *wrote* that speech," Pahner said with another chuckle, "because it was old when I got there. But I did add a few frills. And, speaking of the Mohinga . . ." The captain looked around and shook his head. "I certainly hope we can go around this one."

Cord walked up to look at the swamp as well, then walked over to where Roger and his group stood laughing in the human way. It was apparent that they didn't realize the full import of the marsh.

"Roger," he said with a human-style nod. "Captain Pahner. Sergeant Major Kosutic."

"D'Nal Cord," Roger replied with an answering nod.

"Is there a way around this? I know it's been some time since you came this way, but do you remember?"

"I remember very clearly," the old shaman said, "and this wasn't here in my father's day. The fields of Voitan and H'Nar stretched outward through this region. But as I recall, they had been drained from a swamp that surrounded the Hurtan River." The shaman clapped his false hands in regret. "I fear that this may fill the valley of Voitan. It may stretch all the way to T'an K'tass."

"And how far is that?" Kosutic asked.

"Days to the south," Cord replied. "Even weeks."

"And north?" Pahner asked, looking at the swamp and no longer chuckling.

"It stretches as far north as I have knowledge of," the Mardukan said. "The region to the north, even in the days of Voitan, was held by the Kranolta, and they didn't permit caravans through their lands."

"So," Roger said dubiously, "we have to make a choice between going several weeks out of our way to the south, getting hit by the Kranolta the whole way. Or we can go north, directly into their backyard. Or we can try to navigate the swamp."

"Well, your Marines and my people may have some problems," Cord admitted. "But not the *flar-ta*. They can easily make it through a swamp no deeper than this."

"Really?" It was Kosutic's turn to sound doubtful. "That thing that was chasing you was in a desert. These things—" she jerked a thumb over her shoulder at Patricia "—don't look that different."

"The *flar-ta* and the *flar-ke* are found everywhere," Cord pointed out. "They prefer the high, dry regions because of the absence of *atul-grack*, but they can be found in swamps as well."

Pahner turned and looked at D'Len Pah. The chief mahout had taken over Pat when her original mahout was killed in the first ambush, and now waited patiently for the humans to make up their minds.

"Do you think the pack beasts can cross this, Pah?" the captain asked skeptically.

"Certainly," the mahout said with a grunt of laughter. "Is that what you've been jawing about?"

He tapped the beast in a crease in the armor just behind her massive head shield to get her in gear, and the *flar-ta* whuffled forward. She moaned dolefully when she saw the black muck, but she stepped into it anyway.

The pack beast's feet each consisted of four toes with leathery bases. They were equipped with heavy digging claws, and their pads were broad and fleshy. They were also webbed, and now Patricia spread her toes wide, more than tripling the square area of her foot. That foot sank into the sloppy mud but found "solid" footing well before the belly of the creature touched the water.

"Hmmm." Roger watched thoughtfully. "Can she move out into the swamp?"

Pah prodded again, and the beast grumbled but moved out into the black water. Obviously, she was as at home in the swamp as in the jungle, but a moment later she burbled and started to back up hastily as a "V" ripple started towards her from deeper in the swamp.

Roger picked up his rifle from where he'd leaned it against a tree and flipped it off safe. Beads from Marine rifles started bouncing off the surface as the panicking beast lumbered back up out of the water, but the prince only drew a breath and led the approaching ripple.

Pahner flicked the selector switch on his bead rifle to armor-piercing as he realized that the lighter ceramic beads were simply skipping off the water, but just as he was about to fire, Roger's big rifle boomed, and the ripple turned into a whitewater of convulsions. The creature jerking and flopping at the center of the maelstrom was longer and narrower than a damnbeast but otherwise similar, with the same mucus-covered skin as a scummy. The green and black-striped beast thrashed a few more times as the huge hole blown through its shoulder and neck bled out, then rolled over to float belly-up on the surface.

"Dinner," Roger said calmly, jacking another round into the chamber.

"Well," Pahner observed with a sniff, "that's half the problem solved. We'll pile the rucksacks on the beasts and follow them through the swamp."

"It will make Kranolta attacks less likely, as well," Cord said ruminatively as the mahouts waded into the water to retrieve the kill. "Such swamps are useless to the forest people. They won't be as at home there as in the forest, and they'll never expect us to cross it here. But," he continued, gesturing into the swamp with his spear, "somewhere in there is the Hurtan River. And *that* the *flar-ta* will be unable to cross."

"We'll build that bridge when we come to it," Kosutic said with a laugh. "First, we have to deal with—"

"The Mohiiinga," Roger and Pahner chorused.

Poertena slipped and went under for a moment before Denat could pull him, puffing and spluttering, to his feet. The armorer spat out foul-tasting water, but he'd still managed to keep his bead rifle from going under.

"T'anks, Denat," he began, then broke off as his helmet started to pop and hiss.

"Shit!" He tore off the helmet as the earphones began to howl. "Modderpockers are suppose a be waterproof," he grumped. He'd deal with it later.

The company had been slogging through the waist-to chest-high swamp all the long Mardukan afternoon.

The going was slow and hard, with the black mud sucking at their boots and chameleon suits, and hidden roots and fallen branches grabbing at their ankles. Most of them were coated in muck from top to bottom after repeated falls.

The only exceptions were the marksmen sitting on the *flar-ta*.

"Look at t'at stuck up prig sittin' up there," Poertena grumbled, glaring at the prince who was on the lead pack beast.

"You'd be up there, too," Despreaux said, moving forward to check on her Bravo Team, "if, of course, you could shoot as well as he can."

"Rub it in," the armorer muttered. "An' watch where you step. One o' these modderpocker swamp-beast eat you!"

Roger's head twitched to the right, tracking a ripple in the water, but it was small and heading away. The ride wasn't much different from normal, although it was perhaps a tad smoother. The *flar-ta* crushed most of the fallen limbs or trees they encountered without even breaking stride.

The swamp's flora ran to smaller species than in the jungle, and many of those he'd seen seemed relatively young. Cord had indicated that these areas had been fields in his father's day, so perhaps that explained their lack of age. Which, in turn, might explain their smaller size, now that he thought about it.

He turned to look behind him at the Marines sliding through the swamp and patted the snoring Dogzard on her head. The poor bastards were covered in the thick black mud and looked as worn and dragged as he'd ever seen them. The necessity of holding their rifles up out of the muck and pushing their way through it was obviously telling on them. It was particularly hard on the grenadiers, who had their boxes and bandoliers of grenades piled on their heads and shoulders with the heavy grenade launchers held up out of the slop. All in all, it made him feel like a shit to be sitting on Patricia's back.

The only consolation was that he'd been contributing. The caravan had attracted a host of carnivores as it passed through the swamp, and the Marines' bead rifles, even when switched to the heavier tungsten-cored armor piercing rounds, weren't as effective in the water as his big 11-millimeter magnum "smoke-pole." The lower velocity, heavier slugs punched into the water, rather than tending to come apart on the surface.

But he wasn't happy about it, especially with night coming on.

Pahner moved forward, pushing against the drag of the swamp as he responded to a call from the lead mahouts. He sloshed up alongside, and D'Len Pah looked down from the slow-moving reptiloid and pointed his goad stick in the direction of the descending sun.

"We must rest the beasts soon," he said. "And it will be very difficult to move in the dark."

Pahner had recognized the inevitability an hour before. There was no end to the swamp in sight, and apparently no island-forming uplands. And even if there'd been islands, they would have been inhabited by *something*.

"Agreed," he said. "We're going to have to stop somewhere."

"And we need to unload the packs," the mahout said. "The *flar-ta* will sleep standing up, but we must unload them. Otherwise, they will be useless tomorrow."

Pahner looked around and shook his head in

resignation. It was the same wet, weird vista as it had been for the last few hours, so he supposed here was as good as anywhere.

"Okay, hold up here. I'll go get started on unloading them."

"We can't just dump the stuff in the swamp," Roger said. It was meant as an observation, but his tone made it sound like a protest.

"I know that, Your Highness," Pahner said testily. Just when the prince started to get a grip, he said the wrong thing at the wrong time. "We're not going to dump it in the swamp."

"Going vertical?" Lieutenant Gulyas asked. Because he was a couple of months senior to Jasco, he'd taken over as XO when Sawato was killed, turning his platoon over to Staff Sergeant Hazheir, its senior surviving NCO. It didn't really require more. Second Platoon had been hit hard, both in the ambush and before, and was already down to half its original complement.

"Yep," Pahner responded, looking up. The trees in the area weren't the giants of the rain forest they'd traveled under for weeks. They were lower, more like large cypresses, with branches that spread out to choke the light and red vinelike projections that reached up from their roots to search for oxygen.

"Start setting up slings. We'll sling the armor off one piece at a time, then sling the rest of the gear in bundles." The company had plenty of issue climbing-rope. The lines were rated to support an eighty-ton tank, but the forty-meter length that each team leader carried weighed less than a kilo. There was more than enough to lift all the gear.

"What about the troops?" Roger asked. "Where are they going to sleep?"

"Well, that's the tough part, Your Highness," Kosutic

told him with a grin. "This is how you separate the Marines from the goats."

"Besides the usual method—with a crowbar," Gulyas said, completing a joke as old as armies.

"T'is really suck." Poertena didn't even bother to try to get comfortable.

"Oh, it's not all that bad," Julian said as he adjusted the strap across his chest. The ebullient NCO was coated from head to toe in black, stinking mud, and exhausted from the day's travel, so his manic grin had to be false. "It could be worse."

"How?" Poertena demanded, adjusting his own rope. The two Marines, along with the rest of the company, were tied with their backs to trees. Since they had no choice but to sleep on their feet, the ropes around them were designed to keep them from slipping down into the chest-deep muck. As tired as they were, there was a distinct possibility that they wouldn't wake up if they did.

"Well," Julian replied thoughtfully as the skies opened up in a typical Mardukan deluge, "something could be trying to eat us."

Pahner had the sentries walking the perimeter and shining red flashlights on each individual. It was hoped that a combination of the movement and the light would drive off the vampire moths. Of course, there were also the swamp beasts to worry about, and it was always possible that movement and light would *attract* them, but there wasn't a great deal he could do about that.

All in all, it looked like being a very bad night for the Marines.

"No, Kostas," Roger said, shaking his head at the item Matsugae had produced. "You use it."

"I'm fine, Your Highness," the valet said with a tired

smile. The normally dapper servant was covered in black slime. "Really. You shouldn't sleep in this muck, Sir. It's not *right*."

"Kostas," Roger said, adjusting his chest rope so that he could keep his rifle out of the muck but still get to it quickly, "this is an order. You will take that hammock and sling it somewhere and then climb into it. You will sleep the entire night in it. And you *will* get some goddamned rest. I'm going to be on the back on that damned pack beast again tomorrow, and you won't, so I can damned well spend a night sitting up. God knows I've seen enough 'white nights' carousing. One more won't kill me."

Matsugae touched Roger on the shoulder and turned away so that the prince wouldn't see the tears in his eyes. Without even realizing it, Roger had started to grow up. Finally.

"Now *that* was something I never thought I'd see," Kosutic said quietly.

The sergeant major had managed to rig a line so that she was out of the water, dangling in her combat harness. She didn't know how long she could manage it, but for the time being at least she was off her legs. If she did sleep, she figured she was going to look like something from a bad horror holovid: a dead body dangling on a meat hook.

"Yep," Pahner said, just as quietly. He'd slung himself against a tree like the rest of the company. He had a hammock packed as well, but he'd bundled O'Casey into it. There was no way he was going to use it unless every member of the company had one. And Roger, apparently without prompting, had come to the same decision.

Amazing.

CHAPTER THIRTY-SIX

"Wake up."

Julian shook the private by the arm. The bead rifle-man dangled limply from the tree, her face gray in the predawn light, and pried one eye open. She looked around at her wet, indescribably muddy surroundings and groaned.

"Please. Kill me," she croaked.

Julian just shook his head with a laugh and moved on. A few moments later, he found himself looking up at the sergeant major, spinning slowly on the end of her rope and snoring. He shook his head again, thought about various humorous possibilities, and decided that they wouldn't be good for his health.

"Wake up, Sergeant Major," he said, touching her boot as it swung into range.

The NCO had her bead pistol out and trained before she was fully awake.

"Julian?" she grunted, and cleared her throat.

"Morning, SMaj," the squad leader chuckled. "Wakee, wakee!"

"Time for another glorious day in the Corps," the sergeant major replied, and pulled an end of the rope to release the knot. She splashed into the water, still holding her bead pistol out of the muck, and came up coated in a fresh covering of mud. "Morning ablutions are complete. Time to rock and roll."

"Sergeant Major, you are too much," Julian laughed.

"Stick with me, kid," the senior NCO told him through her brand new mud. "We're gonna see the galaxy."

"Meet exotic people," Pahner said, untying himself and stretching in the early dawn light.

"And kill them," Julian finished.

After changing socks, the company moved out on cold rations and vague dreams of dryness. Pahner, recognizing the danger to the Marines' feet, started cycling the company up onto the *flar-ta* two at a time. Even with the company's reduced manpower, however, it would take most of the day to get everyone up for a brief respite. And it would be brief.

As the morning progressed, there was no sign of a break in the swamp, nor of the sort of increasing depth that might signal a river ahead. In fact, the humans could see no change at all in their surroundings, but the pack beasts seemed to be getting less and less happy about continuing.

Finally, when one balked, Pahner slogged up to D'Len Pah.

"What's wrong with the beasts?" he asked.

"I think we might be in the territory of *atul-grack*," the mahout answered nervously. "They're very frightened."

"*Atul-grack?*" Pahner repeated as Cord's nephew Tratan waded up, and the young tribesman started waving all four arms in agitation.

"We must go back!"

"What?" Pahner asked. "Why?"

"Yes," the mahout said. "We should turn around. If there are *atul-grack* around, we are in grave danger."

"Well," the human said, "are there, or aren't there?"

"I don't know," Pah admitted. "But the beasts act as if they're afraid, and the only thing that would frighten *flar-ta* is *atul-grack*."

"Would someone *please* tell me what the hell an *atul-grack* is?" Pahner demanded in frustration.

His answer was a deafening roar.

The beast that exploded out of the swamp was a nightmare. Solid and low, like a damnbeast, the gray and black-striped monster was at least five times as large—nearly as large as the elephantine *flar-ta*. Its mouth was wide enough to swallow a human whole and filled with sharklike teeth, and it sprinted across the swamp like a tornado, water fountaining skyward from every impact of its six broad feet, as the company's weapons opened up on all sides and the pack beasts erupted in pandemonium.

Roger rolled off of Patty's back as she hot-footed away from the charging carnivore. He came up sputtering, covered in mud, but he'd managed to keep the rifle out of the swamp.

Dogzard had followed him, spinning through the air out of a sound sleep and splashing into the water beside him. The sauroid planted her amphibian hind feet in the muck and shot her head above water just long enough to determine the problem. Then she promptly ducked back under and swam away at top speed. She was a scavenger, not a fighter. And certainly not a fighter of *atul-grack*.

The carnivore was intent on pulling down one of the *flar-ta* as its dinner. It was being bracketed by grenades and hit on either side by dozens of rounds from the bead rifles, but it charged on, ignoring the pinpricks, and Roger realized that it was charging dead at Captain Pahner, who was sliding out of its way as fast as he could while firing a bead pistol at it one-handed.

The prince put the dot of the holographic sight on the beast's temple, led it a little, and let fly.

Sergeant Major Kosutic stood up, coughing and spluttering. One of the pack beasts' tails had hit her hard enough to harden her chameleon armor and throw her ten meters through the air and into a tree. She spun around in place and immediately spotted the bellowing carnivore that had started the ruckus. The friction-sling of her bead rifle was still attached, and she raised the weapon, then froze and checked. A twig frantically inserted into the barrel came out dry, so she switched to armor piercing and took careful aim at the head of the beast.

The two shots sounded as one, somehow echoing clearly in a lull as the rest of the company was reloading. Armand Pahner abandoned dignity and comfort for survival and threw himself into a long, shallow dive out of the way as the beast slid to a halt where he'd been standing in an all-enveloping bow wave of water, muck, and shredded swamp vegetation.

He was back up almost instantly, pistol in a two-handed grip, but the emergency was over. The beast was down and quivering, its tail thumping a slow, splashing tattoo. The back of the tiger-striped beast overtopped the tall Marine by at least half a meter, and he looked over at Roger, who was shakily reloading.

"Thank you, Your Highness," he said, putting his pistol away with a steady hand.

"*De nada*," Roger said. "Let's just get the fuck out of this swamp."

"Yours or mine?" Kosutic asked. She stepped up to the beast and emptied half a magazine of armor piercing into its armored head.

"Uh." Roger examined what was left of the evidence. It sure looked like his 11-millimeter had done the main damage. "Mine, I think."

"Yeah, well," the NCO said as she carefully inserted another magazine, "you shoot it; you skin it."

The good news about the thing Mardukans called an *atul-grack* and the humans just called a bigbeast was that they were very solitary, very territorial hunters who required at least one high, dry spot in their territory. It took a while, but Cord's tribesmen found it.

And the river.

The large mound was clearly artificial, part of a dike system which had once contained the Hurtan River within its banks. The artificial island supported the remains of a burned gazebo, just a few charred sticks succumbing to the Mardukan saprophytes, and the barest outlines of a road paralleling the river it overlooked.

The Hurtan wasn't a huge river by any stretch, but it was big enough. And the current was noticeable, which was unusual in the swamp.

"No way," D'Len Pah said. "*Flar-ta* swim, but not that well."

Their raised elevation also permitted a view of the low mountains or high hills where their intermediate objective lay. They seemed to be within easy reach, no more than one day's march.

If, that was, they could get across the river.

"We could go upriver," Roger suggested. "Look for a crossing point. Was there a ford?" he asked Cord, who shook his head.

"A ferry."

"We could build a raft. . . ." Pah started.

"Huh-uh," Pahner said, cutting everyone else off. He'd been staring at the river and its far bank thoughtfully.

"Bridge it?" Kosutic asked.

"Yep," the company commander replied. "And we'll belay the pack beasts across. Pah," he turned to the mahout, "the beasts can cross on their own, but they have a problem with the current. Is that it?"

"Yes," the mahout said. "They're good swimmers, but we can't ride them while they swim, for if we fall off, we'll drown. Swept downstream, without us to guide them, they might panic and drown as well." He clapped his true-hands in agitation. "You don't want us to lose any, do you?"

"No, no, no," Pahner said soothingly. "But we will cross this river. Right here."

"Why tee pock do *I* have to do t'is?" Poertena demanded as he took off his boots.

"Because you're from Pinopa," Kosutic told him. "Everyone knows Pinopans swim like fish."

"T'at's stereotyping, t'at is," the armorer snapped. He struggled out of his filthy chameleon suit and stood in his issue underwear. The flexible synthetic material made for an adequate swimsuit. "Just because I'm from Pinopa doesn't mean I can swim!"

"Can't you?" Julian asked in an interested tone. "Because if you can't, it's going to be funny as hell when we throw you in."

Dogzard sniffed at the two of them, then walked down to the water's edge. She sniffed at it in turn, then hissed and walked away. Somebody else could swim that river.

"Well, yes," Poertena admitted.

"Fairly well, right?" Kosutic asked. She did have to admit that it was stereotyping. There could be a Pinopan who couldn't swim. It would be like someone from the planet Sherpa, which was basically one giant mountain chain, being afraid of heights. It *could* happen, but it would be like being afraid of oxygen.

"Well, yes," the armorer admitted again, sourly. "I was on a swimming team in high school an' you've gotta believe tee competition was pocking pierce. But t'at's not tee point!" he continued in protest.

"Right. Sure. Anything you say," Julian soothed as he tied a rope around the diminutive Pinopan's waist. "One sacrifice to the river gods, coming up!"

Roger shook his head at the good-natured wrangling going on below his tree and took his rifle off safe. The river appeared placid, but no one intended to settle for appearances.

The rifle normally mounted a three-round magazine to save weight, given how heavy the big magnum rounds were, but the manufacturer also offered a ten-round detachable box magazine as an option. Roger had never understood why anyone who could hit what he was aiming at would need ten rounds—unless, of course, he was trying to kill main battle tanks—but two of the ten-round boxes had come with the rifle, and he'd brought them along without really thinking about it.

Now that he was down on Marduk, he'd discovered that his original contemptuous opinion of the option had undergone considerable modification, and he snapped the first, fully loaded ten-round box into place, then slid an eleventh round "up the spout" before he closed the bolt. He also had additional standard magazines laid out on the broad branch in front of him, a box of ammunition opened on his belt, and Matsugae stood ready to reload empties for him on the fly, but even all of that wasn't enough to banish his fear that he might run out of ammo as the day wore on.

Marine sharpshooters were scattered in other trees

along the river, but more and more, it was Roger the company depended on when an accurate shot was needed. The time he'd spent big game hunting was coming to the fore, as he invariably placed his big bone-smashing bullets in vulnerable spots.

Julian climbed into the tree next to his and Matsugae's and unlimbered his bead rifle.

"You really ought to have one of these," the NCO noted, gesturing with his chin at the ammunition scattered across the tree limb. "Fifty in a magazine beats three—or even ten—all hollow." The sergeant pulled one of the dual magazines out of the bead rifle and replaced it with one filled with armor piercing. "And now I've got a hundred."

"Tell you what," Roger said good-naturedly as he flipped his "smoke pole's" selector switch from bolt action to semi-auto. "What do you want to bet that I get more of whatever comes along than you do?"

Julian considered himself a fair shot, but he recognized it as a tough bet to win. The prince, for all his other faults, was no slouch with that big-game rifle. The entire company had seen ample proof of that, but the Marine couldn't resist.

"Okay. Fifty credits?"

"Three hundred push-ups," Roger retorted. "Fifty credits doesn't mean a thing here, and it's peanuts to me on Earth. But three hundred push-ups is three hundred push-ups."

"Done," Julian agreed with a smile. Watching as the little Pinopan gingerly lowered himself into the water. "But who's gonna judge?" he asked.

"One hundred and twenty-six," Julian grunted. "One hundred and twenty-seven . . ."

"Come on, Julian," Sergeant Major Kosutic said. "He beat you fair and square."

The sound of bugling *flar-ta* and the occasional crack of a bead rifle could still be heard in the distance as the elaborate bridge system was disassembled.

After Poertena had taken the lead line across, the company had swung into gear with a vengeance. The first rope bridge was being tautened within twenty minutes, and a security team went swarming across it. In another half hour, two more rope bridges were in place, and the *flar-ta* were being belayed across.

The first bridge was a simple affair: two taut ropes, one above the other and about a meter and a half apart, strung between trees on either side of the river. The ropes were tightened by tying a metal ring into the side over the river and then running the end of the rope through the ring. A fire team then pulled the rope as taut as possible, and a quick release knot was tied into it. Another rope was run above the first, and then the two lines were lashed together. The resulting bridge was crossed by holding onto the top rope while shuffling across the lower one.

The *flar-ta* crossing was, inevitably, a bit trickier.

That was what the two additional bridges were for. Unlike the personnel bridge, they were single lines, and the Marines attached metal clips to them, then ran a rope from one clip to a sling around each pack beast's middle. Another rope was run from the pack beast to the far shore, and a third ran from the beast to the near shore.

Even if the entire company had grabbed onto the far rope, there would have been no way they could have managed the beast's crossing with raw muscle power. But as it turned out, a simple trick permitted a single fire team of five to pull the beast across the river.

The rope to the far side was first bent around a tree, then back on itself. The team's members held the doubled up rope in their hands as the beast was coaxed into the water, and as slack came into the rope, they pulled it through. But whenever the big beast balked and tried to draw back, they clamped their hands around the rope. The steadiness of the tree and the friction of the clamped rope prevented even the powerful *flar-ta* from backing up.

Once they were in the river, the beasts started to swim. The line run to the taut "bridge" kept them from being swept downstream, and the alternate heaving and belaying of the team on the ropes drew them across whether they wanted to cross the river or not.

In the meantime, the expected wave of carnivores arrived. The Mardukan crocodilia were just pleased as pie to have all those big, toothsome *flar-ta* come into their area, and they decided to welcome them with open jaws. Roger and company, however, had a surprise for them.

Roger was glad he'd brought a couple of cases of ammunition down from *DeGlopper*. He'd thought it was ludicrous to bring more rounds on the expedition than he'd ever shot in his life, but he and his faithful loader Matsugae shot out all the rounds they had in the tree plus a hundred more Roger had asked Despreaux to get for him before the last *flar-ta* was out of the water.

Not all of them hit, of course. Even he missed the occasional shot, but at one point there had been fifty carcasses floating in view, more than two-thirds of them with an 11-millimeter entry wound. That had been the worst point—after the smell of the blood had gotten downriver and attracted the fast-swimming swamp beasts.

Roger, followed silently by Cord, walked up as Julian grunted, "One hundred and fifty-seven . . ."

"I think that's adequate, Sergeant Major," the prince said. He stood his rifle up against a tree and sat on the ground.

The far side of the river had turned out to be higher

and drier, for which the company was giving elaborate thanks. Already, in the midst of constructing a fortified camp, uniforms and allegedly waterproof rucksacks were being dried out.

"We've all had a tough few days," Roger added. He picked up the rifle again and broke open the action to clean it, but that was as far as he could get. "God, I'm tired."

"Let me clean that for you, Sir," Corporal Hooker offered. The lance corporal held out her hand for the rifle. "I've got mine to clean, anyway."

"Oh, thank you, Corporal, but we're all tired," the prince demurred. "I'll get it."

Dogzard walked over to where he sat and sniffed to make sure he was okay after the river crossing, then spun around and curled up against his side. The lizard was growing like a weed. She'd gained at least fifteen kilos in the last two weeks, and it was all Roger could do to prop up her weight.

"Let her take it, Your Highness," Kosutic said. "You probably need to go coordinate with the Old Man while I finish ensuring that the Sergeant here learns to keep his mouth shut."

Roger had opened his mouth to protest, but shut it with a clop and a laugh.

"Very well, Sergeant Major. They say 'Never argue with the Gunny.' I presume that goes double for a sergeant major." He handed the rifle to the lance corporal. "Thank you, Corporal."

He looked at Julian, who gasped: "One hundred and seventy-eight . . . !"

"And to you, Sergeant Julian," the prince said with a twinkle, "good luck."

" . . . can expect an increase in attacks on this side of the river," Lieutenant Gulyas said.

The briefing was taking place in the command tent. The sides were rolled up to let in a bit of breeze, but the troops still kept their distance. Sometimes it was better to get the word through official channels rather than as a rumor.

"Do we stay here and let them concentrate to hit us while we're dug in?" Roger asked, flicking a bug off his pad. "Or do we move on, hoping to cut down on the contacts?" Even with the sun still high, the gray light through the perpetual overcast was dim under the trees. He squinted at the pad, then rolled up the light level. Better. Still not great, but better.

"They can probably figure out that we're headed for Voitan without any difficulty," Pahner said. "And there's something to be said for letting them come to us in a prepared position. But this isn't the sort of location I'd want to defend."

The area was a flat, heavily forested plain, higher than the swamp, but still prone to flooding. The flat plain, however, did not provide anything in the way of terrain features to use in defense. The company could, and had, cut down most of the secondary growth trees to improve their perimeter and fire lanes, but that was about it.

"If we reach Voitan," Cord said, deliberately, "we'll have many places to defend. Not only should there still be walls in places, but the quarries behind the city offer numerous fortifiable spots."

"What do you think, Captain?" Roger asked, yawning. Everyone was exhausted, including him. He just needed to drive on.

"I think that in the morning we pull out carefully, then make the fastest march possible to Voitan. We'll pile the packs on the beasts again and force the pace. I doubt they expected us to cross the swamp here. They probably have a crossing place they use, and if they've begun to assemble to hit us, they'll probably be assembling there. Unfortunately for them, we were too stupid to use the 'good' crossing."

"So we make a run for Voitan," Kosutic said.

"Right." Pahner considered the situation for a moment. "If it's as close as Cord thinks, then we should arrive by mid-afternoon." The long Mardukan day would work in their favor for once.

"And if it's not?" Kosutic asked.

"Then we will have exhausted ourselves for nothing," Pahner told her grimly.

Matsugae sampled the stew and gave the mahout who was stirring it a thumbs up. He walked on to where a Mardukan female was turning strips of meat battered with barleyrice meal on a large metal sheet over a fire. He pulled one of the strips off and blew on it to cool it enough to taste without burning his mouth. Again, he smiled and gave the cook a thumbs up.

The captain had backed the camp up against the river, and the company had spent the remainder of the afternoon digging in and cleaning up. Matsugae, for his part, had spent the same time working hard to put together a decent meal for the first time in three days. Many of the swamp beasts had been lassoed or hooked and dragged to shore. Although there was good flesh all over the carcasses, there were three or four particularly good cuts, and with all the bodies floating in the river, the mahouts had ended up taking only the skins and the very best of the meat.

Most of the mahouts were preparing the skins. The swamp beasts were fairly rare, and their skins brought a high price. The company, possibly Roger alone, had shot the cost of two or three pack beasts in one afternoon.

Matsugae grinned. The mahouts had been picking up the skins of all the beasts that the company shot along the way. The captain had nearly offered them to the drovers as a free benefit, but Matsugae had convinced him not to do that. The mahouts were being paid a straight rate, just as they would for any caravan. The skins, however, even after processing, were the property of whoever shot the beasts they came from. Give the mahouts a bonus for their work, certainly, but the skins of those predators were valuable. The beasts that had harassed them would help pay the company's way, and that gave the valet a simple sense of pleasure.

The dog-lizard wandered into the outdoor kitchen and sniffed at the strips on the fire. The Mardukan female tending them shooed her away, so she wandered over to Matsugae, looking pitiful. The beast had grown steadily since Roger adopted it. It was nearly the size of a dalmatian now, and its growth showed no sign of slowing. In addition, its tail was thickening. The *flar-ta*, which were similar to the dog-lizard in many ways, stored up reserves in their tails, or so the mahouts claimed. Certainly, they were skinnier now than when the company had left Q'Nkok. Apparently, unlike the pack beasts, the journey had been good for the dog-lizard.

Matsugae consulted his toot and smiled as he tossed the dog-lizard the last bit of damncroc tail. Nearly time for dinner.

"Kostas, that was wonderful, as always." A yawn interrupted Roger's compliment, and he grimaced. "Sorry."

"Don't worry about it, Your Highness," Pahner said. "We're all beat. I hope like hell we don't get hit tonight. I don't think Bravo of the Bronze could hold off a troop of Space Scouts tonight."

"I think you underestimate them, Captain," O'Casey said. The chief of staff had begun to adjust to the brutal regimen of the trip, shedding fat and putting on muscle.

When she got back to Imperial City, she intended to recommend shipwreck on a hostile planet full of carnivorous monsters and bloodthirsty barbarians as a sovereign method for attaining physical fitness. Now the former tutor smiled warmly. "Your troops have been just magnificent. Her Majesty will be incredibly proud when we finally get back."

"Well," Pahner said, "we have a long way to go before we find out. But, thank you, Councilor. That means a lot to me, and it will actually mean something to the troopers as well. We don't just fight for pay, you know."

Roger shook his head sleepily.

"I never considered all the little stories around me all the time. Do you know Corporal Hooker's first name?" Roger asked as he fed Dogzard a scrap of gristle from the damncroc.

"Of course, Your Highness. Ima."

"She said her dad had a sick sense of humor," the prince confirmed in a tone of outrage. "I offered to have him thrown out an airlock."

"He's long dead," Kosutic said, taking another fingerstrip of damncroc tail. "Snorted himself to death on dreamwrack."

"Ah," Roger said with a nod. "And Poertena wanted to go to college on a swimming scholarship . . ."

" . . . but he got beat out in the finals," Pahner finished. "There's more to leadership than wearing the right tabs on your collar, Your Highness. Knowing the details of the troops is important, and for knowing the really intimate details . . ."

" . . . you have sergeant majors and gunnery sergeants," Kosutic said with a frown. "Andras' wife was expecting when we left, and I doubt we'll be back before she's due. I don't suppose it will matter one way or the other, though; we're undoubtedly written off as dead."

"That . . . sucks," O'Casey said.

"Being a Marine sucks," Pahner told her with a quiet smile. It was rare for the academic to swear.

"Then why do you do it?" she asked.

"It's something I'm good at. Somebody has to do it, and better someone who's good at it. Not everyone is." The captain looked pensive for a moment. "It's . . . bad, sometimes. When you realize that what you're really good at is either killing other sentients in person or leading others in the killing of them. But everyone in the Regiment is an exceptional Marine. And reasonably presentable. And utterly loyal . . ."

"But there's more," Kosutic said with a grin. "That describes a surprising number of Marines. And even a surprising number that can make it through RIP. It's a big Corps, after all."

"Yes," Pahner said, taking a sip of water, "there is more. Every member of The Empress' Own has some odd skill that the selection board thought might conceivably be of use. You don't get in if the only thing you know is what you've learned since Basic."

"I knew Poertena could swim that river," Kosutic told the prince. "But I wasn't about to tell him that I knew he was an Olympic-class swimmer," she added with a laugh.

"You mentioned Corporal Hooker," Pahner said soberly. "Ima Hooker was an air car thief before a judge gave her a choice between the Marines and a long jail sentence."

"What the hell is *she* doing in The Empress' Own?" O'Casey asked with a gasp as she choked on a mouthful of wine.

"She can open and be driving an air car she's never seen as fast as you can open your own and drive away with a key," Kosutic said seriously. "If you think that's not a skill the Empress might need someday, you're sadly mistaken."

"She is also *utterly* loyal to the Empress," Pahner told the chief of staff. "She actually has one of the most stable loyalty indexes I've ever seen. Better than yours, I might add, Ms. O'Casey. The Marines took her out of a hellish existence and gave her back her honor and purpose. She's somehow transferred that . . . redemption to the *person* of the Empress. She's definitely one of the ones who's going to end up in Gold."

"How strange," the academic murmured. She felt as if she'd stepped through the ancient Alice's looking glass.

"So what's *your* skill, Captain?" Roger asked.

"Ah, well." The CO smiled as he leaned back in the camp chair. "They make exceptions for captains."

"He's taught himself to be a pretty fair machinist, and he can rebuild an air car from the ground up," Kosutic said with a grin at the captain. "You only thought they made an exception for you. He also does decent interior work."

"Hmph! Better than yours."

"What is yours, Sergeant Major?" O'Casey asked after a moment had passed and it was obvious that the sergeant major wasn't going to be forthcoming.

"Well, the main one is . . ." Kosutic paused and glared balefully at Pahner ". . . knitting."

"*Knitting?*" Roger looked at the grim-faced warrior, unable to keep the laugh completely out of his voice. "Knitting? Really?"

"Yes. I like it, okay?"

"It just seems so . . ."

"Feminine?" O'Casey suggested.

"Well, yeah," the prince admitted.

"Okay, okay." Pahner grinned. "Let me point out that it's not just knitting. The Sergeant Major is from Armagh. She can take a hunk of wool, or anything similar, and make you an entire suit, given time."

"Oh," Roger said. The planet Armagh was a slow-boat

colony of primarily Irish descent. Like many slow-boat colonies, it had backslid after reaching its destination and stabilized at a preindustrial technology level before the arrival of the tunnel drive. And unfortunately, also like many, it had broken down into factional warfare. The arrival of the first tunnel drive ships and the subsequent absorption of the planet into the Empire of Man had reduced the blood feuds, but it hadn't eliminated them. It had been suggested that nothing short of carpet bombing the surface with nukes and sowing it with salt would get the residents of Armagh to stop fighting amongst themselves. It was practically a genetic imperative.

"Hey, it's not that bad," Kosutic protested. "You're safer in downtown New Belfast than you are walking around in Imperial City. Just . . . stay out of certain pubs."

"Some *other* time, I'll ask you what it was like being a priestess of the Fallen One on Armagh. Everywhere I turn there are fascinating stories like this," Roger said. "It's like taking off blinders." He yawned and patted Dogzard on the head. "Get up, you ugly beast." The sauroid lifted her red- and black-striped head off his lap with a disturbed hiss and headed for the tent door. "Folks, I'm exhausted. I'm for bed."

"Yes," Pahner said, standing up. "Long day tomorrow. We should all rest."

"Tomorrow," Roger said, getting up to follow Dogzard.

"Tomorrow," O'Casey said.

CHAPTER THIRTY-SEVEN

"We have found the nest of the *basik* outlanders!" Danal Far shouted. "Tomorrow we shall sweep down upon them and rid our lands of them forever! This land is ours!"

The shaman clan-chief of the Kranolta raised his spear in triumph, and the horns of defeated enemies clattered against the steel shaft. It had been long years since the Kranolta gathered in anything like the numbers in this valley. The crushing of the invasion by these "humans" would be the high point of his time as clan-chief.

"This land is ours!" the clan gathering echoed with a blare of horns. Many of them dated from the fall of Voitan, when the horns of champions had been common.

"I wish to speak!"

The statement took no one by surprise, and Danal Far grunted silently in laughter as the limping warrior stepped to the front. Let the young fool say his piece.

Puvin Eske was now the "chief" of the Vum Dee tribe of the Kranolta. As such, he was the representative of the tribe which had supplied the majority of the mercenaries to the N'Jaa of Q'Nkok. But now his tribe consisted only of many hungry females and a handful of survivors of their ambush of the human caravan. The tribe would be gone before the next full moon; the jungle and its competitors would see to that.

Puvin Eske was half the age of most of the leaders gathered for the council. Many of them had participated in the battles to take Voitan, long, long ago, and they remembered those days of high glory for the clan clearly. Few of them, however, saw the truth of the clan as it was, despite their complaints over the loss of spirit among their younger warriors.

"We face a grave decision," the young chieftain said. Only a few days before, he would have been far too hesitant, too aware of his youth, to speak in opposition to the clan elders. Now he'd looked into the face of Hell. After fighting Imperial Marines, no circle of weak, old men would bother him. "Our clan, despite its high standing, has faltered in my years. Every year, we have become fewer and fewer, despite the fertile lands we took from Voitan—"

"What is this 'we,' child?" one of the elders interrupted in a scoffing tone. "You weren't even a thought in your weakling father's head when Voitan fell!"

There were rough chuckles at the jest, but Danal Far raised his Spear of Honor to call for order.

"Let the 'chief' speak," the old shaman said. "Let the words be spoken in public, not in the darkness at the back of huts."

"I asked," the scarred and burned young chief continued, "are we not fewer? And the answer is, 'Yes, we are.' And I tell you this: the reason we are fewer is the fall of Voitan. We lost many, many of the host in the battle against Voitan. Now we recover slowly. Indeed, we seem to be faltering rather than recovering. I had many playmates in my years, but my son plays alone.

"Now the Vum Dee and Cus Mem are a memory. We brought the pride of our tribe against these 'humans,' and the warriors of Cus Mem joined us. We attacked them all unawares, with no warning."

He had, in fact, argued with his own father against the decision to attack. The runners who'd brought the tale of the fall of the House of N'Jaa had also brought word of the terror of the humans' weapons. Hearing that, and fearing for the tribe in its already crippled state, the young warrior had argued against taking losses among the flower of their warriors, but his arguments had been rejected.

"Yes, we surprised them," he continued, "yet still we lost a set of sets while the humans might have lost a hand pair."

The Kranolta's problems, although Puvin Eske didn't know it, were dispersion and death rate. The native sophonts had only two reproductive periods per Mardukan year. With the dispersion of the Kranolta to fill a huge hunting area very sparsely, the males of the tribe had been able to range at will in their hunting quests. Unfortunately, this meant that they weren't always around brooder females when their seed quickened.

Coupled with these missed opportunities to breed were the tremendous casualties taken in capturing Voitan. A single male could only implant a single female with eggs during mating season. With the multiple "pups" that this normally produced and a biannual reproduction, normal death rates were taken care of. But the death rate the Kranolta had suffered in capturing the city hadn't been anything like "normal," and despite the increase in hunting range, child death rates hadn't declined since.

All of which meant that the clan was recovering very slowly, if at all, from its "victory."

"If we lose the greater part of the clan's warriors to

these terrible weapons," Eske continued, holding up an arm cooked by plasma fire, "we shall be ended as a clan. Some few tribes might survive, but even this I doubt."

"Who shall speak to this?" Danal Far asked. He himself would have spoken against it, but an image of impartiality was important. Besides, the answer was a massed roar, and he pointed to one of the other veterans of Voitan. Let him put the young puppy in his place

"The only thing that the loss of Vum Dee shows is that they were and are gutless cowards, as proven by these words!" Gretis Xus shouted. The old warrior limped forward on painful scars won not just in the destruction of Voitan but in constant skirmishing against the other city-states that bordered his tribe. "Vum Dee has sat on its behind since the fall of Voitan. But the Dum Kai have continued to battle against the shit-sitters. We are not so weak and gutless as to accept this intrusion. I say that Vum Dee is no longer true Kranolta!"

Xus' words drew a roar of approval, not just from the gathered tribe chiefs, but from the ring of warriors behind them. Puvin Eske heard it, and bent his head in sorrow.

"I have spoken my words. As I spoke them to my father, who is no more. Puvin Shee, who was the first over the walls of Voitan; who wore the horns of the King of Voitan on his belt. And who I saw cut in half before my eyes by fire from warriors it was nearly impossible to see."

He raised his head and regarded the other tribes.

"Vum Dee will be eaten soon enough by other tribes and the jungle. But if the Kranolta go forth to battle the humans, so also shall the rest of the Kranolta be eaten. You say the Vum Dee, whose fathers led the Kranolta over the walls of Voitan, whose warriors were the spear of the Kranolta all the way out of our ancient tribal lands, whose own flesh was the clan-chief of the Kranolta for the war against Voitan, are not true Kranolta? Very well. Perhaps it is true. But tell me this five days hence, for then it shall indeed be true. For five days hence, there shall *be* no Kranolta!"

The warrior turned and walked out of the circle of hostile faces. Many glared, but none tried to stop him. None would dare even now to touch a chief at the clan meeting. Let them wait the days.

Danal Far took center place again as the Vum Dee chief and his decimated retinue left the circle.

"Are there any other objections?" he asked. "Seeing none, I call for an attack against these humans as soon as we can reach them. They will move out on the morrow, probably for Voitan, but we shall intercept them before they reach there. They move slowly through the jungle, and it will be easy. They are only shit-sitters, after all."

"Move!"

Julian shouldered the private aside, hit the sixth setting on his multitool, held it at arm's length as it flicked into a 130-centimeter blade, and grunted with effort as he brought the mono-machete down on the thick liana. The girder-thick vine parted with a crack and swung towards him, and he grunted again as it hit him in the stomach—then yelled in fear as he had to roll out of the way of a descending pack beast paw.

The point gave him a glance of thanks and hurried to get in front of the pack beast again.

The company moved through the jungle at a trot. It was virtually impossible to maintain that pace, but they were doing it anyway. For the most part, the *flarta* were breaking trail, but occasional larger obstacles had to be cleared the hard way. That meant the point squads were kept busy hacking through the thicker lianas and finding ways around the occasional deep valleys which had begun to appear, none of which was designed to make people who'd survived the first ambush happy at the distraction from keeping an eye out for *future* ambushes.

The ground was rising towards the hills they had glimpsed by the river. Somewhere on the edge of that range of low mountains were the ruins of the city of Voitan, perched, according to reports, on the shoulder of a small peak. And somewhere—either at those ruins, or in the jungle—they were going to be hit again by the Kranolta. Better for it to be in the ruins, where there were places to defend, than in these open, defenseless woods.

Roger leapt a small fallen trunk that hadn't yet been smashed to splinters by the caravan of *flar-ta* and helped the squad leader to his feet.

"No lying down on the job, Julian," he said, and continued on without a pause. Cord, who'd just caught up with the prince, clapped his hands in frustration and trotted off in pursuit.

Julian wasn't sure if the prince was joking or not. The tone had been dead serious, but it could have been a very dry joke. Very dry.

The NCO shrugged and reformatted his multitool to fit into its pouch. If they survived, he might figure it out; if they didn't, it wouldn't matter anyway.

Pahner nodded to himself as his toot flashed a time alert.

"Second Platoon, onto the pack beasts. First Platoon, point!"

Humans, especially Marines, could almost certainly have outrun the *flar-ta* over time and in open terrain. In the jungle, it would have been a toss-up, at best. The company already had several badly sprained or broken ankles, and the strain of jumping logs and dodging limbs slowed them badly.

But the Marines got a breather by cycling the platoons onto and off of the big beasts. It was hard on the *flar-ta*, and Pahner hadn't needed the mahouts to tell him that they would have to rest for at least a couple of days when they reached Voitan, but it was the only way to ensure that the troops would be in any reasonable sort of shape if it dropped into the pot.

Pahner saw the prince pull himself up the ropes onto the *flar-ta* he'd christened Patty, and nodded. Roger had stated that for purposes of rotation he was in Second Platoon, and he'd apparently stuck to that. Which was good. The kid was coming along.

"Captain!" Gunny Lai called. "We've got movement front!"

Cutan Mett heard the tramping sounds of a herd of *flar-ta* and waved his warriors to a halt. They were the vanguard of the Miv Qist tribe, and he felt their hungry anticipation as they realized that the honor of first contact with the invaders was about to be theirs.

"Fire on the contact," Pahner said. Normally, he would have waited for more than a sensor reading. That was not only doctrine, it was also common sense . . . normally. But not here. Whether it was a bolting damnbeast or the vanguard of the attackers, it was time to "plow the road."

"Roger," Lai responded.

The Imperial Marine M-46 was a forty-millimeter, belt-fed, gas-operated grenade launcher. The advanced composition of the grenades' filler gave them the destructive force of a pre-space twenty-kilo bomb, but despite any advances in explosive fillers, the chemical-powered launcher had an old-fashioned kick like that of a particularly irritated Terran mule. Ripping off an entire belt in a mass of fire, as the prince had done a few days before, was the action of an idiot or someone who was very good with the weapon and big enough to handle the recoil.

Lance Corporal Pentzikis was neither a fool nor particularly massive. So when given the order to "flush" the detected Mardukans, the experienced Marine settled the big weapon into her shoulder, made sure the forty-round belt fed over her shoulder without a kink, and started a slow, aimed fire.

The rounds impacted with a deep jackhammer sound that raised the hackles on experienced troopers' necks, and the remainder of First Platoon spread out around her as she fired grenades into the area where the sensors had detected movement. Moments later, the ground and trees flashed white.

Mett shouted as the trees around him started to come apart in eruptions of thunder and lightning, and splinters flayed the warriors of Miv Qist.

"Forward!" he bellowed. *"This land is ours!"*

There were times when Ima Hooker felt like a distilled potion of fury. Whether that was nature or nurture—the father who'd given her her name had been cruel in many other ways—she neither knew nor cared. All that she cared about were the occasional moments when the Imperial Marines gave her an outlet for it.

Like now.

As the scummies burst out of the concealing foliage, she snugged the bead rifle into her shoulder, placed the laser targeting dot on the body of the leader, and flicked her rifle to its three-round burst setting. Time to get some back from the universe.

✧   ✧   ✧

Pahner glanced at his tactical display and made a decision.

"They're trying to close the route," he snapped over the command circuit. "First, stay in place, screening our flank. As we pass, roll in behind us. Everybody but sharpshooters off the pack beasts. Third to the point, Second in the body. Pick up the pace Marines. Let's *go!*"

Roger started to slide off Patty and got slapped on the leg by Sergeant Hazheir.

"Stay up there, Your Highness!" the acting platoon sergeant said. "You're probably who he *meant* by sharpshooters."

Roger laughed and nodded.

"Okay! " he yelled as the staff sergeant slid off the beast and trotted forward. "I'll try to remember who the good guys are!"

Corporal Hooker put another burst into the vegetation and cursed. The bastards were figuring out to stay behind cover.

"Behie! Flush those bastards for me!" she snapped, highlighting the cover with her target designator for the grenadier.

"Roger!" Pentzikis had just finished attaching a new belt and pivoted slightly, letting the launcher's sensors search for the target. "I need more grenades; I'm short."

"Roger," Edwin Bilali acknowledged. The NCO shot at a patch of gray and was rewarded by a scream. "Gelert! Get to the pack beasts and bring back three strings of grenades!"

"On my way, boss!" The newbie private put a burst into the vegetation in front of him and reared up to run for the passing beasts. He thought he knew where he could find the ammunition.

Ima Hooker popped out her first magazine and had just started to reload another of the half-kilo plastic packs when a scummy reared up from behind a log and hurled its javelin.

"Heads up!" she shouted, seating the magazine, and took aim.

The spinning HE grenade beat her to the shot, exploding a meter above the Mardukan's head and turning it into red jelly, but the burst also threw two more targets into her view. The fury within her howled like an enraged beast, for she'd seen the result of her momentary distraction, and she unleashed her rage and flicked the three-millimeter bead gun onto full automatic and cut the unfortunate natives in half.

"*Bastards!*" she screamed, and swept the muzzle onward, seeking still more targets and fresh vengeance.

Sergeant Bilali ran to the rifleman, but he knew he was too late. The private from St. Augustine scrabbled at the muck and loam of the jungle floor, choking on the blood that poured out of his mouth. Bilali pulled off the private's helmet and tried to roll him over, but the javelin pinned him to the forest floor, and the movement jerked a scream through the bright, scarlet flood.

"Ah, Christ, Jeno!" The NCO's hands fluttered helplessly over the wounds. Bullets didn't transfix their targets like specimens in some alien entomologist's collection, so all his training meant nothing. "Ah, God, man."

"Move!" Dobrescu was suddenly at his side. The warrant officer had already learned all he cared to know about wounds like this one. He figured the kid had about one chance in twenty, max, but it was worth going for.

"It's got to come all the way through," the medic went on as he pulled out a monomolecular bone cutter. The scissorlike device sliced open the chameleon suit and snipped the javelin shaft flush with the private's back effortlessly, with absolutely minimal movement, yet even that tiny twitch evoked another scream.

"Now comes the fun part," Dobrescu added through gritted teeth. "Gelert," he said firmly, applying a self-sealing bandage. "Listen to me. I got one way to save your life, and its gonna have to go quick. We are going to *flip* you onto your back. You're probably going to pass out from the pain, but don't scream. Don't."

Even as he spoke, he was running a drainage tube with frantic haste. The wound was going to have to drain somewhere, and if it drained into the lungs, nanites or no nanites, the kid was going to drown in his own blood.

Gelert was twitching and the blood was going everywhere as the company passed them by. Stopping for one casualty would get them all killed, but if Dobrescu couldn't get this kid evacuated soon, the company's advance was going to leave him behind the caravan.

"Bilali, I'm gonna need a stretcher party."

"Who the fuck is going to carry it?" the NCO demanded as fresh firing started to the front and another cry of "Medic!" cut through the bedlam. "We're getting hammered."

"Find someone!" the warrant officer barked. He wondered for a moment if he should just write the kid off and get him lashed to a pack beast until they could bag and burn him. But if he could get the holes patched and the bleeding slowed, the fast-heal nanites sometimes could perform miracles. Fuck it.

"And while you're finding somebody, we're going to need security!"

"Roger," Kosutic answered. "Shit!" She looked over her shoulder. "*Captain!*"

"What?" Pahner never looked away from his HUD. Second Platoon had just passed through in the leapfrog and reported that they were hitting signs of buildings and rock outcroppings. If they made it into the city, it was going to be by the skin of their teeth, and he could hear the howling of the Kranolta horns behind him. It was as if the Huntsmen of Hell had been loosed on their trail.

"Dobrescu is trying to get Gelert stabilized to move. He's already out of Third's coverage!"

That was enough to pull the captain away from his display, and he looked up in disbelief. The sergeant major looked as royally pissed as he felt, not that being in agreement made either of them feel any better.

"Dobrescu!" Pahner keyed his communicator. "Get your ass out of there—now!"

"Captain, I have Gelert stabilized. I think I can save him."

"Mr. Dobrescu, this is in order. Get your ass out of there!" He checked his HUD and realized that none of the private's fire team had moved out. "*Bilali!*"

"Sir, we're pulling out as fast as we can rig a stretcher," the NCO responded.

"Sergeant—!"

The company CO chopped off his furious command. Long, long ago at the Corps NCO combat leadership school, he'd been told something which had stood him in a good stead for fifty-plus Standard years: Never give an order you know won't be obeyed. He never had, and he didn't intend to start today.

"We'll be waiting for you in Voitan, Sergeant."

He knew he'd just written off their only medic, who was also an irreplaceable pilot, and a full fire team, but that was better than losing the entire company trying to cover them.

The line of *flar-ta* was pounding up a slope and through a ruined gateway partially choked by the rubble of the gatehouse. The area beyond was too large to hold for long—a fifty-meter-wide plaza surrounded by over-grown heaps of masonry—but it was a good place to rally.

"Hold it up on the other side," he called over the general company frequency. "Third Platoon on the gate, First and Second in support. I want a headcount."

He stepped up onto a liana-bound pile of masonry that had probably been the wall of a house, and looked around. A quick count showed him that all of the pack beasts had made it through, most of them with bead rifle or grenade launcher-armed Marines on top. Then he took another look at the riders.

"Where," he asked with deadly calm, "is Prince Roger?"

CHAPTER THIRTY-EIGHT

Bilali triggered another burst and the group of scummies disappeared behind their log. He had them pinned for the time being, but he was also low on ammunition.

"Sarge," Hooker called, "you got any ammo? I'm dry."

He cursed silently. Hooker always put her rounds on target, but she always used too many of them.

"I'm about out here, too," he answered.

"I've got some," Dobrescu said. "Take 'em."

The medic had the patient fully prepped and was working on a field expedient stretcher: the trunks of two stout young saplings with the wounded private's chameleon suit stretched between them. It would be heavy and awkward and nearly impossible to get up to the city, but it was the only chance the wounded trooper had.

"Shit!" Hooker spun to the west. "I've got movement between us and the Company!"

"Calm down, Hooker," came the prince's voice. "We're coming in."

✧   ✧   ✧

Roger was positive that he'd killed not only himself, but Matsugae and O'Casey as well. Eleanora was shaking like a leaf, but she still managed to hold up her end of the heavily-loaded standard-issue stretcher. Matsugae was smiling, as usual, as he carried the other end, but the expression was a rictus.

"Roger," the valet told him, "this is quite insane."

"You keep saying that." Roger ducked down behind a tree. "Doc, you're going to have to take the other end for Eleanora on the way back."

He gripped the butt of the grenade launcher between his arm and rib cage, stood up, and ripped out a string of fifteen grenades. The end of the string traveled upward and off target, but most of them hammered into the area where the scummies had taken cover. The shrapnel and splinters of shattered branches scourged the cowering natives like flying knives, and drove them to their feet, screaming.

While Bilali and Hooker blew their flushed targets apart, Roger ejected the mostly-used belt and picked another off the stretcher. The stretcher was covered in belts, as were his shoulders, and more of them bulged his rucksack.

"We'd better move, Doc."

"Got it!" The warrant officer dumped the munitions off the stretcher. "Bilali, Hooker, Penti, get loaded."

Roger kept an eye on the woodline beyond the smashed lane where the *flar-ta* had thundered through the jungle while the remnants of the fire team gathered up the ammunition the civilians had humped in to them and Dobrescu got Gelert strapped into the stretcher.

"Thank you, Sir," Bilali said. "But this is goddamn stupid."

"My blood for yours, Sergeant," the prince replied.

"Why the hell should you try to save my life if I'm not willing to reciprocate?"

"Break out the armor!" Pahner shouted furiously over the general circuit. "Roger, where the *hell* are you?!"

"Ah," Roger said as Matsugae and Dobrescu lifted the stretcher. "Our master's voice."

Pentzikis was so nervous that she broke into giggles and put a few rounds into the woodline from the twitch.

"We're fucking dead," she giggled. "If the goddamn scummies don't kill us, Captain Pahner will!"

"I don't think so." Roger lifted another belt of grenades out of his rucksack and draped it across the top. "Personally, I refuse to die today."

"Come on, you stupid hunk of crap!"

Julian watched the power levels rise in his helmet HUD. The suit wasn't even on completely, but he could feel the crash of grenades through the heels of his armored boots.

Despreaux hooked on his gloves, working with furious haste as the crack of bead rifles got closer. A moment later came the furious blast of another string of grenades in the distance, and she knew that Roger, at least, was still alive.

"You'll make it," she said.

"I know I'll make it. But will I make it before Pahner decides to just kill us and start over with scummies as bodyguards?"

"It's not *our* fault Roger went haring off!" Despreaux protested, furious with the prince.

"No, but after we save ourselves, Pahner is going to kill us. We were supposed to be *watching* the little shit."

"Now that's not fair," the female sergeant snapped as she hooked up the gravity feed to the stutter gun. The quad-barreled bead gun hooked to an ammunition storage box on the back of the armor, but despite the mass of rounds in the box, it could still run through its ammunition in a surprising hurry. And they had only so many boxes. "Roger was trying to save a wounded Marine," she went on. "And watch your ammo."

"I will," Julian said. "And he was. But he's still a little shit. If he gets killed, I'm gonna frag his ass."

"You're up!" Despreaux made the last connection and flipped his visor up to give him some air. Until the things came online, the armored suits could be sweltering.

"Still waiting for the God *damned* computer to settle down," Julian snarled. Why the damn thing took so long to load was always a mystery to the Marines. It was worse than a pad.

"*Julian?*" Pahner roared from his perch on the rubble.

"Waiting for warm-up to complete, Sir!" Julian yelled back, looking around his troops. He couldn't even do his status check until the damned computer completed dumping its memory or pulling its cheek or whatever took so . . . so . . . so modder pocking long. Finally, the damned light turned green.

"*Up!*" He shouted, and raised one hand, thumbs up. A moment later, two more hands came up, then a third. But that was it.

"What the fuck?" He'd lost Russell earlier, but that still left nine in his squad. "Status check!"

"Red lights," Corporal Aburia reported tersely, stepping up to Cathcart and looking into his helmet. The plasma gunner was yelling behind his visor, and the team leader lifted it just in time to hear ". . . motherfuckingcocksuck . . ."

"We've only got four, Sir," Julian told Pahner over the captain's private channel.

"*Poertena!*"

"How you doin' for ammo, Behie?" Roger yelled as he laid down another string and a screen of lianas vanished in the explosions. A javelin had come from beyond that screen, and Roger had become a major proponent of peace through superior firepower. A ghastly shriek sounded even through the thunder of grenades, and something thrashed and bled in the bushes. "Fuck with a MacClintock, will you?" he yelled.

"I've got five belts left, Sir!" The grenadier popped a single round into a suspicious looking bush, exercising an economy of ammunition expenditure His Highness seemed constitutionally unable to match. "You might want to conserve your ammunition a little, Sir."

"We can conserve ammo when we're dead," he retorted. "Move, I'll cover you."

The grenadier just shook her head and darted from behind the fallen tree she'd been using for shelter. The stretcher team—the struggling doc and Matsugae, with the prince's chief of staff holding a bottle of drip fluid—was nearly twenty meters ahead of them, closely protected by the bead gunners as the grenadiers covered the retreat. She'd already tried to argue about who should move out first and who should stay behind in a movement. And lost. She was done arguing.

She ran to where Hooker sheltered behind another fallen tree. They'd cursed all day long at the obstacles the passage of the *flar-ta* had thrown down, but now they were lifesavers.

"Move, Sir!" Pentzikis shouted, and fired a round into another likely looking clump.

Roger pushed himself up with both hands and turned to run . . . just as a massive flight of javelins erupted out of the brush.

"Oh, fuck," the grenadier said mildly. She'd become expert at judging the flight of the spears, and she realized they were all aimed at their previous positions. Hers . . . and the prince's.

Roger didn't even think—not consciously, anyway. He simply bolted straight towards the source of that massive flight, grenade launcher blazing. There was no way he could outrun the flock of javelins, but he might be able to run *under* them.

Their angle of flight, partially because of the slope of the ground, was high, and the speed he'd found so useful on soccer fields finally came into its own somewhere else. As the steel-tipped rain fell all around and behind him, he charged forward, grenade launcher spitting a metronome of fire.

Julian and his three armored companions passed the stretcher team, bounding by in run mode at nearly sixty kilometers per hour. They could have gone faster on better ground, but not on a track torn by *flar-ta* and covered in fallen trees.

"Man, Bilali," Julian said as he passed. "You are fucked."

"What the hell was I supposed to do?" the squad leader demanded, falling back to cover the stretcher team. "Knock him over the head and throw *him* on the stretcher?"

"Probably," the squad leader snarled, then tripped over one of the fallen trunks and plowed into a tree that was still standing. *"Shit!"*

"You okay, boss?" Gronningen called. The big Asgardian had his M-105 plasma cannon trained outward. The company hadn't expected to be using them so quickly, so they hadn't been inspected with the same care as the M-98s. On the other hand, they were an older and more robust design which had never given any trouble. Yet.

"Yeah, yeah," Julian growled, scrambling to his feet. The impact had done far more damage to the tree than to his now sap-coated armor. It would take more than a sixty kilometer per hour impact to damage ChromSten. "I'll be right there," he added as another flurry of grenades exploded ahead of them.

Roger dropped the empty grenade launcher and pulled his sword over his shoulder. The sensei in school was always talking about *The Book of Five Rings*, but the prince had never bothered to read it all. Another of those little acts of rebellion he was beginning to regret. Still, he remembered the technique for battling multiple opponents: reduce it to one at a time.

Nice to know, he thought, surveying the fifteen or twenty Mardukans filtering out of the brush with a variety of swords, spears, and other sharpened artifacts. *Now, how the hell do you do it?*

Some of them were wounded, a few quite seriously. Most of them, however, were just fine. And seemed really upset about something. Worse, the clear notes of hundreds of hunting horns sounded, coming up the hill behind them. All in all, it looked to be just a little dicey. Maybe they would leave him alone because his forehead didn't offer any trophies? Right.

The first Mardukan charged, holding a spear at waist height and screaming to wake the dead. Roger parried the spear down and to the side, let the momentum carry him through a spin and took off one of the scummy's arm as he passed. Then the rest of the group charged, and he picked out the weakest: a Mardukan with a bloody shrapnel wound on one leg.

Roger charged the wounded warrior, parrying another's spear and carrying the sword into a high parry of the wounded Mardukan's own blade. A butterfly twist, and the katana-like weapon came down and across, opening the Mardukan from shoulder to thigh as Roger passed through the closing circle.

He found himself several meters from his opponents, gazing at the group of warriors. He'd laid out two of them for nary a scratch, and the Kranolta seemed to be reevaluating the situation.

Roger was doing the same. He was fully aware that so far he'd survived on luck and a few tricks, but these Kranolta didn't seem to be very well trained. There were standard counters for both of the attacks he'd used. Cord knew them, and he'd taught them to the prince, but none of these tribesmen seemed aware of them. If all of them were this inept, he might last, oh, five more minutes.

But realistically, unless something broke soon, he was dead. Unfortunately, if he turned tail and ran, those spears could fly faster than he could run. So far, nobody seemed inclined to simply pincushion him and be done with it, and as long as it was hand-to-hand and more or less one-on-one he had a chance, however small.

Let's hear it for Homeric customs, he thought.

One of the scummies stepped forward and drew a line on the ground. Roger looked at it and shrugged; he had no idea what the gesture meant. He thought about it, then drew a line of his own.

The scummy clapped his false hands and stepped over his own line and fell into a guard position.

As he did, Roger thought of his pistol for the first time. There were only four spearmen; the others carried only swords. He could draw his pistol and kill all of his missile-armed opponents before the first spear could fly—he'd proven that conclusively in Q'Nkok—and he almost did it. It was the right thing to do, and he knew it. The idea of a prince of the Empire of Man fighting some four-armed barbarian with a sword on a neo-barb planet on the ass-end of nowhere was something from a really bad adventure novel. And if, by some fluke, he survived the experience, Captain Armand Pahner would personally break his neck for it.

He stepped over the line.

As he did, the scummy charged, sword held over his right shoulder. The weapon was one of the Mardukan two-handers and weighed nearly ten kilos. If Roger tried to block it, it would smash through his parry as if it weren't even there, so he waited patiently, sword at low guard, until the scummy began his swing. Then he darted in close to his towering foe, his sword held practically overhead.

The clash of steel was frighteningly loud as Hooker pounded into view. At every step, she'd expected to see the prince's dead body, for the ground was a pincushion of javelins. Instead, she found him in the midst of a half-circle of yelling scummies. She nearly tripped over a dead Mardukan as she skidded to a stop, but she managed to keep her feet . . . and not open fire as a dozen more scummies trotted up to join the shouting crowd. She knew instinctively that if she fired, the prince was dead.

Roger panted and looked at the next scummy in line. Already, three bodies had been pulled out of the de facto arena, and he was beginning to learn the rules. The line he'd drawn was a safe point. As long as he stayed on "his" side of it, they wouldn't attack, and if they were on the other side of their line, he couldn't attack in turn. However, the one time he'd waited too long to come out to meet an opponent, they'd gotten agitated. Obviously, he couldn't just sit and wait for rescue.

He didn't look around as he heard running feet behind him, but from the stiffening of some of the Mardukans, it had to be a Marine.

"There's a line behind me on the ground. Don't cross it!"

"Yes, Sir." He recognized Hooker's voice and hoped the angry little Marine would keep her cool. "Armor's on its way."

Roger nodded and flexed his shoulders. He'd long since dropped his rucksack, ammunition harness, and anything else that threatened to weigh him down. His sparring with Cord had taught him much that had, so far, kept him alive. As a mass, these scummies might be the most terrifying thing on this part of the planet, but as individuals, they were almost woefully ill-trained. On the other hand, it had been a long day already, and he was getting tired.

"Tell them to get here fast, but keep their cool," he said as another set of boots pounded up behind him. Then he looked at the scummy. "Come on, you four-armed bastard. I'm getting bored."

Julian passed the Mardukan shaman, hurrying towards Roger's position. The NCO wasn't sure exactly what the old scummy was saying, but it sounded a lot like cursing. The old geezer, who was fast enough on open ground, was having a bunch of trouble with the fallen trees, which was obviously the reason Roger hadn't included him on this little jaunt.

"Glad to see you're as happy with him as we are," the Marine yelled over his external speakers as he thundered by.

"I'll kill him," Cord snarled. "*Asi* or no *asi*, I swear I will!"

"Okay by me, but you'll have to get in line," Julian said as he passed out of sight. "A *long* line."

"I'm gonna kill him," Pahner said, almost calmly, as Bilali and the stretcher team pounded into view.

"Bilali?" Kosutic asked rubbing her ear.

"Roger. Maybe Bilali, too."

The team leader marched up to the company commander and saluted.

"Sir, Sergeant Bilali reporting with party of one."

"And that one isn't the Prince, I see," Pahner said coldly. "I am far too enraged at the moment to deal with this. Get out of my sight."

"Yes, Sir." The sergeant walked over to where the medic was working on Gelert.

"Don't go ballistic, Armand," Kosutic whispered. "We have a *long* way to go."

"I keep telling myself that," Pahner replied. "And I'm trying not to. But if we lose the Prince, finishing the journey is next to pointless."

Kosutic could only nod at that.

Roger stepped back across his line and turned around. "Who is the leader here?" he asked.

Over a hundred scummies had gathered to watch the contest by now. So far, Roger had won each match handily. A gouge on his helmet indicated the closest anyone had come to hitting him, and several of his own supporters—including Julian and his armored companions—had assembled with Hooker behind him. So far, the scummies had left his cheering section strictly alone while they concentrated on the main event.

A handful of seconds passed, and then a single Mardukan stepped carefully onto the blood-soaked ground. He was older than most of the others, much scarred, and wore a necklace of horns around his neck.

"I am the senior tribe chief. I am Leem Molay, chief of the Kranolta Du Juqa."

"Well," Roger flipped the sword sideways to flick off the blood pooling on it, "I am Prince Roger Ramius Sergei Alexander Chiang MacClintock, of the House MacClintock, Heir Tertiary to the Throne of Man. And I finally have enough firepower to turn your pissant little tribe into meat for the *atul*." He took a rag from Hooker and began wiping down his blade as Cord came scrambling across the fallen tree trunks at last. "I don't intend to kill you one by one until I'm exhausted, and I don't intend to stand here jawing until darkness. So I propose a truce."

"Why should we let you live?" the chief scoffed.

"Julian?" Roger hadn't been able to see who was in the suits, and he'd long before turned his radio off. Listening to Pahner bitch had gotten on his nerves.

"Yep," one of the suits answered over its external speakers.

"Leem Molay, how many of your warriors do you want slaughtered to prove that you should let us walk away?" Roger sheathed his cleaned sword and took his reloaded grenade launcher from Pentzikis, but his icy eyes never left the Kranolta chieftain.

"Let me ask it this way," he went on calmly, tilting his head to the side. "Which half do you want us to kill to prove our point?"

"If you could truly kill us all, you would!" the chief retorted. "We are the Kranolta! Even Voitan could not stand before us! We will wipe *your* pissant little tribe from these lands!"

Roger inhaled sharply through his nostrils. The stench of dead Mardukans barely affected him at this point; he was far too deep into that dark world of battle.

"Watch carefully, old fool," he hissed.

The impromptu challenge matches had occurred on an open spot on the southern edge of the main battle zone. The Mardukans, for the most part, had been appearing from the northern woodline, so the southern one would make a better neutral target zone.

"Sergeant Julian." The prince gestured to the south. "Demonstration, please."

"Yes, Your Highness," the squad leader replied over his external speakers. He'd directed the response at the Kranolta, and his toot automatically translated it into the local dialect. "Gronningen, make these fine people a clearing to bury their dead in."

"Aye," Gronningen acknowledged, and turned to the south. "Shaman Cord, you might want to cover your ears."

The M-105 was a much heavier system than the M-98. That meant that, despite the all-pervasive, humid dampness of the jungle, the first shot from the plasma cannon left a trail of flickering fires on a ruler-straight line from the big Asgardian to the plasma bolt's impact on a tree in the middle of the area Roger had indicated. Where it shattered a divot into the woods.

The cannon's *"CRAAACK!"* was the loudest sound any of the Mardukans, even the survivors of the first brush with the company, had ever heard. It set their ears ringing, and the thermal pulse dried the surface of their mucus-covered skin, burning several of them painfully. And that was just from the secondary effects.

Twenty meters of the jungle giant which had been the gunner's target simply vanished as a lightning bolt carved from the heart of a star devoured it. The massive trunk shredded explosively for another five to ten meters above the impact point, and splinters longer than Roger was tall shrieked through the air far more lethally than any Kranolta javelin. The top of the tree flipped away into the burning jungle beyond, and the vegetation around it was turned into a finely divided, drifting ash surrounded by a dozen other burning, fallen trees.

And then Gronningen fired another round. And a third.

With those three rounds, he'd cleared a section of jungle fifty meters on a side and ringed with smoldering vegetation. Within that semicircle of hellfire, the ground steamed and smoked.

After a moment's stunned reflection, the chieftain turned from the destruction and asked the question.

"Why?"

"Because I don't intend to fight my way into Voitan. We walk into the city unmolested, or we kill every scummy in sight. Your choice."

"And on the morrow?" Molay was beginning to understand Puvin Eske's objections to this attack.

"On the morrow, you do your damnedest to kill all of us. Good luck. You had your chance to kill me as an individual . . . and couldn't. I suggest that you go home. If you do, we . . . I, Prince Roger Ramius Sergei Alexander Chiang MacClintock, will let you live."

The Kranolta chieftain laughed, although, even to himself, the sound was hollow. Or perhaps it was only the ringing in his ears.

"You think much of yourselves, humans. We are the Kranolta! I myself was one of the first over the walls of Voitan! Don't think to impress me with your threats!"

"We are The Empress' Own," Roger replied in a voice of iron, "and The Empress' Own does not know the meaning of failure." He smiled grimly, baring his teeth in that way which bothered most species except humans. "We rarely know the meaning of mercy, either, so count your blessings that I'm willing to show it to you this once."

The Mardukan glanced again at the flaming clearing and clapped his true-hands.

"Very well. We will let you go."

"Unmolested," Roger said. "To the city."

"Yes," the old Mardukan said. "And on the morrow, we will come, Prince Roger Ramius Sergei Alexander Chiang MacClintock. And the Kranolta will kill you all!"

"Then you'd better bring a bigger army!" Roger snarled, turning his back, and switched on his radio. "Julian, take the back door."

"Oh, yeah," the squad leader said. "Bet on it."

CHAPTER THIRTY-NINE

Most of the company was already gone when Roger walked through the gates. The hill ascended through the ruined city to a citadel on the upper slope, and it was obviously there that Captain Pahner had decided to make his stand.

Not everyone had been sent on to the citadel, however. A security detachment consisting of most of Second Platoon covered the gates, and Pahner sat waiting on his mound of rubble.

Roger walked up and saluted the captain.

"I'm back," he said, and Pahner shook his head slowly and spat out his gum at the prince's feet.

"First of all, Your Highness, as you've pointed out to me time and again, you don't salute me, I salute you."

"Captain—"

"I won't ask what you were thinking," the Marine continued. "I know what you were thinking. And I will admit here and now that it has a certain romantic attraction. It will certainly play well to the newsfeeds when we get home."

"Captain—"

"But it doesn't play well to *me*," Pahner snarled. "I've spent Marines like water to keep you alive, and having you throw that away on a stupid little gesture really pissed me off, Your Highness."

"Captain Pahner—" Roger tried again, beginning to get angry.

"You wanna play games, Your Highness?" the officer demanded, finally standing up. The two were of a height, both of them nearly two meters, but Pahner was by far the more imposing, a modern Hercules in bulk and build.

"You wanna play games?" he repeated in a deadly quiet voice. "Fine. I'm a master of playing games. I resign. *You're* the fucking company commander." He tapped the prince on the forehead with one finger. "*You* figure out how to make it across this goddamned planet without running completely out of ammunition and troops."

"Captain—" Roger was beginning to sound desperate.

"Yes, Sir, I'll just toddle along behind. What the hell, there's not a damn thing I can do *anyway*!" Pahner's face was turning a truly alarming shade of red. "I am really, really pissed at Bilali, Your Highness. You know why?"

"Huh?" Roger was confused by the sudden *non sequitur*. "No, why? But—"

"Because he can't forget he's a goddamned Marine!" Pahner barked. "I was a Marine before his *mother* was born, but when I came to the Regiment the first time, do you know what they told me?"

"No. But, Captain—"

"They told me to forget about being a Marine. Because Marines have all sorts of great traditions. Marines always bring back their dead. Marines never disobey an order. Marines always recover the flag. But in The Empress' Own, there's only *one* tradition. And do you know what the tradition of *your* regiment is, Colonel?"

"No, I guess not, but, Captain—"

"The tradition is that there is only one task. Only one mission. And we've never failed at it. Do you know what it is?"

"To protect the Imperial Family," Roger said, trying to get a word in edgewise. "But, Captain—"

"Do you think I *liked* leaving Gelert behind?!" the captain shouted.

"No, but—"

"Or Bilali, or Hooker, or, for God's sake, Dobrescu? Do you think I liked leaving our only *medic* behind?"

"No, Captain," Roger said, no longer even trying to rebut.

"Do you know why I was willing to lose those valuable people, troopers I've trained with my own hands, some of them for years? People I love? People that until recently you didn't even realize *existed*?"

"No," Roger said, finally really listening. "Why?"

"Because we have only one job: get you back to Imperial City alive. Until Crown Prince John's kids reach their legal majority and Parliament confirms their place in the succession, *you*—God help us all—are third in line for the Throne of Man! And whether you believe it or not, your family is the only damned glue holding the entire Empire of Man together, which is why it's our job—the *Regiment's* job—to protect that glue at any cost. Anything that stands in the way of that *has* to be ignored. Anything!" the captain snarled. "That's our mission. That's our *only* mission. I thought about it, and determined that I couldn't persuade them to retreat and abandon Gelert. But the company probably would have been lost if we'd settled into a meeting engagement on that ground. So I ran," he said softly.

"I abandoned them to certain death, cut my losses, and beat feet. For one reason only. And do you know what that was?"

"To keep me alive," Roger said quietly.

"So how do you think I felt when I turned around and you weren't there? After sacrificing all those people? And finding out it was for *nothing*?"

"I'm sorry, Sir," Roger said. "I didn't think."

"No," Pahner snapped. "You didn't. That's just fine, even expected, in a brand new, wet-behind-the-ears lieutenant. The ones who survive by luck and the skin of their teeth learn to think, eventually. But I can't take the chance on *your* not making it. Is that clear?"

"Yes," Roger replied, looking at the ground.

"If we lose you, we might as well all cut our throats. You realize that?"

"Yes, Sir."

"Roger, you'd better learn to think," the Marine said in a softer tone. "You'd better learn to think very quickly. I nearly took the entire company back out to get you. And we would all have died on that slope, because we couldn't have extracted you and then withdrawn successfully. We would have died right here. All of us. Bilali and Hooker and Despreaux and Eleanora and Kostas and all the rest of us. You understand?"

"Yes." Roger's voice was almost inaudible and he was looking at the ground again.

"And whose fault would that have been? Yours, or Bilali's?"

"Mine." Roger sighed, and Pahner looked at him unblinkingly for several moments, then nodded.

"Okay. As long as we have that straight," he said, and waited again until Roger nodded back.

"Colonel," he went on then, without a smile, "I think it's time we gave you another 'hat.' " He reached out again and tapped the prince on the forehead once more, more gently this time. "I think you need to take over as Third Platoon leader, Colonel. I know it will be a step down in rank, but I really need a platoon leader over there. Are you up for it, Colonel?"

Roger took his gaze off the ground at last, looked up at him, and nodded with slightly misty eyes.

"I'll try."

"Very well, Lieutenant MacClintock. Your platoon sergeant is Gunnery Sergeant Jin. He's an experienced NCO, and I think you could learn a lot from listening to his advice. I remind you that platoon leader is one of the most dangerous jobs in the Corps. Keep your head down and your powder dry."

"Yes, Sir," Roger said, and produced another salute.

"You'd better get up there, Lieutenant," the captain said soberly. "Your platoon is hard at work digging in. I think you should familiarize yourself with the situation as soon as possible."

"Yes, Sir!" Roger saluted yet again.

"Dismissed," Pahner said, and shook his head as the prince trotted up the ruined road towards the citadel. At least he finally had Roger unambiguously slotted into the chain of command, although he hated to think how the Regiment's CO was going to feel about the expedient to which he'd been driven. Now if he could only keep the young idiot alive! Platoon leader really *was* the most dangerous post in the Corps; which didn't mean that it wasn't *less* dangerous than watching Prince Roger ricochet around like an unaimed rifle bead on his own.

He watched the prince for a few more moments, then decided that he should hurry himself. He couldn't wait to see Jin's face.

"Gunnery Sergeant Jin?"

"Yes, Your Highness?" The gunnery sergeant turned from specifying positions and fields of fire with Corporal Casset and glanced at the prince. "Can I help you?"

The city of Voitan had been vast, but the citadel was

the simplest of constructions. It was built into the slope of the mountain, backed up to a cliff which had been quarried sheer, undoubtedly for building material for the rest of the city. A seven-meter curtain wall ran in a more or less semicircle from cliff to cliff and surrounded a three-story inner keep. The curtain wall was thick, three meters across at the top and tapered outward as it descended, with a heavy bastion built right into the cliff face at either end. The only entrances to the bastions were through small doors on the inner side at the level of the top of the wall. The original doors were long since gone, but temporary doors were already being constructed. The upper stories of the bastions had been of wood and had burned down long ago, as had the upper story of the keep, but the lower stories were built into the wall, and the interior partitions were stone. These had withstood not only the Kranolta assault but also the ravages of time and even the unceasing onslaught of the Mardukan jungle.

Slits for javelins and spears were arrayed on the "wall-level," pointing outward. No inner first-story slits faced the top of the wall, but upper-level slits did just that, designed so that if the top of the wall were taken, fire could be poured into the attackers. There were also slits at the level of the bailey, so that if the attackers made it over the wall they could be attacked as they assaulted the keep.

The keep itself was a large, burned-out, vine-covered shell. The upper story, like those of the bastions, had been constructed of wood and was now charcoal. The rear of the keep, however, was dug deeply into the hillside, its roof supported by cleverly constructed stone buttresses, which provided a large, cavelike area that could be used to shield the pack beasts, wounded, and noncombatants. The *flar-ta*, kept from stampeding by chains stapled into the naked rock, were on the ground level, while the wounded and noncombatants waited on a raised shelf on the north side, along with Julian and the other power-armored Marines.

There were spear slits at the keep's bailey level, but the only exterior door was on the second floor, up a staircase. Vines covered the walls, and trees had grown up through the flagstones of the bailey, but other than the vegetation and the damage to the gates, the gray stone of the fortress was intact.

Third Platoon, which was still more or less at full strength, had been assigned the left side of the wall, while First and Second shared the right. Teams from both groups were working feverishly to construct barricades to replace the broken and decayed gates, and Sergeant Jin had been noting the locations of the platoon's troopers and their fields of fire. It was important to ensure that all possible approaches were covered and that the heaviest fire could be directed at the point where the enemy would be most likely to attack in force.

With that in mind, Jin had placed his grenadiers in locations covering the primary avenues of approach. He'd also pointed out to them the locations that the enemy was most likely to use for cover. There were, unfortunately, a lot of those. The citadel overlooked what had once been a densely populated city, and the shells of buildings still loomed above narrow, twisting streets. That would have been enough to mask the approach of any attackers by itself, but the ruins were also massively overgrown with vines, creepers, small trees, and jungle ferns, producing what were effectively well-screened trenches up to the foot of the citadel wall. Those would be the particular target of the grenadiers, since they were the only troopers whose weapons would allow them to drop indirect fire behind obstacles.

The platoon also had two plasma cannon. Given the failure of the power suits and the fact that this would be a stationary defense, the heavy cannon had been set up on their tripods. Jin intended to use them only against the heaviest concentrations of enemies, both because the Marines had developed a healthy distaste for the possible repercussions of firing them and because of the need to conserve their precious ammunition.

He was going to be without Julian and his team of suit-users. The inoperable suits had been lashed back onto the pack beasts, with their cursing users still trapped inside them, and carried out into the citadel. The gear was now scattered on one side of the bailey with Poertena working on it, but the personnel whose suits did work were going to be used as a reserve for the company as a whole. So it was with too few troops to man the section of wall he'd been given, with his heavy troopers missing, and the possibility, however remote, of losing half his platoon to exploding plasma cannon, that the gunnery sergeant found out he had a new responsibility.

"I'm your new platoon leader," Roger said.

"Pardon me?" Jin looked around. Corporal Casset was standing with his jaw dropped, but other than the corporal (and the pissed-off and tired-looking shaman standing behind the prince) no one else had heard Roger's announcement. "Is this some sort of joke, Your Highness?"

"No, Gunnery Sergeant, it isn't," Roger said carefully. "Captain Pahner has asked me to 'wear another hat.' He's appointed me to be your platoon leader."

"Oh," Jin said. He did not add "joy," for some unknown reason, but after a moment he went on with slightly glassy eyes. "Very well, Your Highness. If you'll give me a moment, I'll walk you through the defenses and explain the placements. I would ask for your comments and suggestions after that."

"Very well, Gunny. And, I think 'Sir' would be

appropriate. Or 'Lieutenant.' I'm not really a prince in this assignment, as I understand things."

"Very well, Your . . . Sir," the sergeant said, shaking his head.

"Captain, we've gotten our people into position, and—"

"Shhh!" Pahner's hand waved Lieutenant Jasco to silence as the captain turned his head from side to side.

"Pardon me, Sir?" the lieutenant said after trying for a moment to figure out what he was looking at. All the lieutenant could see was the idiot prince talking to Gunny Jin.

"*Shhh!*" Pahner repeated, then grunted in satisfaction as he finally managed to get the directional microphone onto the conversation just as Jin realized what his company commander had done to him.

Lieutenant Jasco maintained a straight face as Captain Pahner did something the lieutenant would have flatly denied was possible. He giggled. It was an amazing sound to hear out of the tall, broad officer, and Pahner cut it off almost immediately. He listened for a few more seconds, then switched off the mike and turned to Jasco with a seraphic smile.

"Yes, Lieutenant?" he asked, still chuckling. "You were saying?"

"We've gotten all of our people into position, Sir. When do you think they're going to attack?"

"Lieutenant," Pahner looked at the sky, "your guess on that is as good as mine. But I think they'll wait until morning. It's getting late, and they've never hit us at night. I'll come by your positions in a bit. Go get with your platoon sergeant and figure out a chow rotation for right now."

He could smell Matsugae starting something on a fire.

❖   ❖   ❖

Roger sniffed and looked towards the keep where Kostas had dinner well under way. The valet might just have put himself in harm's way to rescue a nobody trooper, but it didn't seem to have affected him at all. He'd simply gone back to organizing the camp. Maybe there was a lesson to learn there.

Roger turned and swept his gaze over the troopers still working all around him. Now that the basics had been done—setting up the heavy weapons, assigning fields of fire, putting up sandbags where stones had fallen from the battlements of the citadel wall—the Marines were improving their individual positions. Despite the intense heat, even more focused here inside the stone walls, the troopers worked without pause. They knew it would be too late to improve their chances of survival *after* the Kranolta hit.

Despreaux walked over to him, and he nodded to her.

"Sergeant," he said, and she nodded back and tossed him the small object in her hand.

"Nice folks."

Roger caught the item and blanched. It was a very small Mardukan skull, one side crushed. The horns were barely buds.

"There's a big pile of bones over in the bastion," she continued. "That was part of it. It looks like the defenders made some sort of stand."

Roger looked over the wall at the crumbled city below. He had enough experience now to imagine the horrors the castle's defenders would have observed as the rest of their city went up in roaring flame and massacre. And to imagine their despair as the gate crumbled and the Kranolta barbarians poured through. . . .

"I'm not really very happy with these fellows," he said, setting the skull gently on the parapet.

"I've seen worse," Despreaux said coldly. "I made the

drop on Jurgen. Pardon me if I'm humanocentric, but . . . it was worse."

"Jurgen?" Roger couldn't place the name.

Despreaux's sculpted profile hardened, and a muscle in her jaw twitched.

"No place that mattered, Your Highness. Just a stinking little fringe world. Bunch of dirt-poor colonists, and a single town. A pirate ship dropped in for a visit. It was a particularly unpleasant bunch. By the time we got there, the pirates were long gone. The results weren't."

"Oh," Roger said. The attacks on border worlds were so common that they hardly ever made the news in the Home Regions. "I'm sorry."

"Nothing for you to be sorry about, Your Highness. Just something to remember; there's bad guys out there all the time. The only people who usually see them are the Fleet and the Marines. But when things get screwed up enough, this isn't so uncommon. The barbs are always at the door."

She touched the skull gently, then gave him another cool nod and walked back to where her squad was digging in. Roger continued looking out over the city, stroking the skull with a thumb, until Pahner walked up.

"How's it going, Lieutenant?"

"Just fine . . . Sir," Roger said distractedly, still gazing out over murdered Voitan. "Captain, can I say something as 'His Highness' instead of 'Lieutenant'?"

"Certainly," Pahner said with a smile. "Your Highness."

"I don't think it would be a good idea to leave an existing force in our rear, do you?"

"You're talking about the Kranolta?" Pahner glanced at the skull.

"Yes, Captain. How are we fixed for power for the suits?"

"Well," Pahner grimaced, "since we only have four of them up, not bad. Days and days with just four of them.

But we need to get the rest up to have a hope in hell of taking the spaceport."

"But we have enough for a pursuit, don't we?"

"Certainly." Pahner nodded. "And you have a point about leaving remnants in our rear. I don't want to have to fight off ambushes from here to the next city-state."

"Good." Roger turned and looked the captain in the eye. "I don't think that the cause of civilization on this world would be advanced by leaving a single Kranolta alive, Captain. I would prefer that that not be the case after tomorrow."

Pahner regarded him steadily, then nodded.

"So would I, Your Highness. So would I. I think tomorrow we'll be building a samadh. To the honor of the Corps."

CHAPTER FORTY

Roger looked out from the citadel wall as the first overcast light of dawn stole across the dead, jungle-devoured cityscape.

The company had been up for nearly an hour, getting breakfast and preparing for these first moments of early morning light. This time, Before Morning Nautical Twilight, had been considered the most dangerous time of all for millennia. It was the time preferred for a "dawn attack," when sleepy-eyed sentries were at their lowest ebb and attackers could slip up under cover of darkness but attack with the gathering light.

The Marines' answer was the same one armies had used for centuries: get up well before time and be awake and alert when the moment of "stand to" came. Naturally, as had also been the case for centuries, there were some complainers.

Roger wasn't one of them. He'd been up for hours

the previous night, reviewing his actions of the day before and worrying about what was to come. For all that he'd been fighting monsters and the occasional skirmish or ambush all the way across the continent, this would be his first true battle. Today the Kranolta would come to kill the company, and someone would lose, and someone would win. Some of them would die, and some would live. While it seemed likely that casualties would be light, there was still a risk. There was even a risk that the humans would lose, and then word of the treachery aboard the *DeGlopper* would never reach Earth. Roger had smiled at himself when he reached that point in his ruminations. It was amusing to realize that the main thing he thought about was that the word wouldn't get back to his mother, not that he himself would be dead.

Sergeant Major Kosutic padded up silently behind him and leaned on the lip of the adjoining embrasure.

"Still quiet," she said, and glanced over at Cord who stood silently at Roger's back. Since the events of the day before, the old shaman had attached himself firmly to his "master," and was rarely to be found more than five meters away.

The sergeant major had been up from time to time the night before. Not worried, just running through the practiced actions of an experienced warrior checking on changes. Still, she'd become slightly perturbed as every sentry throughout the night had reported more and more fires. The tactical computers were having a hard time pinning down numbers, but each fire sent the estimates up and up. The current balance of forces didn't look good.

"I wish we had some razor wire," she said.

"Do you think it will come to that?" Roger asked in surprise. "They've only got spears; we have plasma cannon."

"Your Highness—I mean, Lieutenant," Kosutic said with a smile, "there's an old story, probably a space story, about a general and a captain. They were fighting some indigs and an air car came in with a spear sticking out of the side. The captain laughed and asked how they could lose against people armed only with spears. But the general looked at the captain and asked how she thought they could win against people willing to *fight* an air car with only a spear."

"And the moral is?" Roger asked politely.

"The moral, Lieutenant, is that there is no such thing as a deadly weapon. There are only deadly people, and the Kranolta—" her hand waved over the battlements at the broken city "—are fairly deadly."

Roger nodded and looked around, then back into the sergeant major's eyes.

"Are we?" he asked quietly.

"Oh, yeah," Kosutic said. "Nobody who gets through RIP is a slacker in a firefight. But . . . there's gonna be a lot of those scummies, and there ain't many of us." She shivered slightly at the smell of woodsmoke from the thousands of fires in the jungle. "It's gonna get interesting. Satan damn me if it ain't."

"We'll get the job done, Sergeant Major," the prince said confidently.

"Yeah." Kosutic looked at the sword hilt jutting up over his shoulder. "I suppose we will."

Captain Pahner strolled up, checking the positions, and looked out at the mists curling around the ruined city.

"Beautiful morning, fellas," he remarked, and Roger chuckled.

"It'd be even more beautiful if half 'my' platoon were in armor, Captain. What's the status?"

"Well," Pahner said with a grimace, "it isn't pretty, 'Lieutenant.' Poertena found the fault, which is a mold eating the contacts coating of the joint power conduits.

You can't remove the coating; it's a dissimilar metallic contact. The problem seems to be in a new 'improved' version."

"Oh shit," Kosutic chuckled grimly.

"Yeah." Pahner nodded with a grim smile. "Another improvement. The suits that hadn't been 'upgraded' are okay. But that's just the four."

"What are we going to do?" Roger's eyes were wide, for Pahner had stressed repeatedly that they had to have the suits to take the starport.

"Fortunately, the contacts tend to wear out, so each suit has a spare in its onboard spares compartment. The ones sealed up in the storage packets are okay, but . . ."

"But there's only a couple of spares per suit, normally." Kosutic shook her head. "So we're down to four sets of armor for everything except taking the spaceport."

"Right." The captain nodded. "We can cannibalize from suits that we lose the users for, or that go down with other problems we can't fix. So we can put His Highness in a suit if things look particularly bad. But until then, it's just 'The Four Horseman.' "

"I guess that will have to do," Roger said with a shrug, then changed the subject. "So what's the plan for today, Captain?"

"Well," Pahner replied with his own shrug, "we wait until they have the majority of their forces in close, then engage with all the firepower we have. I won't say that I agree or disagree about whether they should be wiped out as a tribe, but we can't afford to have a large force following us to the next city-state. So they have to be eliminated as an operational threat at least."

"Can we do that?" Over the night, Roger's ardor had cooled, and he looked at the scattered weapons positions worriedly.

"Against what I'd estimate the maximum threat to be, yes," Pahner said. "There's a big difference between barbarian warriors and soldiers, and today these Kranolta are going to discover that."

"What's your estimate?" There were hundreds of fires in the jungle according to the taccomp in Roger's helmet—just under a thousand, in fact.

"I'm estimating a maximum of five thousand warriors with some camp followers. More than that is really hard to maintain logistically."

"Five *thousand*?" Roger choked. "There are only *seventy* of us!"

"Don't sweat it, Your Highness." Kosutic gave him a cold smile. "A defensive position like this gives us a ten-to-one advantage all by its lonesome. Add in the fire-power, and five thousand isn't an impossible number." She paused and looked thoughtful. "Tough? Yeah. But not impossible. We're gonna get hurt, though."

"We'll make it through," Pahner said grimly. "That's the only thing that matters."

"What did Cord think of those numbers?" the prince asked, looking over his shoulder at the shaman. Despite the Marines' confidence, it still seemed like a lot of scummies to him.

"The Kranolta are said to be as numerous as the stars in the sky," the shaman said quietly. "They cover the ground like the trees."

"Maybe they do," Pahner said, "but that's not what you could call a hard and fast number. And it's really difficult to support more than five thousand in these sorts of conditions. I don't see any sign of a baggage train, for example."

"And if it *is* more?" Roger asked dubiously.

"More than the stars in the sky?" Pahner smiled wryly. "If it's more than five thousand, well . . . we'll just handle it. The important part is to survive and damage them badly enough that they decide that fucking with Imperial Marines is a short road to Hell."

✦   ✦   ✦

"Oh hell," Corporal Kane whispered.

The humans had been working in shifts throughout the night to prepare their defenses, and she stood on one of the recently constructed platforms within the burned-out bastion, monitoring the sensor remotes planted along the approaches to the citadel. That gave her the dubious pleasure of an advanced look at the approaching horde, and a horde it was. She took one more look at the numbers estimate, blanched, and keyed her radio.

"Sergeant Despreaux, could you step over to the west bastion?"

The company command group had gathered atop the curtain wall gatehouse, watching the gathering horde on their visor HUDs. Captain Pahner's maximum estimate had unquestionably been exceeded.

"How the hell could they have gathered fifteen thousand warriors?" Pahner demanded irately. He couldn't seem to decide whether he was more incredulous or more offended that the Kranolta had not abided by his professional estimate.

"Between fifteen and eighteen, actually, Sir," Lieutenant Gulyas corrected, looking at the readout on his own helmet heads-up display.

"Should I have Poertena start warming up the other suits?" "Lieutenant" MacClintock asked.

"No," Pahner said, thinking furiously.

"We could engage them at longer ranges," Lieutenant Jasco suggested. "The plasma cannon would range from here, and they've got the punch to burn through the undergrowth. Hell, for that matter, they could blow through most of those *walls* without much sweat."

"No," Pahner said again, shaking his head. He pulled out a stick of gum and popped it into his mouth without any sort of ritual.

"This is gonna get real interesting, boss," Kosutic said, taking another look between the battlements.

"Pull the plasma cannon off the walls," Pahner said abruptly. "Put them in the bastions ready to move up. Put one on each of the bottom floors, and the rest at wall level. When we come to grips, it's bead rifles only. No grenades, no plasma."

"But—" Lieutenant Jasco said. "Sir, we'll lose the walls!"

"Yep," Pahner agreed with a grim smile. "Better make sure the door to the keep is heavily reinforced. And tell Julian his people stay put in there until I tell him different. And make sure those damned pack beasts are tied down!" If the elephant-sized *flar-ta* got loose in those close confines, it would doom anyone who wasn't in armor.

"I'll take care of that," Jasco said, heading out the door.

"Get those plasma cannon moved back," Pahner continued to Gulyas. "Remember, at least one downstairs in each of the bastions. We have five, so two upstairs in Third Platoon's bastion, and one downstairs. One up, one down in the east bastion."

"I'm on it," the lieutenant replied, already leaving, and Pahner turned back to the oncoming Kranolta.

"I still don't believe this." He shook his head. "Where do they get the food?"

"They've had word of our coming for some time now," Cord pointed out. "Undoubtedly they heard through rumors from Q'Nkok, and with that warning, the warriors would have gorged and gorged for days, then set off with packs of food for Voitan. We were lucky to arrive before the main host."

"They were probably waiting for us wherever the crossing of that Satan-damned swamp was," Kosutic agreed, nodding her head. "Good thing *we* didn't know where it was, or we'd be dead in the jungle."

"They can't stay together long," Cord admitted. "Only a few days, at most. But they don't intend to stay long; only long enough to kill us."

"And if we just hold them off," Roger continued, "they'll be waiting for us every few kilometers in the jungle."

"Which is why we have to do more than drive them off," Pahner confirmed. "And we will."

"Let's hope so," Roger said. "Let's hope so."

CHAPTER FORTY-ONE

All through the long morning, the enemy gathered in a swarm just inside the ruined outer wall of the city. The mass of natives blew their horrible trophy horns and pounded drums, taunting the humans hunkered down in the citadel. Finally, when their numbers were fully gathered, they started in good order for the citadel.

Pahner, watching the approach from the gate bastion on the HUD fed by the remotes, nodded as he surveyed their formation. The lead group carried scaling ladders, and about a third of the way back from the front of the formation a mass of warriors with ropes carried a large ram. They'd prepared well, he decided, but then, they'd taken this city before.

Of course, they've never tried to take a city away from The Empress' Own, he thought grimly.

"Third Platoon, when that ram gets to a hundred and fifty meters from the gate, take it out with plasma fire."

Roger watched from a position on the wall. The heavily reinforced firing point had been prepared for one of the plasma cannons, so it was a "safe" spot from which to watch the approach of the enemy. It seemed folly to wait for the Kranolta to overrun the company before using heavy weapons, but he was taking Pahner's lead. He keyed his microphone and passed on the order.

Corporal Cathcart was almost over the failure of his armor, but he was still pissed about being taken off the wall and told to hold his fire. So when the word came down to engage the ram, he was happy to oblige.

The designers of Voitan's original defenses had faced only muscle-powered weapon threats, and that had dictated the clear areas they had allowed as fire zones. The citadel's approaches had been paved and flat for approximately a hundred and fifty meters from the curtain wall gatehouse, and just a bit over a hundred meters from the rest of the wall. The city's buildings had begun beyond those ranges, and the wrecked, decaying, luxuriantly overgrown ruins of those buildings were what cut up the company's fire lanes and would have deprived it of the full use of its range advantage even if Captain Pahner hadn't opted to let the barbarians close. But those ruins were also liberally seeded with remote sensors, and Cathcart had been using them to watch the big log approach.

Now he rolled his plasma cannon over to a handy spear slot and mentally licked his chops as he positioned it carefully. The cannon was designed for use as either a crew-served weapon or from a powered armor mount. In its crew-served configuration, its mount included retractable wheels, which were really quite useful in situations like this. He got the gun lined up, and hit the switch to take it off the wheels and drop its firing platform firmly into place.

"Everybody stand back. There's liable to be some backblast."

The barrel of the weapon was aligned with the exterior of the mini-fort as he hunted until he spotted the ram again. It had advanced another fifty meters as the lead elements approached the wall. In fact, it was in direct line of sight from his position now, and he punched a button and grunted as the entire ram was outlined in red on his sighting screen. The computer recognized it as a target and began to track automatically.

There were quicker ways to do things like this, but he had plenty of time, and it never hurt to do the job right. He designated the entire ram as a target, then designated three specific target points along its length before he took his eyes from the display to look carefully around his position one last time. He was behind the blast shield, but anyone else nearby might be caught by backscatter as the plasma charge exited the spear slit. Fortunately, everyone was well under cover . . . helped, no doubt, he reflected, by memories of exploding plasma rifles.

"Fire in the hole!"

The three plasma charges hit like the micro-nuclear explosions they were. They didn't splinter the ram; they vaporized it, along with every one of its carriers and every Kranolta warrior within forty meters. Beyond that immediate kill zone, there were actually some survivors, although the mucus-covered Mardukans suffered horribly from the flash burns of thermal bloom. The entire horde bellowed in shock, but they hadn't been totally surprised, for the story of Julian's "demonstration" had spread among them.

Worse, from the humans' perspective, the narrow, twisting streets, choked with rubble, and encroaching jungle wreckage, split the Kranolta advance into channelized tentacles, exactly as the Marines had feared. Had the horde been a more organized force, that might have wreaked havoc with its attack, but the barbarians' lack of organization actually worked in their favor in this instance. They were scarcely discommoded by the confusion of their approach to the citadel, even as the Marines were denied the full advantage of their weapons' range.

That was one main reason Pahner had selected his chosen deployment plan. If the scummies were prepared to accept sufficient casualties, they could close with the citadel whatever his people did, so he'd decided to make a virtue out of his weakness.

The trickiest element of his battle plan was the need to inflict sufficient casualties to enrage the barbarians into pressing the attack without hurting them badly enough to convince them to do the intelligent thing and back off until simple starvation forced the Marines to abandon their defensive position and run a gauntlet of endless ambushes in the jungle. Not that this particular bunch of barbarians seemed to require much in the way of enraging, he reflected as they surged forward around the huge, half-fused hole the plasma cannon had torn in their ranks.

Cathcart's shot had also acted as an effective start for the rest of the company's fire. The citadel's elevated position helped some, but the furthest out aiming stake was barely a hundred and fifty meters from the curtain wall. That was short range for a bead rifle . . . and meant the scummies had only a soccer field and a half to cross.

"*Fire!*" Gunnery Sergeant Jin snapped over the platoon net, and set the example himself. The first wave of burst fire from the company tumbled a windrow of the ladder-carriers in piles, but the mass of natives simply kept coming as the following ranks picked up the ladders and charged the walls.

Pahner nodded. The enemy was coming on more or less as expected, although the ladders were a surprise. There were even more Kranolta than the taccomp had

estimated, though, and that was causing a few jinks in
the plan. They were also much heavier on the west flank;
Roger's side. It might be a good idea to thin them out
a bit.

"I want two grenade volleys," he called. "Aim into the
middle of the mass, about seventy-five meters out. I want
to create a break in the assault."

"Roger," Lieutenant Jasco acknowledged. He'd taken
over command of the right wall while Lieutenant Gulyas
was in the keep.

The grenadiers filed out of the bastions and got into
position as the bead riflemen on the parapets continued
to pour aimed fire into the attacking Mardukans. The
grenadiers readied their weapons and awaited the word
as Pahner followed the timing. Right . . . about . . .

"*Now!*"

The twelve remaining grenadiers fired upon his command. For most of them, it was their first clear look
at the enemy, but the numbers coming at them didn't
throw off their aim. The twenty-four grenades arced
out into the mass of the Mardukans, dropping behind
sheltering walls and heaps of rubble which had blocked
the bead fire, and detonated. The double string of
explosions ripped holes in the Kranolta army, and hundreds of the four-armed natives writhed in shrieking
agony as shrapnel from the mini-artillery scythed
through their packed ranks.

"Again," Pahner called. "Down fifty meters."

Again the belt-fed launchers spat out their packages
of death, tearing the ranks of the enemy apart. But still
the natives closed up over the mangled bodies of their
comrades and came on, blowing their horns and bellowing war cries.

"Okay," Pahner said, satisfied. "Back under cover." He
pursed his lips and whistled. " '*When you're wounded
and left on Marduk's plains—*' "

Most of the grenadiers filed back into the bastions, where the hastily constructed doors were wedged in place. The few who stayed on the wall picked up their bead rifles and opened fire again. The enemy was about to assault.

"Sir," Lieutenant Jasco said, with a grunt that carried clearly over the com, "I've got more ladders coming up than I've got hands to push down. I need some support here."

"Same here," Roger reported, and Pahner heard the distinctive sound of steel meeting flesh over the prince's radio. "We're about to lose the wall!"

"Too soon," Pahner whispered, peering through the slit that overlooked Roger's position. There were already Mardukans on the wall, in close combat with the Marines, and he saw Roger lop the head off one, while Cord speared another.

"Call out your grenadiers and plasma gunners! Push them off the walls!" he ordered. He'd held the grenadiers and plasma gunners under cover to protect them from the anticipated wave of javelins from the Mardukans, but very few javelins were flying. Instead, the Kranolta concentrated with fanatical determination on getting over the walls and coming to close grips with their smaller opponents. *When are they going to follow the plan?* he wondered with a grim mental chuckle. *Guess they've learned a little about the disadvantages of matching javelins against bead rifles at range. Too bad it's really true that no plan survives contact with the enemy!*

The fresh infusion of Marines and a barrage of grenades pushed the enemy off the walls, and Pahner was relieved to see no prone bodies and only a few Marines nursing wounds.

"Switch out weapons. Put the wounded in the bastions." He looked out the slit facing the enemy, who seemed to be getting back in shape rather quickly. "And get ready for another attack!"

"Inside, Despreaux." Roger thumbed towards the bastion.

"I'm not hurt that bad, Sir." She hefted her rifle with her left hand, and started to try to reload it one-handed.

"I said, get in the bastion!" Roger snatched the weapon out of her hand. "That's an order, Sergeant."

Her jaw clenched, but then she nodded.

"Yes, *Sir!*" She saluted with her left hand.

"And get Liszez to replace you."

"Aye," she answered, and he nodded and turned towards the gate.

"Kameswaran! I thought I told you to get your ass into the bastion!"

Jimmy Dalton stroked the butt of the bead rifle and shook his head. There sure were a shit-load of the damned scummies.

The plasma gunner had carried a bead rifle through about half his service, so he was familiar enough with the operation of the weapon. But he'd also inherited Corporal Kameswaran's ammo harness, and that was unfamiliar. Everyone had his own idiosyncrasies about what went where, and the corporal's were more idiosyncratic than most.

Dalton ran his hand across the positions of all the gear and shook his head. Just had to hope he didn't need any of the stuff in a hurry.

The prince came up and looked out of the mini-bunker the private occupied.

"Looks like they're getting ready to come back."

"Yes, Your Highness." The private wished he had his plasma rifle; that would slow them up. "When do we open fire?"

"When Gunny Jin gives the word." The prince grinned. "Even I don't fire until the gunny says it's okay!"

"Yes, Your Highness." The plasma gunner ran his hand across the ammo harness again and shook his head. They'd made it onto the walls the last time. Why not open fire further out?

The prince seemed to read his mind.

"This is hard, waiting for them to come to us. But it would be worse worrying about being ambushed from here to the sea. We need to suck them in and kill them all, Jimmy, not just drive them off."

Dalton hadn't thought the prince even knew his name.

"Yes, Your Highness."

"I'm not Prince Roger right now, Jimmy. I'm just your platoon leader. Call me Lieutenant MacClintock."

"Yes, Your—Lieutenant," the private said. As if he didn't have enough to worry about.

Most of the ladders were still at the base of the wall, so the Kranolta came on at an unburdened run in the second wave.

"*Fire!*" Jin barked as they passed the hundred-meter stake and picked out his own target—one covered with horn trophies. "Take that, you bastard," he whispered, as the chieftain and two followers fell away from the burst of fire.

Roger pulled out another magazine and inserted it even as he maintained fire. The double magazine system was made for situations like this. His accuracy was somewhat degraded during the switch, but as long as he fired into that incredible mass of targets he was bound to hit *something*.

The Kranolta packed the ground before the wall as they reached its base and the ladders started coming up again. They were more tangled than in the first assault, but a little thing like that was nothing in the chaos at the wall's foot. Thousands of them were packed dozens deep, each and every one of them determined to be the very first over the battlements.

"Grenades, Gunny?" Roger heard his own voice over the radio and was surprised by how calm he sounded. He triggered another burst into the back of the mass; leaning out over the wall to fire directly down at its base was hazardous to health.

"Yes, Sir," Jin approved and called the order. A dozen grenades sailed into the close-packed Kranolta, exploding with deadly effectiveness, but the close press of bodies actually lessened their effect by absorbing blast and fragments, and the holes they opened closed rapidly as the feet of fresh waves of tribesmen pounded their less fortunate fellows into paste.

Roger charged forward as the first ladder came up in his sector. He and PFC Stickles managed to heave it back over the side with a descending scream from the scummies on it, but three more came up in the time it took to push one off. The Kranolta were pushing forward again through sheer weight of numbers and there were nowhere near enough humans to cover the full length of the wall.

"*Grenades!*" Pahner barked. "All you've got!"

Roger ripped one of the hundred-gram cylinders off his belt with his left hand, thumbed the activator, and tossed it over the wall just as the first scummy appeared at the top of a ladder. The prince put two rifle beads into the attacker one-handed even as he threw two more grenades, but by then the Kranolta were over the wall.

His magazine clicked suddenly empty, and he tossed the rifle into "his" bunker and waded in with the katana as he had before. This battle was a complete madhouse, with dozens of screaming barbarians clambering over the parapets, their false-hands holding the ladders and both true-hands filled with weapons. Trading parries with a scummy who was better than usual, Roger found himself back-to-back with Cord and realized they were practically alone. Most of the Marines had retreated into the bastions, but there were a few human bodies scattered along the wall.

"Cord!" Roger ducked a swing and opened the attacking Kranolta from thigh to breastbone. "We have to get off the wall!"

"No doubt!" the shaman shouted back, and speared another attacker. The barbarian dropped, but Cord suddenly found himself facing three replacements, and they did not appear to be taking turns. "How?"

Roger was about to reply, when his eyes widened and he spun and lunged at Cord. He tackled the much larger shaman hard enough to drive both of them into his mini-bunker . . . just as the flight of grenades from Third Platoon's bastion landed.

The grenades temporarily cleared the wall, turning the Kranolta who'd scaled it into hamburger. Most of the Marines' chameleon-suited wounded were unaffected by the air-burst grenades, but the unarmored barbarians were slaughtered.

Fragments also tore into Cord's legs. Roger had thrown himself across the shaman's torso, preventing instant death, but the native was horribly injured, and Roger himself was considerably the worse for wear.

He was stumbling to his feet, ears ringing, vision doubled, and more than half stunned, when he felt himself lifted and thrown across a shoulder.

"Okay," Despreaux snapped. She seemed, he noticed, to be upside-down. "Are you done playing hero, Hero?"

"Get Cord," he croaked. It had to be either St. John or Mutabi carrying him, he decided; nobody else was big enough.

"Already done," she said, taking one corner of the

shaman's stretcher. Wounded Marines were being dragged off all along the wall while others recovered their weapons.

The last thing Roger remembered was an upside-down scummy coming over the parapet, with his ax raised over Despreaux's head.

Pahner listened to the reports and nodded.

"One more time on the walls. But make sure everyone makes it back to the bastions this time."

He looked out at the sea of scummies and shook his head. The jam-packed mob looked as if it hadn't been reduced at all, but that was an illusion. They'd already lost almost a fifth of their force to the wall assaults and the grenades. Now it was time to start the real killing.

"Blow the gate."

The timber barrier replacing the ruined gates had been carefully constructed. The original purpose of the emplaced demolition charges had been to permit a sally by the armored suits, but the explosives designed to let Marines out worked just as well to let Mardukans in.

The loss of their ram had reduced the Kranolta at the gate to clawing and hacking at the timbers. Their howls of frustration had been clearly audible even through the din of battle . . . and so were their shrieks of agony as the demo charges' explosions mangled them and blew them backwards. The warriors behind them paid them no heed, however, except to stream forward over their writhing bodies, screaming exultant war cries as they fanned out across the bailey. The gate was down; the fortress was theirs!

"Oh, Captain, that was mean," Julian whispered as he peered through the firing slit at the open gateway. He watched the tide of scummies split, some charging for the keep, and others for the inner stairs to the bastions, and then he poked his bead cannon through the slit.

There were a number of available munitions for the weapon. Besides the standard ten-millimeter ceramic-cored, steel-coated beads, there were both armor piercing and "special actions" munitions. The armor piercing beads were designed to be effective against any known suit armor, and against most armored vehicles, as well. The "special actions" munitions were mixed. Some were crowd-control devices: sticky balls to coat rioters in glue, knockout gas, or puke gas. And some of them were for close quarter conditions where the object was pure, unmitigated slaughter. The company didn't have many of those with them, but this was just about the perfect time to use the one magazine he had.

He stroked the stock of the bead cannon with a feral grin.

"Come to Poppa," he crooned.

Pahner gazed down into the courtyard from the gatehouse's upper story, calmly masticating his gum and waiting. He blew a bubble when First Platoon reported that spears were being thrust into the ground floor slits of its bastion. He nodded when the keep reported that the Mardukans were chopping at its door, and he steepled his fingers when the sound of ax blows started beneath his own feet. Then he nodded again.

"Fire," he said, and stepped back from the spear slit.

Julian had already programmed his visor HUD to show the round's footprint, and he aimed his first shot carefully. The ten-millimeter cylinder was fired at very low velocity, relatively speaking, but the instant it exited the barrel, it blossomed like some hideous flower to deploy its twenty-five depleted uranium beads in a beautiful geometric pattern like a high-tech spider's web.

Strung with monomolecular wire.

The advanced adaptation of the ancient concept of chainshot was lethal almost beyond belief, yet it never made it across the courtyard. Its designers wouldn't have believed that was possible, for the wire sliced through weapons, limbs, and bodies almost effortlessly. But only *almost*. If enough flesh and bone was crowded together in its path, eventually even wire a single molecule thick would find sufficient resistance to stop it.

This wire did, but not before it had torn over a third of the way across the bailey and sliced every native in its path into neatly severed gobbets of flesh. The destruction sprayed blood and bits of Mardukan in every direction, and so did the second shot in Julian's magazine. And the third. And the fourth.

The paved courtyard was an abattoir, filled with Kranolta who'd finally seen sufficient concentrated slaughter to stem even their frenzied advance for just a moment. The survivors were frozen in momentary shock and disbelief, like lifesize sculptures coated in the blood of their hideously dismembered fellows.

Sculptures which were cooked an instant later by plasma cannon.

There were four of the weapons at ground level: one in each bastion, and two mounted in armored suits in the keep. Some of the natives had begun poking spears into the firing slits before Pahner gave the word, but a few blasts from bead rifles had cleared the Kranolta away. Now all four plasma gunners thrust the muzzles of their weapons outward, a moment after the "special actions" cartridges had scythed across the bailey, and filled the courtyard with actinic silver fury.

The charges from the cannon were five times as powerful as those from mere plasma rifles, and the volcanic impact of four of them within the confined space of the bailey flashed all of the remaining vegetation into flame and cooked every Kranolta inside the gates.

The remaining plasma cannon on the wall level opened up simultaneously. Their blasts of silver fire were less intense and concentrated than in the confined space of the bailey, but that made them no less effective. They turned the Kranolta attacking the bastions into charred stumps and flaming torches. The hydrophilic Mardukans were particularly susceptible to burns, and the silver death of the plasma cannon was pure horror to them as it swept the top of the wall.

The handful who survived threw themselves shrieking from the wall's height, accepting broken bones or death itself—*anything*—to escape that ravening, hideous furnace.

Pahner stepped back up to the spear slit and looked out over the area in front of the citadel. The true horror within the bailey and atop the walls had been invisible to most of the enemy outside the fortress, and its impact had been lost on them, for all their attention was concentrated on gaining entry themselves. As he'd expected, the horde continued to push forward into the citadel, although with slightly less haste.

"Check fire," he said calmly, face and voice leached of all expression as he gazed down upon the unspeakable carnage.

No need to rout them. Not yet.

"Pull back, you old *fool*!" Puvin Eske shouted. "*Now* will you believe us? This is the death of the clan!"

"Great rewards require great sacrifice," the clan leader said. "Do you think we took this town before without loss?"

"No," the chieftain snapped. "We obviously lost everyone with any sense! I'm taking the rest of my people to the camp. We will prepare to try to hold off the humans when they come forth to take our horns. And may the forest demons eat your *soul!*"

"You shall be cast out of the clan," the elder said calmly. "Coward. We shall deal with *you* after the victory."

"Go into that hell yourself, coward," the younger Mardukan hissed. "Then come tell me of *'victories'*!"

Eleanora O'Casey wore one of the "spare" helmets and the same uniform as the Marines, but unlike them, she'd never been trained to break down the net's clipped transmissions or the military technobabble which comprised them. For her, the majority of the bursts that came over her radio were cryptic "Tango at two-fifty" conversations which, unfortunately, her translator software was useless for deciphering, so she generally depended on some friendly Marine to interpret for her.

In this case, however, the only available translator was Poertena. Which created its own problems.

"What's happening?" she asked the armorer. She, Matsugae, and three of the pilots sat on a pile of ammunition boxes halfway back into the cave that made up the majority of the keep's interior. The noncombatants shared the space with the wounded, Doc Dobrescu, the mahouts, and nineteen nervous *flar-ta. Flar-ta* reacted in a predictable animal way to nervousness. It was a hot, smelly existence.

"Tee scummies, they off tee wall," the diminutive Pinopan said with a shrug, "but they getting ready to 'tack again. Tee Cap'n is gonna say somethin' soon."

"How is Roger?" Matsugae asked quietly. He had his own helmet and had heard the terse report of the prince's injury.

"He fine," Poertena said. "Jus' shock. He be fine."

"I'm pleased to hear that," Matsugae said. "Very pleased."

❖   ❖   ❖

"Great," Pahner said, nodding as he listened to the transmission. "Great. Get him to Doc Dobrescu as soon as possible. I know you don't dare now, but as soon as we open that door, I want him in the keep."

He looked out the slit at the reforming enemy and shook his head. Bravo Company had really whittled them down that time, but the barbs were still coming back for more, and he sent his toot the command that opened the general frequency.

"Okay, people, they're coming back for another round. We took some wounded that time, so we're a little thin on the walls. I want platoon sergeants to select your best walking wounded for bead rifles and send out everyone else you can to stand by as grenadiers. They don't seem to be bothered by casualties, so I'll call for fire a little further out this time.

"Grenadiers, when they start coming through the gate, I want you to fill the bailey with their dead. I think they'll still come on in, so when they start coming up the stairs or over the walls, retreat to the bastions."

He thought of trying to say something stirring, but the only thing that came to mind was "once more into the breach, my friends," which was both technically inaccurate and too theatrical for him. Finally he just keyed the mike.

"Pahner, out."

There was silence over the com for several seconds, except for the occasional laconic transmission of firing points and targets. But then Julian's distinctive voice came over the Third Platoon net.

"Okay, Second Squad. I know I can't be up there with you, but I want you to remember that . . . that . . . you're members of The Empress' Own, damn it." There was a cracked sob, and he choked out the next words. "I want you to do me *proud*. Remember: long, *wildly* uncontrolled bursts!"

A tide of laughter welled up over the net. Gunnery Sergeant Jin was faintly audible, protesting the bad radio discipline, but it was almost impossible to understand him through his own barking belly laughs.

"Remember," the squad leader continued with another sob. "You're Marines, and The Empress' Own! We're the best, of the best, of the best. Well, maybe not the last best. That would be *Gold* Battalion, actually, but—"

"Juliannn," Jin wailed, "stoppp!"

"And, I just want to say . . . if these are our last moments together . . ." the NCO continued.

"Company, stand by to open fire!" Captain Pahner's voice crackled over the general frequency, oblivious of the transmissions on the platoon net.

"Gronningen," Julian said, with another choking sob, to the biggest, ugliest, most straightlaced private in the entire company, "I just want you to know: *I love you, man!*"

Eleanora looked up in surprise and fear as one of the armored plasma gunners fell over on her side, bent nearly double. The academic started to get up to try to render assistance, but Poertena held up his hand to stop her as he switched frequencies on his helmet radio. She watched in fear as his expression slid from worry through annoyance while the plasma gunner first tried to get to her knees, and then fell over again, twitching. O'Casey couldn't imagine what could have happened to the woman, but then the armorer began to laugh. He slid down from his perch on the ammunition boxes, holding his sides, and the civilian's eyes went wide as Doc Dobrescu opened his mouth and began to howl with laughter of his own.

❖   ❖   ❖

"Third Platoon!" Pahner barked as a burst of bead fire went flying off into the distance and a grenade volley rolled through the enemy's ranks like a surf line of fire and death. "Sergeant Jin! What the hell is happening down there?"

"Ah . . ." Jin replied, then burst into laughter. "Sorry," he choked out. "Sorry, Sir, ah . . ."

A wild rip of bead fire lashed out from Third Platoon's position and sliced into the Kranolta like a hypervelocity bandsaw. Then another. The Mardukans went down like wheat before a reaper, and Pahner heard the distant sound of almost maniacal laughter from the parapet.

"Sergeant Jin! *What the hell is happening down there?*" He couldn't fault the effectiveness of the platoon's fire, but it wasn't like they had ammo to spare.

"Ah—" It was all the gunnery sergeant could say as he tore off his own wildly uncontrolled rip of automatic fire . . . and dissolved into helpless laughter of his own.

Pahner started to bellow furiously at Jin, but the firing quickly got itself back under control, and he clamped his jaw tightly. Then he tilted his head to the side and flipped to the platoon frequency just in time to hear " . . . no, man, really. I *love* you!" followed by hysterical laughter as Gronningen explained exactly what was going to happen to the NCO when he got his extremely heterosexual fingers around Julian's throat.

"*Juliannn!*" Pahner began, then paused as he realized that not only was the firing steadier, but he could actually see smiles on the faces of the troopers on the parapet. Some of those smiles might be a little crazed, but it was obvious that at least one platoon had stopped contemplating the likelihood of death in the near future.

"Buuut, Caaaptain!" the NCO whined.

"And," sobbed Jin, who was well known for his own interests, "I've gotta tell the Sergeant Major I love her, tooo!"

"Okay, people," Pahner said, shaking his head but unable not to do a little laughing of his own. "Let's settle down and kill us some scummies, okay?"

"Okay, okay," Julian said. "Sorry, boss."

"I'm still gonna kill your ass, Julian," Gronningen growled. A burst of fire echoed over the open link. "But I've got other things to do in the meantime."

And so Bravo Company, Bronze Battalion of The Empress' Own, went into battle against overwhelming odds . . . with an uncontrollable chuckle on its lips.

Morale is to the physical as ten is to one.

CHAPTER FORTY-TWO

"Are these stupid bastards ever going to realize that they're beaten?" Pahner wearily asked no one in particular.

Damage from repeated plasma blasts had finally forced him to abandon the gatehouse, which was now a pile of rubble, and move into the Third Platoon bastion. The Kranolta had taken unspeakable losses throughout the long Mardukan day, but still they insisted on charging the castle. And in so doing, they'd whittled their opponents down to practically nothing.

Of the seventy-two members of The Empress' Own who'd survived the initial Kranolta ambush, barely half were still on their feet. Pahner had come to the point of regretting his decision to immure Poertena and Cord's nephews in the keep. They were safe there, but he could have used them on the walls.

He shook his head. There were still several thousand Kranolta out there, and they'd stopped trying to take the keep. The last wave had avoided the smoldering killing ground of the bailey and hurled itself solely against Second Platoon's portion of the wall and its bastion. The attack had crashed in behind a massive javelin launch, and Second Platoon had taken terrific casualties before it could beat off the assault.

As always, the Mardukans' losses had been enormously higher than the humans'. Unfortunately, the Marines could kill hundreds of the barbarians for every one of their own casualties and still lose. It was insane. Whatever happened to the company, the slaughter of the Kranoltas warriors had already been so extreme that the clan itself was almost certainly doomed to extinction, but they didn't seem to care. Or perhaps they did. Perhaps they knew their people had already been effectively destroyed this bloodsoaked day, and all they wanted now was to drag down and kill the aliens who'd slain them.

Whatever they were thinking, they were also lining up for yet another attack on Second Platoon, and he lifted the visor of his helmet to scrub his eyes in exhaustion.

He could shift some of Third Platoon over to Second's area, but if he did that and the scummies hit Third's bastion simultaneously, they would sweep away the reduced defenders. No. The only option was to order Third to fire everything it had into the flank of the assault. That hadn't stopped the last one, but maybe it would work this time. Something *had* to break these bastards.

He shook his head again as the scummies surged forward. The ground was so thickly covered with their dead that they literally had to climb over drifts and hills of bodies just to reach the wall, but they didn't even seem to notice. They just came on through the hail of bead and grenade fire from front and flank until they hit the wall. Then the ladders went up again, and the Kranolta swarmed upward.

The plasma cannon in the keep and Third Platoon's

bastion could bear on them as they topped the battlements, but the gunners had to be careful. Not only was there the danger that they might inflict human casualties in the wild melee atop the wall, but one twitch to the side, and the plasma bolts could blow the door right out of the other bastion.

Now that door rang to the sound of axes again, and bead gunners from Third Platoon's bastion picked off the axmen carefully. Again, a burst of beads in the wrong spot would do the scummies' work for them.

Only three of Third Platoon's spear slits overlooked the other platoon's doorway. Against any rational foe, that should have been enough, but these were Kranolta. A bead rifleman stepped back with a jammed rifle, and for the flicker of time required for someone to replace him, a single scummy was able to survive long enough to drive three more blows into the hastily assembled timber barricade.

The barrier had finally taken all it could stand. It crumbled, and a wild, hungry scream of triumph went up from the Kranolta as they saw their chance at last.

Pahner dropped down to the plasma cannon and slapped the gunner on the helmet. He pointed to the open doorway and the line of scummies clawing towards it against a solid wall of bead fire.

"Fire it up!"

"But, Captain—" the gunner began. The angle to the doorway was acute, and it the odds were better than even that none of the plasma bolt itself would carry through it. But they were just *barely* better than even, and even if the bolt itself didn't, blast, fragments, and thermal bloom through the doorway and its covering spear slits would be more than sufficient to turn the bastion's interior into a vision of Hell.

"Do it!" Pahner snapped, and keyed the general frequency. "*Second Platoon! Duck and cover!*"

The gunner shook her head and triggered three rounds into the mass around the doorway, clearing the narrow walkway. Someone shrieked over the radio as the rounds impacted, but there was no time to think of that, and Pahner leapt back to his previous perch as the Kranolta recoiled again.

But they didn't recoil far, and the Marine cursed. They'd barely retreated at all this time, dropping below the level of the now unmanned wall, which put them just out of the angle of fire from the defenders clinging to the bastions and the keep. His taccomp threw fresh strength estimates up on his HUD, and he swore again. There were still three thousand or so of them left. Which wasn't very many for a force which had begun with *eighteen* thousand, but his readouts showed only thirty-one of the company still mobile.

We can still win this thing, he thought. *They're wearing us away, but we're wearing them away even faster. Two more assaults. Maybe three. That's all we've got to make it through, and—*

The enemy's horrible trophy horns brayed as they worked themselves up for yet another assault, and Pahner's nerves tightened. But then he heard another sound, an answer to the Kranolta horns. A harsher, deeper braying came from the west, and Pahner looked in that direction and his heart seemed to freeze.

Another entire army was deploying out of the forests beyond the ruined city. It was barely a fraction of the original Kranolta host, but it was also fresh and unbloodied as it marched to join the assault. The new warriors were heavily armed and armored, and they were accompanied by *flar-ta*—the missing baggage train the initial Kranolta army had left behind, no doubt. Some of the pack beasts seemed to be covered in glittering bronze, and as the taccomp projected the new numbers, Armand Pahner knew utter despair.

The Kranolta reinforcements outnumbered the mangled force at the foot of the wall, and their addition to the next assault would break the Marines' back at last.

He stared at the death of every one of his people for perhaps ten seconds, then sucked in a deep breath. If he and his people were going to go down, he would be damned if they died cowering in these holes like Voitan's last defenders.

"If you can make a heap of all your winnings . . ." he whispered then opened the company frequency. "Bravo Company. All units, prepare to sally. A new force has just arrived. If we can hammer them badly enough in the open field, it will give us a little time to regroup. Immediately upon return to this position, I want everyone to fall back to the keep. We'll reform our line there." As if any of them were going to return, he thought bitterly. "All units, arm your wounded and prepare to sally."

"Oh, fuck," Julian muttered as he began to tear at the barrier across the keep door. Like the curtain wall gate, the keep doorway had been too large for them to hang a portal that could be easily opened and closed. Instead, it was barricaded by a pile of braced tree trunks, hammered together by the armored suits. Taking it down was a permanent operation; putting it back would not be an option.

"It's cool," Macek said unevenly. "We can do this."

"Sure, sure," Julian said as he ripped down another support with the mechanically enhanced power of the armor. "We'll live until the juice gives out. While we watch the damned Kranolta kill everybody else. Then we'll have a choice between opening up or suffocating."

"We'll kill them at the same time," the private said. "We'll kill most of them that are left."

"Sure, but they'll wipe out the company while we do it. Which is why the Old Man didn't send us out in the first place."

He pulled down the last support and opened up the door to the bailey.

The door to Third Platoon's bastion was already open. Nobody was in sight, yet, but Julian figured they would be coming out as soon as Captain Pahner gave the word. Second Platoon's door was just . . . gone. He didn't want to think about what it must be like inside that tower.

He looked out over the rubble where the gatehouse had been. From the elevated "porch" in front of the keep, he could just make out the distant army that Pahner had spotted, and it looked formidable indeed. He dialed up the magnification on his helmet, and his jaw tightened. Most of the new force was armored, and if bronze armor wouldn't do the Mardukans much good against the rifles, it would let them hammer the Marines right under when it got down to hand-to-hand. And it would.

He jumped off the platform and onto the rubble in two long "bounces," then checked to be sure his chameleon system was engaged. The active system on the suits was more effective than that of the uniforms and made the armor virtually invisible, although the suits were "loud" both electronically and audibly, which gave advanced enemies many ways to target them. There were ways to counteract that as well, but not easily or when the suits were moving fast.

Not that it mattered in this case. The Mardukans weren't going to see anything but a flicker and bursts of bead fire punctuated with plasma bolts. It should seem like evil demons in their midst . . . as long as the juice lasted.

The original Kranolta force had moved around the

shoulder of the hill and was preparing to hit Second Platoon again. He thought about triggering a burst of bead fire into them, but waited for orders. They would be coming soon enough, and he saw Third Platoon filing out of its bastion even as the army by the jungle started up the long slope to the battleground. The scummy reinforcements were at least four or five thousand strong, and their banners flapped in the breeze. Their horns brayed again, and some of the survivors of the original Kranolta force turned and spotted them. They blared on their own horns, and waved their weapons in excitement as the newcomers hurried towards them.

"Who is that?" Danal Far asked.

"I don't know," his second in command replied, but he sounded uneasy. "It looks like . . . the host of Voitan."

"Hah!" It was the first good laugh Danal Far had had since this slaughter began. But they'd nearly taken the outer defenses, now. But for the damned fire-weapons, they would have already. The next push would see them in firm control of the bastion, and from there they could roll up these damned humans easily.

"Ghosts!" he scoffed. "No, it's some other tribe come to help us against these humans. Perhaps the Talna or the Boort."

"Nooo," Banty Kar said dubiously. "Neither use armor. The last time I saw such a host was in the fighting for T'an K'tass."

"Ghosts," the chieftain grunted again, but with a nervous edge. "All of those lands are ours, now. We took them, and we keep them. Even against these 'human' demons."

"Took them, yes," Kar said as he started toward the walls. "Keep them? Maybe."

❖   ❖   ❖

"How's it going, Julian?" Pahner asked over the radio. Third Platoon—what remained of it—had gathered on the gatehouse rubble while Second and First pulled their dead and wounded out of the damaged bastion.

"Oh, fair, Sir. Looks like they're getting ready to come back."

"Very well." Pahner looked around at the pitiful remnants of his company, and shook his head. "Swing around to cover our front. Third Platoon, prepare to deploy over the rubble."

"It *is* T'an K'tass!" Banty Kar cried. The Kranolta second in command gestured at the flag that had just been unfurled atop one of the armored *flar-ta*. "That's the Spreading Tree!"

"Impossible!" Far shouted, refusing to believe his eyes. "We killed them all! We destroyed their warriors, and scattered their people to the winds."

"But we didn't kill their sons," his second grated in a voice of bleached, old bone, and a groan of despair went up from the Kranolta host as another banner was unfurled and the long-lost symbol of the Fire and the Iron soared over the battlefield.

"Nor all the sons of Voitan."

"Captain," Julian called, "you might want to hold up. Something just happened with the two forces. The new one just raised some flags. I don't know scummies real well, but I don't think the Kranolta are all that happy to see these new guys after all."

"Understood," Pahner replied. "Keep me advised," he finished just as the Kranolta broke into a chant.

"Do you hear that?!" T'Leen Targ demanded. "That's the sound I've waited to hear most of my life: the sound

of the Kranolta Death Chant!" The big, old Mardukan
hefted the battle ax attached to his stump and waved
it high. "Suck on this, you barbarian bastards! *Voitan
is back!*"

"Aye!" T'Kal Vlan shouted back. The last of the
princes of T'an K'tass grunted in laughter as he listened
to the mournful dirge. "It's time for T'an K'tass to collect
a debt!"

Much of the force consisted of mercenaries, gathered
from all over the lower city-states. But the core of the
army were the sons and grandsons of the cities fallen
before the Kranolta. Both Voitan and T'an K'tass had
managed to evacuate not only noncombatants, but also
funds. Those funds had been scattered in businesses
ventures in multiple city-states, awaiting the day when
Voitan could rise again.

And this day, the humans had cleared the way.

"Oh, the demons are feasting well this day!" Targ
clapped his remaining true-hand to the ax in delight as
he surveyed the mountainous piles of corpses. "Look at
the souls these humans have sent on!"

"And it looks as if they're still holding out." Vlan ges-
tured at the smoking citadel. "I think we should hurry."
He turned to the force at his back. "Forward the Tree!
Time to take back our own!"

"Forward the Tree!" the roar came back to him.
"Forward the Flame!"

"Hammer those Kranolta bastards into *atul* food!"
T'Leen Targ howled, waving his ax overhead.

"Forward the Tree! Forward the Flame!"

CHAPTER FORTY-THREE

Despreaux knelt beside the prince in the dim light.

The wounded had been gathered in a line on the ledge on the north side of the cavernous keep, and the bandaged and burnt Marines were mostly asleep, courtesy of Doc Dobrescu. Their wounds were horrible, even by modern standards. Most of the wounded seemed to be from First and Second platoon; despite the protection of their flame resistant chameleon suits, most of them looked like so many pieces of barbecued chicken, and she shook her head and turned away when she realized that the white thing sticking out of Kileti's uniform was his ulna.

Horrible though it was, the damage would heal. Even the severed limbs would regrow over time, and the nanites and regenerative retroviruses the Marines were pumped full of were already hard at work repairing the gross wounds. As skin grew over burns and muscles mended at impossible speeds, the limbs would start regrowing, as well.

There was a metabolic penalty, of course. For the next

several days, the wounded would be able to do nothing but eat and sleep as the nanites worked feverishly to repair the wounds and combat infections. But in time—short or long, depending mostly on the *amount* of damage rather than its severity—the terrible wounds would reduce themselves to nothing but scars. In time, even those scars would fade. To be replaced by new ones, undoubtedly.

She touched the prince's face and picked up the diagnostic tag attached to his uniform. There were only a few of those, and she was surprised Dobrescu had used it on him. Or maybe she wasn't. There were more seriously wounded—the tag told her that immediately with its readout of his alpha rhythms, blood pressure, pulse, and oxygen—but there were none so precious.

She touched his face again, gently.

"He gets to you, doesn't he?" a gravelly voice asked.

She froze and looked up at the sergeant major.

"You look like a rabbit in a spotlight," Kosutic told her with a quiet chuckle. The senior NCO had propped herself up on her uninjured right arm to contemplate the squad leader with a quizzical smile.

"I was just checking on Third Platoon's wounded, Sergeant Major," Despreaux said guiltily . . . and almost truthfully. That *had* been her rationale for the visit, but she'd realized almost immediately what she was really after.

"Try to tell the Old Man that, girl—not me!" the sergeant major snapped, shifting her burnt and mangled left arm into a better position. Or, at least, one that was marginally less uncomfortable. "You haven't so much as looked at any of the other wounded. You've just been making cow eyes at Roger."

"Sergeant Major—" Despreaux began.

"Can it, I said! I know exactly what's going on. It was obvious even back on the ship, if you had eyes. And I do."

"But . . . I *hated* him back on the ship," the sergeant protested. "He was so . . . so. . . ."

"Snotty?" Kosutic suggested with a chuckle that cut off abruptly. "Shit, don't make me laugh, girl! Yeah. And you were making cow eyes at him, snotty attitude and all."

"I was *not* making cow eyes," Despreaux insisted firmly.

"Call it what you want, girl," the older woman said with a grin. "*I* call it cow eyes."

Despreaux looked around almost desperately, but all the other wounded seemed to be asleep. If they weren't, they were being incredibly disciplined in not laughing at her. Then she looked back at Kosutic.

"What are you going to do about it?"

"Nothing," the sergeant major said, and chuckled again at her look of surprise. "We've got bigger things to worry about, Sergeant. And so far he seems to be either oblivious or beating you off with a club. I'm not sure which."

"Neither am I," the squad leader admitted sadly.

"Look," Kosutic said, "when I'm not feeling like a pounded piece of liver, come talk to me about this. I don't know if I can do anything, but we can talk. No reports, no notes, no counseling. Just . . . girl talk. About boy problems."

"Girl talk," Despreaux repeated incredulously. She looked at the sergeant major, then down at the line of combat ribbons and the burnt and mangled arm. "You realize that that sounds . . . odd."

"Hey, you've got boy problems," the senior NCO said, pointing at the sleeping prince with her chin. "Think of me as your older sister."

"Okay," Despreaux said, shaking her head slowly from side to side. "If you say so. Girl talk."

"Later," the sergeant major agreed, lying back down. "When I don't feel like pounded liver."

❖   ❖   ❖

The first thing Roger noticed was a raging thirst. Hard on the heels of the thirst, though, was a headache that put it to shame.

He groaned and tried moving his fingers and toes. Something seemed to happen, so next he tried opening his eyes.

Well, he thought, cataloging his sensory impressions, it was hot and close, and there was a rock roof overhead. There was also a distinct stench of *flar-ta* droppings, and he swore, as he gagged on the dreadful smell, that he would never complain about grumbly oil again. He'd found so many, many smells that were worse.

Starting with burnt pork.

He turned his head to the side and groaned again. He didn't know what had happened to the Marine, but it been bad. Bad enough that he wasn't too sure, right offhand, whether it was a man or a woman.

"Plasma blast," a voice said from his other side. Roger turned his head, slowly and carefully, and looked up into the ugly face of Doc Dobrescu. "Only the bloom from it, actually. Not that that wasn't bad enough." The warrant officer gazed at his other patient for a moment, then back at Roger.

"Morning, Your Highness."

"My head," Roger croaked.

"Kinda hurts?" the medic asked cheerfully.

"Yeah."

The former Raider leaned forward and administered a stim shot to the prince's neck. In a moment, a wave of blessed relief flowed through him.

"Ooooh."

"Don't get used to it," the medic cautioned. "We've got lots of wounded. And on that subject, I need you to get your ass in gear, Your Highness. I've got other people to attend to."

Roger felt a hand on his shoulder, pulling him up, and looked back to discover that it belonged to Matsugae.

"Kostas?" he asked him blearily. He listened, but there was no crash of plasma cannon or crack of bead rifles. "What happened? Did we win?"

"Yes, Your Highness," the valet said, propping him up and handing him a cup of deliciously cool water. "Welcome back."

An image flashed suddenly across Roger's memory.

"Despreaux?" he said sharply.

"Sergeant Despreaux?" the valet asked with a puzzled expression. "She's fine. Why do you ask?"

Roger thought about explaining the memory of an upraised ax, but decided against it. He might also have to explain the strange, unsettled feeling that the image caused him.

"Never mind. What's the situation?"

"We won, as you surmised," the valet told him. "But things are complicated at the moment."

Roger looked around the fetid keep and blanched.

"How many?" he asked, gazing at the rows of wounded.

"Thirty-eight," Dobrescu replied, coming by checking monitors. "That aren't walking wounded. Twelve KIA . . . including Lieutenant Gulyas, I'm afraid."

"Oh, God." Roger's eyes returned to the burn patient next to him. So many of the wounded seemed to have terrible burns. "What happened?" he repeated.

"Plasma fire," Dobrescu said simply. "Things got . . . a little tight."

"We need to get them out of here," the prince said, waving a hand around in the stinking dimness. "This is no place to put a hospital."

"They're working on it, Your Highness," the medic

told him. "We'll have them out of here by nightfall. In the meantime, it's the only roof we've got."

"Okay." Roger levered himself up with help from the valet. "Make sure of it."

The prince stumbled across the floor to the open doorway and stopped at the view that greeted him. The interior of the citadel was a scene from some demented vision of Hell.

The eastern bastion, Second Platoon's redoubt, was a blackened ruin. The curtain wall on that side was still covered in Mardukan dead, and the doors and spear slits were blasted, blackened, and broken.

The gatehouse was nothing but rubble, and half-fused, still-smoking rubble, at that. And the bailey was covered in Mardukan dead, piled five and six deep . . . where the piles weren't even deeper. Since the gate had been the only drain for the torrential Mardukan rains, the courtyard had started to fill with water. The line of natives who were working to clear the area already waded ankle deep in the noisome mess as they bent over the dead, and it was getting deeper.

Roger peered at the natives picking up bodies and bits of bodies in the gruesome, deepening soup.

"Are those who I think they are?"

"Kranolta," Kostas confirmed.

"They have weapons," Roger pointed out in a croak. He took another sip of water and shook his head. "What happened?" he asked for the third time.

"We won," the valet repeated. "Sort of. Forces from the other city-states showed up right at the end. They hit the Kranolta from the rear, and drove them back over the wall, where they finally took the eastern bastion. By then, Captain Pahner had evacuated it anyway, and it was the only cover they could find. Between the pressure of the new forces and having them pinned down, the Marines more or less wiped them out.

"But quite a few of them had withdrawn to their encampment before the city-state forces arrived. Only a handful of their original army, but enough that they could still have caused lots of problems, so Pahner arranged a cease-fire. The Kranolta that are left don't have any interest in facing Marines or the 'New Voitan' forces, but they'll fight if forced to. So the Captain and our new . . . allies agreed to let them keep their weapons and bury their dead."

"What a disaster," Roger whispered, looking over his shoulder back into the keep.

"It could have been worse, Sir."

"How?" Roger demanded bitterly.

"Well," the valet said as the rain began again, "we could have lost."

CHAPTER FORTY-FOUR

"If you hadn't come, we would have lost."

Roger took a sip of wine. The vintage was excellent, but then, all of the tent's appointments were excellent, from the finely tooled leather of its walls, to its hammered brass tables. The cushions on the floor were covered in a cloth the humans had never seen before, silky and utterly unlike the more common rough and wool-like material found in Q'Nkok. Obviously, T'Kal Vlan traveled in style.

"Perhaps so." The last ruler of T'an K'tass picked up a candied slice of kate fruit and nibbled it. "Yet even so, you would have destroyed the Kranolta. That's surely worth something even in the eyes of gods of the most distant land!"

Captain Pahner shook his head.

"I'm sorry, Your Highness, but it isn't. We come from an empire so vast that the Kranolta and all the valley of the Hurtan are an unnoticeable speck. I'm glad that you're glad, but the losses we took might mean the prince won't make it home." He grinned at the Mardukans. "And that would really disappoint his mother."

"Ah!" Roger exclaimed. "Not that! Not Mother angry! God forbid!"

"A formidable woman, eh?" T'Kal Vlan grunted a laugh.

"Rather," Roger told him with a shrug. "He has a point, though. I'm sure that if I died, Mother would visit me beyond the grave to chastise me for it."

"So, you see," Pahner continued, "I'm afraid I have to count this one as a straight loss."

"Not really, Captain," the prince said, swirling his wine gently. "We've cleared the way. One way or another, we had to get to the other side of this range of hills, and *none* of the choices were particularly good. There's no reason to second-guess this one. If we'd gone south, we would've been walking through a war, and we would undoubtedly have second-guessed ourselves then and said 'I bet those Kranolta pussies wouldn't have been *this* much trouble.'"

"Well, I for one thank you for clearing out most of those 'Kranolta pussies,'" T'Leen Targ said, with his own grunt of laughter. "Already, the ironworkers we brought with us are building the furnaces. We have gathered all the surviving masters of the art and their apprentices. Soon the lifeblood of Voitan will flow once more."

"Aye," T'Kal Vlan agreed. "And the sooner the better. My own treasury is flowing away like blood."

"You need to capitalize," O'Casey said. The chief of staff had been quietly sipping her wine and listening to the warriors' testosterone grunting with amusement. This, however, was her specialty.

"Agreed," Vlan said. "But the family has already liquidated most of its holdings to fund the expedition. Short of borrowing, at extortionate rates, I'm not sure how to raise more capital."

"Sell shares," O'Casey suggested. "Offer a partial ownership of the mines. Each share has a vote on management, and each gains equity and shares in the profits, if any. It would be a long-term investment, but not a particularly risky one if you're sufficiently capitalized. "

"I didn't understand all the words you just used," Vlan said, cocking his head. "What is this 'equity'?"

"Oh, my." O'Casey grinned widely. "We really must have a *long* conversation."

"Don't worry," Pahner told her with a shrug. "We're not going anywhere for a while."

Roger sat up in his tent, damp with sweat and panting and looked around him. All clear. Tent walls faintly billowing in the wind that had come up. Camp gear. Eyes.

"You should be resting, Your Highness," said Cord faintly.

"So should you, old snake," Roger said. "You don't heal as fast as we do." He sat up on the camp cot and took a deep breath. "It just, you know, comes back."

"Yes, it does," the Mardukan agreed.

"I wonder how . . ." The prince stopped and shook his head.

"How?" the shaman queried, lifting himself up with a grimace.

"You should be flat on your back, Cord," Roger said with another headshake.

"I grow weary of lying about like a worm," the Mardukan countered. "How, what?"

"Not one to be distracted, are you?" Roger smiled. "I was wondering how the Marines handle it. How they handle the fear and the death. Not just ours, God knows I got enough Marines killed here. But the Kranolta. We've ended them as a tribe, Cord. Piled them up against the wall as if they were a ramp. They . . . don't seem affected by that."

"Then you have not eyes, Young Prince," the shaman countered with a grunt. "Look at young Julian. Your people, too, have the laughing warrior who hides his pain with humor, as did our Denat, he who I lost to the *atul*. Always he faced danger with laughter, but it was a shield to the soul. I'm sure that he jested with the very *atul* as it ate him. Or young Despreaux. So young, so dangerous. I am told that she is beautiful for a human. I don't see it myself; she lacks . . . many things. Horns for one. And her shield is that face like a stone. She holds her pain in so hard it has turned her to a stone, I think."

Roger tilted his head to the side and played with a stray lock of hair. "What about . . . Pahner? Kosutic?"

"Ah," Cord grunted. "For one, you notice that though they are capable warriors, they control from afar. But mostly they have learned the tricks. The first trick is to know that you are not alone. While I was in the cavern still, Pahner came to visit, to see the wounded, and we talked. He is a font of wisdom is your captain. We talked of many things but mostly we talked of . . . song. Of poetry."

"Poetry?" Roger laughed. "What in the hell would Pahner be doing talking about poetry?"

"There is poetry and poetry, my Prince," the shaman said with a grunt. "Ask him about 'The Grave of the Hundred Dead.' Or 'Recessional.' Or 'If.'" The shaman rolled over to find a more comfortable position. "But ask him in the morning."

"Poetry?" Roger said. "What in hell would I want with poetry?"

"Eleonora?" Roger asked. The chief of staff was on her way to another of the numerous meetings she had arranged with the Voitanese forces. She apparently considered herself a one-person social reengineering team, or at least the best equivalent available. She was determined that when she left, the Voitanese would have the strongest governmental structure available to the situation. Since that was probably a rational oligarchy it fit in well with the Voitanese plans.

"Yes, Ro . . . Your Highness?" she asked hurriedly. Her pad was almost overloaded with notes and there were only a few days left to get everything in place. Whatever Roger wanted had better be quick.

"Have you ever heard of a poem called 'The Grave of the Hundred Dead?' "

The chief of staff stopped and thought then consulted her toot. "The name is familiar, but I can't quite place it."

"Or 'Recessional.' " Roger's brow wrinkled but he couldn't think of the other. "Or something like 'If?' "

"Ah!" the historian's face cleared. "Yes. That one I have. Why?"

"Uh," Roger stopped, caught. "Would you believe Cord recommended it?"

O'Casey laughed merrily. It was a twinkling sound that Roger realized he had never heard. "Not without some sort of body transference, Your Highness."

"I think he heard of it from someone," Roger explained stiffly.

"Set your pad," she said with a smile and transferred the file.

There was a blip and Roger looked at the translation remark on his pad. "You keep it on your toot?" Roger asked, surprised.

"Oh, yes," O'Casey said as she started back down the path. "I love that poem. There are very few prespace poets that have even one poem known. Kipling has to be right up there with the Earl of Oxford. You might see Captain Pahner. I believe Eva said he has the collected works in his toot."

⋄   ⋄   ⋄

Warrant Officer Dobrescu tossed the chunk of reddish ore from hand to hand as he gazed up at the towering wall of red and black.

And, lo, the answers come clear, he thought.

The last two weeks had been good for the company. The troops had been given time to rest and get some separation from the terrible losses inflicted in the battle. Since Voitan was going to be held by "friendly" forces, Captain Pahner had decided to leave all of their dead. If they made it through alive, they would come back for them. If they fell along the way, these Marines, at least, would be honored.

The Voitanese had opened a vault in their own catacombs, which had been looted by the Kranolta. The sepulcher had been the resting place of the city's royal guards before its fall, and there were still a few of their bones moldering in the back. The Marines had been bagged but not burned and laid to rest along with their brethren. Sergeant Major Kosutic, as the only registered chaplain in the company, had performed the ceremony, and if any of the Marines had objected to their honored dead being prayed over by a High Priestess of Satan, they hadn't mentioned it.

The pause had also given the wounded time to recover, and a regimen of heavy eating and bed rest had done wonders. All but the most critically injured were back on their feet and training, and, from a purely selfish point of view, it had given Dobrescu time to scratch a few itches.

The first itch had to do with the local steel. The point had been made again and again that only the "water steels" made in Voitan were of the finest quality. That steels from other areas, even if processed in what they thought was the same way, did not possess the "spirit" of Voitan's Damascene steels.

The second itch had to do with the Mardukan

biology. Something had been bugging him ever since they landed and ran into D'Nal Cord, and the down-time and necessity of working on Mardukan wounded, as well as human, had given him the opportunity to do a little studying. What he'd discovered would startle most of the company, but the warrant thought it was hilarious. He hated it when people made assumptions.

Time to go watch some people cringe, he thought with an evil smile.

"So the steel has a high percentage of impurities," O'Casey said. "So what?"

"It's not just that it has a high percentage," Dobrescu said, consulting his pad. "It's what the impurities are."

"I don't know what this 'impurity' is," Targ said.

"That's going to be difficult to explain," Eleanora said with a frown. "It involves molecular chemistry."

"I'll give it a shot," Roger said. "Targ, you know how when you first smelt the ore, you get 'black iron.' The brittle stuff, right?"

"Yes," T'Kal Vlan agreed. "It's what was given to Cord's tribe, that broke so easily."

"You have to remelt it," Cord put in. The wounded Mardukan was seated behind Roger, as was proper, but stretched out on cushions to save his ravaged legs. "Very hot. It's hard and expensive, which is why black iron is cheaper."

"Okay," Roger went on. "Then when you heat it in a crucible, 'very hot,' as Cord said, you get a material that's gray and very easy to work."

"Iron," Targ said. "So?"

"That's what we call 'wrought iron,' and it actually is almost pure iron. Iron is a molecule. Black iron is iron with carbon, which is what's in charcoal, mixed into it."

"What about steel?" T'Kal Vlan asked. "And why do I think we need an ironmaster here?"

"Somebody else can explain it later," Roger said with a laugh. "The point is that iron is a pure element, a kind of molecule. Is that sort of clear?"

"I hear the words," Targ replied, "but I don't know their meaning."

"That would be hard to really explain without teaching you basic chemistry first," Dobrescu said. "You're just going to have to take our word for most of this and I'm not sure how much you can do with it."

"The point is that steel is also iron with carbon in it," Roger said. "But less carbon, and heated to a much higher temperature."

"That much is well known to our master smiths," Targ said, with a human-style shrug. "Yet mere heat and tempering does not produce the water steel. Even in exile, our smiths have forged weapons far superior to those of other city-states, but never the water steel of Voitan."

"No, steel is complicated," Roger agreed. "Especially 'water steel'—what we call 'Damascene.' We—well, I— was really surprised you had it and of such quality. It's unusual at your technology level."

"I think it's driven by their pumping industry," O'Casey interjected. "They have quite a bit of refined technology dedicated to pumps. Once that starts to spread out a bit, look for an industrial revolution. I wish they were just a bit further along. If they were, I'd introduce the steam engine."

"Let's stick to the subject, if we can," Pahner suggested with a slight grin, "and reengineer their society when we can do it with a regiment at our back. Okay?"

"His Highness is right," Dobrescu went on to Targ, ignoring the captain's amusement. "Normal steel is specially formed iron with a bit of carbon and high temperature, but you need some other impurities, if you want *good* steel, which explains Voitan blades. The first thing to realize is that the local ore is what we call 'banded iron.' "

"I know," Roger said. "Geology, remember? It's formed by early oxygen-generating organisms. Prior to their evolution, atmospheres are mostly reducing, and iron can remain on the surface in a mostly pure state. But once the first green or blue-green organism occurs and starts producing oxygen, the iron rusts. Then the oxygen gets used up over millions of years, and there's a band of non-rusted ore, then another band of rusted ore. Right?"

"Right," the warrant officer agreed. "Which makes it some of the best possible taconite, so it's comparatively easy to work. But, even better, it's contaminated with vanadium, which is one of several possible hardening agents for steel. Molybdenum and chrome are a couple of others."

"Molybe—molby—?" Cord grimaced. "I can't pronounce that."

"Don't worry about it," Dobrescu said. "The point is, Targ, that it really *is* the local ore, and your know-how, that's special. And I ran a tap in on one of your main mines, and it's all laced with impurities: vanadium and molybdenum. In fact, I'd give odds that by the time you get back into full swing, you'll hit a vein that makes the best steel you've ever seen."

"Ah, good," Targ said. "We have long wondered what it was that made our water steel. That's part of it, surely."

"Hold on a minute," Roger said, frowning at Dobrescu. "Vanadium and molybdenum are important, yeah, but not really critical for *sword* steel, Doc." The warrant officer blinked at him in surprise, and the prince chuckled with a humor that was more than slightly sour. "I won't claim to be an expert on the topic," he said, "but no MacClintock can avoid learning at least a little about ancient weapons . . . no matter how hard he tries."

"Oh?" Dobrescu cocked an eyebrow, and Roger shrugged.

"Oh," he replied. "Vanadium helps produce a finer grain structure in heat-treated steel, which helps with the tempering process and eliminates some of the problems in overheating steel. And it helps prevent loss of temper in reheated metal, so steel with vanadium in it can withstand higher temperatures before losing its temper.

"Molybdenum does some of the same thing by helping to transmit the temperature deeper into the steel, and it also increases hardness some and helps reduce the fatigue factor. But carbon is the most critical element in hardening steel."

Both of Dobrescu's eyebrows had risen during the prince's explanation, and the warrant officer's surprise was not an isolated phenomenon. Even O'Casey was staring at her one-time student, and Roger shrugged.

"Hey, like I said, I'm a MacClintock," he told them.

"According to something I read years ago, though," Dobrescu said, "vanadium and molybdenum were what produced Damascene steel."

"Almost right," Roger told him. "The 'water pattern'— those white lines on the black background—are a crystalline damask that's largely the result of those sorts of impurities. But you can have that kind of pattern on a blade that really sucks. Good Damascene steel hits a carbon content of something like one and a half percent, if I remember correctly, but even then, the trick is in the tempering. There are some beautifully patterned blades in the Roger III Collection that were never properly heat treated. I think their Rockwell number was only thirty or so, which would make them pretty useless as real weapons. You need to hit a Rockwell of around fifty if you want something to cut through mail and bone like this baby." He touched the katana lying beside him even in T'Kal Vlan's tent

"Really?" O'Casey asked, trying to hide her delight at hearing Roger—*her* Roger!—in professorial mode. Sort of.

"Yeah. There were different techniques for making the good stuff back on Old Earth," Roger told her. "Europeans did it with pattern welding, the Japanese used mechanical construction, but the Indians probably did it closest to the way Voitan smiths did it, judging from this." He touched the katana again. "They heated the steel in sealed clay crucibles that allowed the iron to soak up lots of carbon."

"That is, indeed, how our craftsmen work," Targ said, regarding Roger narrowly. "It is part of our closely held craft secrets," he added, and Roger grinned.

"Don't worry, Targ—I don't plan on telling anyone else. But the humans who used that technique produced something called 'wootz' steel that happened to have the very impurities the Doc here was talking about thanks to the local ores. And he's probably right that their presence helps account for at least some of your weapons' superiority, but don't let that distract you. The real secret's in the tempering and how well you judge temperatures and what quenching techniques you use. You might not get as pronounced a 'water' pattern using steels without the impurities, but your people would still be turning out some of the best weapon-grade steel in the world!"

"But it is the water steel which warriors associate with the superiority of our blades," Targ pointed out. "It shows the soul of the steel."

"And it's flat out beautiful, too," Roger agreed. "I'm not saying the nature of your ore isn't important, just that you shouldn't sell yourselves or your smiths short. The hardest thing of all in making a true master blade is the tempering, and you guys obviously have that down. For the rest—" He shrugged. "Now that you've got access to the right ores again, everyone else will see that the true 'water steel' is back. I imagine that's going to do good things for your income while you rebuild the city."

"True," T'Kal Vlan put in. "It is what warriors and merchants will look for when they judge the quality of our blades, and it is well to know what creates it. But where else do we find these ingredients? If we do start to have problems, we could mine them separately and add them, no?"

"Yes," Roger said with a frown. "The problem is finding them and separating them. I'd say that for the time being, you should probably just use what you have. I'll talk to a couple of your ironmasters if you want. Between us, Dobrescu and I might be able to explain it and point them in the right direction. If I recall clearly, chrome is actually easier to detect and separate."

"It is if you have an acid," Dobrescu agreed. "Less so, otherwise. And it's tricky to hit the right proportions and heat treatments. Humans didn't turn out good chromium steel until, oh, the last century and a half or so before space flight, I think. Of course, they didn't have anyone from the outside telling them how it worked, either."

"No, but they had more or less started figuring out chemistry on their own by then," O'Casey pointed out, and frowned thoughtfully. "I wonder if we could help them make that jump," she mused, and Pahner snorted.

"It sounds to me like we could probably spend a year or three just trying to remember what we don't remember about the processes," the Marine observed. "It would be better to just come back with a lander filled with science texts."

"Agreed." Roger chuckled. "Or, hell, a lander filled with a social reconstruct team. I don't want to crack Mardukan society; I like most of what I see. But I do want to bring them into the Empire."

"We can do that," O'Casey said. "God knows we've

brought in enough devolved human societies without smashing their forms."

"Like Armagh?" Roger asked with a grin.

"Well," the chief of staff said, "there's something to be said for a planet full of battling Irishmen. Look at the Sergeant Major."

"True, true," Pahner said. "However, to bring back a Soc team, we need to get to the port. And to get to the port . . ."

"We just have to put one foot in front of the other," Roger said. "And that means breaking up this little party."

"Yep." Pahner nodded. "Targ, Vlan, thank you for coming."

"Not a problem," Vlan said. "We're at your disposal until you leave."

"Thank you," Pahner said, carefully not raising an eyebrow at the surreptitious signal Dobrescu flashed him. "I think we'll see you tomorrow. Until then?"

"Yes," Targ said. "Thank you. And good night."

Pahner waited until the Mardukans had left the tent, then turned to the medic.

"Yes, Mister Dobrescu? You had something to add without the Mardukans present?"

The warrant officer glanced at the shaman behind Roger.

"Yes, Sir. But I'm not sure about Cord."

"He stays," Roger said coldly. "Whatever you have to say, you can say in front of my *asi*."

"All righty, Your Highness," the medic said. "It's about the Mardukans. And about some assumptions we've been making."

"What assumptions?" Pahner asked warily.

"Oh, it doesn't relate to security, Captain," Dobrescu said with an evil grin. "I'm not sure it matters at all, actually. But, you see, we've got their genders confused."

"What?" O'Casey demanded. As the manager for the

translation program it was her job to make sure that that sort of thing didn't happen, and she started to bristle indignantly. Then she remembered all the times the program had tried to switch gender, and looked at Cord, stretched out behind Roger.

"But . . ." she began, and blushed.

"What you're looking at, Ms. O'Casey," the medic told her with an even wider evil grin, "is an ovipositor."

"An ovi . . . What?" Roger asked, checking his impulse to turn around and look. Dealing with the habitually nude Mardukans had slowly inured the humans to the size of the natives' . . . members, but he wasn't about to turn around and get all depressed again.

"Gender is a slippery term when you start discussing xenobiology," the medic continued, pulling up a different entry on his pad. "But the current 'definitive' definition is that the 'male' gender is that which supplies numerous gametes to fertilize a single gamete. However that's done."

"I take it, then, that Cord and his 'gender' do not supply numerous gametes," Pahner said carefully. "They certainly look . . . capable of doing so."

"No, they don't, and yes, they do," Dobrescu responded. "The gender we've been calling 'male,' Cord's gender, that is . . . implants, is the correct term, between four and six gametes that are functional cells, with the exception of a matching set of chromosomes. Once these have been implanted, they're fertilized by free swimming zygotes resident in the egg pouches of what I suppose should technically be called 'brooder males.'" The medic pursed his lips. "There are a few terrestrial species of fish that use a similar method, and its common on Ashivum in the native species."

"So, Cord is actually a female?" Pahner asked.

"Technically. However, there are sociological aspects that make the 'males' fill traditional female gender roles and vice versa. That and the physiology are what have been confusing the program."

"And me," O'Casey admitted, "but I'll bet you're right. We didn't have much of a language kernel to start with, and I never tried to get at its fundamental, underlying assumptions. Even if I'd thought about it, I wouldn't have known how to access them or what to do with them once I had. But given what Mr. Dobrescu just said about 'definitive' definitions, I'd guess that whoever prepared the kernel in the first place knew that Cord and his gender were *technically* 'female.' It tried to switch gender a couple of times, which is just the sort of literal-minded lunacy you might expect out of an AI with partial data, and I wouldn't let it."

"I am *not* a female," Cord stated definitively.

"Shaman Cord," Eleanora said, "we're having a problem with our translator. Try not to pay any attention to the flipping gender discussions."

"Very well," the shaman said. "I can understand problems with your machines. You have them all time. But I am *not* a female."

"What was the word he actually used there?" Dobrescu asked.

"'*Blec tule*'?" O'Casey consulted her pad. "The etymology looks to be something like 'one that holds.' 'One that holds the eggs'? 'One that broods'? I bet that's it."

"What about Dogzard?" Roger asked, looking at the faintly snoring lizard.

"Another interesting aspect of local biology," Dobrescu answered. "There are two dominant families in Mardukan terrestrial zoology. You can think of them as equivalent to reptiles and amphibians if you want. Cord is from the 'amphibian' type. So are damnbeasts and damcrocs and bigbeasts. They all have slimy skin and similar internal organ structures.

"But the feck beasts, the dogzards, and the *flar-ta* are

completely different. They have a dry integument with some scaling and radically different internal structures. Different heart chambers, different stomachs, different kidney analogs."

"So is Dogzard a he or a she?" asked Roger in exasperation.

"She," Dobrescu answered. "The 'reptile' analogs are set up, sexually, much like terrestrial reptiles. So Dogzard will eventually have puppies. Well, eggs."

"So what do we do about the translator?" Roger asked.

"We don't do anything about it," Pahner said. "We inform the troops of the physical aspects, and explain to them that the Mardukans are flipped gender, but we'll continue with our current distinction. As Elenora just suggested, the difference is purely technical, and since none of us are xenobiologists, I think we can get away with ignoring it. I can't see that it matters one way or the other, anyway, and this way we keep from confusing the troops. And the software."

"Just make sure that they're aware," Cord said stiffly, "that I am *not* a brooder."

"He's a female?" Julian asked.

"Sort of." Roger laughed. "But just keep treating him like he's a male. And hope like hell the software doesn't slip up when you get a visualization miscue." The implant-based software had already miscued once, with Poertena and Denat. Fortunately, it was a minor wound. The Pinopan would heal quickly, and the tribesman had accepted the explanation.

"Oh, man," Julian said, shaking his head. "I cannot *wait* to get off this planet. I got so much culture shock I feel like my dick's stuck in a culture socket."

Roger touched PFC Gelert on his shoulder as he strode past. The Marine grinned back at him, and hefted the spear over his shoulder. He obviously still found it an odd item for a Marine to carry.

All the Marines were armed with Mardukan weaponry. There'd been thousands of ex-Kranolta weapons available to choose from, and the New Voitan forces had let no time pass getting the first forges lit. They weren't up to custom work yet, but they were able to modify most of the weapons to fit the smaller humans, so the company was now well armed with short swords—long daggers, to the Mardukans—and Mardukan-style round shields, as well as at least one spear or javelin per Marine.

During the three weeks of rest while the company recovered, the Marines had begun their training. They had nowhere near the ability of the Mardukans, who'd practically been born with weapons in their hands, but unlike the natives, they were *soldiers*, not warriors. All of their training emphasized teamwork and cooperation, not individual, uncoordinated prowess, and they only needed to be good enough for one platoon to hold a shield wall—which no Mardukan seemed ever to have heard of—while the other one got out the real weapons.

Roger grinned back at the private and jabbed a thumb to indicate the sword over his own shoulder. The entire company looked better for the rest, although a few of the most seriously wounded were still going to be riding *flar-ta*.

Roger tossed a salute toward Corporal D'Estrees. She'd been one of the worst burn cases, and Dobrescu had eventually been forced to remove her left arm from the elbow down. Now she waved in return with her pink stump and scratched at the growing bulb of regenerating tissue. It itched like mad, but in another month or so, she'd be back in gear.

Roger finally reached the pack beast assigned to Cord. The shaman gestured to the straps holding him in place.

"This is most undignified."

Roger shook his head and waved at the endless row of grave mounds along the woodline. Figures could be seen moving down there, cutting wood for the charcoal pits and clearing brush from the beds of former roads.

"Be glad you're not in one of those."

"Oh, I am," Cord said, with a grunt, "but it is still most undignified."

Roger shook his head again as Pahner approached from the opposite direction.

"Well, Captain, are we ready?"

"Looks that way, Your Highness," the captain answered as a delegation headed by T'Leen Targ and T'Kal Vlan approached.

"We're leaving a lot of good people behind," Roger murmured, his smile fading just a bit as he glanced at the entrance to the city catacombs.

"We are," Pahner agreed quietly. "But we're leaving them in good company. And to tell the truth, Your Highness, I think it's better this way. I know it's a Marine tradition to bring our dead out with us, but I've always thought a soldier should be buried where he fell." He shook his head, his own eyes just a bit unfocused as he, too, gazed at the catacomb entrance. "That's what I want if my time ever comes," he said softly. "To be buried where I fall, with my comrades . . . and my enemies."

Roger looked at the Marine's profile in surprise, but not as much of it as he might have felt before reading "If." Or the other dozen or so Kipling poems Elenora O'Casey's toot had contained. There were depths to the captain which the old prince had never suspected . . . and which the new one respected too deeply to mention out loud.

"Well," he said cheerfully, "I'll bear that in mind if the time comes, Captain. But don't go getting any ideas! You're strictly forbidden to die until you get my royal butt home where it belongs! Clear?"

"Aye, 'Colonel,'" Pahner agreed with a grin. "I'll bear that in mind."

"Good!" Roger said, and the two of them turned back towards the approaching delegation together.

"I'd say this is the farewell committee," Kosutic observed, coming around the pack beast. She gestured at the groups of soldiers gathering along the route out of the rebuilding city. "I think they're getting ready for the big sendoff." She scratched at her own pink skin.

"I'll put on a bigger hat," Roger said jokingly, and flicked at a bit of leaf on the front of his chameleon suit. The suit was indelibly stained in places, but it was still self-cleaning, to an extent, and was more or less intact. Many of the company's uniforms were in tatters from where they'd been cut off in the course of hasty first-aid.

"Well, if you can find one, you can wear it," Pahner said calmly.

"Why, thank you for that permission, Sir." The prince grinned. "Should I go look?"

"I wouldn't suggest it at the moment, Your Highness," O'Casey said tartly. The little chief of staff had snuck up behind them so quietly that her unexpected voice made Roger start. "I think we need to thank our benefactors."

"I suppose," Roger answered impishly. "Of course, they might have saved our bacon, but we wiped out the Kranolta for them," he pointed out, and Pahner smiled again as Targ approached.

"I suppose there is that," the captain agreed.

It took an hour, but the company finally broke free of its brothers in arms, after profuse expressions of eternal friendship and undying mutual fealty, and started back on the long trail to the sea.

Marching upcountry.

CHAPTER FORTY-FIVE

The messenger lay prostrate in front of the throne. He couldn't think of any bad news in what he had to convey, but that didn't really matter. If the king was in a bad mood, the messenger's life was forfeit, anyway, no matter how important he was.

"So, 'Scout,'" the king said with a grunt of humor, "you say that the humans will come out on the Pasule side of the river?"

"Yes, O King. They follow the old trade route from Voitan."

"Insure that they bypass Pasule." The monarch picked at the ornate intaglio of his throne. "They must come to Marshad first."

"Yes, O King," the messenger said. *Now to figure out a way to do that.*

"You may go, 'Scout,'" the king said. "Bring them here. Bring them to me, or kill yourself before We lay Our hands on you."

"It shall be done," the messenger said, wiggling backwards out of the king's presence. *Cheated death again*, he thought.

✧   ✧   ✧

"Cheated death again." Julian sighed as the company broke through the final screen of trees into obviously civilized lands.

"Yeah," Despreaux said. "Damn, but I'm glad to be out of the jungle."

The passage over the hills from Voitan hadn't been terrible. In fact, they hadn't lost even one person to the jungle flora and fauna, although Kraft in Second Platoon had been badly mauled by a damnbeast.

The march from Voitan had also given them time to shake down into their new organization. The reduced company had separated into just two platoons, Second and Third, and they were getting used to all the empty files. Not happy about them, but adjusted.

All in all, they were probably in better shape both physically and in morale than at any time since leaving Q'Nkok, and the vista stretching out before them would help even more.

The region was obviously long and widely settled. Cultivated fields, interspersed with patches of woodland, spread for kilometers in every direction, and the river the old path had been following was flanked in the middle distance by two towns, one clearly larger than the other.

Captain Pahner waved for the column to hold up as it cleared the jungle completely. The bare track they'd been following for the last day had suddenly become a road. Not much of one these days, perhaps—weeds and even small trees thrust up through the roadbed's cracked, uneven flagstones—but it showed that this had once been an important route.

The company stopped by the ruins of a small building. The structure was set on a raised mound, one of many scattered across the floodplain, and its construction had been massive. It looked as if it had been a guardhouse or border station to receive the caravans from Voitan, and Pahner stepped up onto its two-meter-high mound to watch the caravan pull to a halt as the company deployed.

The Marines had been training hard with their new weapons, and it showed. Bead rifles and grenade launchers were still slung over their shoulders, but their primary weapons were clearly the short swords and spears they carried, and the small units spread out in a cigar perimeter, one swordsman to each spear carrier. Once Pahner had the shields designed, the formation would be quite different, but that was going to have to wait. The tower shield was another thing the Mardukans had apparently never discovered, so he would have to have them built somewhere.

And that somewhere would, hopefully, be here.

He made another gesture, and his "command team"—a grandiose term for a small group of battered Marines and civilians, but the only one he had—gathered about him. Sergeant Julian was filling in as Intel officer in the wake of Lieutenant Gulyas' death, but other than that, it was the same group he'd faced in Voitan.

"Okay," he said, gesturing to the two towns, "it looks pretty much the way the Voitan contingent said it would. This has to be the Hadur region." Heads nodded, and he wished—again—for an even half-way decent map. According to the Voitanese, the Hadur region took its name from the Hadur River, which had to be a truly major stream even for Marduk from the descriptions. He had no reason to doubt them, but he hated trying to fix his position without a reliable map. "If we're where we think we are," he went on with a crooked smile, "that larger town should be Marshad. And that," he pointed to the smaller town "must be Pasule."

Heads nodded again. Marshad had been the primary destination for caravans from over the hills before the fall of Voitan, which had made it a wealthy mercantile center. Pasule, on the other hand, was just a farming town, according to T'Leen Targ.

"I'd almost prefer to get our toes wet locally in Pasule before we tackle the big city," he went on, "but if we're going to get the shields and armor made, it will have to be in Marshad. On the other hand, we need resupply, too, and Pasule might be a better source for that."

As he spoke, he looked around the nearer fields, where peasants had stopped their work to gawk at the force coming out of the jungle. Most of the workers were breaking ground for another crop of barleyrice, but other laborers were harvesting the ubiquitous kate fruit. That was good. It meant that both the fruit and the previous barleyrice harvest would be fully available when it was time to buy.

"Yeah," Jasco agreed, with a grunting laugh that sounded almost Mardukan, as he, too, watched the workers, "these damn pack beasts go through some grain."

"Sergeant Major, I want you and Poertena to handle the resupply and procurement of the shields."

"Got it." The NCO made a note in her toot. They'd discussed the possibilities before, of course, but now that they were actually able to see the lay of the land, it seemed clear that Pasule would be a better, and probably cheaper, source for the food.

"We've seen that they can make laminated wood, plywood," said Roger, who'd been quietly listening. "We should have the shields made out of that."

"Plywood?" Jasco sounded incredulous, but, then, he hadn't been present to hear the prince discuss sword making with the Voitanese leaders. "You've got to be joking . . . Your Highness. *I'd* want something a little more solid than that!"

"No, he isn't joking." O'Casey shook her head. "The Roman shield was probably the most famous design ever to come out of Terran history, and *it* was made out of 'plywood.' The histories always call it 'laminated wood,' but that's what plywood *is*, and it's enormously tougher than an equivalent thickness of 'solid' wood."

"They have to have metal or leather rims to protect the edges," the prince continued, "but the bulk of the shield is plywood."

"Okay." Pahner nodded. "Kosutic, coordinate with Lieutenant MacClintock on the design of the shields." He looked around and shook his head. "I hope I don't have to remind anybody that we need to maintain as low a profile as possible. We can't afford another butt-kicking like Voitan. Hopefully, we'll be greeted as heroes for taking out the Kranolta and be able to pass on quickly. But if we get into a hassle, we have to think our way out of it. We're way too short on ammo to shoot our way out!"

Corporal Liszez trotted toward the command group with one of the locals. The Mardukan wore a haversack full of tools and appeared to be some sort of tinker.

"LT?" the corporal said as she approached Roger.

"Whatcha got, Liz?" the prince replied with a nod.

"This scummy's gabbling something, but the translator can't make anything of it."

"Oh, great," O'Casey sighed. "Dialect shift. Just what we needed."

"Get on it," Pahner said. "We have to be able to communicate with these people." The local was gesturing across the river at the distant city, obviously agitated about something. He either wanted the company to go there, or else he was warning them away. It could have been either, and Pahner nodded and gave him a closed-lip, Mardukan-style smile. "Yes, yes," he said "we're going to Marshad."

Either the smile or the words seemed to calm the local. He gestured, as if offering to lead them, but Pahner shook his head.

"We'll be along," he said soothingly. "Thank you. I'm sure we can find our own way."

He smiled again and started to wave the still-gabbling local politely away, then paused and looked at O'Casey. "Do you want to talk with him?"

"Yes." She sounded a bit absent, obviously because she was concentrating on the translation—or lack thereof—from her toot. "I'm starting to pick up a few words. Let him walk with us to the town, and I'm pretty sure I can have most of the language by the time we arrive."

"Okay," Pahner agreed. "I think that's about it. Questions? Comments? Concerns?"

There were none, so the company reassembled and moved on up the road.

The ancient high road became even more cracked and damaged looking as it entered the planted areas, despite clear indications of repairs. Heavy deposits of silt had been thrown up to either side, obviously as the result of post-flood road clearing, which forced the company to move between low, brown walls. In places, the walls built up to true dikes to protect the barleyrice crops, and in places the dikes were planted with the tall kate trees.

The peasants harvesting the kate fruit dangled from ropes or perched on tall, single-pole ladders that were unpleasantly reminiscent of scaling ladders, but they paused in their labors to gape at the human contingent as it headed toward the distant city-state. Whether because of the humans' outlandish look, or the fact that they came on the road from dead Voitan, the locals' reaction to them was far different from reactions in Q'Nkok.

"You'd think they'd never seen a human before," Denat snorted.

"Buncha rubes," Tratan agreed with a grunt. "Ripe

for the plucking." He looked down at the diminutive human striding along beside him under his huge rucksack. "What should we teach them first?"

"Poker," Poertena replied. "Always start wit' poker. Den, I dunno. Maybe acey-deucy. If they really stupid, cribbage."

"They pocked," Cranla said with a grunt of laughter. He waved at one of the harvesters. "Hello, you stupid peasants. We're going to pluck your merchants for all they're worth."

Julian pointed at the Mardukan tribesmen with his chin.

"They've taken quite a shine to Poertena," he said to Despreaux.

"Birds of a feather," the other squad leader responded absently. "Is it just me, or does this place look fairly run down?" she went on.

The company was approaching a fork in the road, where the travelers had to choose between Marshad or Pasule. There was another official looking building on a mound where the roads diverged, but although it was in better repair, it had obviously been converted into an agricultural outbuilding.

"Yeah," Julian said, glancing at the structure. "I think the loss of the Voitan trade must have hit them hard."

The company took the left fork and headed for the river. The solid stone bridge which crossed it was the only structure they'd so far seen which appeared to have been properly kept up. In fact, there'd been some obvious renovations—the well-fortified guard posts on either bank looked like fairly recent additions.

The guards on the near bank gestured for the caravan to halt, and Julian looked around as the long train of *flar-ta* dragged to stop. An outcropping of the underlying gneiss of the Hadur region rose steeply on the right side of the road, he noted. The oxbow river took a bend around it, and an extension of the outcropping acted as a firm base for the bridge.

The hill was surmounted by trees and what appeared to have once been a small park. A well-made road in very poor repair wound to the summit, but it was obvious that the track was rarely used anymore. Only a thin path cut through the layered silt and entangling undergrowth on its lower sections. Despreaux followed his eye, and shook her head as Captain Pahner argued with the guards on the bridge. They obviously felt that the travelers ought to keep themselves—and the business they represented—on this side of the river.

"This place has really been hammered," she observed.

"No shit," Julian agreed. "It looks like it used to be a pretty nice place, though. Maybe it'll get that way again with Voitan back in business."

"We'll see," Despreaux said. "The old Voitan wasn't built in a day."

"No," Julian acknowledged as the caravan lurched back into movement, "but that guy from T'an K'tass looked like he was going to try to do it pretty damned fast."

"That he did," Despreaux said, but her tone was a bit distracted, and she nodded at the sour looking guards on the bridge as they passed. "Those guys don't look happy."

"Probably pissed at all the money they're losing," Julian said. "We're about to pump a lot of cash into the local economy . . . on the other side of their bridge."

"We hope," she answered.

The approaching city-state was huge, much larger than Q'Nkok, but it had a seedy air. Once past the bridge area, the road was once again rutted and cracked from traffic and ill repair. In fact, it was in worse shape than it had been on the other side of the river, and the

peasants plowing the fields to either side of the roadbed also seemed less interested in the passage of the
company.

Flar-ta were useless as draft animals, because they
were far too large to move effectively in the fields. That
meant that the only way to plow was to use teams of
Mardukans for traction, which was a remarkably inef-
ficient method. It was also extremely hard work, but
while the plowers on the far side of the river had taken
the opportunity for a break while they watched the
company march by, those on this side all kept their heads
down, concentrating on their tasks. And while the
majority crop had been barleyrice on the far side of the
river, on this side most of the fields were being sown
with legumes or a crop the humans didn't recognize. The
Marines had encountered the legumes before, and
promptly christened them bullybeans, but they'd never
seen the other crop, and the locals seemed to be planting
a lot of it. At least two-thirds of the fields they could
see seemed to be dedicated to producing whatever it
was.

"I wonder why there's a difference," Julian said, pointing it out to Despreaux, who shrugged and gestured
across the wide expanse of fields. There was another hill
barely visible in the distance, but it was apparent that
the local city-state dominated a vast area.

"They've got plenty of room," she pointed out. "This
is probably just their area for bullybeans and . . . whatever
that other stuff is."

"I guess," the intel NCO said. "But that much change
just from one side of the river to the other?" He
shrugged. "I'm no farmer, but it seems kinda strange to
me."

"I suppose we'll find out why they do it eventually,"
Despreaux said with a shrug of her own. "But I wonder what that other plant is?"

❖ ❖ ❖

"*Dianda*," the itinerant tinker said to the chief of staff. "It is . . . *urdak* into *wosan* . . . like that," he finished, gesturing to the chameleon cloth uniform the civilian wore.

The local was named Kheder Bijan. It was obvious he expected some sort of reward from the company for guiding them to the clearly evident city which the ignorant foreigners could never have found on their own, but the chief of staff was happy to have him along, anyway. He'd been a good way to update the language program, and he was a mine of information about conditions around Pasule. He was strangely uninformative, however, about Marshad.

"Ah!" Eleanora said. "Something like flax or cotton!" The software had updated the local dialect well enough for Pahner to talk their way across the bridge. She was puzzled by the fact that the officials of Pasule had been more trouble than Marshad's. The local guards had simply stepped aside, almost as if the humans had been expected.

"Yes," the local said. He rubbed a horn in thought while he considered the best way to explain. "We make cloth from it for trade."

"A cash crop." The chief of staff nodded. "Where are the subsistence crops?" she asked, looking around. "I'd think you'd be planting more barleyrice than this."

"Well," Bijan said, fingering his horn again, "I don't really understand farming. I fix things." He gestured with his haversack. "I suppose there must be other farms around here somewhere."

"Who owns the land?" Eleanora had been pleasantly surprised to discover that in the Q'Nkok region the farmers owned their own land, for the most part. The farms were passed down through complicated cultural "rules" that moved them from generation to generation more or less intact. That denied inheritance to most of the "younger sons," but that was a common problem for agrarian societies the galaxy over, and the important thing was that the farms weren't broken into minuscule lots that were impossible to manage. Nor were they sold or lost in chunks to form giant latifundia. The Houses of Q'Nkok had been well on their way to the sort of backward agricultural "reform" which would strip the peasantry of land ownership, but hopefully the destruction of their power would stop that in its tracks. At this level of technology, small-scale "yeomanry" farming was as good as it got.

"I'm not sure who owns it," the tinker said, fingering his horn again. "I've never asked."

The chief of staff blinked, then smiled cheerfully. The "tinker" had blithely nattered on about the minutiae of the inner workings of the council of oligarchs who ruled Pasule, and the different groups of independents and sharecroppers who farmed the land on that side of the river. Now, on the side that he claimed he was from, he suddenly clammed up. She wouldn't have survived a day in the imperial court if *that* hadn't set off some alarm bells.

"That's interesting," she said with complete honesty. "I suppose a tinker wouldn't really care, would he?"

"Not really," Bijan said. "I just look forward to returning to my beautiful city!"

"Nice city," Kosutic said tugging at an earlobe.

"It's okay," Pahner replied.

Marshad was larger than Q'Nkok, but smaller than the former Voitan had been, with streets that wound up the hill from several gates in the curtain walls.

The gates were unusual. They were constructed of thick wood, well joined and even caulked, and their bottoms were lined with copper, which must have cost a fortune. There was also a base upon which they were, apparently, supposed to seat, but it was shattered, and any metal which might once have sheathed it was long since gone.

Much of the city appeared to be in the same dilapidated condition. The walls were higher than Voitan's, but in even worse shape. Numerous parapets had fallen to lie in rubble at the base of the main wall, leaving gaps like broken teeth in the battlements, and in places the outer stones had worked out, exposing the rubble interior fill. One section was so badly damaged that it might as well have been called a breach, and they discovered even more signs of neglect once they entered the city proper.

The area immediately inside the gate was clear, but beyond that the city reared up the hill in a maze of alleys and tunnels. The houses were mostly built of stone, pink granite and blinding white limestone, erected in a crazy quilt of warrens, with one house on top of another in a widely varying mixture of styles and quality.

The main thoroughfare was wide enough for the passage of the company, but only barely, and the boulevard was lined with wide gutters which were joined by thin streams leading out of the alleyways. This lower section clearly wasn't the best place to live: the noisome stew in the streams which obviously provided the entire city's drainage was a noxious compound of fecal matter and rot that was practically explosive.

As they continued inward, the road presented a graphic cross-section of the city. The lower slopes showed the best quality of work, with well cut blocks of feldspar and gneiss cunningly fitted, mostly without mortar. The surfaces had been coated in white plaster, and the lintels and trim still showed signs of colorful paints. But now the plaster was patched and fallen, with caved-in roofs and shattered corners, and the once bright paint was pathetically faded in the blazing gray light.

There were signs of flooding, as well, with brown high-water marks well up the sides of the houses. Many of the buildings were deserted, but shadows moved in some of the wreckage—furtive inhabitants who clearly only showed their faces under the friendly cover of night.

The quality of the stonework fell as the procession headed up the hill, but the upkeep improved. More houses were inhabited above the level of the floods, and the warren became truly mazelike, with houses piled on houses and built across alleyways which their floors turned into tunnels.

Business was being conducted in this labyrinth, but with a definitely desultory air. A few vendors lined the road with sparse offerings of half-rotten fruits, moldy barleyrice, cheap and poorly-made jewelry, and assorted minor knickknacks. The obvious poverty of the area was crushing, and the stench of rotting garbage and uncleaned latrines hung in the air as young Mardukans sat in doorways, scratching listlessly at the dust in the street.

The slums ended abruptly in a large square. Its downhill side was lined with tall townhouses which had apparently been carved out of the warren beyond at some time in the past. They fronted on a broad, flat, open area that was partially natural and partially Mardukan-made. The centerpiece of the square was a large fountain around the statue of an armed Mard-ukan, while the upper side of the square was occupied by a large ornamental building. The building seemed to climb—without a break, but in a myriad of differing styles—up to the citadel at the hill's summit. It appeared to be one vast palace, and a ceremony was in progress at its entrance.

It was apparently a public audience. The ruler of the city-state sat in a resplendent throne set up at the front door of the palace. As with the throne in Q'Nkok, this was made of many different inlaid woods, but the local monarch's throne was also set with precious metals and gems. The entire edifice gleamed with gold and silver and the twinkle of the local sapphires and rubies in their rough "miner's" cut.

The king was the first Mardukan the company had seen wearing any significant clothing, and he was garbed in a light robe of lustrous saffron. The outfit was slit down the sides, gathering only at the ankles and trimmed in bright vermillion. Traceries of silver thread ran through it, and the collar was a lace of silver and gems.

The monarch's horns had also been inlaid with precious metals and gems and were joined by a complex web of jewel-strung gold chains that caught the gray light and refracted it in a dull rainbow. As if all of that weren't enough, he also wore a heavy chain of jeweled gold around his neck, dangling far down his chest.

Arrayed to either side of the king were persons who were probably advisers. They were unclothed, except for one obvious commander in armor, but their horns were also inlaid and gemmed. The display was an obvious indication of rank, for it grew less expensive and spectacular in direct proportion to the owner's distance from the monarch.

About six hundred guards lined the steps at the front of the palace, standing at parade rest in two ranks. They were more heavily armored than the guards in Q'Nkok, with metal thigh-guards and bracers in addition to breastplates shining gray-silver in the clouded light. They carried the same long spear as the Q'Nkok guards, but they also wore palmate swords, about a meter in length, and despite their carefully polished breastplates, their purpose was obviously more than merely ceremonial.

The crowd before the monarch was a mixed bag. Most of them seemed to be from the Mardukan "middle class," to the extent that the planet had one. They also had decorations on their horns, but the displays were generally simple and made of base metals or brass. A few of the poorest of the poor were mixed in here and there, and it was one of them who was currently making some plea to the refulgent monarch.

The petitioner was in full prostration before the king, all six limbs splayed out as he abased himself. Whatever he was saying was unintelligible at this distance, but it didn't really matter, since the king was sitting half across his throne and paying virtually no attention to him.

As the company watched, the suppliant apparently finished whatever he was saying, and the monarch picked a kate fruit off a platter and nibbled on it. Then he threw the fruit at the petitioner and gestured to a guard.

Before the first protest could leave the unfortunate Mardukan's mouth, the guards had seized him and cut off his head. The head rolled to the edge of the crowd as the stump spurted a red spray and the body of the serf slumped into a twitching heap.

There was not a sound from the gathered Marshadans.

"We may have a problem here," Pahner observed.

"Oh, my," O'Casey said. A few months earlier, she probably would have lost her breakfast, but after Voitan, she was going to have a hard time finding anything that truly shocked her. "I agree."

"Well, if we turn around and leave," Roger said, "which is my first instinct, we *will* have a problem."

"Agreed," the captain said. "Stick to the prepared speech Your Highness. But I want the up squad right on you. Sergeant Major!"

"Captain?"

"Fall in the company in extended formation, Sergeant Major. I want a snappy movement. And drop the pig-stickers. Rifles and cannon front and center!"

❖   ❖   ❖

The caravan devolved into an organized frenzy as the Marines prepared to "present" their noble lord to the local monarch. Roger, for his part, rehearsed his speech and checked his pistol, on the assumption that he was equally likely to need either of them.

"Credentials, credentials," O'Casey muttered, diving into the packs on the *flar-ta* called Bertha. Somewhere she had the now much travel-stained, vermillion-sealed documents of Roger's credibility, along with letters from the King of Q'Nkok and the new council of Voitan, but she hadn't expected to need them so soon. They'd assumed that they would have to deal first with a functionary just to find shelter, then the king—not the other way around.

"Snap it, snap it, snap it," Kosutic chanted subvocally. The change from a tactical formation to one intended for parade had to be made as cleanly and professionally as possible. Any trace of disorder would not only reflect poorly on the Regiment, but would create an opening. If you looked professional, it stopped nine out of ten fights before they started; the tenth, of course, was Voitan.

The post guide had found a mark, and the squad leaders fell in on her, with their squads in turn falling in behind them. On command, the company—less one squad, which was "tight" on the prince—deployed in a double line facing that of the local guards. The Marines were pitifully few in number, but soon enough the locals would know what that pitiful few had accomplished at a place called Voitan.

Then let them get ideas.

Roger looked behind him into the unsmiling blue eyes of Sergeant Nimashet Despreaux.

"We've got to quit meeting like this. People will talk," he told her, but her demeanor didn't change.

"I'm on post, Sir. I'm not supposed to carry on a conversation."

"Ah." Roger turned back to the front and tugged at his braid as Pahner and O'Casey walked up to find him. "Sorry. I'll put myself on report."

"Ready?" Pahner subvocalized over the com.

"Bravo in position," Lieutenant Jasco replied almost as quietly.

"Inner team in position." Despreaux's voice was the ghost of a whisper at the back of Roger's head.

"Documents," O'Casey said, handing them to the prince.

"Then let's do it, Captain," Roger said calmly, and hid a silent snort of mental laughter. The presentation ceremony they were about to use was the same one they'd planned and rehearsed for Net-Hauling on Leviathan. The only difference was that the survivors of the company were on a hair trigger, and if anything went wrong he was hitting the deck at about Mach 3. Fifty-eight weapons would turn the square into an abattoir at the slightest sign of threat, and anything he personally might have added to the carnage would be purely inconsequential.

The group started forward in a slow, hieratic half-step which was used for only two purposes: formal presentations, and funerals. Since Marines did a lot more of the latter than the former, they referred to do it as "The Death March," which, in Roger's considered opinion, did not bode well in this circumstance.

The crowd before the throne parted to let them through. It was surprisingly silent; the only sound in the entire square was the slow tap of the humans' boots and the distant rumble of thunder.

Roger reached the sticky red stain where the previous petitioner had pled his case and stopped. He bowed deeply and held out the documents as the iron and shit smell of a fresh kill rose around him.

"Your Majesty, Great Ruler of Marshad and Voice of the People, I, Prince Roger Ramius Sergei Alexander Chiang MacClintock, of the House MacClintock, Heir Tertiary to the Throne of the Empire of Man, greet you in the name of my Imperial Mother, Her Majesty, Empress Alexandra MacClintock, Empress of Man, Queen of the Dawn, and Mistress of the Void."

Eleanora took the documents ceremoniously back from him and stepped forward and to the side. Dropping to both knees at the edge of the stairs, she held them out, hoping that one of these glittering idiots would figure out her purpose.

One of the advisers—a senior one, by the decoration of his horns—trotted down the steps and accepted the documents as Roger continued his speech about the magnificence of Marshad and its ruler, whose name he had yet to find out.

She backchecked the translation and winced. The program had reversed genders on Empress Alexandra, making her "Emperor Alexander," which was historically humorous but a pain otherwise. Eleanora locked that description in for this culture (they were never going to know the difference anyway), and checked the other gender settings. Sure enough, the program had reversed gender in the dialect. Fortunately, the translation glitch hadn't come up yet, so she suppressed a snarl and fixed it, then dumped the patch to the other toots and went back to listening to Roger's speech

" . . . bring joyous news: Voitan is restored! The Kranolta in all their fury came against us when we entered the fallen city, but that was a grave mistake. Aided by the forces of New Voitan, we defeated them in a terrible battle and destroyed their war host utterly. Even now the foundries and forges of fabled Voitan ring once more with the sound of forming metal! Soon the caravans will come once more on a regular basis. We are the first, but we shall not be the last!"

The prince paused in a planned break for the expected applause, but there was only a quiet murmur, and even that was almost instantly hushed. Roger was clearly nonplussed by the lack of reaction, but he carried on gamely.

"We are foreign emissaries on a voyage of exploration, and we are to be met by ships on a distant shore to the northwest. Thus we ask the boon of permission to pass through these lands in peace. We also wish to rest and enjoy the hospitality of your city, and we have brought rich booty from the conquest of the Kranolta which we wish to trade for supplies to continue our journey."

He bowed again as the king sat up. The entire company tensed, although an outside observer might have been pardoned for not realizing that it had, as the saffron-clad monarch leaned forward and examined the documents. After a brief, whispered consultation with one of his advisers, concentrating on the letter from the King of Q'Nkok, the monarch clapped his hands in agreement and stood.

"Welcome, welcome, Your Highness, to the land of Marshad, you and all your brave warriors! We have heard of your exploits in defeating the Kranolta and raising Voitan to its ancient and honorable place! In Our name, Radj Hoomas, King of Marshad, Lord of the Land, We welcome you to Marshad. Rest here as long as you like. A place has been prepared for you and your great warriors, and there shall be a great feast in your honor tonight! So We declare! Let there be merriment and celebration, for the way to Voitan is open once more!"

CHAPTER FORTY-SIX

"I don't think I understand your reasoning, Sir." Lieutenant Jasco shook his head and gestured around the sumptuous quarters the officers had been given. "They certainly seem friendly enough."

"So does a spider, Lieutenant," Pahner replied. "Right before it eats a fly."

The room was paneled in blond wood, the pale grain cut to expose abstract swirls. The floor was covered in cushions a shade or two darker than the wood, most of them piled to one side, and the single window revealed a breathtaking view of the city and the river, with a glimpse of Pasule and the vast stretch of cultivated land beyond.

All in all, it was a pleasant place. Now if they could just decide whether or not it was a prison.

"We've been dealing with Mardukans for a while now," Roger said. "They're not the gentlest people in the galaxy, but they have more regard for life than we saw this morning."

"Roger is correct," O'Casey said. "This town, the

whole local culture, appears atypical. And the focus of that would seem to be Radj Hoomas." She fingered the silken cover of the pillow on which she sat. "*Dianda*. Everywhere you look, you see this flaxsilk. All the fields, throughout the citadel. I bet if we peeked behind doorways, we'd find that everyone is weaving the stuff."

"Well, okay," Jasco said. "But that doesn't necessarily mean there's anything wrong. There have been plenty of societies where everyone was a weaver, or whatever. It doesn't make this culture evil."

"No, but it does make it dangerous," Pahner said definitively. "We need to back off from thinking like Marines and start thinking like bodyguards again."

Cord nodded in a gesture he'd picked up from the humans.

"A monarch like this Radj cares only about himself and his needs. And this *atul* has obviously been in power long enough to put his stamp on the entire kingdom."

Pahner nodded back at the shaman and looked at Kosutic.

"What are the major assassination methods?"

"You think he's going to try to assassinate Prince Roger, Sir?" Jasco asked. "Why?"

"Maybe not Roger," the sergeant major rasped, "but if he thinks there's some profit to be made from killing the guards and taking Roger hostage, he might try." She looked at the ceiling and began ticking methods off. "Poison, bomb, hand, knife, smart-bot, close-shot, long-shot, heavy weapon, weapons of mass destruction."

"This society has hand, poison, and knife," Pahner said. "So we need to concentrate on those."

"We already have analyzers," Roger pointed out, "they'll pick up poisons."

"If they come at us with swords, we respond with guns," Jasco said.

"And if they come at you with knives?" the sergeant

major asked with a grim smile. "*En masse*, from every side? What then, Lieutenant?"

"Exactly." Pahner turned to O'Casey. "You're going to be handling point on the negotiations again. Make sure they're aware that Roger has to have," he paused and thought for a moment, "seven guards at all times. Seven is a mystic number to us humans. Not to be trifled with. So sorry if that's a problem."

"Okay," Eleanora said, making a note on her toot.

"I don't trust him as far as I could throw Patty," Roger said.

"Why not, Your Highness?" Jasco asked, perhaps just a trifle more dismissively than he really ought to have spoken to the Heir Tertiary to the Throne of Man. "They've given us everything we wanted on a silver platter, and no wonder. I mean, obviously, they're happy they'll be getting the Voitan trade back. Look at the slums we passed through on the way up."

"That's exactly why," Roger said quietly. "Look, I might have been a clotheshorse. Well, still am," he amended with a chuckle, looking down at his stained chameleon uniform. "But," he continued seriously, "it wasn't the same as this place. Right down the hill from us there's crushing poverty. In case you didn't notice, most of those kids were literally starving. And the guy who should be working on fixing that is sitting on his ass at the top of the heap, sucking on fruit, having his horns inlaid, and cutting peasants' heads off. And there are all these fields where food could be grown, but it isn't. They're being planted in flaxsilk. So the people are starving, and I don't think that that's the *farmers'* plan. I think it's the plan of the son-of-a-bitch we're about to have a 'Victory Dinner' with." The prince's jaw flexed in anger, and his nostrils twitched as if they'd scented something foul. "So that, Lieutenant, is why I don't trust that Borgia son-of-a-bitch."

"Seven guards, Chief of Staff, Sergeant Major," Pahner said emphatically. "Fully armed. Especially at this 'Victory Party.' And extra especially," he added dryly, "after all the trouble 'our friend' the monarch went to making sure we came here."

"Yeah," Roger said. "A 'tinker.' "

"You caught that, too?" Eleanora observed with a smile.

"I wonder what he really is?"

"You succeeded, Kheder Bijan," the king observed. He took a nibble out of a kate fruit and tossed the remainder on the floor. "Congratulations, 'Scout.' "

"Thank you, O King," the commander of the Royal Scouts replied. The Scouts actually did some scouting, especially when meeting with the informants they maintained among the surrounding tribes, but he was in fact the commander of the Marshad secret police.

"Once again you have avoided having your head lopped off," the monarch added with a grunt of humor. "One of these days, you won't be so lucky. That day will be a great pleasure to me. A day of comfort."

"I live to serve, O King." The spy knew he was on the edge of the knife, but that was what gave the role spice.

"Of course you do." The king gave a disbelieving chuckle. "It is a well-known fact, is it not?"

He turned to the commander of the Royal Guard. The commander had been nothing more than a common mercenary before being given his position, and the king had been careful to ensure that plenty of hatred was directed at him. It was one way to ensure the Guard's total loyalty, for if the king fell, so would the Guard.

"We will continue with the original plan."

"Yes, O King," the guard commander replied with a

brief glance of fury at the spy. "The forces are at your command."

"Of course they are," he whispered. "And with Our mighty army and the power of these humans, We shall rule the world!"

Roger took another bite of the spiced meat. He'd run an analyzer over it and gotten all the usual warning about alkaloids, but it wasn't poisonous. It just tasted that way.

The locals used a spice that tasted exactly like rancid fennel, and it was apparently wildly popular, because it was in every dish. Roger picked a bit of the purple leaf off the meat and checked. Yep, that was it. He surreptitiously spat, trying to get the rotten taste out of his mouth, then gave up. At least there were only fourteen more courses to go.

The diners were seated on cushions, arranged in pairs and trios around low, three-legged tables. The courses were borne in by silent servants, and the empty platters were borne back out picked over or finished off. Most of the diners were members of the Marshad court, but there were also some representatives from other city-states. They were neither exactly ambassadors nor simple visitors, but seemed to occupy some place in between.

Roger was seated with two such representatives near the king. He had initially engaged them in desultory conversation, but they'd rapidly dropped into a complex discussion of trading futures that drifted first out of Roger's interest, and eventually out of the local dialect. Since then, the prince had occupied himself picking at his food and observing the dinner party.

He looked over at Pahner. The captain was seated on a cushion, legs crossed as if he'd been born to this society, calmly chewing and swallowing the horrible food and nodding as if he actually heard every word his seat mate was saying. As always, the Marine was the perfect diplomat, and Roger sighed. He was *never* going to be that good.

Eleanora had stopped eating after only a couple of mouthfuls, but she could excuse that on the basis of the steady conversation she'd been maintaining with both her table mates. The chief of staff was doing her usual job of probing every nuance of the local culture, dissecting it as a biologist would dissect an invertebrate.

He didn't look over his shoulder, but he knew the Marines were standing at the ready. They lined the wall at his back, weapons at low port and ready for instant use if it dropped in the pot.

He felt mildly naked without the additional presence of Cord, but the shaman lacked the nanites of his human companions and was still recovering from the terrible shrapnel wounds he'd taken in Voitan. Whatever might happen, the shaman would have to ride it out from a pile of cushions in the visitors' quarters.

Everyone was still as nervous as cats in a roomful of float-chairs. Including, unless he was much mistaken, Radj Hoomas.

The king sat at the head of the room, with his back to the large double doors leading into one of his many throne rooms. He was surrounded, literally, by guards and hard to observe through the obscurement of the armored behemoths. From what Roger could see of him, however, he, too, was picking at his food, speaking occasionally with the armored commander seated beside him and glancing nervously around the room. It might be a victory party, but the host didn't look very victorious.

"The Prince isn't eating!" the king whispered angrily.

"He's eaten enough," Mirzal Pars responded. The old mercenary clapped his hands and grunted in humor. "They're so smart, but they don't even recognize *miz* poison. It may be tasteless, but you can see the leaves clearly. Everyone knows about it . . . except these *humans*." He grunted another laugh.

"But will it be enough?" Radj Hoomas demanded. The plan had to be executed flawlessly, for the power of these humans was terrifying to contemplate. Holding onto it would be like holding an *atul* by the tail.

"It will be enough. They've all eaten more than a large enough dose. If we withhold the antidote, they'll die within a day."

"And the guards are ready?"

"Assuredly," the commander chuckled. "They look forward to it."

CHAPTER FORTY-SEVEN

The celebration had moved into the throne room, where the king presided over the conversation swirling around him from his throne. Much of the court had excused itself after the dinner, pleading the excuse of work to complete, and the majority of the room was sparsely filled with the prince's party and the representatives from the surrounding city-states.

Eleanora sipped from a cup of warm, flat water and squinted at the representative from Pasule.

"The king is the *sole* landowner?" she asked incredulously. Even in the most despotic regimes in Earth's history, power had been more diffuse than that.

"Yes. Radj Hoomas owns not only the agricultural land, but all of the buildings of the town, and all of the houses of the Council outside the city wall." The representative, Jedal Vel, was short for a Mardukan, but he still towered over the chief of staff. She'd ended up talking exclusively to him after finding him a mine of information. The "simple trader" from Pasule was a student not only of commerce, but of government and history. He was, naturally, biased towards Pasule's oligarchical form of government, but having Marshad as a horrible counterexample would tend to do that.

"Two generations ago, in the chaos after the fall of Voitan, there was a great rebellion among the Houses of Marshad. Three of them were the most prominent, and the king of that time, Radj Kordan, Radj Hoomas' grandfather, allied with one of them against the other two. It was a terrible battle, but the king finally prevailed over all but his single surviving ally. Most unfortunately, he was, in turn, assassinated shortly after the end of the war by a son of one of the defeated Houses. He had intended simply to reduce their power, fine them heavily, and strip them of guards, but his son, Hoomas' father, killed every member of the defeated Houses. Then he forced a marriage with a daughter of the single surviving ally, and absorbed that House, leaving the House of Radj as the only power in Marshad."

The representative sipped his wine and gave a lower handclap, a Mardukan shrug.

"Pasule's actions in this were not the best. We supported both sides, trying to drag the war out and damage Marshad as much as possible. We've always seen the city as a rival, and since the fall of Voitan it's come to war more than once. But when Radj consolidated all the power under itself, it was clear we'd made a serious mistake. Since then, Radj has taken more and more power and treasure, and left less and less for others.

"The only thing that Marshad exports anymore is *dianda*, but it makes a tremendous profit on it. The crop is hard to grow, and takes up valuable land which might otherwise be used to grow food. Naturally, Radj Hoomas could care less. The land produces barely enough food to support the farmers; the city poor are left to starve and work the looms."

"It seems like a situation ripe for a revolution,"

O'Casey said. "Surely there's some group that might rise up?"

"Perhaps," Jedal Vel said carefully. "However, the profits from the *dianda* trade also permit him to support a large standing army. Most of it is composed of mercenaries, but they recognize that they need Radj in power as the only way to preserve their own positions. They've crushed the few attempted rebellions easily."

"I see," O'Casey said. *Take the army out of the picture though,* she mused silently, *and things might change.* She glanced at the guards lining every wall. Another, separate contingent formed a half-moon crescent around the throne, and the ostentatious display of force finally made sense to her.

"Millions for defense, not a penny for the poor. . . ." she murmured with a low chuckle.

"Pardon?" the Pasule asked, but it was only an absent courtesy, for he was looking towards the throne. Radj Hoomas had called over the guard commander, and it looked like he might finally be ready to make the announcement that would permit everyone to leave gracefully.

Pahner nodded to the prince as Roger walked up to him. The squad parted as the prince neared the captain, and the Marines expertly swallowed up both officers in a protective ring.

"Roger," the captain greeted him, and glanced at Despreaux. The Marines had been specifically tasked with eavesdropping on the king and his guard captain, but the sergeant shrugged her shoulders. Nothing clear to report.

"Radj is definitely planning something," the prince said, tucking a stray hair back into line. "But so far, so good."

"That's what the jumper said as he passed the

thirtieth floor," Pahner pointed out. He looked at Despreaux again. "What?"

"Just something about the guards, Sir," the sergeant said. "Maybe something about poison, too, but that wasn't clear."

"Joy," the company CO said.

"I don't like being surrounded like this, Sir," she added. "We could take the king if it dropped in the pot, but I'm not sure we could keep the Prince alive."

"If that happens, Sergeant," Roger said quietly, "take the king. That's your primary mission. Understood?"

Despreaux glanced quickly at Pahner, but the captain only looked back at her without expression.

"Yes, Sir. Understood," she said.

"Let's be on our toes," Pahner suggested as conversation died down and the king climbed to his feet. "Looks like time to party."

"We are gathered here tonight," Radj Hoomas said, "to honor the brave warriors who crushed the Kranolta and reopened the road to Voitan. Puissant warriors, indeed," he said, and his voice echoed hollowly through the wood-paneled hall.

"Puissant warriors, indeed," he repeated, and glanced around at his own massed guards. "I ask you, Your Royal Highness, Prince Roger Ramius Sergei Alexander Chiang MacClintock, could your puissant warriors defeat all the guards in this room? Before you fell yourself?"

"Possibly," Roger replied calmly. "Quite probably. And I would be trying very hard to survive."

The king gazed at him for a moment, then glanced at one of his guards . . . who stepped forward, and, with a smooth motion, shoved his spear into the back of the representative from Pasule. Jedal Vel screamed in a froth of aspirated blood as the bitter steel spearhead emerged from his chest, but the guard only grinned cruelly and twisted his wrist as he jerked his weapon free once more and the envoy thudded to the floor.

"Are you so confident?" the king asked, grunting in humor.

"What?" Roger asked, with a smile he didn't feel, as O'Casey recoiled towards the Marines and away from the twitching corpse at her feet. "You think that the 'puissant warriors' who defeated the Kranolta have never seen blood?"

He booted up the assassin program he'd used in Q'Nkok, and as the aiming reticle appeared, superimposed on his vision, he dropped it onto the forehead of the laughter-grunting guard captain.

It required more than well-written software to be truly phenomenal with an assassin program. Even with hard encoding, it required smooth, practiced muscles that could handle the high twitch-rate strains placed upon them. But Roger *had* practiced, and the pistol came up with the blinding speed which had so surprised Pahner in the Q'Nkok banquet hall. The weapon simply *materialized* in his hand, and the supersonic crack of the bead's passage blended with a meaty thump as the decapitated guard captain hit the floor.

The king opened his mouth to shout, his face covered in the bright crimson spray of the captain's blood, then froze as he found himself looking down the barrel of the bead pistol.

"Now, there's an old term for this," Pahner said quietly, his own pistol out and trained as he transmitted furious orders to hold fast over his toot. The orders had to be in text, because the subvocalization equipment was part of the combat helmet he wasn't wearing at the moment, and his toot had to rebroadcast it through the systems of the bodyguards' helmets. That meant the orders were necessarily one-way, but he could imagine Kosutic's distant cursing just fine.

"It's called a 'Mexican standoff,'" he continued. "You try to kill us, and our company blows your little town to the ground. Not that you personally will care, Your Majesty, because you'll die right here, right now."

"I don't think so," the king said with a grunt as guards moved to interpose their bodies between him and Roger's weapon. "But I don't intend to kill any humans today. No, no. That was never my intent."

"You don't mind if we doubt your word, do you?" Roger asked, deflecting the pistol's point of aim to the ceiling as the tension eased slightly. "And, by the way," he added, nodding to the guards between him and Radj Hoomas, "we'll cut through those fucking bodies like they were so much cloth when we start. Bodies aren't going to stop us."

"But doing that would take time and prevent you from killing all the *other* guards that would be killing *you*," the king said. "But, again, that was never my intent."

"Ask him what his plan *is*," O'Casey hissed, now relatively safe between the bulks of Pahner and Roger. She was a fair negotiator, but these were not, in her opinion, optimal conditions. In fact, her mouth was dry with fear and her palms were sweating. She couldn't imagine how Roger and Pahner were staying so calm.

"All right, O King, what's your plan?" Roger asked, carefully not swallowing. If he did, it would be obvious his mouth was as dry as the lakebed they'd landed on.

"I have certain desires," the king said, with another grunt of laughter. "You have certain needs. I think we could come to mutually acceptable terms."

"All right," and Pahner said grimly. "I can see that. But why in hell did you choose to open negotiations like this?"

"Well," the king responded, with yet another grunt that this time turned into a belly laugh, "your need is food, supplies and weapons. Unfortunately, there is no great supply of either in Marshad. My desire, on the other hand, is to conquer Pasule, where it chances that both are readily available. I was fairly sure you wouldn't care to conquer Pasule for me, so it seemed advisable to discover an incentive to . . . *encourage* you."

"An incentive," Pahner repeated tonelessly.

"Precisely. I feel confident that your warband will take Pasule for me when I tell them it's a choice between that and the death of their leaders."

"Okay, okay," Kosutic said, waving for quiet. "Let's just stay cold here, people."

"We should extract them immediately," Jasco said. "I know those aren't our orders, but orders given under duress are invalid."

"Sure, Sir," Kosutic said. "Tell it to the Captain."

"Well . . ."

The conversation was taking place in the third-floor "officers' quarters" of the visitors' area. The pale yellow room where the prince had prepared for the fateful dinner party was now filled with the temporary command group.

"Lieutenant," Julian said, tapping his pad, "we have upwards of a battalion of scummies outside this building. They hold the high ground, and our pack beasts. We would have to fight our way out and up to the throne room."

"The Captain's right, Lieutenant Jasco," the sergeant major said. "We wait for the right moment, and play along in the meantime. We have to wait until the odds favor us, instead of the other way around. We have the time."

"This isn't right!" the exasperated officer said. "We should be taking down that throne room right now. This is a member of the *Imperial Family!*"

"Yep," Kosutic said equably. "Surely is. Dangerous one, too."

✧   ✧   ✧

Roger listened calmly to the brand-new guard commander's bloodthirsty pronouncements about what would happen to any human who did not obey orders. The new, heavily-armored commander explained at considerable length, and when he finished, Roger bared his teeth in a smile.

"You're next," he said pleasantly.

The guard captain glared at the prince, but the Mardukan's eyes fell before Roger's did, and the scummy withdrew, closing the door behind him.

Roger turned from the door and looked around. The suite was large and airy, with several windows which overlooked the back side of the castle. The far curtain wall, he noticed, was covered with torch-bearing guards watching the shadows for any attempt to escape.

The floor was scattered with the ubiquitous pillows and low tables of the Hadur, and there were "chamber buckets" for relieving wastes. It was quite pleasant, all things considered.

"We have to get out of here," he muttered.

"And you propose to do that, how?" Pahner asked, handing Despreaux back her borrowed helmet. Unlike the prince, the captain was the very picture of sangfroid.

"Well, I feel like taking a rifle and killing a guard an hour until they either let us go or figure out to stay out of sight," Roger snarled, glaring at the guards manning the wall.

"Thereby suggesting retaliation," the captain said coolly. "Until we're actually in combat, we aren't decisively engaged. We should maneuver for room until then. Violence at this stage will only limit, rather than expand, our maneuver room."

"Do you have a plan?" O'Casey asked. "It sounds like you do."

"Not as such," Pahner said, glancing out the window.

The lesser moon, Sharma, was rising, and its glimmer could be sensed rather than seen in the darkness beyond the windows. "On the other hand, I've often found that waiting for your opponent to move reveals the weakness in his own plans."

CHAPTER FORTY-EIGHT

Kostas Matsugae watched the line of stooped figures carrying in the sacks of barleyrice. These Mardukans were the first females, outside their mahouts' families, the company had seen since Q'Nkok, and they were clearly being used for this task because they were both nonthreatening and of subnormal intelligence. They were also thin as rails.

The valet nodded and looked around as the last sack of grain was carried in. The area where the food supplies were being piled was out of sight of the Mardukan guards stationed outside the visitors' quarters, and he quickly opened up a pot and gestured to the Mardukans.

"This is stew with some barleyrice in it." He gestured to a stack of small bowls. "You can each have a bowl. Only one, please."

After the almost pathetically grateful females had left, he looked up and noticed Julian watching him from the doorway. The alcove to one side of the entrance was technically a guard room, but since there were nothing *but* guards in the building, it had been converted to storage.

514

"Do you have a problem with my charity, Sergeant?" Matsugae picked up one of the sacks and headed for the doorway; it was time to start work on dinner.

"No." The Marine plucked the twenty-kilo sack easily from the slight valet's grip and tossed it over his own shoulder. "Charity seems to be in short supply in this town. Nothing wrong with changing that."

"This is the most detestable town it has ever been my displeasure to visit," Matsugae said. He shook his head and grimaced. "It defies belief."

"Well," the sergeant said with a grim smile, "it's bad— I'll grant that. But it's not the worst in the galaxy. You ever read anything about Saint 'recovery worlds'?"

"Not much," the valet admitted. "Rather, I've heard of them, but I don't really 'know' about them. On the other hand, I believe the overall concept that the Saints espouse has some justice. Many planets *have* been damaged beyond recovery by overzealous terraforming and unchecked mining. That doesn't make me a SaintSymp," he added hastily.

"Didn't think you were. You couldn't have made it past the loyalty tests if you were. Or, at least, I hope you couldn't have. But have you ever read any reports about 'recovery worlds'? Unbiased ones?"

"No," Matsugae replied as they reached the kitchen area. A blaze had already been started in the large fireplace at one end of the guard room, and a pot hung from a swing arm, ready to be put into the fire. The room was amazingly hot, like an entrance to Hell, and Matsugae started gathering the ingredients of the evening meal. "Should I have?"

"Maybe." The sergeant set the bag of grain on the floor. "You know the theory?"

"They're former colonized planets that the Saints are trying to return to 'pristine' condition," the valet said as he began measuring ingredients into the pot. "They're

trying to erase any evidence of terrestrial life on them."
He smiled and gestured at the pot. "It's stew and barleyrice tonight, for a change."

Julian snorted, but didn't smile.

"That's the theory, all right," he agreed. "But how are
they actually doing it? How are they 'unterraforming'
those worlds? And what worlds are they? And where are
the colonists who lived on them?"

"Why the questions, Sergeant?" Matsugae asked.
"Should I assume that you know the answers, whereas
I don't?"

"Yeah." Julian gave a mildly angry nod. "I know the
answers. Okay. How are they 'unterraforming' the planets? They started with the colonists. Dirt poor farmers, mostly—none of these are worlds that produce
anything the Saints give a damn about. That's why
they're willing to drop them. So they have these people
rounded up and put to work undoing the 'damage' that
a couple of generations have done to the planets. Since
they were farmers and terraformers—or the descen-
dants of farmers and terraformers, anyway—before they
were picked up, they were, *de facto*, guilty of 'eco-
logical mismanagement.' "

"But . . . ?" the valet began in a puzzled tone.

"Hang on." The sergeant held up a hand. "I think I'll
answer your question in a bit. Anyway, they put them
to work 'reversing' the process. Mostly with hand tools,
'to minimize the impact.' And since humans, just by their
excretions, if nothing else, tend to change the environment around them, the 'Saints' have to make sure that
any fresh damage is minimized. Which they do by
reducing the food supplies of the workers to under one
thousand calories per day."

"But that's—"

"About half the minimum necessary to sustain life?"
the sergeant said with a vicious smile. "Really? Gee."

"Are you saying that they're starving their own colonists to death?" Matsugae asked in a disbelieving tone. "That's hard to believe. Where's the Human Rights Commission report?"

"These are planets near the center of the Saints own empire," Julian pointed out. "HRC teams aren't let anywhere near the recovery planets. According to the Saints, they're completely abandoned and quarantined, so what interest could the HRC possibly have in them? Besides," he added bitterly, "they worked their way through the colonists years ago."

"My God, you're serious," the valet said quietly. He accepted the help of the obviously angry NCO to fill the pot with water and swung it over the fire. "That's insane!"

"'Insane' describes the Saints to a 'T,'" Julian snarled. "Of course, the job is never really 'complete,'" he added with a ghastly smile.

"Oh?" Matsugae said warily.

"Sure. I mean, there's always some damned humanocentric weed cropping up somewhere on these pristine beauties," the sergeant said lightly. "That's why they still have to send humans down there to root them out."

"And where do they get those humans?"

"Well, first there's political prisoners," Julian said, ticking off the groups on his fingers. "Then there are other 'environmental enemies,' such as smokers. And there are general prisoners that are just going to be a bother to keep around. Last, but most certainly not least, there are nationals from other political systems that have, in the opinion of the Saint higher-ups, no utility," he finished with a snarl.

"Like?" Matsugae asked even more warily.

"Raider insertion teams, for starters," the Marine said bitterly. "We've lost three in the last year, and all we get out of the Saints is 'we have no knowledge of them.'"

"Oh."

"The hell of it is, that there are all these rumors that NavInt knows where they are." The NCO sat down on one of the tri-legged tables and hung his head. "If they'd just tell us, we'd go in in an instant. Shit, we've put Raider teams on the planets and *documented* what's going on—that's how we lost our people in the first frigging place! I know we could get at least some of them out!"

"So these are *rumors*? That makes sense. I can't believe that sort of thing is going on in this day and age."

"Oh, get a fucking grip, Kostas!" Julian snapped. "I've seen the damned pictures from Calypso, and they look like one of the internment camps from the Dagger Years! A bunch of skeletons wandering around with wooden tools and digging at *dandelions*, for God's sake!"

The valet regarded him calmly.

"I believe that *you* believe this to be true. Would you mind if I tried to corroborate it?"

"Not at all," the NCO sighed. "Ask any of the senior Marines. Hell, ask O'Casey when we get her back. I'm sure she's up to speed on it. But the point is that, bad as this place is, humans do ten times worse to each other every day."

Poertena watched the Mardukans carefully. He'd long since stopped regretting his "cheating" demonstration. There wasn't much point in regret, since he couldn't put the genie back into the bottle whatever he did, but it turned out that four arms made for hellacious cardsharps.

He'd first noticed the problem shortly after his brief demonstration to his cronies on the march from Voitan. Suddenly, where he'd been winning fairly consistently at poker, he started losing. Since his play hadn't changed, it meant that his companions' play must have gotten better, but it wasn't until Cranla fumbled a transfer that he twigged to what was going on.

Even though the Mardukans' "false-hands" were relatively clumsy, it was easy enough for them to palm one or two critical cards, and then it was a simple matter of switching them off. He caught them once on the basis of an ace that was covered in slime; Denat, the tricky bastard, had figured out that he could embed a card in the mucous on his arm and even show that his "hands were empty."

So now, they played spades. There were still ways to cheat, but with all fifty-two cards in play, it was trickier. Which wasn't much consolation at the moment, he thought, as Tratan dropped an ace onto the current trick and cut the Pinopan's king.

"Be calm, Poertena," the big Mardukan snorted. "Next you'll think these brainless females are giving us tips!" He gestured at the nearest one, who was slowly shuffling along in a squat, sweeping the floor with nothing more than a handful of barleyrice straw while she crooned and murmured tunelessly to herself.

A group of the simpleminded peasant women had been sent in the previous day to clean and had stayed. Not surprisingly; they were treated better among the humans than anywhere else in the city. But in the short time they'd been there, while the company waited for word on what the king intended, the inoffensive little creatures had faded into the background.

Poertena looked up at Tratan's gesture, and snorted.

"I don't t'ink so," he said.

The small, retiring Mardukan noted their regard and ducked her head, raising the volume of her croon slightly, and Poertena grunted a laugh and started to look back at his cards, then paused as his toot's translation program started to cycle. The system had tried to react to his unconscious desire to listen to the words of the song and detected that it was in an unknown dialect. He started to disengage the translation protocol's furious cycling, but decided to let it finish the run when the first phrase to pop out was "stupid man."

He hid a chuckle and picked at the program. The tiny female, very little more than normal human height, was apparently cursing the three Mardukan tribesmen.

> "O, most stupid of men, am I not singing
> in your language?
> "Look at me, just a glance is all I ask.
> "I dare not call attention, for there
> may be spies among my fellows.
> "But I am the only one who
> knows your language,
> "You stupid, foolish, gutless, idiotic men.
> "Will you not listen to me
> that your prince might live?"

Poertena wasn't quite certain how he managed to keep a straight face as he shifted from humor to panic, but he was a long-experienced negotiator, and that experience wasn't limited to legal goods and services. Individuals had made clandestine contact with him in public places before, and as soon as he realized the song was an attempt to do just that, he probed the translation program.

The problem was that the female was *not* using language of The People. Nor was she using the dialect of Q'Nkok, which was very similar. Instead, she was using a third dialect which was significantly different, and between those differences and the fact that she was trying to avoid calling anyone *else's* attention to herself, the three tribesmen had been totally oblivious to her.

"The problem is you language, O silly female," Poertena said. The translator, noting who the target of the statement was, automatically used the odd dialect. "They do no' speak it. So, who is tee foolish one, I ask you?"

"Ah," she sang. "I had wondered how any three boys could be so stupid. It is the language of the city you have passed through, a city restored." The song was almost atonal and, sung in a whisper, it could have been a lullaby in an unknown language. No threat. Despite that, the contact shifted to a completely wordless hum as another female passed through carrying a tray of food. She let the other female draw out of earshot, then glanced up discreetly while she continued her aimless sweeping.

"Move it or lose it," Cranla said, thumping on the table, and Poertena jerked out of his reverie and threw a card without even looking at it.

"Hey, *partner*," Denat began with a snarl, "what—"

"No, no, no table talk," Tratan chuckled as he covered the king with a spade. "Gotcha."

"Su', su'," Poertena said quietly. "We jus' stopped playing anyway. We gonna continue to throw cards until t'is hand is done, then *we* done."

"Hey, it's not that bad . . ." Cranla started to say.

"I jus' got word t'at there's a problem," Poertena lied. "So, me, I'm not really pay attention to tee game. We need to stop. Soon."

"I can quit," Tratan said. There was half a hand left, but he flashed his cards. "We just throw them down, tot up the score like it's real, and deal a hand of poker. And pretend to play until you have to move." He looked casually around for any immediate threats. "We need to get our spears?"

"What?" Cranla said. "I don't—"

"Shut up," Denat said mildly. "Just do it."

"Oh." The young Mardukan finally caught the drift and tossed his cards into the middle of the table with a shrug. "Not a great hand, anyway."

"Yeah," Tratan said. "I think it was a lousy hand we were just dealt."

"Okay, Lady," Poertena said. "What you message?" He deliberately kept his eyes on the table and addressed the apparent nonsense syllables to Tratan.

"I think I caught a bit of that," the tribesman said in return, glancing involuntarily at the female and then down at the table. "So it wasn't one of your mystical radio communications?"

"There is one who needs to talk to your leaders," the female sang, dusting the walls beside the table now. "One who must meet with your leaders."

"T'at will be hard," Poertena said, but he glanced up at Cord's nephews. "Cranla, go get tee Sergeant Major?"

"Okay," the Mardukan said, using the actual Standard, and got up and trotted towards the stairs.

"I will meet you near the fireplace downstairs, in a little while," the female sang, sweeping her way towards the door. "In the time a candle takes to burn a finger's breadth."

Poertena thought about it but decided against trying to get her to stay put. She was obviously working to a game plan, and if the humans wanted to use it, they had to have some idea what it was.

"All right," he answered, picking up the poker hand. "A half-hour." He glanced at his cards and grimaced. "A full house on deal. Jus' my luck."

"Not really," Tratan said soothingly. "I just didn't want you to be distracted trying to decide what to draw."

CHAPTER FORTY-NINE

"You're sure about this, Poertena?" Lieutenant Jasco asked dubiously.

The blazing fireplace made the kitchen an inferno which was normally empty, but for Matsugae and the mahout's wives who helped him with meals. Now, however, it was crowded with the sergeant major, the lieutenant, Poertena, and Denat, along with Julian and one of his fire teams. Matsugae and his current assistant continued preparing the evening meal, stepping around the Marines and Mardukans crowding the room, but it wasn't exactly easy.

"T'is is where she said, Sir."

"She's late, then," the lieutenant said.

"The time is ambiguous," Pahner said over the radio. "A 'finger's breadth' on a candle. Human or Mardukan, and what kind of candle?" The captain, Roger, and O'Casey were attending the assembly through the suit cameras from Despreaux's squad.

"But it still should have been about half an hour, Sir,"

Jasco argued. "This is a fool's errand," he added with a glance at the armorer.

"So you think we should have dismissed it, Sir?" Kosutic asked.

"I think," the lieutenant replied as the wall behind him swung silently open, "that we should all get ready to be hit. We don't know what might be coming at us," he finished as the female menial, moving in a much less menial fashion and accompanied by a familiar face, stepped out of the secret passage.

"Shit," Kosutic said mildly, and flipped her helmet sensors to deep-sonar. The view of the "visitors' quarters" in that frequency was interesting. "Captain, we got us a honeycomb here."

Jasco looked at her very strangely, then noticed where everyone else was staring, looked over his shoulder, and jumped half out of his chameleon suit, then backed hastily over to join the other humans.

Julian wrinkled his nose and chuckled.

"Well, if it isn't the tinker!"

Kheder Bijan nodded as the female, no longer looking either meek or unintelligent, padded across the room to secure the door.

"Please pardon my deception on your approach. It was necessary to prevent your destruction."

"What do you mean?" Jasco's natural suspicions had not been particularly eased by having someone step out of a "solid" wall behind him. "Trust me, nobody would be destroying *us*, bucko!"

"You can be killed," Bijan replied. "You were badly hurt at Voitan. You lost, I believe, some thirty out of your total of ninety."

"Slightly off," Kosutic told him with a thin smile. "You must have had someone counting wounded they assumed would die, but we're tougher than that."

Bijan clapped his hands quietly in agreement.

"Yes, my own count showed that the numbers were off. Thank you for that explanation. Nonetheless, if you hadn't come to Marshad, you would have been destroyed on the road to Pasule. Even if Radj Hoomas had needed his entire army to accomplish it, you would have been destroyed."

"Why?" Jasco demanded. "What the hell did we do?"

"Not what we did, Sir," Julian said. "What we are. We're his ticket to power."

"Exactly." Bijan nodded at the sergeant. "You are his 'ticket' to control of the *Hadur*. Make no mistake, Pasule is but a stepping stone. After Pasule comes Turzan and then Dram. He'll use you until you're used up."

"That's more or less what we figured," Pahner said to Kosutic and Jasco. He was using a discrete frequency to avoid having the rest of the company listening in; this was not a morale-boosting conversation. "And we can't afford the time. He has a plan, so ask him what it is."

"What's the plan?" Kosutic asked, cutting Jasco off.

"Let Kosutic take the lead, Lieutenant," Pahner coached when the lieutenant looked sharply at the noncom. "It's customary to let a lower-level person take point. That way if you decide to hang somebody out to dry, it's the Sergeant Major, not you."

"You have to have a reason to contact us," the sergeant major continued, suppressing a smile. The captain would be hard pressed to ever "hang somebody out to dry," but it certainly made a good excuse to let the grown-ups do the planning.

"You have a schedule to keep," the spy told her with a Mardukan grunt of humor. "Yes, I know even that about you. You have to reach this far distant coast within a set time frame. You can't afford to spend a year here campaigning."

"How in the hell—!" Jasco exclaimed.

"Nice piece of information," Kosutic said. "But you still haven't mentioned the plan."

"There are those who don't look with favor upon Radj Hoomas, obviously," the tinker said. "There are many such in Marshad. Perhaps even more, at least among those with power and funds, in Pasule."

"And you are what? A friend of these people? A believer?"

"Call me a friend," the spy said. "Or a humble servant."

"Uh-huh. Okay, humble servant, what's the plan of this anonymous group of people?"

"They simply wish to change the status quo," the spy said unctuously. "To create a better Marshad for all its inhabitants. And, among those in the group who are from Pasule, to save themselves from conquest by a madman."

"And why should we help them?" Kosutic asked. "Given that we might be 'monarchy: like it or die' types."

"You aren't," Bijan replied calmly. "My conversation with the O'Casey made that clear. She was very interested in the ownership of land, and pleased when I told her Pasule practiced free ownership by the farmers themselves. Furthermore, you're trapped; you must destroy the House of Radj or miss your rendezvous. Nor will your part be difficult. On the day of the battle, you will simply switch your allegiance. With the aid of your lightning weapons and the forces of Pasule, the local rebels will be able to overcome Radj Hoomas' forces, most of whom will be involved in the attack on Pasule in your support."

"And what about our commanders?" Kosutic could see that the plan was as full of holes as Swiss cheese, but she also suspected that those holes were traps for the humans. "How do they survive our 'switch in allegiance'?"

"There are partisans within the palace," Bijan replied easily. "Between them and your leaders' guards, the purely Radj forces can be overcome. Certainly they can secure your leaders' safety until either you arrive to relieve them or the palace is taken by the city partisans.

"However," he continued, with a hand slap of regret, "whether we can guarantee your leaders' security or not, you have little choice. If you don't assist us, you will be here a year hence, trapped, I suspect, in this horrible little backwater for the rest of your lives. Which, given that Radj intends to use you over and over again for shock troops, will probably be short ones."

Kosutic made sure her smile was broad and toothy; Mardukans didn't show teeth except in aggression.

"You've figured all the angles, haven't you?"

"You need our help," the spy said simply, "and we need yours. It's a simple meeting of needs. No more."

"Uh-huh." The sergeant major glanced over at the female. "Is that our contact?" she asked, gesturing with her chin.

"Yes," Bijan answered. "Her family was from Voitan and has . . . different customs. She's an excellent conduit."

"Nobody notices me," the diminutive female said, standing by the door with her broom and dusting idly. "Who would notice a brainless female? Even if she heard something, how could she remember it?"

The girl grunted evilly and Kosutic smiled, then nodded at the spy.

"Stay here. We need to go talk." She jerked her head at the command group to precede her out of the kitchen's Stygian heat. They went as far as the second guardroom, where she made the "rally here" hand sign.

"Captain, you there?" she asked.

"Aye. We got it all, too," the CO said.

"Yeah," Roger chimed in. "Every goddamned bit of it."

"I want suggestions," Pahner went on. "Julian, you first."

"We need to go with the plan, Sir. At least at first.

Like the guy said, right now I don't see a way around it."

"Don't worry about us," Roger said. "I don't know if Captain Pahner fully agrees, but I believe we'll be able to hold our own if most of the guards are involved in the assault."

Pahner's sigh was audible over the radio.

"I don't like it, but I more or less agree."

"We should be able to turn the tables on the ground," Jasco said, shaking his head. "But it's gonna be a helluva fight at the bridge, and then we'll be in a running battle all the way up to the palace."

"Actually, Sir," Kosutic said, thinking about the terrain, "the problem will be on this side."

"Correct," Pahner agreed. "If formed forces make it to the city, you'll be fighting every step of the way through that warren. That sort of fighting will whittle us down to nothing. If you have to fight street-to-street, we might as well surrender now."

"So you think that if the Marshad army is on the Pasule side of the river—and stays there—then the Company can relieve us?" Roger asked carefully.

"Yes," the Marine said after a moment's thought. "We'll still take some casualties. But if we can get some assurances that the Pasule forces will cover our retreat, we should be all right. However, we still face the problem of how to keep them from cross . . ." His voice trailed off. Then—"Are you thinking what I think you're thinking, Your Highness?" He asked carefully.

"Maybe. It depends on whether or not we can smuggle one of the Mardukans out of the visitors' quarters."

"Yeah," Julian and Kosutic said almost simultaneously. The two NCOs looked at each other and laughed.

"If we can get some armor for one of the Three Musketeers, I can rig a camera and radio," Julian said. "I've got the gear packed."

"I can coach him through the rigging, and Denat is fairly good with knots," Kosutic added rubbing her ear.

"What are we talking about?" Jasco asked.

The group trooped back into the stifling kitchen to confront the spies.

"We're in agreement," Kosutic said. "However, we have a few questions to ask and some requirements that must be met for us to be willing to proceed."

"Oh?" Bijan said. "And if I reject your demands?"

"We tell the king about your treason just before we tear this pathetic city to the ground," the sergeant major said quietly. "It will practically wipe us out to do it, but the 'not difficult' plan you just suggested will do the same thing. So are you going to listen? Or do we start now?"

The spy looked down at her for a moment, then grunted in laughter.

"Very well, Sergeant Major Kosutic. What are your demands?

"Questions first," the NCO said. "How secret are all these passages?"

"There's only one to this building," Bijan said, "which is why we came in here, but there are a few others in strategic spots throughout the city. As far as I know, Radj Hoomas doesn't know a thing about this one . . . or about any of the others, for that matter. This one was created during the construction of this building, which predated the rise of the House of Radj."

"Then how did you know of it?" Jasco asked, deciding that he had to get at least one word in.

"I showed him," the female spy replied. "My mother's family was involved in the construction. They were masons from Voitan, and my mother knew of it from her mother."

Kosutic was sorely tempted to ask why Voitan women

seemed to be the only ones on Marduk with any freedom, but decided it was a side issue. Fixing the problems of the Company came first. Although, she reflected,
Roger's plan would certainly free up a few social con-
straints in Marshad.

"Okay," she said. "That has that covered. The reason
we needed to know is that we need to smuggle one or
two of our Mardukan allies out."

"Why?" Bijan demanded angrily. "This will make it
much more likely that we'll be discovered! Those barbarians don't even speak the language!"

"What?" Julian snapped. "You have no barbarians in
your city? No visitors whatsoever?"

"A few," Bijan admitted reluctantly. "But they're
mainly from Kranolta tribes, and there are very few at
the moment. They're mostly traders in hides and jungle
medicines."

"Good," Kosutic said. "We have a mass of those we
collected on the march, and he can take some with him
as a cover. Also, before he goes, he'll need an armor
apron and a helmet."

"No!" Bijan snarled. "No fighting. I don't know what
your plan is, but he won't destroy all I've worked for!
I'll wait for a better chance, if that's what it takes!"

"No, you won't," Kosutic told him with another toothy
smile, "because if this goes wrong, I will follow you to
Hell to spit on your soul. Do I make myself clear?"

They stared at one another for a long time, until,
finally, the Mardukan clapped his hands reluctantly.

"Very well. *One* of them. I'll get appropriate armor
and a helmet." He paused. "But if he gives away our
preparations, on your head be it."

"He'll have a mission, which he'll divulge to you as he
goes," the sergeant major said. "You will support it fully."
She gestured with her head at the female spy. "And that
one will be the primary control. Do you understand?"

"I'm in charge here—" Bijan started to say.

"No," Kosutic interrupted with a shake of her head. "Fate, chaos, and destruction are in charge here, *spy*. The faster you figure out how to ride the whirlwind, the better."

CHAPTER FIFTY

Denat padded through the trackless dark of nighttime Marshad, following the dimly perceived shape of the female in front of him.

The stench of the lower warrens was unbelievable, an effluvia of chemicals from dyes, rotting carcasses, shit, and misery. He'd visited Q'Nkok often, and although there had been many poor, it had never seemed as if the entire city was destitute. But in Marshad, he hadn't seen a single sign of relative wealth. It appeared that there were only king's advisers, and the penniless.

As his guide passed one of the tunnel-like alleys, a figure emerged from the deeper shadows and grabbed the little female by the arm.

Denat's orders had been to follow and, as much as possible, to avoid notice, so he stepped sideways into the deeper blackness along the alleyway, turning to put the heavy sack he carried against the wall. The little guide, Sena, had heartily endorsed the importance of his avoiding attention, and added an injunction against coming to her aid. She was confident of her own abilities. Or so she said.

Now Denat saw why. The confrontation was brief, and ended when the accoster suddenly flew into a wall. There was another flicker of movement as the two shapes merged, a horn flashed, and then the little female continued on, leaving a crumpled, life-oozing shape sprawled in the noisome alley.

Denat stepped around the growing, sticky puddle and followed his guide into the deeper blackness. There was just enough filtered light in the intersection for him to see that the thug's head was barely attached to his body. He'd heard of the *enat* techniques, but Sena was the first practitioner of the art he'd ever met, and he resolved to treat the guide with the greatest possible respect.

They took a fork away from the slightly wider alley they'd been following into a smelly path barely wide enough for the broad tribesman to pass. The alley's clay walls were intermittently coated in waterproofing, but much of it had worn away, exposing the walls to the rains. There were runnels in the material, and if it wasn't fixed soon, the houses to either side would collapse.

The narrow slit dropped into one of the tunnels that was a bit wider. It was impossible to see in the lightless passage, so the guide took the tribesman's hand and put it on her shoulder. The passage was half-flooded with a river of sludge—runoff from the evening's rains and rancid beyond compare—through which they were forced to wade. Denat steeled himself and refused to wonder what the things bumping against his legs or disintegrating beneath his feet might be.

That passage was blessedly short, however, and soon Sena led him up onto a slightly elevated platform and stopped. There was an almost unheard tapping, and the creak of a hinge, and then the guide stepped forward once more.

Denat started to follow . . . and slammed his nose into

a lintel. He stifled a venomous curse, ducked through the doorway and stepped forward until he felt a hand on his chest. There was another creak behind him, a thump as a door closed, and the click of a bolt shooting. Then light flared from a tinderbox.

The candle that the tinder lit revealed a space which seemed too tiny for the group filling it. Besides his guide, there were three other females of about the same age, two older females, and half a dozen children. The only male in the room was obviously old, the lighter of the candle.

Two of the younger females cringed back at the sight of the armored tribesman in their midst, but the rest simply regarded Denat calmly.

"Unexpected visitors, Sena?" The old male sat creakily on a stool and gestured for the visitor to seat himself, addressing Denat's guide in the Voitan dialect which Denat, now that he was paying attention, could fuzzily understand.

"Yes," the guide agreed, wiping the filth of the sewer off her legs. "A requirement of the humans. They must have one of their own perform some mission. Also, we must smuggle communiqués to and from their commanders. They must have permission to help us."

She added something else in the dialect, speaking much too rapidly for Denat to follow.

"That was to be expected," one of the older females said, coming forward. "Welcome, tribesman. I am Selat, which my daughter would have told you, if she'd any manners."

"D'Nal Denat." The tribesman bowed. "I greet you in the name of The People." He hoped he'd all the sounds right. Some of the words were the same, but accented so differently as to make them nearly unintelligible.

"Denat," Julian said over the earbud the intel NCO'd installed, "if you're having translation problems, ask me.

I'll give you the right words. You just said 'I sneeze you in the name of The Idiots.' "

The Mardukan had been seeded with more listening devices than a Saint embassy, and the company now had a way out of the building. The sergeant major was hard at work tracing out the other hidden passageways, and if Denat truly needed help, it was possible the Marines could come to the rescue.

The locals looked at one another, and then the older female bowed slightly towards him.

"I . . . greet you in the name of our house. Won't you take a seat?"

Denat nodded as reassuringly as possible at the worried females in the corner, guarding the children, and sat on the floor. The walls of the room were well-set stone and the room itself was a snug, out-of-the-way burrow.

"I . . . have . . ."

"A mission," Julian prompted.

" . . . a mission to put a human . . ."

" . . . thing . . ."

" . . . thing on the . . ."

" . . . bridge . . ."

" . . . *bridge*," the tribesman finished with a snarl and a triple cough, the agreed-upon code for: GO AWAY.

"Okay, okay," the NCO whispered. "Going into lurk mode."

"Are you quite well?" his host asked. The old Mardukan leaned forward in concern; if the contact became unwell, it would ruin all their plans.

"Yes," Denat answered. "I am well."

"What is this device?" the older female asked as she poured their visitor a drink of water and proffered the cup.

"I don't know," Denat lied easily. He'd quickly learned the expression Poertena called a "poker face," an apt description. "However, the humans say that it's vital to their plans."

"How large is it? How do you have to attach it? And where?" Sena clapped her hands in agitation. "It will be difficult to do. The bridge is well guarded."

"It has to be attached anywhere on the underside," Denat said.

" . . . underside," Julian corrected. "You just said anywhere on the 'butt.' Well, 'ass' is closer." The NCO chuckled.

"Underside," Denat amended.

"Ah," his host said. The old Mardukan male looked at the ceiling of the dwelling. "This is perhaps possible."

"How large is this package?" Sena asked, taking a seat as well.

Denat pulled the sack he'd been carrying around in front of him and opened it. Pulling out several hide-wrapped packages and partially prepared hides, he removed a final package covered in red leather. It was done up with thongs which he untied to reveal a strange shape. It looked like a small box attached to a cube of clay the size of his hand.

"How do you attach it?" Sena asked, for there were no strings or ropes in evidence.

"They told me that if I pushed it on stone, it would stay." Denat tried it, and it adhered to the nearer wall, which was in easy arm's reach. He pulled at it, and it came away with difficulty.

"Like glue," Selat observed. The older female looked at the device curiously. "Very interesting. What does it do?"

"That I don't know," Denat lied again. He knew very well what it did, but he wasn't about to tell the locals. "I also need to be near the river on the day of the battle," he added.

"That won't be hard," Sena assured him. "Right on

the river would be difficult, but there are several places on that edge of town where you'll be outside the walls and within easy running distance. Will that do?"

"Yes. Now, how do we get the item attached?"

"How well do you swim?" Sena asked with a handclap of humor.

"Well enough to swim that little puddle you call a river."

"There's a landing beneath the bridge," the little female said. "We can put you in the river upstream. You swim down to the bridge, climb up and attach your item, then swim downriver to another point, where someone will meet you to lead you back."

"Very well," Denat said with satisfaction. "Now, I suppose we wait."

"Indeed," Sena said. "And starve," she added sourly.

"Oh, it isn't that bad, dear," the host rebuked. "We have enough to share with our guest. The House of T'Leen is not so fallen as to be unable to provide hospitality!"

"T'Leen?" Denat repeated, startled. "Was that a common name in Voitan? Because I know a T'Leen Targ."

"T'Leen Targ?" The host sounded surprised. "I am T'Leen Sul. He's my cousin on my father's side! Where do you know him from?" he asked eagerly. "I haven't seen him since before the fall of S'Lenna! How is he?"

"He's well," Denat said, glad to be able to impart some happy news. "He was one of the leaders of the force that relieved us in Voitan. They're rebuilding the city, and he'll be one of the leaders of that, as well."

"Ah!" Sul clapped his hands in joy. "The shining city shall rise again!"

"Let it not be too late for us," his wife said quietly. "Would that we could go to it before our deaths."

"We shall," Sul said with quiet firmness. "We shall

return to the shining city. We might have only our hands to offer, but it will be enough."

There was no doubt in his voice, but the whole group had lost its animation. Even if they returned to Voitan, it would be as beggars.

"I was surprised by your choice of messengers," Denat said, deliberately moving away from what was obviously a painful subject. "My people wouldn't have entrusted such a grave responsibility to a female."

"Because we're worthless and unintelligent?" Sena snorted. "Good only for birthing babies and cooking?"

"Yes," Denat said calmly. "I was surprised that the people of Voitan were so accepting of women working other than in the fields and home. You keep to the Voitan customs?"

"With difficulty," T'Leen Sul said. "Marshad doesn't agree with those customs. A female cannot own property and she must obey the orders of any male. Such are both customs and law in this land, so it's hard for one raised among the customs of Voitan to put up with. Females are common in weaving, but that's because it's work males don't want." The old male grunted in laughter. "But Sena was raised in the Voitan way, and she's proof that not all females are worthless and weak."

"So she is," Denat grunted. He looked at the little female out of the corner of his eye. "So she is." He gave himself a shake. "But returning to the matter of starvation." He reached back into his sack. "I brought some food. When that runs out, we'll have to see what we can think of."

"Well," Sena said, clapping her hands in resignation, "that means we can stay out of sight until we have to go to the bridge. Of course, staying out of sight means being stuck in the company of a smelly tribesman for all that time, but at least one part of the plan is working."

CHAPTER FIFTY-ONE

"This is going too smoothly," Pahner complained, shaking his head.

"Really?" Roger looked around the room and chuckled. "I suppose Voitan was your idea of just the right amount of friction?"

"Yes, Your Highness, it was." The captain turned dark eyes on the prince and nodded. "We survived." He shook his head again. "Something is bound to screw this up, and there's not much in the way of a backup."

"Blow the town down and take what we can?" Despreaux suggested.

"More or less." The CO straightened and kneaded the small of his back with both hands. "I'm getting too old for this shit."

"Seventy isn't *old*," Roger told him with a laugh. "Look at my grandfather. He lived to the ripe old age of one hundred and eighty-three senile years."

"Not a record I hope to beat, Your Highness." The

captain smiled. "Time for bed. We'd better be on our toes tomorrow."

Roger nodded a good night to Pahner as he left the room, then looked over at O'Casey.

"You've been particularly quiet this evening, Eleanora," he observed, taking off the borrowed helmet he'd been using to monitor the operation.

"Just thinking about our host," the chief of staff replied with a smile. "And about universality."

"How so?" Roger asked, mopping at his sweaty forehead. The evening was unusually hot, even for Marduk. It usually cooled off a bit after nightfall, but not tonight, apparently.

"If you don't mind, Your Highness," Despreaux said, "I'm going to turn in as well. I have guard duty in a few hours."

"Take off, Nimashet." Roger waved one hand in a shooing gesture. "I think we can guard ourselves for a while."

The sergeant smiled at him and left the room behind the captain. Roger watched her go, and then turned back to O'Casey.

"You were saying?" he said, then noticed her slight smile. "What?"

"Nothing," his former tutor said. "I was talking about universality. It's not quite a given that fops aren't to be trusted, but rulers who pay more attention to their wardrobes than their subjects have a habit of coming to bad ends."

"Did you have anyone in mind?" Roger asked coldly.

"Oh," O'Casey chuckled, "that wasn't directed at you, Roger. Although, at one time it might have been," she added pensively. "But, frankly, son, there's not much of the peacock left in you."

"Don't be too sure of that." Roger gave her a wry smile now that he realized the comment wasn't directed at him. "I'm definitely looking forward to getting back into some civilized clothing."

"That's fair." O'Casey looked down at her own stained uniform. "So am I. But I wasn't speaking of you. I was actually thinking of Ceasare Borgia and your father."

"Now that's a comparison you don't often hear," Roger said tightly.

"Perhaps *you* don't," O'Casey acknowledged, "but before I was your tutor, I used it frequently in lectures. I suspect that was one of the reasons I was assigned to you in the first place. That and the follow-through, which is that, frankly, it's an insult to the Borgias. They never would've screwed up their plot the way New Madrid did."

"You know the whole story?" Roger asked in an odd voice. "I never realized that."

"I'm sorry, Roger," O'Casey said sadly. "I'm surprised you weren't aware of how widely it's studied. I only learned the details after becoming your tutor, of course, but the broad outline is used in political courses as a case study. It's right up there with the takeover of the Solarian Union by the Dagger Lords."

"Really?" Roger's eyes were wide. "Well, you never discussed it with *me!*"

"It's a sensitive subject, Roger." His chief of staff shrugged. "I didn't want to hurt your feelings, and I felt that you must have already learned any lessons it could teach long before I was named your tutor."

"Really," Roger repeated, sarcastically, this time, and leaned one elbow on the table and fixed her with a glare. "That's just absolutely fascinating, Eleanora, because I have *never* known what it was that got my father exiled from Court, which makes it rather difficult to *learn* anything from it, wouldn't you say?" He let out an exasperated hiss and shook his head. "I'm so glad that you were respectful of my feelings, *teacher!*"

"But . . ." O'Casey stared at him, her face white. "But what about your mother? Or Professor Earl?"

"Ms. O'Casey," Roger snarled, "I don't remember my mother from when I was a young child at all. Only a succession of nurses. From the time I started to know who she was, I have a general impression of seeing her—oh, once a week or so, whether I really needed to see her or not. She would comment on the reports from my tutors and nannies and tell me to be a good boy. I saw John and Alexa more than I ever saw my mother! And as for Professor Earl, I asked him once—just once—about my father. He told me to ask my mother when I was older." Roger shook his head. "The good doctor was a fair tutor, but he was never very good with the personal stuff."

It was O'Casey's turn to shake her head, and she pulled at a lock of hair.

"I'm sorry, Roger. I just assumed— Hell, *everybody* probably assumed." She grimaced in exasperation, then inhaled sharply.

"Okay. Where do you want me to begin?"

"Well," Roger said with a smile, "I had this tutor once who was always telling me—"

"To start at the beginning, and go through to the end," she finished with an answering smile. "This will take a long time, though," she said more seriously, and Roger gestured around the room.

"You may not have noticed, but I've got all night."

"Hmph. Okay, let me think about how to begin."

She gazed into an unseen distance for several seconds, then made a little moue of annoyance which was clearly directed at herself.

"You know, I never really covered recent history with you too well, did I? I just let that little detail slide. Renaissance or Byzantine politics, yes, but not what was going on right under your nose. Of course," she flashed a quick grin, "most of the time it was stuck so far up you'd never have noticed anyway."

"True, unfortunately." Roger chuckled ruefully. "But I have to get the story."

"New Madrid," she said, nodding. "As you know, there were few major military actions during your grandfather's reign. This is sometimes pointed at as an indication that he was a great emperor, but what was actually happening was that your grandfather was almost completely ineffectual. The Fleet and Marines were being slashed to the bone, and we lost several border systems to treaties we accepted out of weakness—or disinterest—or small actions that never got much press coverage back home. There weren't any *major* actions because no one was drawing any lines to stop the gradual erosion of the frontiers. And while they were crumbling, the Empire was self-destructing internally with plots and counterplots.

"New Madrid was part of that action, but not as a central player." She sighed and looked at the prince in the glow from the camp light. "Roger, you got almost all your brains from your mother, thank God. If you'd gotten your mother's looks and your father's brains, you would have been shit out of luck."

"That bad?" he asked with a chuckle. "He's as smart as Mom is good-looking?"

"Say rather that he's as good-looking as your mother is smart. Which is where you come in."

"What a line!" he observed.

"John Gaston, John and Alexa's father, died as you know in a light-flier accident. The Duke of New Madrid was part of the Court at that time, fairly recently arrived. He was, and is, a gorgeous man, and quite the ladies man, as well. However, he was very circumspect at Court. He and your mother struck up an acquaintance shortly after the death of Count Gaston, and the acquaintance slowly changed to . . . um . . ."

"Me," Roger said with a raised eyebrow.

"Well, the 'proto' you. Empress Alexandra—Heir Apparent, at that time—might have been having a hard time, but she was no fool. She was more or less swept off her feet, which is why she wasn't on a contraceptive, but she landed back on them quickly. Especially when the head of the IBI brought her a report on New Madrid's contacts among factions known to be maneuvering to control the Empire.

"There'd never been a question of marriage, because she had to leave the way open for a dynastic alliance. With the IBI report in hand, though, she had to know if New Madrid's interests were from the heart or the scent of power. So she let herself appear to weaken."

Eleanora twisted her lock of hair again, and let a smile quirk.

"I understand New Madrid can be somewhat dominant, and he apparently found nothing odd in Alexandra's suddenly becoming compliant during her pregnancy. Which was when he tipped his hand. He began forcefully lobbying her for some of the precise policies that the Jackson Cabal had been promoting."

"Are you talking about Prince Jackson of Kellerman?" Roger asked. "He's one of the most important noblemen in the Senate!"

"Ummm-hummm. And doesn't he just know it?" O'Casey wrinkled her brow. "Towards the end of your grandfather's reign, it became apparent even to him that the Saints were becoming very expansionist. That caught him by surprise, since he'd felt that the Saints were . . . well, saints. Once he realized he was wrong, and possibly *because* he recognized that he had been and felt somehow 'betrayed' by them, he began giving a great deal of weight to the more militant factions in the House of Lords."

"And Jackson was one of those." Roger nodded.

"He's always been one of the more, um, hawkish members."

"Indeed. However, your grandfather began making most of his appointments on the basis of Jackson's advice. Many of them weren't appointments, whether to the House of Lords or to the imperial ministries, which Alexandra thought were wise. She had long argued against the military drawdown, but when it became apparent even to her father that the Empire was in trouble, he turned not to her, but to Prince Jackson.

"It might have appeared on the surface that there was little difference, since both she and Jackson supported many of the same policies. But even then, Alexandra was more interested in loyalty to the concept of the Empire of Man than in a specific cant. Worse, all of Jackson's choices for appointments were people he could depend upon to follow *his* lead.

"So when Alexandra found New Madrid spouting the Jackson line, after having been handed that damning report, she saw the situation with amazing clarity. One of the few things she managed to convince her father of in his waning years was to have New Madrid banished from Court."

"However . . ." The former tutor gave her former student a winsome smile.

"That left me," Roger said, his eyes wide. "I'm surprised she didn't . . ."

"Oh, it was contemplated. She'd already had the fetus, you," she pointed out with another smile, "transferred to a uterine replicator, so it would have been a simple matter of—"

"Turning a tap," Roger said woodenly.

"Sort of." O'Casey nodded. "For whatever reason, though, she didn't." She began twisting another lock of hair. "I understand that she spent quite a bit of time with you when you were an infant, Roger. It was only as you matured that she started spending more and more time away."

"As I began looking more like my father," he said in a deathly tone. It wasn't a question.

"And acting more like him, frankly," O'Casey confirmed. "There were other reasons. Things were getting very tense at Court as your grandfather began to fail, and Alexandra was desperately trying to line up partisans against the coup she could see in the offing. In the end, of course, she was able to. But even so she's spent the last decade trying to repair the damage to the Empire."

The chief of staff shook her head again.

"To be honest, I don't know if she ever will be able to truly repair all of it. Things were getting tense again before we left. Most of the Fleet has been pulled away from home systems towards the Saint sector, which is Jackson's sphere of influence, and she doesn't trust the Imperial Inspector's Corps. At least she can trust the chief of the Fleet and the IBI, but those are thin reeds with the Saints pressing the border and the House of Lords deadlocked most of the time.

"So," she finished, "that's the tale. Both the one that I used as a case study of blown political conspiracies, and the additional data I was made privy to as your tutor." She looked at the prince, who was staring at the far wall. "Questions?"

"A million," Roger said. "But one simple one first. Is this why no one has ever trusted me with anything important? Because of my *blood*?" he ended angrily.

"Partially," she admitted with a nod. "But more of it was, well . . . *you*, Roger. *I* certainly didn't realize you'd never been 'briefed,' so I'm guessing that, just like me, everyone else around you must have assumed that someone *else* had told you. They thought you knew. So if you knew the problems that had been associated with your father, and yet chose to emulate him in every way, then one logical conclusion was that you'd chosen *him* as your role model rather than your mother."

"Oh, shit," Roger said, shaking his head. "So all this time . . ."

"Captain Pahner asked me, early in the voyage, if you were a threat to the throne," Eleanora said quietly. "I had to tell him that, frankly, I didn't know." She looked the prince in the eye. "For that, I'm sorry, Roger. But I *didn't* know. And I doubt that *anyone*, except probably Kostas, was sure about you."

"Is that why we're here?" Roger asked, with a hand over his eyes. "Is that why we're stuck in this rathole?" he grated in an iron tone. "Because everyone thought I was in a conspiracy with Prince Jackson? To overthrow my own *mother*?"

"I prefer to believe you were being protected," the chief of staff said. "That your mother saw a gathering storm and chose to put you out of harm's way."

"On Leviathan." Roger dropped his hand and looked at her with tight eyes. "Where I'd be safe if it 'dropped in the pot,' as Julian likes to put it."

"Um," O'Casey said, thinking about the company's incredible battle to have reached even as far as Marshad. "Well, yes."

"Oh!" Roger began to laugh even as tears welled up in his eyes. "Thank God she didn't let me stick around for something *dangerous*! I'd hate to think what *Mother* might find *dangerous*! Maybe facing the Kranolta with a *knife*?!"

"Roger."

"*Aaaahhhhh!*" he screamed as the door burst open to admit a worried Marine sentry. Kyrou panned his bead rifle around the room, looking for the threat, as the prince slammed both fists down on the table. "Fuck, fuck, *fuck*! Pock, *pock it*, and pock *you*, Mother! Fuck you *and* your fucking paranoia, you secretive, Machiavellian, untrusting, coldhearted *bitch*!"

Kyrou stepped aside as Pahner slid through the door, pistol in a two-handed grip.

"What the hell is going *on* here?" the captain barked.

"*Out!*" Roger screamed. He picked O'Casey up by one biceps, and shoved her towards the door. "Out! All of you, *out!*" He pushed Kyrou so hard the heavyset private skittered backwards on his butt through the doorway. "If you're not out of here in *one fucking second*, I will fucking *kill* every fucking *one* of you!"

The solid door of the suite slammed shut with an ear-shattering boom, followed almost instantly by the sounds of complicated destruction.

"I think I could have handled that better," Eleanora said judiciously. "I'm not sure how, but I'm almost certain I could have."

"What just happened?" Kyrou said, lurching upright and looking around the main room of the suite, where the Marines were all staring at the door.

"Did he just say what I *think* he said?" Corporal Damdin asked, his eyes wide. "About the *Empress*?"

"Yes," Eleanora said calmly, "he did. But," she continued, raising her voice, "he just found out something very personal and unpleasant. He's very upset with the Empress, not as the Empress, but as his mother. I think that once he calms down," she suggested as the sound of breaking wood came through the door, "he'll be less—"

"Treasonous?" Pahner suggested lightly.

"He's angry at his *mother*, Captain—very angry, I might add, and not completely without reason—and, not at the Empress," the chief of staff said coldly. "There is, in this instance, a distinct difference. One you and I need to discuss."

Pahner looked at her, then glanced at the door as the

sound of hacking came from the far side. The door shook to the pounding blows of the prince's sword.

"What did you *say* to him?" the captain asked incredulously.

"I told him the truth, Captain," the former tutor said tautly. "All of it."

"Oh," the Marine said. "You're right. We do need to talk." He looked around the room. "Kyrou, back on post. The rest of you—" He glanced at the door and winced at the sound of steel skittering on stone. Roger loved that sword; if he was willing to bang stones with it, his fury was even more towering than the captain had thought.

"The rest of you, go back to sleep," he said finally, and beckoned for O'Casey to follow him out of the room.

CHAPTER FIFTY-TWO

The next day passed quietly, especially in the hostages' suite.

Roger failed to emerge from his room even when a breakfast of barleyrice and vegetables was brought to the suite. The food no longer contained the obnoxious herb that had been so prevalent in the first dinner, but there was still a weird, bitter aftertaste. Despite that, Roger had been able to stomach it on the previous two days, but he obviously had no interest in it at all today.

An hour after the breakfast had been cleared, Pahner opened the door to make sure he was all right. Roger was sprawled on his camp bed, in the middle of a mass of broken fixtures, his forearm across his face. When the door opened, the prince simply glanced at the captain and resumed his position. Recognizing a deep funk that was in no mood for semi-parental bitching, the Marine shook his head and closed the door.

Back in the troop barracks, however, the mood was quiet but active. Rumors were still the only method of faster-than-light communication the military had discovered.

"I heard he called the Empress a whore!" St. John (M.) said.

"I heard it was just a bitch," St. John (J.) said. The older twin had often had to control the outbursts of his younger brother. "But still."

"It was a bitch," Kosutic confirmed, appearing as if by magic behind them. "To be precise, a 'paranoid bitch.' But," she added, "he was also referring to the Empress as his mother, not the Empress. It's a big difference."

"How?" St. John (M.) asked. "They're the same person, ain't they?"

"Yes," the sergeant major agreed. "But calling one of them a bitch is treason, and calling the other one a bitch is just being really, really pissed at your mother." She looked from twin to twin. "Either one of you ever been upset with your mother before?"

"Welll . . ." St. John (M.) said.

"He always calls her a damnsaint when he's mad at Momma," St. John (J.) said with a grin.

"Well so do you!" St. John (M.) protested.

"Sure, Mark. But not to her face!"

"The point is," the sergeant major said before the family feud could go any farther, "that he was mad at his mother. *Not* at Empress Alexandra."

"Well, why?" St. John (M.) asked in a puzzled tone. "I mean, Her Majesty's not exactly here to get mad *at*. I mean, I don't get mad at Momma back on New Miss just 'cause, well, she ain't here."

"You got mad at Momma just the other day 'cause she had twins," St. John (J.) said slyly.

"Well, the Prince ain't got no twin," his exasperated brother said, then he got a puzzled expression and turned back to the sergeant major. "He doesn't, does he? We'd a heard, right?"

Kosutic kept the smile off her face only with difficulty. She knew why the St. John brothers had made it into the Regiment; they were both very, very good soldiers with the protective instincts of Dobermans. But the younger twin was no Hawking.

"He doesn't have a twin," she said precisely. "However, he was told something yesterday about some of his mother's decisions that really upset him."

"What?" St. John (J.) asked.

"What it was is between him and his mother. And he really wants to talk to her about it. The thing for all of you to keep in mind is that our job is to make sure that that conversation takes place."

"Okay," St. John (J.) said with a snort. "Gotcha, Sergeant Major."

"Now, I want you guys to pass it on. What happened yesterday is between Roger and his mother. Our job is to make sure that he gets home to ask her why she's a paranoid bitch in person."

Roger emerged without a word just before dinner was delivered. There'd been sounds of movement for some time before that, and he carried a pile of crushed and broken fixtures from the room. He took them to the door to the suite, deposited them in the guarded hall beyond, and turned to Pahner.

"What's the status of the Company?" he asked coldly.

"Nominal," the CO replied in a neutral tone. He was seated on a cushion, tapping on a pad, and he cocked his head as he looked up at the prince. "They've been doing some training with the new weapons, and they're waiting for the word on when we move." He hesitated, then went on. "They got the word about last evening. The Sergeant Major has been spending most of the day quelling rumors."

Roger nodded in acknowledgment, but didn't respond directly to the last sentence.

"We have a problem, Captain," he said instead.

"And that is?"

"I don't think we have enough troops or ammunition to make it to the coast." The prince pulled up a pile of cushions beside the Marine and dropped down onto them, and Pahner regarded him calmly as O'Casey looked up from her own pad.

"To an extent, I agree, Your Highness. Do you have an answer?"

"Not directly." Roger picked up a canteen and took a sip. The water was tepid, but his chilled camel-bag was in the other room. "But I was thinking about Cord and his nephews. We need more Mardukan warriors attached to us, whether that be by cash or loyalty oaths."

"So we keep an eye out for a group of mercenaries to attach?" Pahner sounded dubious. "I'm not sure about using mercenaries to protect you, Your Highness."

"Let's not look too far down on mercenaries," Roger said with a bitter smile. "After all, we're about to take still another city so that we can get the gear to continue our journey. I don't think we should be calling the kettle black."

"That is a point, Your Highness," Pahner said ruefully. "However, it's not like we're doing it by our own choice."

"Let's go," Denat hissed. "It's not like we have a choice!"

The little female didn't even look around. She was totally focused on the path from the walls to the water, and a part of Denat wished he could match her total concentration.

Unfortunately, he couldn't. He didn't know what was happening back at the barracks, but whatever it was, it was making Julian nervous as hell, which hadn't done a great deal for Denat's state of mind, either. The good news was that the NCO had steadied down when the time to move arrived, and now he was monitoring the sensors scattered over the Mardukan's gear.

"Well," the earbud whispered. "There's nothing large moving between you and the water. By the way, I'm glad it's you and not me."

Denat wrinkled his nose but forbore to comment. The exit from the city was a sewer, and although the run-off stream was currently a mere trickle, the first hint of rain would transform it into a flash flood of obnoxious matter. It was high time to make a bolt for the river.

"Come *on!*" he hissed again.

"Great hunter," Sena said derisively, "I have learned not to move too fast. You have to know what the next step is. Otherwise, you find yourself paste between the toes of the *flar-ke.*"

Denat shook his head and stepped forward.

"Julian," his subvocalized, "have you got anything?"

"Guards on the bridge," the human responded, detecting the movement at a hundred meters. "Other than that, there's no movement."

The tribesman tried to sniff the air for the musk of a hidden enemy, but the sewer stench overrode any other scent.

"Stay here," he whispered to Sena, removing the encumbering armor. When he was finished, he wore only his normal garb, a belt with a knife and a pouch. The pouch bulged with the human gift to the King of Marshad.

He stepped out of the sewer-stream and moved forward slowly but naturally. The bridge guards were using lanterns, which would destroy their night vision, so the two conspirators should be impossible to see at this distance.

He was confused by the little female's timidity. She'd been practically fearless up until this moment, and the change was baffling . . . until he suddenly realized that all the previous action had taken place within the confines of the city walls. Now, out in the open, the spy was no longer on familiar ground facing familiar threats.

Denat, on the other hand, was close to his element. He had grown up hunting the jungles of the east, and was one of the few of his tribe who was as willing to hunt the night as the day. The nighttime jungles were a pitch black mine of hazards, both inanimate and animate alike; from quagmires to *atul*, night was when death stalked the forests.

And was stalked in turn by D'Nal Denat.

Now he moved away from the stench of the sewer and let his senses roam. The way to move by night was without focus. Trying to concentrate, straining to see, fighting to hear—those were the ways to die. The way to live was the way of intuition. Place the feet just so, and the leaf did not stir. Open the eyes wide, but look at nothing; open the ears, but hear nothing; and breathe the air, but smell nothing. Become one with the night.

And because that was the way he moved, he was instantly aware when the faint sound out of harmony with its surroundings came to him. He stopped, motionless, like a darker hole in the night, as a furtive shape stole past him. The figure was short—a small male or a female—returning from the river and bent under a dripping pack, and the tribesman's stomach dropped as he realized there was smuggling across the river.

If there was smuggling, there might be patrols, and he paused for several seconds to consider the problem, then made a small gesture of resignation. The plan was the only one possible, so if there were patrols, he would simply have to avoid them. And from what he'd seen thus far of the locals, at least that shouldn't be difficult to do.

He continued his slow but steady movement, stopping occasionally and making a little natural noise, scuffing a foot, rattling a leaf. The noises blended into the natural night sounds, the sounds of little animals rustling in the *kur* grass for seeds and roots. If anyone was there to hear his slow passage, they would dismiss him as a *stap* or *basik*. Now if only no *insheck* pounced on him, everything would be fine. In the past, he'd been attacked by *insheck* or juvenile *atul* while moving this way because the diminutive predators had mistaken him for natural prey.

He reached the banks of the river without incident, however. The current was fast, but nothing to deter someone who'd been swimming in worse since he was a cub. The humans had assured him that the package was waterproof, so he lowered himself into the water, moving as carefully as if he were stalking an *atul-grack*.

The current caught him and swept him away from the low earthen bank. The water was warmer than the night, a soothing bath that washed away the stench of the city. He let the current swirl him like a bit of flotsam, keeping his head just above water and breathing through his nose while he kept an eye out for *asleem*. If he met one of those, the entire plan was forfeit . . . as was his life.

He approached the bridge quickly under the impetus of the current and ducked under to swim towards the bank. There was a danger in this—the danger of striking an underwater obstruction, as much as anything. But it was a calculated risk, for the guards might well be watching the water as much as the banks.

He surfaced carefully when his air ran out and found himself nearly to the bridge, with a guard directly above him, looking up the river. The guard was not, however, looking *down*, and the tribesman suppressed a grunt of laughter. These shit-sitters were as blind and stupid as *basik*.

He drove himself towards the edge, where the bridge's foundation shelf was clearly evident in the reflected light of the lamps. He grabbed the rock and held himself still, head out of the water, letting his senses adjust to conditions under the bridge.

The chuckling water echoed oddly in the arches of the structure, gurgling and sucking air into their watery vortices. He heard the echoing footsteps of guards overhead and smaller night sounds—the hissing calls of *feen* and the chittering cracks of water *slen*.

Finally, when he was sure he had all the sounds cataloged, he began to lift himself out of the water. The movement was painfully slow, but it allowed all the water to run off his body, leaving nothing to drip-drop-drip and betray him by the out-of-place sound.

He crept up the rock to the junction of the bridge and its foundation. The humans had been careful in their instructions on this point: the package must be in contact with the bridge, but out of sight. He placed the box against the cool stones of the arch, and spread some of the wiry *flir* grass that thrived in the shadow to cover it. Then he began his slow progress back down the slope.

With any luck at all, there really would be a guide on the downstream side.

"That's half the plan in place," Roger said, and Pahner nodded.

"Now if we can just be in place for the other half."

"About that—" Roger began, then paused as someone thumped on the door.

Despreaux stepped back with most of her squad, covering the door as Corporal Bebi jerked it opened.

The new commander of the Guard was revealed in the doorway, and looked at the leveled weapons evenly.

"I was sent by His Majesty. You are to write a

message to your company. It will command them to follow my orders until you are reunited."

Roger looked at Pahner, then back at the visitor.

"How long do you want to be the new commander?" the prince asked. "I can cut that tenure short, if you'd like."

"If you kill me, another will take my place," the commander said in indifferent tones. "And if your company isn't given help in the battle, it will be wiped out. I'll be in command of the support forces. If you anger me, I guarantee that you'll have no soldiers left after the morrow."

"Ah," Roger said with a feral smile. "Nice to know we're all on the same sheet of music." He pulled a pad over, tapped on the interface for a moment, then threw it to the Mardukan. "Take that to them. It gives them all the orders they need."

"Very well," the Mardukan said, holding the pad upside down as he studied it. "Tomorrow morning, you will join my lord in observing our glorious battle." He grunted evilly, the first expression he'd made other than contempt. "To Victory!"

"Yeah," Roger said. "Whatever."

CHAPTER FIFTY-THREE

The day dawned bright and almost clear. The lower layer of clouds had pulled away, leaving only the permanent thin upper layer, which actually raised the temperature a few degrees.

The human troops gathered in front of the visitors' quarters, checking their gear, making sure their rucksacks rode well, and getting their mission faces on. The fight was looking to be short, sharp, and unpleasant. They were critically short of bead and grenade rounds and had no plasma rifles, so unless they got more support than they expected from the Marshadans, it would get down to hand-to-hand.

At least they had their swords, but they still didn't have the proper shields to go with them, and without the shield wall, the superior individual training of the Pasule forces would weigh against the humans. All in all, it looked to be a bad day.

Julian was running a whetstone over the blade of his sword when his helmet radio came to life on the general frequency.

"Mornin', Marines," Roger's voice said. "I thought you should understand something before we start the ball.

"I'm not going to get into my bitches about the way I was raised. We've all got complaints about our parents, and I'm no different from anyone else in that respect. But I want you to know that no matter how angry I was the other day, I love my mother, both as my mother and as my Empress.

"What happened was that I found out why we're really here. Sure, there was an assassination attempt, and that was the final cause that put us *here*, on Marduk. But the reason we were on the cruise, the reason we were in an assault ship and not a carrier, had to do with a personal problem between me and my mother. One I didn't even know existed.

"So I have a few things to apologize for. I'd like to apologize for causing any of you to wonder about my loyalty. We're just going to have to get in out of the cold and let me discuss it with my mother to straighten that one out. And I want to apologize for not forcing my mother to have that talk with me before we left. We could all be in Imperial City having a beer right now, if I had. So, last, I'd like to apologize for getting you stuck in this goddamned situation with me. And I pledge, on my word as a MacClintock, to do everything in my power to get each and every one of you home."

The prince paused, and Julian looked around at the company. Every Marine sat as still as he did himself, listening. It wasn't often that you heard a member of the Imperial Family open up his heart . . . and it was even rarer to hear one apologize.

"Now, you've got some things to do today," Roger went on after a moment. "And I'm not going to be there with you. But we all need to go home. We all need to get our asses back to Imperial City and have that beer together. Today, in my opinion, is the first step on the road home. So let's get it done.

"Roger, out."

The new commander of the Royal Guard walked over to the humans as they began to break out of their strange stasis.

"What are you doing?" he snapped. "Why have you stopped preparing? Get moving, you stupid *basik*!"

Lance Corporal Moseyev was closest to the spluttering Mardukan, and the Bravo Team Leader looked up at the native coldly.

"Shut your gob, asshole." He turned to his team and gestured at the folded up plasma cannon. "Jeno, give Gronningen a hand with that." He turned back to the Mardukan commander who had been spluttering at his back, and looked the taller native in the eye. "You can move out of our way, or you can die. Your choice."

"Move," Roger said coldly.

The Mardukan guard seemed disinclined to obey, but he stepped aside at a head gesture from the king, and Roger walked forward to the parapet and looked down. The balcony was located at one of the highest points in the hilltop castle and permitted a breathtaking view of the town laid out below. He could see the company moving through the local forces gathered around the gate and heading for the bridge.

Radj Hoomas stood a short distance down the balcony's low, stone wall, watching the same deployment. There were only a few guards between him and the humans, but at least fifty lined the back of the balcony, ready to fill the hostages full of javelins at his command.

The king looked over at Roger and grunted.

"I believe you and Oget Sar came to an understanding?"

"If you mean your new guard commander, yes," Roger said without a smile. "He'll use up my troops, and I'll try my best to kill him. We understand each other perfectly."

"Such a way to talk to your host," the king said crossly, clapping his cross hands in displeasure. "You need to learn better manners before someone gets hurt."

"I always have had that problem," Roger admitted as the company deployed across the fields along the river. "I guess it's my short temper."

"Everybody stay cool," Moseyev said. "We're almost at the deploy point."

In traveling configuration, the Marine plasma cannon was a meter and a half long, a half meter square, and nearly seventy kilos in weight, which made it marginally portable for one unarmored human. Fortunately, it also had a pair of handy carrying handles at either end, so two Marines could lug it for short distances without any problems. Except, of course, for the inevitable bitching.

"God," Macek said. "This is one heavy mother."

"You'll be glad to have this heavy mother along in a few minutes," Gronningen chuckled.

"Yeah," Macek admitted. "But that don't make it any lighter."

"Okay," Moseyev said, eyeing the bridge guardhouses. "This is a good angle. Set 'er up."

The two Marines dropped the featureless oblong in the half-grown flaxsilk, and Gronningen hit an inconspicuous button. A door opened, and he flipped the key switch within and stood back as the M-109 cannon deployed like a butterfly from a chrysalis.

The surrounding matrix was a set of memory plastic

parts. The first part to open was the tripod, which pushed down a small pre-tripod to hold the weapon off the ground, then deployed the main supports. Once the main tripod legs had reached their maximum extent and done a pre-level, they deployed spikes into the ground with a susurrant hiss-thump. Then the tripod elevated the gun to its full extension, and the blast shield deployed.

The shield was, arguably, the most important feature of the support module. The thermal bloom when the cannon fired was immense, and without the shield, the firer would incinerate himself. That would have been enough to endear it to any gunner, but it also acted as armor against frontal fire. Now it opened like the ruff of a basilisk lizard or a *flar-ta's* head shield, deploying in a rectangle to either side. It offered ample vertical coverage above and below the weapon, but most of it spread to the sides in a shape largely governed by the expansion pattern of the plasma shot.

Gronningen tapped a control on top of the weapon and sat down cross-legged behind it. He looked at the bridge where the Mardukan soldiers in both guardhouses were watching the company deploy. None of them appeared to have noticed the team's preparations.

"We're up," he announced.

"Plasma cannon's up," Moseyev relayed over the com.

"Copy," Kosutic replied. "We're in position. Take the shot."

"Why haven't they jumped yet?" Kidard Pla snarled. The Pasulian watched the wings of the fearsome weapon deploy and fingered the stone rail of the bridge nervously.

"Maybe they weren't told?" his companion suggested.

The Pasulian guards had been specially detailed to the bridge because all of them could swim. They'd been informed of the plan just before they went on duty, and now they watched their Marshad counterparts, waiting for them to abandon their posts. The plasma weapons were supposed to sweep the Pasule defenders off the bridge, but they would kill or severely wound the Marshad guards as well, unless they got themselves safely out of the way. But none of them were moving. Either they hadn't been informed that their "allies'" weapons were dangerous to them, as well, or else they were playing a game of *basik*. Whichever it was, Kidard Pla wasn't playing along.

"I'm going to start yelling and pointing," he said. "Then we jump."

"Sounds good to me. Hurry."

"*Look!*" the guard leader called. "The human lightning weapons! *Everyone off the bridge!*"

He took his own advice without further ado and launched himself over the low wall of the bridge and into the water. He was *not* sticking around to see what happened next.

Gronningen had already started to depress the firing stud when he saw the Pasule contingent start pointing. He paused for only a moment, all the time it took the keyed-up guards to hit the water, and then fired.

The plasma charge traveled at nearly the speed of light and smote the nearer Pasule guardhouse in a flash of actinic light and a bellowing explosion. The Marshadan guards were swept effortlessly from the bridge by the thermal bloom, vanishing like gnats in a candle flame, and the plasma bolt carved a ruler-straight line of blazing vegetation across the fields between the cannon and the bridge. The center of that line was bare black to the soil, which steamed and smoked in the blazing gray light.

The Marines broke into a trot, heading straight for the bridge with bead rifles and grenade launchers at port arms, and the rest of the Marshad forces poured out of the city gates behind them.

Gronningen flipped the safety back on and hit the collapse key, and the fire team waited while the cannon reabsorbed itself, then looked at their leader.

"Mutabi," Moseyev said, slinging his bead rifle and taking one of the handles. "Let's go."

The team hefted their weapons and followed the rest of their company. Walking through the fire.

"Glorious! Glorious!" Radj Hoomas clapped all four hands in glee. "The bridge is clear! Pity their guards got away, though."

"You didn't inform your own guards?" Roger's tone was wooden.

"Why should I? If they'd panicked early, it might have given away our attack." The king looked towards the distant city. "Look, they still haven't even begun to issue forth. We've caught them completely by surprise. Glorious!"

"Yes," Roger agreed, as Pahner stepped up beside him, obviously to get a better view of Pasule. "It's going well so far."

Eleanora O'Casey nodded at the group of guards around the king, who waved for them to move aside. It was well known that the chief of staff was an academic, not a fighter, and so tiny a person hardly posed a threat to Radj Hoomas.

"What do you intend to do with them when you capture their city?" she asked, stepping up on the far side of the king from the prince and captain and gesturing at the other city.

"Well, the market for *dianda* is fully satisfied at the moment," the Mardukan said, rubbing his horns. "So after stripping the Houses, I will probably permit them to raise barleyrice. Well, that and use them to support my combined army as it conquers the rest of the city-states."

"And, of course," O'Casey said, "we'll be free to pass on our way."

"Of course. I will have no further need for you. With the combined force of Marshad and Pasule, I'll control the plains."

"Ah," the academic said. "Excellent."

The king grunted as the gates of the distant city opened at last. It was difficult to see much at this distance, but it was obvious that the city's forces were pouring out into the plain to defend their fields.

"I'd hoped they would take longer to respond," he grumped.

"Well," O'Casey smiled, "they say no plan survives contact with the enemy." She tried not to smile too broadly as she recalled Pahner's explanation of the sole exception to that rule—the first few moments of a surprise attack

"Look." The king pointed to the struggling plasma cannon team. "Your lightning weapon is almost to the hill."

Moseyev's team had reached the parklike hill, and were toiling up the overgrown path, and Radj Hoomas pointed again, this time to a small group of his own forces which had separated from the main body.

"I hope no one minds, but I sent along some of my own troops." He grunted in laughter, looking down at the chief of staff. "Just in case your soldiers should meet up with stragglers or brigands. You can never be too careful, you know."

"Oh, I agree," the academic said with a slight frown. "War is a terrible business. One never knows what might go wrong."

"Okay," Gronningen said. "We've got nursemaids." The big Asgardian frowned. "This is going to fuck things up."

"I see 'em," Moseyev grunted. "Stay with the plan."

"There's nearly twenty of 'em," Macek's tone wasn't nervous, just professional.

"Yeah," Moseyev said, grunting again—this time under the combined weight of their overloaded packs and the plasma cannon. "And there's four of us, and we planned for this. When we get in place, put out the gear right away. Even *with* this heavy mother, we can make it to the top of the hill in plenty of time."

The king grunted in laughter as the Marshad forces came to a halt on the plain. The formation's wings were composed of standard mercenary companies, professionals who would stand and fight as long as they felt the battle was going for them, and not a second longer. They could be expected to lend weight to a successful attack, but only a fool would depend on them for more than that.

No, the critical point was in the center, where the strongest and deepest companies stood. The humans formed the front rank, "supported" by the majority of the Royal Guard immediately behind them, ready to cut them down if they attempted to flee or to exploit the expected breach the human weapons were about to rip through the Pasulians.

The Guards had stopped to dress their ranks before attacking . . . which gave the humans an opportunity to make one last communication.

"Fire it off, Julian," Lieutenant Jasco said.

"Yes, Sir." The NCO dug the star flare out of his cargo pocket and prepared it, then fired it into the air over the human forces—where both the Pasulian army and their Marshadan allies in the city could see it— with a thump.

✧   ✧   ✧

"What was that?" the king demanded suspiciously as the green firework burst in midair.

"It's a human custom," O'Casey said indifferently. "It's a sign that the force is here for battle and that no parley will be accepted."

"Ah." The mollified monarch gave another grunting laugh. "You seem eager to enter battle."

"The sooner we finish, the sooner we can be on our way," O'Casey said with absolute sincerity.

"There's the signal," Denat whispered.

"You don't need to whisper," Sena said grumpily. "No one can hear us here."

They were back in their sewer tunnel, but Denat wasn't paying any attention to the smell this time. The two of them were too busy watching the humans who had just topped out on the small hill across the river.

"What's that they're setting up?" Sena asked. The activity could barely be seen at this range.

"A lightning weapon," Denat replied offhandedly. "One of their largest. It will cut through the enemy like a scythe."

"Ah," the spy said. "Good. It looks like they're ready."

"We're up, boss."

"Roger." Moseyev looked to where Macek and Mutabi were putting in the last of the crosslike stakes. The stakes ran in a semicircle ten meters back from where the plasma cannon was set up. "You set, Mutabi?"

"Yep." The grenadier dusted his hands. "Limit line's all set."

"Good, because here comes our company." The team leader raised a hand at the group of Mardukans struggling up the hill. "Hold it. Why are you here?"

The Mardukan in the lead swatted at his hand.

"We were sent to keep an eye on you, *basik*," he grunted. "Make sure you didn't scuttle off into the bush like the cowards you are."

"Did you see what this thing did to the bridge?" Moseyev snapped. "I could give a shit why you're here, frankly, but if you don't follow our instructions *exactly*, you're all going to be a pre-fried lunch for the crocs, got it?"

"We're going to do as we damned well please," the leader shot back angrily, but there was more than a hint of fear under his belligerence, and the troops behind him muttered nervously. "We'll stay out of the way, but only where we can watch you," he said in slightly more moderate tones. Clearly, he had no more interest in dying than the soldiers he commanded.

"Okay." Moseyev pointed to the line of stakes. "There's enough room behind the gun shield for the four of us, but no more, and we all have jobs to do so we can't put any of you behind it. The stakes are the limit line—you'll be safe enough as long as you stay behind it, but you'll be close enough so that if we try to run or do any other funny stuff you can fill us full of javelins."

The leader examined the situation and clapped his hands in agreement.

"Very good. But remember—we'll be watching you!"

"You just do that," Moseyev said, and turned back towards the gun so the idiot couldn't see his feral smile.

CHAPTER FIFTY-FOUR

"Captain, this is Lieutenant Jasco," the field commander said. He looked around at the bare platoon of soldiers and shook his head. "We're in place with the Marshad forces. The plasma gun is in place, with its line out. Denat and the package are in place. I would say we're a go."

"Roger," Pahner replied over the circuit. "Plasma team, you're the initiators. When the Pasule forces charge."

"Roger, Sir," Moseyev responded nervously. "We're ready."

"Pahner, out."

Moseyev looked over Gronningen's fire plan one last time.

"Wait for my call," he said.

"Got it," the Asgardian grunted. "We're locked and cocked."

"Corporal," Macek whispered. "We've got movement."

"Let's get ready to rock and roll, people," Sergeant Major Kosutic said as a leader of the Pasule contingent stalked to the fore. The two armies had stopped just beyond javelin range from each other, and the Pasulian now waved his sword overhead, clearly exhorting his smaller force to attack. His words, probably fortunately for the humans, couldn't be discerned, but whatever he said worked, for the mass started into a trot behind him.

"Showtime."

"Fire," Moseyev whispered, and Gronningen tapped the fire button.

The plasma cannon spat out three carefully calculated bursts. One into each flank of the Marshad contingent, and the third directly into the rearmost ranks of the Royal Guard.

Pahner drew, turned, and fired three carefully aimed beads. The only three guards between him and the king went down like string-cut marionettes, and he sprinted forward.

The anticipated explosions roared behind them, and Bravo Company, Bronze Battalion, The Empress' Own, executed a perfect about-face and opened fire into the forces at their back.

Eleanora O'Casey hit the ground and covered her head.

Sergeant Despreaux dropped her bead rifle to hip level and followed her HUD aiming point as the grenadiers to either side of her went to continuous fire.

Corporal Moseyev pressed the hand unit detonator button, simultaneously firing the semicircle of stake-mounted directional mines and detonating the kilo charge of C-20 catalyst under the bridge. The charge was half the company's total supply . . . and sufficient to take down a three-story office building.

Pahner's first kick took Radj Hoomas in the groin. Anecdotal evidence had suggested that the area was nearly as vulnerable for Mardukans as for humans, which proved to be the case as the monarch doubled over in agony. The captain followed up with a spinning sidekick that intercepted the descending head on the temple. Mardukans, unlike humans, had thick bone there, but the impact still spun the king off his feet and stunned him.

The ruler of Marshad hit the balcony's stone floor and bounced, and Pahner grabbed the heavy Mardukan by one horn, yanked his head up, and shoved the muzzle of his bead pistol against it. Then he looked up, prepared to threaten the king's life to control the guards.

But there were no guards to control.

Those who had lined the back wall of the balcony had been reduced to so much paste by the impact of hundreds of beads and a dozen grenades in the confined space. Stickles was down, with a javelin in the side, but he would live, and that was the only casualty the humans had taken.

All eight of the guards who'd been directly around the king were dead. Most of them appeared to have been caught flat-footed, watching the plasma cannon, but one, at least, had apparently reacted to the captain's attack. That one had his sword out . . . and a bloody hole in his stomach. All the others had been hit in the head, neck, and upper chest.

Roger holstered his pistol and rotated his shoulder. "I really have to find the guy who wrote that program and thank him when we get back."

Gronningen pounded rounds into the two flanks. The company was too intermixed with the Royal Guard now for him to fire into the center, but the flanks were fair game. He winced as he saw another Marine go down, but there was nothing he could do from here. Nothing but give covering fire and keep the flanking mercenaries off their backs.

Moseyev picked up one of the shredded guards' javelins. The directional mines had stripped away a few centimeters of the end, but aside from that—and the dripping gore—it was intact, and he tied the first line to its haft and waited.

Denat sprinted to the water's edge, then skipped aside as the javelin came scything through the air. The last rocks were still raining down from the demolished bridge when he picked the weapon up and threw it over the chosen tree limb. He motioned for slack and quickly tied a bowline slipknot in the rope and signaled complete. The rope twitched upward, and he smiled. Company was coming.

Roger heaved on his end, and the Mardukan he'd been sharing with Kyrou thumped soddenly into the pile against the door. He skipped aside and shook his head as Pahner and Surono came out with another.

"I've heard the expression before," he said, "but I never thought I'd do it."

"You see anything else to barricade the door with, Your Highness?" Pahner asked with a frown. "This is what war is all about: doing things you don't like to people you don't like even more."

"Sergeant Major," Julian said, jumping over a small mountain of Mardukans, "remind me never, ever to make that joke again."

"What's that?" Kosutic asked. She was simultaneously trying to walk sideways over the mounded bodies of the

Royal Guard, tie a bandage on Pohm's neck, and make sure nobody was being left behind.

"Join the Marines . . ." Julian said.

"Travel to fascinating planets," Georgiadas chorused as he fired at one of the flankers who'd stopped to throw a javelin at them. The Marshad contingent's instinctive retreat to the city had come to a screeching halt when the bridge disintegrated in its face. Unable to fall back, it was beginning to reform south of the original battlefield, and even after the terrible pounding it had taken, the Marshadans were almost as numerous as the Pasulians.

"Meet exotic natives," Bernstein yelled, dropping a line of grenades across the line between the humans and the Marshadans.

"And kill them," Julian finished somberly as he shouldered the rolled up bag of ashes that was all that was left of Lieutenant Jasco. "Somehow, it's just not funny anymore."

"It never was, Julian." Kosutic finished the bandage and clapped the "repaired" private on the back. She looked around the battlefield and pointed to the marked assembly area. "*Assemble at the O-P!*" she yelled, then looked at the NCO who was jogging alongside her.

"So I should just shut up and soldier?"

"No. But you might wait until we're done with the mission," the sergeant major said, "and that will be a long time. Or at least wait to have your moral dilemma until the battle's over. In case you hadn't noticed, it isn't. And afterwards, you can drown your sorrows in wine, like the rest of us.

"I'm not saying that you have to be one of those guys who drinks from the skulls of dead enemies," she said as the company started to gather and tally off the dead and wounded. "But we have a few to pile yet. So wait until we're done to start the bitching."

❖   ❖   ❖

"So you're just gonna leave me here, huh?"

Gronningen triggered another shot at the distant Marshadans. There were at least a thousand warriors in the mass, but it was nearly three thousand meters away. Maximum effective range for the cannon was only four thousand meters in atmosphere, due to energy bleed, so shots at this range were relatively ineffectual, but they still served to keep the Marshadan force off the backs of the rest of the Marines as they trotted steadily back towards his hilltop position. And, of course, the cannon would become increasingly effective if any of the Marshadans were stupid enough to come into shorter range.

"Bitch, bitch, bitch," Macek said nervously. Dozens of Mardukan soldiers had appeared at Marshad's gate, and more were coming from around the backside of the hill. If the main contingent didn't arrive soon, the bridgehead Denat had established across the river from them would be lost.

"Think of the poor bastards back in the barracks," Moseyev said. The word had come down that the first assault on the "guests' quarters" had been repulsed, but the group of walking wounded, mahouts, and tribesmen had been hard pressed.

"I'll think about them when I can quit thinking about myself," Mutabi said, hooking a clip onto the overhead rope. "I hate heights."

"Let's move out, people!" Kosutic snarled as she reached the foot of the hill and the plasma cannon atop it began firing across the river at Marshad. She glanced back at the stretcher teams toiling to keep up with her and shook her head. "Hooker!"

"Yes, Sergeant Major?" the corporal, who'd been promoted to team leader to replace Bilali after Voitan, responded.

"Your team stays with the stretcher bearers." There were three stretcher cases and four walking wounded, one of them in Hooker's team. "And St. John (J.), Kraft, and Willis," she added, naming off the other three walking wounded. "The rest, follow me," she finished, and went from the dog trot that they'd been maintaining to a loping run.

Macek ducked behind the tree as another flight of javelins rained down. There were only a few dozen Marshadans in the sewage ditch, but their last charge had nearly made it to the riverbank where the team crouched.

"This *sucks!*" he yelled.

"Oh, I don't know," Mutabi opined. "It could be worse."

"How?" Macek shouted back. "We're pinned down, the Company's not gonna get here in time, and there are more of them coming. How could it be *worse?*"

"Well," the grenadier said, pulling out his last belt of grenades. "We could be *completely* out of ammo."

"I can't get the angle into the ditch, Sergeant Major!" Gronningen reported furiously.

The senior NCO sucked in deep, cleansing breaths as she stepped to the edge of the hilltop to look the situation over.

"Grenadiers," she snapped, "flush those bastards. Gunny Lai!"

"Yes, Sergeant Major!"

"Your team first—go! Everybody else, lay down covering fire!"

Lai pulled the loop of rope out of her cargo pocket and hooked to the clip on the overhead line. She slung her bead rifle across her back and smiled.

"I always wondered why we did this in training." She laughed, and jumped off the cliff.

The company began to pour fire down on the scummy positions surrounding the sewage ditch bridgehead as the gunnery sergeant slid down the rope. The Marine gained speed rapidly as she felt another body hit the rope behind her, but there was an uplift at the bottom that slowed her. She let go near the top of the swing, and landed lightly a few meters from the riverbank.

"Ta-*Da!*" she said with a grin, and pulled the rifle off her back.

"Gunny," Macek told her, "you're a sight for sore eyes." He had a red-stained pressure bandage clamped on the side of Mutabi's neck, and there was a bloody javelin head next to the unconscious grenadier.

"Where's Moseyev and the scummy?" she asked as Pentzikis came off the rope, followed by St. John (M.). The latter had a rope trailing out of his rucksack and trotted off to the north, flipping it up and out of the river's current as he went.

"They're somewhere over there," Macek said, pointing south. "They're not responding anymore."

"Okay." The NCO looked around as more and more of the remnants of her platoon came down the rope. "Dokkum, Kileti, Gravdal—go find Moseyev and Denat." She waved to the south. "The rest of you, follow me!"

Roger's sword lopped the head off the spear as it thrust at him and opened up the scummy's chest on the backstroke. He spun in place to take the one grappling with Despreaux in the back, and then took the arm off of one fleeing towards the smashed-in door.

The wounded Mardukan slipped on the pool of blood which covered most of the floor and slid into the pile of bodies barricading the door. He started to scramble up again, but before he could, Captain Pahner took off his head with a single powerful blow of the broad, cleaverlike short sword he carried.

Roger straightened up, panting, and looked out over the city. The sounds of fighting carried clearly up to the balcony.

"We should have figured out how to smuggle in ropes. We could have gotten them in with the camping gear."

"No way." Despreaux disagreed, jerking hard to retrieve her own sword from the Mardukan in whose ribs it had wedged. "They were looking for stuff like that." She looked over at the remnants of the squad in one corner of the balcony. "How you doin'?"

"Oh, just fine, Sergeant," Kyrou said. He gestured at the securely trussed up king. "His Majesty's a bit put out, but we're fine."

"Right," Pahner said. "We may be low on ammunition, but that was too close. Next time we use the rifles and pistols as our primary weapons." He waved the remaining team to the door. "Your turn to cover."

Roger wiped at his face with a sleeve, trying to get some of the blood off, but his sleeve was even more sodden than his face.

"Anybody got a hankie?" he asked. "Yuck."

"Captain," Damdin shouted. "We've got movement!"

"Check-fire," the sergeant major called from the landing. She peeked around the corner until she had the corporal in sight, then stumped wearily up to the top of the stairs. "Check-fire, Damdin. The cavalry has arrived."

"Great," Roger said, looking at the sergeant major. She was just as blood-covered as he was. "So what took you so long?"

CHAPTER FIFTY-FIVE

Roger glanced at the fresh bloodstains on the floor as he approached the throne. Some things never seemed to change in Marshad, he reflected. Or not, at least, without a little nudge from the outside.

"Tinker!" He smiled at the throne's new occupant. "You seem to have come up in the world."

Kheder Bijan did not return his expression of pleasure.

"You are to bow to a ruler, Prince Roger," he said. "I would suggest that you get used to it."

"You know," Roger said, glancing at the full platoon of Marines behind him, "I can understand how Radj Hoomas made the mistake of underestimating us, but I'm surprised at you. Surely you don't think *you* can bully us? Although, if you really are that stupid, I imagine that explains why we haven't received any of our agreed upon equipment yet. You were supposed to have the barleyrice, *dianda*, and shields to us three days ago, Bijan. Where are they?"

"You humans are so incredibly arrogant," the new ruler observed. "Do you think that we're simple provincials?

That there was only one javelin in the quiver? Fools. You're all fools."

"Perhaps," Roger said with a thin smile. "But we're starting to be angry fools, Bijan. Where's our gear?"

"You're not getting any gear, human," the ruler snorted. "Nor are you going anywhere. I have far too much to do to lose my most important contingent of troops. Become accustomed to these walls."

Roger cocked his head and smiled quizzically.

"Okay, what neat trick do you have up your sleeve now, spy?" he asked brightly.

"You will address me as 'Your Majesty,' human! Or I will withhold the antidote to the *miz* poison you ate the first night you were here!"

"Unfortunately, we didn't have any poison," and Roger told him. "I'm fairly sure of that. For one thing, we're still alive."

"It was in your dishes at the banquet," the former spy scoffed. "It is visible as small flecks of leaf, but it's virtually tasteless. And it only takes one dose. Only a fool would have missed it, but you ate it nonetheless. Since then, we've been keeping you alive with the antidote. If you don't have it, you'll die, *basik*!"

"Hold it," and Roger said, thinking back. "Little green leaves? Taste like raw sewage?"

"They're tasteless," Bijan said. "But, yes, they would have been bright green."

"Uh-huh," and Roger said, trying not to smile. "And, let me guess—the antidote has been in all the food you've been giving us since, right?"

"Correct," Bijan sneered. "And if you don't have it, you'll die. It starts within a day, but it takes days of agony to end. So I suggest that you avoid it at all costs. But enough discussion of this, we must plan the next conquest and—"

"I don't think so," Roger interrupted with a chuckle.

"Haven't you been keeping up with recent news, Bijan?"

"What are you talking about?" the new ruler asked. "I've been doing many things..." he continued suspiciously.

"But obviously not keeping up with who's been cooking my meals for the last few days," Roger purred like a smiling tiger.

Bijan gazed at him for a few seconds, then gestured to one of the guards standing by the throne. There was a brief, whispered discussion, and the guard left.

"Sir," Julian said, leaning forward behind Roger, "is this a good idea?"

"Yeah, it is." Roger never took his eyes off of Kheder Bijan. "In fact, send somebody to collect up T'Leen Sul. That seems like a capable family. Oh, and tell Captain Pahner that it looks like we're going to be staying a little longer then we'd planned."

He stopped talking as the guard returned to the throne room. The guardsman crossed to the new ruler and said a few words, and Roger had become sufficiently familiar with Mardukan body language to tell Bijan was suddenly one worried scummy.

The new king turned to the prince and placed his true-hands on the arms of the throne.

"Uh . . ."

"We're not Mardukans, Bijan," and Roger told him with a deliberately Mardukan laugh. "In fact, I'll tell you a little secret, Tinker. We're not from anywhere on this planet. We have no similarity to anything on it, we're not vulnerable to the same poisons you are, and we most especially aren't *basik*."

"Ah, Prince Roger, there seems—" the ruler began.

"Bijan?" Roger interrupted, as the door opened to admit Pahner.

"Yes?"

"Say goodbye, Bijan."

✧   ✧   ✧

Including the representatives from Voitan and all the surrounding city-states, there must have been two or three hundred diplomats, alone, in Marshad. The exact number was open to some debate, since no one had ever gotten a definitive count, but there were certainly enough to make the goodbyes both long and fulsome. Roger smiled and shook hands, smiled and waved, smiled and bowed.

"He's getting good at this," Pahner said quietly. "I hope he doesn't get to liking it too much."

"I don't think he's a Caesar, Captain," Eleanora said, just as quietly. "Or even a Yavolov. Besides, he has Cord beside him muttering 'You, too, are mortal.'"

"I don't really think he is either," the Marine said, then grunted in laughter. "And you know what? I'm beginning to think that it wouldn't matter, anyway."

He surveyed the troops surrounding the prince. You always knew the ones who should be in the Regiment, even before RIP. They were the ones who always looked out. Even when they joked, they were the ones who watched others, and not just whoever they were talking to. The ones who saw their whole surroundings in one gulp. The ones who were human anti-assassin missiles.

Sometimes those weren't the ones who made it. Sometimes, rarely, you got those who were straight plodders. And sometimes even the missiles lost their edge. He'd felt that in the company before leaving Earth. Too many of the troops hadn't cared; it was only the prince, for God's sake.

Not now. The survivors were like a Voitan blade. They'd been tempered over and over, folded and refolded. And, at their core, it wasn't Pahner or even the sergeant major who'd given them their true temper. It was the prince—the trace element that made them hard and flexible. That was where their loyalty lay now. Wholly. Whether it had been his admission of fault, or his swift and decisive removal of the spy who, more than anyone, the company blamed for putting them in the noose of Marshad, or the realization that he'd removed Bijan not simply out of vengeance but because he'd finally learned the responsibility that came with power, as well, the captain didn't know. But whatever it was, it had worked. This was no longer the company of Captain Armand Pahner, escorting a useless prince; it was a detachment of Bronze Battalion, The Empress' Own, Colonel Roger MacClintock, commanding, and the captain smiled.

"Yours is the Earth and everything that's in it, *And— which is more—you'll be a Man, my son!*"

Roger thanked the representative from Sadan for his kind words. The broad, well-watered Hadur River valley was heavily settled, and the trade routes ran far and wide. And throughout that entire region the word had spread over the last several weeks that you didn't want to mess with the *basik*. Sadan was the city-state furthest along the route, and its representative had already promised that not only was the way open through his lands, but also in the lands beyond.

Roger looked up at the *flar-ta* loaded with wounded. The two beasts were crowded with stretchers, but most of the Marines in the stretchers were recovering from leg wounds. They'd be back on their feet in a week, and getting used to marching again, he thought, and smiled at one of the exceptions.

"Denat, you lazy bum. You just wanted to ride!"

"You just wait until I get out of this stretcher," the tribesman said. "I'll kick your butt."

"That's no way to address the Prince," Cord said severely, and Roger looked over his shoulder at his *asi*.

"He's permitted. By your laws, Moseyev would be *asi* to him, so I give him leave to be a lousy patient." The prince reached up to clap the towering shaman on the shoulder. "But it's good to have you behind me again. I missed you."

"And well you should have," Cord sniffed. "It's past time to begin your teaching again. But I had a fine time in the barracks. Great fun." The still-recovering Mardukan had emerged coated in red, as had Matsugae and Poertena.

"It's still good to have you back," Roger said, and passed up the line of *flar-ta* and Marines, touching an occasional arm, helping to adjust a shield or commenting on a recovery, until he reached the head of the column, where he smiled broadly at T'Leen Sul.

The Mardukan nodded to him. The human expression was accepted now throughout the Hadur region, and the new council head clapped his lower hands in resignation.

"It won't be the same here without you," he said.

"You'll do fine," Roger said. "The land distribution was more than equitable, although you and I both know there'll be complaints anyway. But the trade from Voitan will soon mean you can relieve the tax burden and still maintain the public works."

"Any other points I should remember, O Prince?" the Mardukan asked dryly. "Should I, perhaps, think about a fund to restart the forges? Reduce the crops of *dianda* and balance it with barleyrice? Remember to use my chamber bucket and not the floor?"

"Yeah," Roger chuckled. "Something like that." He looked back along the line, where the natives of Pasule were pressing forward to offer baskets of food to the Marines.

Roger looked up and smiled as the sergeant major walked up the line of packbeasts but the smile slid off his face at her expression.

"What?" the prince asked.

"D'Estrees picked up a transmission," said the sergeant major. "No direction and it was only a tiny snip of encryption. But it looks like somebody found the shuttles and reported them to the port."

"Grand," Roger snarled. He glared up at the clouds for a moment, then looked back at Kosutic. "You've told the Old Man?"

"Yep."

"And he said?"

"He said it may be a good thing you and Elenora talked him into telling our friends along the way the truth," the sergeant major said with a small, crooked smile. "Something about covering our back trail."

"That was the idea," Roger agreed, then sighed. "I just hope we don't really need it in the end."

"You and me both, Your Highness."

"All right, SMaj," the prince said, and punched her lightly on the shoulder. "Guess we'll just have to improvise, adapt, and overcome."

"Like always, Sir," Kosutic agreed, and moved off to complete her own final check.

Roger watched her go, then turned to look to the northeast, where the mountains which were probably their next major obstacle loomed. They were reported to be high, dry, frozen and impassable. Of course, that was the judgment of a species which would find the Amazon drought stricken.

"I guess it's time to get this train a-moving," he murmured, and grasped Patty's armored head glacis, stepped on her knee, and lifted himself onto her back. Another mahout had been killed, so somebody had to drive, and he plucked the mahout stick from his belt and lifted it.

The line of drivers behind him, Marine and Mardukan, lifted their sticks in response. Everyone was ready to go, and Roger looked to Captain Pahner, who waved in reply.

"Okay," the prince said to the packbeast. "Time to head upcountry."

"*Move 'em out!*" he shouted. He pressed the forked head of the stick into the tender flesh under the armored collar, and as the *flar-ta* lurched into motion, he looked up at the mountains once more.

They weren't going to be fun.

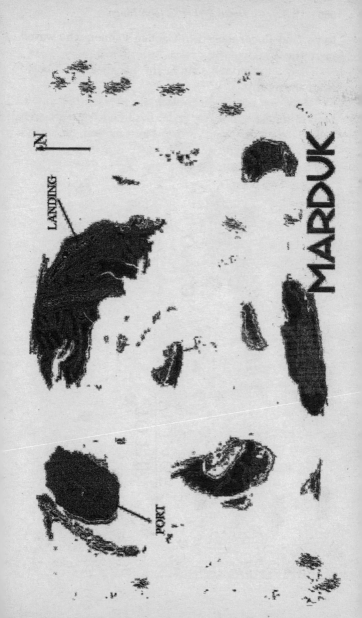

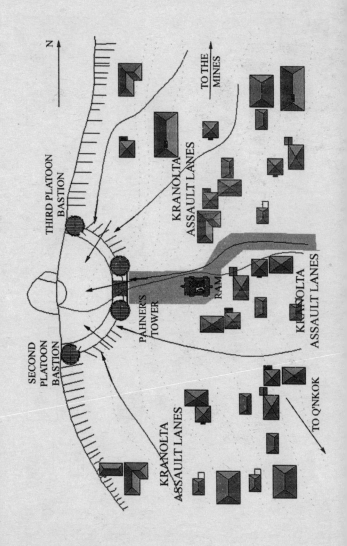

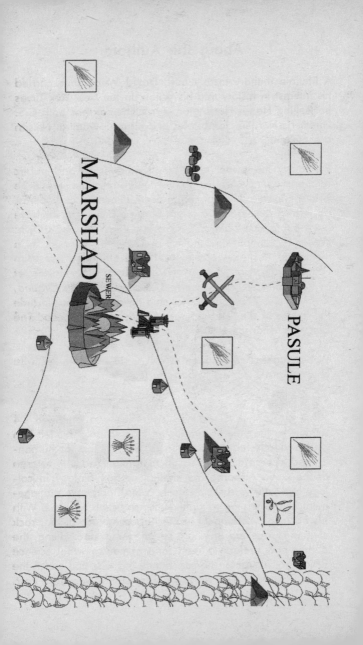

MARSHAD

SEWER

PASULE

About the Authors

A lifetime military history buff, **David Weber** has carried his interest in history into his fiction. In the *New York Times* bestselling Honor Harrington series, the spirit of both C.S. Forester's Horatio Hornblower and history's Admiral Nelson are evident.

Previously the owner of a small advertising and public relations agency, Weber now writes SF full time. While he is best known for his spirited, modern-minded space operas, he is also developing a fantasy series, of which two have been published: *Oath of Swords* and *The War God's Own*. Weber's first published novels grew out of his work as a war game designer for the Task Force game *Starfire*. With collaborator Steve White, Weber has written four novels set in that universe: *Insurrection*, *Crusade*, *In Death Ground*, and *The Shiva Option*. Other solo novels by Weber include the novels of the "Dahak" series, *Path of the Fury* and *The Excalibur Alternative*.

Weber makes his home in South Carolina, with his wife Sharon and their many dogs.

John Ringo had visited 23 countries and attended 14 schools by the time he graduated high school. This left him with a wonderful appreciation of the oneness of humanity and a permanent aversion to foreign food. A veteran of the 82nd Airborne, he studied marine biology in college and later worked in quality control database management before turning to writing science fiction full time. With his bachelor years spent in the Airborne, cave diving, rock climbing, rapelling, hunting, spear-fishing, and sailing, the author now prefers to read (and of course write) science fiction, raise Arabian horses, dandle his kids and watch the grass grow. He also writes op-eds for the *New York Post*.

DAVID WEBER

<u>The Honor Harrington series:</u> *(cont.)*

Flag in Exile
Hounded into retirement and disgrace by political enemies, Honor Harrington has retreated to planet Grayson, where powerful men plot to reverse the changes she has brought to their world. And for their plans to succeed, Honor Harrington must die!

Honor Among Enemies
Offered a chance to end her exile and again command a ship, Honor Harrington must use a crew drawn from the dregs of the service to stop pirates who are plundering commerce. Her enemies have chosen the mission carefully, thinking that either she will stop the raiders or they will kill her ... and either way, her enemies will win....

In Enemy Hands
After being ambushed, Honor finds herself aboard an enemy cruiser, bound for her scheduled execution. But one lesson Honor has never learned is how to give up!

Echoes of Honor
"Brilliant! Brilliant! Brilliant!"—*Anne McCaffrey*

Ashes of Victory
Honor has escaped from the prison planet called Hell and returned to the Manticoran Alliance, to the heart of a furnace of new weapons, new strategies, new tactics, spies, diplomacy, and assassination.

continued ☞

PRAISE FOR
LOIS McMASTER BUJOLD

What the critics say:

The Warrior's Apprentice: "Now here's a fun romp through the spaceways—not so much a space opera as space ballet.... it has all the 'right stuff.' A lot of thought and thoughtfulness stand behind the all-too-human characters. Enjoy this one, and look forward to the next." —Dean Lambe, *SF Reviews*

"The pace is breathless, the characterization thoughtful and emotionally powerful, and the author's narrative technique and command of language compelling. Highly recommended."
—*Booklist*

Brothers in Arms: "...she gives it a genuine depth of character, while reveling in the wild turnings of her tale.... Bujold is as audacious as her favorite hero, and as brilliantly (if sneakily) successful." —*Locus*

"Miles Vorkosigan is such a great character that I'll read anything Lois wants to write about him....a book to re-read on cold rainy days." —Robert Coulson, *Comic Buyer's Guide*

Borders of Infinity: "Bujold's series hero Miles Vorkosigan may be a lord by birth and an admiral by rank, but a bone disease that has left him hobbled and in frequent pain has sensitized him to the suffering of outcasts in his very hierarchical era.... Playing off Miles's reserve and cleverness, Bujold draws outrageous and outlandish foils to color her high-minded adventures." —*Publishers Weekly*

Falling Free: "In *Falling Free* Lois McMaster Bujold has written her fourth straight superb novel.... How to break down a talent like Bujold's into analyzable components? Best not to try. Best to say: 'Read, or you will be missing something extraordinary.'" —Roland Green, *Chicago Sun-Times*

The Vor Game: "The chronicles of Miles Vorkosigan are far too witty to be literary junk food, but they rouse the kind of craving that makes popcorn magically vanish during a double feature." —Faren Miller, *Locus*

MORE PRAISE FOR
LOIS McMASTER BUJOLD

What the readers say:

"My copy of *Shards of Honor* is falling apart I've reread it so often. . . . I'll read whatever you write. You've certainly proved yourself a grand storyteller."

—Lisa Kolbe, Colorado Springs, CO

"I experience the stories of Miles Vorkosigan as almost viscerally uplifting. . . . But certainly, even the weightiest theme would have less impact than a cinder on snow were it not for a rousing good story, and good story-telling with it. This is the second thing I want to thank you for. . . . I suppose if you boiled down all I've said to its simplest expression, it would be that I immensely enjoy and admire your work. I submit that, as literature, your work raises the overall level of the science fiction genre, and spiritually, your work cannot avoid positively influencing all who read it."

—Glen Stonebraker, Gaithersburg, MD

" 'The Mountains of Mourning' [in *Borders of Infinity*] was one of the best-crafted, and simply best, works I'd ever read. When I finished it, I immediately turned back to the beginning and read it again, and I can't remember the last time I did that."

—Betsy Bizot, Lisle, IL

"I can only hope that you will continue to write, so that I can continue to read (and of course buy) your books, for they make me laugh and cry and think . . . rare indeed."

—Steven Knott, Major, USAF